PRAISE FOR KATR

"A haunting, unflinching portrait of new mothe_____ _____ chilling terror and staggering empathy. With nimble pacing, genuine scares, and a riveting central mystery, *Graveyard of Lost Children* is a bona fide page-turner that will have your heart racing and breaking, that will linger long after the final chapter. Magnificent."

—**RACHEL HARRISON**, author of *Such Sharp Teeth*, for *Graveyard of Lost Children*

"*They Drown Our Daughters* is the best kind of story—one that will both break your heart and scare the hell out of you."

—**JENNIFER McMAHON**, *New York Times* bestselling author of *The Invited* and *The Children on the Hill*, for *They Drown Our Daughters*

"*They Drown Our Daughters* is a stunner. Beautifully written, deeply creepy, and carefully plotted—but above all, a fantastic meditation on what it means to be a parent."

—**ROB HART**, author of *The Warehouse* and *The Paradox Hotel*, for *They Drown Our Daughters*

"An atmospheric, absorbing, multigenerational novel, which explores the way historical events can impact the present. I was at turns terrified by the air of ghostly myth and compelled by the excellent prose. A brilliant achievement!"

—**MELANIE GOLDING**, author of *The Hidden*, for *They Drown Our Daughters*

ALSO BY KATRINA MONROE

They Drown Our Daughters
Graveyard of Lost Children

THROUGH
THE
MIDNIGHT
DOOR

KATRINA MONROE

Copyright © 2024 by Katrina Monroe
Cover and internal design © 2024 by Sourcebooks
Cover design by Sarah Brody/Sourcebooks
Cover images © Patrick Ziegler/Shutterstock, Castleski/Shutterstock,
Valentina131313/Shutterstock, Kichigin/Shutterstock, levan828/Shutterstock

Published by Poisoned Pen Press, an imprint of Sourcebooks
P.O. Box 4410, Naperville, Illinois 60567-4410
(630) 961-3900
sourcebooks.com

Library of Congress Cataloging-in-Publication Data

Names: Monroe, Katrina, author.
Title: Through the midnight door / Katrina Monroe.
Description: Naperville, Illinois : Poisoned Pen Press, 2024.
Identifiers: LCCN 2023058025 (print) | LCCN 2023058026 (ebook) | (trade paperback) | (epub)
Subjects: LCGFT: Horror fiction. | Novels.
Classification: LCC PS3613.O53696 T54 2024 (print) | LCC PS3613.O53696
    (ebook) | DDC 813/.6--dc23/eng/20240116
LC record available at https://lccn.loc.gov/2023058025
LC ebook record available at https://lccn.loc.gov/2023058026

Printed and bound in the United States of America.
SB 10 9 8 7 6 5 4 3 2 1

For Allison, who always opened the window so I could sneak back in.

And:

For Emily, who makes me laugh hardest.

I love you both.

AUTHOR'S NOTE

This book contains themes of mental illness and self-harm, as well as suicide and the loss of a young child. Please practice self-care before and after reading.

If you or anyone you know is struggling, in the United States, call 988, where the folks at the Suicide and Crisis Line are ready to listen.

Fear and guilt are sisters.

—*The Haunting of Hill House*, Shirley Jackson

CHAPTER ONE

MEG

R ain pummeled Meg's car, dripping onto her shoulder and thigh through the gap in the window that never closed properly. The air was hot and humid, thick as soup. Her car's ancient air conditioner only managed to pump out enough cold, burnt-smelling air to fog up the windshield. Every mile or so, she leaned hard against the steering wheel, the sleeve of her Indiana University sweatshirt tucked around her hand, and tried to wipe the fog clear. With the pressure of the wheel on her chest, she imagined a car careening through every intersection. It would hit her head-on, driving the wheel into her body. Her ribs would crack like twigs and her head would whip forward into the dash. It'd be a race between choking on her broken teeth and the wheel crushing her heart, and even if neither was enough to kill her right away, the metal shrapnel in her belly—the shrapnel she wouldn't feel until after the shock had worn off—would. Eventually.

But this was Blacklick, a town just big enough and old enough and don't-fuck-with-me enough to not have been absorbed by one of its neighboring cities at the tail end of the industrial age. This time of night, everyone was either in bed or leaning over some bar at last call, stinking of booze and fryer grease. She hadn't seen headlights for ages, doubted she would at all. Still, she held onto those bleak thoughts, imagined in painful detail the way her body would jerk and fly, a rain-soaked rag doll, to be found by some poor asshole who'd slept it off in the parking lot. Thinking about the blood and the pain was better than thinking about the phone call that put her on the road in the first place.

Cruiser lights flickered in the distance and soon she came upon a cop pulled over to the side of the road behind a dark-colored truck. She couldn't tell if someone was inside. Didn't care. Still, she slowed as she drove past. If she got pulled over, precious time would be wasted. She would be too late.

She slipped her phone, upright, into the cupholder. It'd be sticky with spilled coffee later, but that wasn't important. She kept shooting worried glances at the thing, expecting it to ring, to pick it up and hear a stranger's voice on the other end. *I'm so sorry...*

She shook her head, focused on the road that was barely visible for more than a few feet in front of her. There would be no phone call. No apologetic stranger. Because Meg was on her way. She pressed a little harder on the accelerator, white-knuckling the wheel as she felt her back end fish tail a little.

Come on, old girl, she thought. *Keep it together. Almost there.*

The call had jerked her out of a dead sleep, her first in ages, and Meg's half-asleep reaction was to stuff the phone under her pillow. Whoever it was, she'd deal with them in the morning. Juggling a handful of gigs meant swinging between day and night shifts with no buffer in between. She slept when she could. It wasn't often. But as she'd pulled her hand away, her thumb slipped across the screen, accepting the call. With the pillow muffling the noise and her mind caught somewhere between dream and awake, the voice on the other end sounded too close and far away at the same time.

"—wrong. Not *wrong*, but wrong, you know? And it's—"

Meg had fished the phone out from under the pillow intending to hang up on whoever thought they needed to rant into her ear at two in the morning.

But then she saw Claire's name on the display.

"It's just—it was right there. Under our stupid noses." Claire paused. "Meg?"

"Yeah," Meg said, voice like a garbage disposal. "I mean—yeah, I'm here." Then, "What's going on?"

She sat up. Ran her tongue over fuzzy teeth that tasted like the cigarettes she wasn't supposed to be smoking anymore. For a long time, all she heard on the other end of the line was Claire's breath. Calm, but a little ragged, like she'd just been crying.

It made her think of another time her little sister had called her crying in the middle of the night, making promises and threats. Meg stiffened against a shiver.

"Everything okay?" she asked carefully.

"It looks different at night," Claire said finally.

"What does?"

"The house."

Meg didn't need to ask which house. "What are you doing there?"

She could almost hear the shrug. "I had a feeling."

"Oh yeah?" Wide awake, Meg climbed out of bed and started hunting in the dark for a pair of jeans. Her shoes.

"I couldn't sleep. Couldn't stop thinking about that room. What it showed me."

"When most people can't sleep they pour a drink. Take an Ambien." Meg stuffed her phone between her head and shoulder as she wriggled into questionably clean jeans.

"I don't drink."

"Warm milk, then."

Claire chuckled. "You ever actually tried warm milk?"

Meg shoved her feet into her shoes, working her heels in as she made her way to the door. "Nope."

"Me neither."

"Good. We can try it together. I'm sure I've got some around here."

"Cookies too or no deal."

"Obviously."

Meg heard the brush of fabric through the phone. Keys jangling. She dared to hope it was Claire getting back into her car. Then the line went silent. Meg froze, hand reaching for her own keys, heart pounding.

Finally, Claire sighed. "You ever think about it? What we saw?"

Meg thought about lying. Thought of burying the darkness just a little deeper, beneath more platitudes, and false positivity. It wouldn't help. "All the time."

"Me too." Then, "For a long time I thought it would never go away. But it's so easy, I don't know why I didn't see it before. It's like with the hornets, remember? That tree in the backyard?"

Meg's brain glitched, struggling to conjure the memory while staying firmly here, in the moment. "I—hornets? I don't—"

"I think I know how to make the darkness go away."

Something in her sister's tone sent a chill down Meg's spine. "Let's talk about it." Meg started out the door, down the narrow stairs from her third-floor apartment to the parking lot. "We can stay up all night, like we used to."

"You hated that."

"Only sometimes." Meg paused. "Claire?"

"Hmm?"

"What are you really doing up there?"

"It followed me, like it followed you and Esther. I could be wrong. It could... come back. But I have to try, right? We missed it. All of us."

Meg swallowed. "What do you mean?"

"Nothing. I—nothing." She sighed again. "Go back to sleep. I'm sorry I woke you up."

"It's fine. Just come over, okay? We don't even have to talk if you don't want. We can—"

The line went dead.

Meg dove for her car door, choking back a curse.

The rain had picked up, roaring louder than her engine. She almost missed the turn from the main road onto Hill Street, where a single streetlight shone pitifully through the flailing branches of trees left to grow wild for more than a decade.

There were dozens of abandoned properties around Blacklick, but driving along Hill Street was like driving through a graveyard, all black dirt and bones, every sagging porch a gaping maw. She was too busy eyeing the power lines, which snapped and pulled between the poles. She didn't see the pallet in the road until she was almost on it.

"Shit!"

She pulled too hard on the wheel and sent the car drifting toward the rain-water ditch. She pumped the brakes, but they were almost as bad as her bald tires, practically useless against the pull of water flooding the road. The side of her head hit the window, not hard enough to hurt but enough to scare the shit out of her. Her hands, slick with sweat and rain, slipped off the wheel as the tires caught. When the car finally skidded to a stop, front end hanging at an uncomfortably low angle, she pressed her fist to her chest, willing her heart to slow. The engine still rumbled, but when she tried to turn the wheel, it wouldn't budge. She glanced over the dashboard and saw nothing but darkness. Smashed headlights probably, she thought. Great. Still, she forced the gear shift into reverse and hit the gas. The tires whined and the car jerked, but it didn't move. She tried again, stomping on the gas pedal, but only managed to lodge herself deeper in whatever hole she'd landed in.

"Come *on*."

One more time on the gas pedal. The engine roared and she could smell smoke, but she didn't let up. Couldn't. Finally, the car shook with a loud clank, and the engine died.

"No." Meg punched the steering wheel. Pain shot up her arm, but it only made her want to keep hitting things. "No, no, no," punctuated with punches to the wheel, the dash, the radio, until her hand throbbed.

She was still a block away from the house.

Taking deep, measured breaths, she leaned over the center console and groped the floorboards until she found her phone, flung away as the car spun. At least her phone was okay. She scrolled until she found Claire's number and hit Dial as she pulled open the car door.

Thunder rumbled overhead as she jumped out of the car, casting a quick glance back to see the right, front wheel dangling over the side of a ditch, and ran for the sidewalk where the thick canopy of trees shielded her at least partially from the rain. She pulled the collar of her sweatshirt over her head to protect the phone.

It rang and rang and—

You've reached Claire Finch. I'm not around right now, so please leave a message—

"Pick up the phone, Claire."

She hung up. Dialed again.

You've reached Claire Finch—

"Fuck."

She slipped on a patch of mud, nearly dropping the phone. She was already soaked through, but the rain came down harder, making it almost impossible to see.

She tucked her phone in her front pocket and pulled her now sopping sweater low over her waistband to try to protect it.

Lightning lit up the street, and the shadows flinched back just long enough for her to make out the chain-link fence surrounding *The House*. She was out of breath—too many cigarettes, too much takeout—but she pushed on, forcing her legs to move faster, push harder, until finally she reached the gate.

Another flash of lightning and she spotted Claire's car: a small, blue hatchback with an *I brake for Little Free Libraries* bumper sticker. Meg pressed her face against the window, but the inside was empty. With her hands shielding her face from the rain, she peered over the top of the car to the house. She'd never been here at night—never wanted to be. The shadows that lurked beneath the eves and under the porch really spread out at night, greedily covering every inch of the place. It looked like someone had tried to put up a swing, but all that was left on the large oak tree in the yard was a frayed bit of rope that twitched and writhed in the wind. The windows were black holes, the splintered glass like spiderwebs.

She really didn't want to go inside.

She had to.

The chain-link gate swung open, almost in welcome, as she started up the narrow, cracked sidewalk to the porch. The awning at least provided some shelter from the rain, but she could hear the roof rattling above her. It was a miracle the place hadn't collapsed yet.

"Claire!" she called, but her voice was snatched away by the wind and rain. She nudged the door with her foot, already cracked open, and called again. "Claire?"

A mournful groan in the walls followed her to the front room. From the moment she crossed the threshold, an eerie, prickling sensation fingered its way down the back of her neck and over her shoulders. Head on a swivel, she strained to see into the corners of the room, to the hallway and the stairs, feeling both horribly alone and like she was being watched.

It was smaller than she remembered.

"Claire!"

Her voice echoed, startling what sounded like bats somewhere in the house. She suppressed a shudder and made her way deeper into the house, using the flashlight on her phone to navigate. The first hallway was clear. Same with the kitchen. She wrinkled her nose at the moldy wallpaper and drooping cabinets.

She pulled up Claire's number and hit the Call button. It rang and rang. Just when Meg almost had herself convinced this was all a big misunderstanding, that she needed to do some serious soul-searching—tomorrow, today, whatever—the soft, tinny sound of music pulled her attention upstairs. She stared, unblinking, at the stairwell, and hung up. Immediately, the tinny music stopped.

Her stomach rolled.

"Claire!"

Meg ran for the stairs, taking them two at a time, the light from her phone brushing the floor, the railing, the walls covered in rot. At the top was another hallway, which led to several rooms. There was a landing off to the side with a stained-glass window overlooking the back yard. She absently wondered how it hadn't been stolen yet. She tried to dial Claire's number again, but her hands were shaking too hard, and she kept closing out of the screen.

Cursing under her breath, she shoved her phone into her pocket and started kicking in doors. The frames splintered, each one she broke more satisfying than the last. It felt good. She imagined knocking down every door, ripping the railings out of their sockets, and smashing every burned-out bulb until the place was destroyed. But for every room she found empty, a fist closed tighter around her stomach. Where was her sister?

Finally, at the end of the hall was the last room. Claire's room, she thought, images of that day, so many years ago, flickering through her mind like a film reel sped up too fast. The door was much smaller than the others, its white paint chipped and stained yellow. Meg touched the place where, a million years ago, the wood thrummed with possibility, promising dangerous secrets.

Shaking, she got down on hands and knees and opened the door.

In the faint glow of her phone light, she saw Claire's shoes first: bright-red sneakers dangling impossibly off the ground. Her gaze lifted, following the light up Claire's legs to her middle—gray cardigan hanging like a shroud—and finally her head, leaning limply forward, hair dangling like straw over her front. Meg stopped breathing. She gripped the door handle to pull herself up, standing on shaky legs. It was like the connection between her mind and her body snapped. She trembled so hard she dropped her phone, and the sound of it crashing onto the wood floor finally shoved her forward. Screaming, she wrapped her arms around Claire's knees and lifted.

"Claire! Jesus, fuck, no—Claire! Help!"

Meg's ankle hit something hard, and when she looked down, she saw a small toolbox. It looked like the one Claire kept in her trunk. There were dusty footprints on the top. Struggling to keep Claire aloft and the strain of the rope off her neck, Meg nudged the toolbox closer, but each time she managed to get the tread of her shoe to grip it, her arms slipped, and Claire fell hard. The sound of something cracking made bile rise in her throat.

Tears and snot streamed down her face. She could barely see, but finally she got the toolbox close enough to climb onto it. Draping her sister's limp body over her shoulder, she removed the makeshift noose from her neck and dropped it like it had bitten her. She sank gratefully to the floor just as her arms gave out. Claire fell against Meg, her skin barely warm.

Meg held her tightly and cried into her hair. "Goddamn it, Claire," she muttered.

She gritted her teeth, chest aching with each hitching breath, as a twisted sort of déjà vu took over.

She held Claire until she was cold, and then held on a little longer. She stared unblinking at the ancient fan in the middle of the ceiling. A fan that should have crumbled like the rest of the damn house, but had clung stubbornly, cruelly, just strong enough to hold Claire's weight.

Finally, her hands quit shaking long enough for her to call for help. The words sounded far away, not her own, and when she hung up, she stroked Claire's face. She closed her eyes, head leaning against the wall. A low thrum came from somewhere in the hallway and she realized she could no longer hear the storm, though the lightning still flashed, casting shadows just outside the open door. She squeezed Claire a little tighter, the need to protect her sister too little, too late.

It was all Meg's fault.

CHAPTER TWO

MEG

N O W

The police threw questions at her while she sat in the back of the police car, feet firmly planted on the street. More than once they reminded her that she wasn't under arrest, she wasn't in any trouble, which only made it sound like she *was* in trouble. Anyway, she should have been—if she'd gotten out of bed faster, if she hadn't skidded out in her shitty car, if she'd just been *better*, Claire might not have had time to lug her toolbox into the house, to tie a rope around the fan. But Meg had, and Claire did, and now Claire was dead and the weight of it hung around Meg's neck, so heavy she could barely look up from the crumbling asphalt.

Her parents stood on the curb, arms wrapped around each other. Her mom was still in her pajamas—sweatpants and a T-shirt from their one Disney vacation, so long ago that even Meg didn't remember it—but her dad had managed to get dressed. She could almost see him getting out of bed, checking the clock, and deciding it was better to dress, to be ready for work. Because of course he would go to work after this. Wasn't hell or high water that could keep Brian Finch from the Sunshine Plastics plant so long as there was overtime to be got. It wasn't heartlessness, just a fact. There'd been months, damn near a full year, when the hours were piecemeal. Meg could always see the memory of those extra-lean times in the corners of his eyes, even when he smiled. Especially then.

She watched her mom fall into him. They wobbled a little on their feet, but Dad kept them upright. Meg wondered if Claire's death would be the thing to reconcile them for good. Her parents were each other's bad habits, never divorcing despite years of sleeping in separate beds, of living entirely separate lives, tied together only by a mortgage refinanced too many times and a constantly dwindling bank account.

"Ma'am?"

Meg blinked. Looked up at the cop who'd been standing over her for what felt like hours. "Sorry. I was… Did you ask me something?"

The cop was tense, shoulders up around his ears. Young. Well, younger than her anyway. Once she hit thirty-five everyone started to look either like a child or like they had one foot in the grave. This was probably his first suicide. A cynical part of her wanted to tell him to get used to it.

"I asked if you knew whether your sister had made prior arrangements."

"Arrangements?"

"For her…remains." He winced as he said the word. "Sometimes people make plans. We want to make sure she's taken to the right place."

Meg scowled. "She was barely thirty."

"Of course." He scribbled something in his little notebook, cheeks blazing. "Sorry, ma'am."

Remains.

She felt sick all over again.

The cop scuttled away, likely thankful to be done dealing with her, so she pulled out her phone and tried, again, to get Esther to pick up.

Despite it being early in the morning, she knew Esther was awake, which meant she was screening her calls. What kind of person saw dozens of missed calls and thought, *never mind, if it's important they'll leave a message?*

Esther. That's who. But only because it was Meg's number on the caller ID.

When the calls started going directly to voicemail, Meg decided she'd had enough. Gritting her teeth, she typed out a text.

Claire's dead.

Less than a second after she sent it, her phone rang.

Before Meg could get a word out, Esther started in on the rant.

"It's five in the morning, Meg. I don't answer the phone because I don't want to answer the phone. That doesn't mean you keep calling, and it sure as hell doesn't mean you send me some sick text just to get me to answer. This is low, even for you."

At the sound of her other sister's voice, Meg's throat tightened. Tears streamed soundlessly down her face and neck, soaking the collar of her already damp sweater. She pressed the phone tighter to her ear, taking comfort in the familiar bark of Esther's frustration, in this brief moment of normalcy.

She sniffed, and Esther stopped mid-sentence.

"Meg?" Her voice became guarded. "It was a joke, right? Tell me it was a fucking joke."

"They keep asking me if she had *arrangements*. I don't even know what that *means*."

"Meg—"

"And the police are here and there's this white van and all I can think about is that winter break when she was, like, six, and I got honor roll and you got that stupid attendance trophy and all she wanted was for Mom to be proud of her, too, so she told us she was outside and this guy came up to her out of his big, white van and tried to give her candy but she screamed and ran away, just like Mom had told her to—"

"Meg!"

The next words caught in her throat and she choked and it was like she was dying and—God, is this what it had felt like?

Esther was on the razor edge of hysterical, "Tell me what happened!"

When she could finally speak, Meg told her everything, about the phone call and the house. About the stained-glass window and the fan and toolbox, and at the end of it, she felt eviscerated.

Voice shaking, Esther said, "Is Mom there? Let me talk to Mom."

Meg stood and walked the phone over to her mom. "Esther," she said when her mom frowned.

Her dad squeezed her shoulder, but she barely felt it.

The door to the house banged open. Her dad must have seen before she did, because he hustled her mom away from the sidewalk. Then Meg saw the gurney, wheeled carefully out by the police and some guy in blue booties and a surgical mask dangling off one ear. The white sheet covering Claire's body rustled with the wind, a holdover from the storm. The corner flicked sharply upward and Meg caught a glimpse of Claire's red sneaker. A wave of nausea rolled over her too quick to swallow back. Bracing herself on her knees, she puked in a patch of dead grass.

Getting the bad out, her dad used to call it.

As she stood, wiping her mouth with her sleeve, the memory of a long-ago conversation moved across the front of her mind.

"It's *badness*," Claire had said. "I can feel it clogging my veins like mud."

The doors slammed on the white van, making Meg jump.

All conversations seemed to stop as the van pulled slowly out of the driveway. Meg tried to see the driver, but the windows were tinted. She waved anyway, a tic she couldn't help. On the patchy, yellow lawn in front of the house, police officers watched the van leave, their expressions somber. One of the female officers rubbed her nose with the back of her hand. Meg felt a stab of anger. They didn't know Claire. They didn't get to mourn.

You don't either, a small voice whispered. *You saw it, and you didn't stop it. It's your fault.*

"Here you go, Peanut."

She turned and her dad stood on the curb holding her phone out.

"Esther's coming," he continued. "Be here in an hour or so."

"Okay," Meg said. "Good."

"I'm gonna take your mom home. She don't need to be standing here with all this…" He nodded at the cops, who'd started poking around in Claire's car. "You'll come too, right?"

It wasn't a request.

Meg nodded. "Yeah. I just, uh, I need to make some calls first."

The corner of his mouth lifted. It made the wrinkles in his cheeks look like caverns. "Sure thing. Don't take too long, though, okay?"

As he walked back to her mom, Meg scrolled through her contacts: people she didn't talk to or couldn't remember, old bosses and girlfriends. There had to be someone here, she thought. Someone who could tell her what to do. Being the eldest, Meg was expected to handle the big stuff. The disasters. Except a lot of the time, it was Meg that was the disaster. Meg that needed handling, and more often than not, it was Claire who'd done it.

In the end, Meg only called Claire's office. She was a social worker with the county, mostly with kids in high-risk environments, and there was no doubt somewhere Claire was supposed to be today. She navigated the automated system at the Human Services office and, gratefully, reached someone's voicemail where she left a stunted message and her phone number and hoped no one would call her back because there were only so many times she was willing to say, out loud, that her baby sister was dead.

She looked up at the house, at the window of the room where she'd found Claire. The shudders were dangling by their top hinges and the glass was clouded with dirt. Movement behind the window made her stop mid-breath. *Cops are still looking around the room,* she told herself, but the figure in the window had long hair and Claire's slight frame. The figure put its hand on the window, the heat of it fogging the rest of the glass. As Meg raised hers as if to meet it, the figure backed away and disappeared into the dark.

CHAPTER THREE

ESTHER

Esther had lied about being asleep.

When her phone had started buzzing on her nightstand, she had already been awake for more than an hour, pulled out of a deep sleep by the thought of an unlocked door. She stared at the ceiling, ignoring the shadows cast by the glow of the bathroom light, which shone from beneath the door. Her husband hated it, claimed he couldn't sleep with any lights on, but light or no light, he was always snoring before Esther's head even hit the pillow. The light stayed on. No discussions. No exceptions. It was essential, just like every other step in her routine.

Every evening, she moved through the house flipping switches and turning locks and double-checking the oven, the dryer, the furnace, and anything else that could conceivably catch fire in the middle of the night, then circled back to start all over again, ensuring she hadn't missed a single step. Only then was she allowed to go upstairs, brush her teeth and wash her face, and finally climb into bed. It was a foolproof routine that provided her the sense of security necessary to be able to sleep unmedicated.

But last night she'd been distracted. Not by anything specific, just a general feeling of unease. What her son would have called a *disturbance in the force*. She had lain there in bed, remembering how she finished her kitchen checks (oven, dishwasher, microwave, all disarmed), then walked into the living room only to stop in front of the couch. She remembered feeling suddenly very, very tired, and a soreness throughout her entire body. She sat down, massaged her temples…and then the memory stopped. She went to bed—she remembered that bit—so she must have locked the front door, because she always locked the front door before going upstairs. Still, it nagged her, like hooks in her subconscious.

And then the text came, and the first thought to cross her mind was, *It's my fault. I did it again.*

She still had the phone pressed against her ear when her mother hung up. She held it there for a long time because she knew the second she stopped, the reality of it would come crashing down.

"Babe?" Ryan's hand on her shoulder was cold through the flimsy material of her T-shirt. Goosebumps pinched painfully along her skin. "Everything okay?"

"I have to go." She studied the dark, just making out the shapes of her dresser, her closet where her overnight bag hung deep in the back, behind her wedding dress carefully packed in its pink garment bag. "I have to go," she repeated, like it would force her up and out of bed.

Ryan clicked on his bedside lamp. "Go where? What happened?"

"Home." She stood on shaky legs. Walked to her dresser and began pulling clothes out. "Claire died."

"Claire—what?" She heard the mattress protest as he climbed out of bed.

"Died," she said.

"How? I mean—" He stood next to her at the dresser. Grabbed her shoulders and turned her to face him. His hair was turned up at the front like a duck bill, and a cushion scar marred his face, bisecting his eye. A pirate scar. *Arrr*, she thought, and laughed.

Ryan frowned. "Esther. Talk to me."

She opened her mouth, but all that came out was more laughter. She laughed until tears blurred her vision, and she doubled over the dresser. She laughed as her stomach clenched and she couldn't breathe and she slammed her fist on the wooden top over, and over, and over until finally Ryan pulled her into him, smothering the laughter in his chest until it became deep, wrenching sobs.

"It's okay," he said, smoothing her hair back. "It'll be okay."

No, she thought. *Nothing will ever be okay again.*

He offered to go with her, because of course he would, but Esther brushed it away. Their son, Brandon, had midterm exams in a little over an hour. No makeups. The emails had been very specific.

"I'm sure they'd make an exception," Ryan said, following her to the kitchen. "Besides, are you sure you want to go alone?"

Esther nodded, though the thought of getting behind the wheel for the first time in—God, it couldn't have been that long, could it? "I'm sure. I just—I'm not sure what's happening. Meg said something about arrangements, but you and I both know she can't handle that, and Mom isn't in any state to do anything, so I'll go and get everything sorted and then I'll call you. Okay?"

He sighed. "Okay. But you'll call me before you do all that. The second you get there."

"Sure. Fine." She slipped a couple of slices of wheat bread into the toaster. Brandon's alarm would be going off soon. "And don't tell Brandon."

His eyebrows furrowed. "What? Why?"

"Just—not before his exams, okay? Tell him after school."

"He's not a toddler, you know."

"After his exams." Esther pulled the strawberry jelly and a tangerine from the refrigerator, setting them next to the toaster. "Make sure he eats the fruit."

"I will."

"And if he says his stomach hurts, he's lying."

"Got it." Then, "Hey." He gently took her hands and pulled her toward him, a deep V in the center of his forehead, dark eyes full of concern. In the harsh kitchen light, she noticed the gray at his temples and around his forehead made his ash-blond hair look almost silver. She absently pushed it out of his face.

"You're sure you're gonna be okay?" he asked.

She briefly touched her forehead to his collarbone. Took a deep breath. When she looked up, she forced a smile. "I'll call you."

Ryan put her overnight bag in the back of the car while she watched from the window. He made a show of looking under the car and in the trunk, all to try to put her at ease but it only made her hands sweat. He would wait for her at the car, keys in hand. All she had to do was walk out the door.

It shouldn't have been this hard.

She wasn't afraid, exactly. She was wary. Implicitly aware of her surroundings.

It was hard to explain the way she felt, especially to someone like Ryan. It was like she somehow had complete control and none at the same time. Like she could see the beams shuddering, could feel the walls shake and the ceiling tremble, but if she did exactly what she was supposed to, in the exact order, if she took precautions, then she could keep it all from crashing down on her.

But sometimes she slipped.

Sometimes it all fell down anyway.

Ryan waved and she waved back, thinking the hedges on either side of their property were too high. She liked the privacy, but hadn't realized how easily someone could hide in the thick foliage. She'd ask him to cut them when she got back.

It was Brandon's alarm that finally pushed her out the door. She knew it was selfish, leaving Ryan to deal with their son's first brush with death on his own, but Esther had managed to build paper-thin walls around the idea of Claire's death, a breath from crumbling. She needed to keep it together—and she couldn't do that faced with the kind of morbidly curious questions only a twelve-year-old boy would ask.

Heart pounding, she slipped outside just as she heard the creak of Brandon's bedroom door.

Ryan ushered her into the driver's seat and handed her the keys. Once she was settled—ignition on, seatbelt clipped—he leaned down, kissed her forehead, then opened his mouth like he was going to say something, only to shake his head.

"What?" she asked.

"Nothing. It's just—" He paused. "I don't know if it'll make you feel better... It should, I think. But when I came out here, the front door was unlocked."

Her panic must have shown on her face.

"No! It's a good thing, right? You didn't lock the door, and nothing happened." He paused, cheeks going a little pale as he clocked her expression. "You know what I mean. We're safe. Brandon's safe. Doesn't this show you that you don't need to obsess so much?"

No, she thought. It showed her she was slipping.

"I have to go," she said, shutting the car door just as Ryan jumped out of the way.

She put the car in reverse, nodding at the reassuring clunk of the automatic locks.

It wasn't that her husband didn't care. He lived in a world where an open door was an opportunity, not a threat. It was the same world her son would grow into, and though part of her was grateful, she wished that just once they could climb inside her head, that they could see through her eyes: the shadows that lurked in every corner, fingers creeping slowly, surely, toward her.

Esther got all the way to the highway on-ramp before the low fuel light came on. It was only forty minutes to Blacklick from Chicago, but she'd be lucky to get to the next exit running on fumes.

"Goddamn it," she muttered. How many times had she asked Ryan to make sure the tank was full? It wasn't just a convenience issue. It was a safety issue. He'd seen just as many horror films as her, had watched as some young, blond woman found a car and perceived safety, only to discover the tank was empty.

She carefully drove through to the next exit and bounced anxiously in her seat as she hit not one, but two red lights that took ages to change. She threw the car around in an illegal U-turn as it sputtered and jumped, and finally pulled into a gas station, just as a light she'd never noticed before started flashing at her from the console.

She put the car in park and quickly hit the button when the car door locks automatically released.

"A convenience feature," the dealer had said when they first bought the car, but Esther had taken one look at the lock and broken out into a cold sweat.

"That's not how it's supposed to work," she'd muttered, though by that point no one was listening.

Now, she hit the Lock button one more time to be sure, and set her hands on the wheel. She took a deep breath and tapped her fingers on the worn leather.

One. Two. Three.

A voice like viscera through wet fingers wriggled up from the back of her mind, *Four.*

She shook her head and counted again, tapping with the fingers of her other hand.

One. Two Three.

She waited for the voice to resurface, but the darkness had disappeared as quickly as it had come.

Holding her breath, she released the lock.

A woman about Esther's age stood at the pump across from hers. She figured if she only pumped her gas for as long as the woman was there, she was safe. She didn't need much anyway. A quarter tank would do.

But as soon as she managed to cajole herself out of the car and got the tank cap off, the woman returned the nozzle to the pump.

Cursing under her breath, Esther fought with the credit card reader, and then, when she grabbed her nozzle, she grabbed the release and spilled gas all down the side of her car and onto her shoes.

"Need some help there?"

Her gaze snapped up to see a man with dark hair and sharp features standing at the back of her car, a plastic bag hanging from his wrist. She spotted the fingers of gloves sticking out of the top. Her face went cold and hot at the same time and she gritted her teeth, willing her hands not to shake. Where were her keys? Her pocket? There was pepper spray on the key ring, but there was no way she'd have time to get it out before he attacked.

"I'm fine," she said.

"You don't look—"

"I said I'm *fine.*"

He put his hands up. Rolled his eyes. "Whatever. Crazy bitch."

She stuck the nozzle in her fuel tank and watched him walk to a car on the opposite side of the parking lot, committing its features to memory. Blue sedan. Rust on the rear driver's side wheel well. Plate starting with W1.

"You're spilling."

Esther jumped, then looked up to see the woman on the other side of the pump staring at her. She was right. Esther had somehow missed her tank completely. There was a puddle of gas on the ground, seeping toward her.

"Sorry, I—" Esther began, but the woman was already in her car.

She pumped another few dollars into her tank, holding the nozzle with both hands this time. She counted the seconds she stood there, vulnerable, until she couldn't take it anymore and slammed the nozzle home. When she turned to get in the car, she noticed Blue Sedan guy sitting in his vehicle, staring at her.

She tapped her finger and thumb together—One. Two. Three—careful to keep her eyes on her own car. When she looked up, his car was gone.

Get in, she ordered herself. *Get in and drive away.*

The smell of the gasoline was almost too much when she got in, but she didn't dare roll her windows down. Not until she was safely on the highway. She tried not to breathe.

Finally on the highway again, she rolled down all the windows, relishing the feel of the wind whipping through her hair and across her chest. She'd done it. She was okay.

But for the rest of the drive, every few seconds, she glanced at the rearview mirror, eyes peeled. Just in case.

Blacklick had been dying for the better part of half a century. Like an ancient miner still wearing his coveralls, with one booted foot in the grave, it was a stubborn place for stubborn people. A plague of abandoned homes and warehouses and factories and churches crept through the place, inching ever closer to the small community of people who'd managed to hang on to their houses and their jobs, despite massive layoffs and frequent restructuring, at the oldest and largest employer for fifty miles. Sunshine Plastics had, at one point or another, employed at least one person from every household in town, including the Finches. Folks were happy to look the other way while Sunshine dumped sludge barely a mile off the coast into Lake Michigan, and pumped the air full of smog and burning hair smell, so long as they delivered steady paychecks. Esther couldn't get out fast enough.

A Stars and Stripes bunting hung across the street, wrapped noose-like around the light poles that lined the main drag, likely left over from the Fourth of July. It was September. She remembered talking to Claire that months-ago weekend, trying to convince her to come to Chicago for fireworks and a cookout at Esther's house.

"The kiddos need me," Claire had said. What she always said when Esther tried to get her to leave for more than a few hours.

It didn't matter what the coroner said. Esther knew the truth. It was Blacklick that'd killed her sister.

The morning fog had just started to lift when Esther pulled into the driveway of her parents' house. The gray siding was in dire need of a pressure wash, and it looked like the lawn hadn't been mowed in a month. One of the gutters on the carport roof was dangling off the side, and the wood fence at the edge of the property was green with mold and moss.

She left her bag in the back seat—even with her keys sticking knife-like between her fingers, she didn't trust turning her back on the street for longer than it took to get to the front door. The porch was littered with cigarette butts. A pair of paint-splattered work boots lay next to the mat like they'd just been kicked off, their bottoms worn down almost to the quick. A vague dog shit smell drifted from somewhere upwind. She remembered one of their neighbors used to breed German shepherds and would let them squat wherever they pleased, even in her parents' front yard.

She let herself in without knocking. The door wasn't locked—it had never been locked, as far as Esther could remember, her parents believing firmly in small-town sanctity. Inside, the only light came from the kitchen. She walked through, noting a stain on the arm of her mother's white couch, and then noticed the framed pictures sitting on the fireplace mantel. There were two of Claire at the far end. A school picture from probably her sophomore or junior year in high school, her gray eyes dim. The other was of the three of them—Esther, Claire, and Meg. Esther was maybe six, which meant Claire would have been four. They were all squeezed together in front of the television, Meg's arms wrapped tight around their necks. Claire's tongue was stuck out, stained purple from the ring pop on her finger.

Esther ached once, hard, like the period at the end of a sentence.

She followed the scents of burnt toast and coffee into the kitchen where her mother stood at the sink. The water was running and she had a sponge in her hand, but she wasn't moving, just staring at the water disappearing down the drain. Dad ate standing over the garbage, but still managed to crumb all over the floor.

"Knock, knock," she said.

Dad looked up, mid-bite, and waved. Mom dropped the sponge, jumpy. She turned and, seeing Esther, seemed to collapse under her own weight. Dad and Esther rushed to catch her but she managed to grip the side of the sink. She shooed Dad away and then pulled Esther into a hug. The skin of her arms felt like rice paper against Esther's neck. Soon her cheek was damp with Mom's tears.

"I just don't believe it," Mom said, breath hitching. "I can't believe it."

Behind her, Esther heard the door waft open. She stiffened.

"Meg?" Dad said.

"It's me," Meg said from the living room.

"We're in here," Mom said. She released Esther, who turned just as Meg walked in. Esther hadn't seen her big sister face-to-face in over a year, and they didn't talk much more often. Meg's dark blond hair hung limp down her back and there were streaks of dirt on her sweater and jeans. Before Esther got the chance to say anything, Mom pulled Meg and Esther into a tight embrace. The three of them stood with their heads pressed together, arms tangled at the center. Meg's shoulder was cold and damp and she smelled musty—like rain and old.

Meg's breath hitched, and as she started to shake, the fragile calm Esther had pulled over herself like a blanket unraveled. Hot tears streaked down her face, dripping onto their clasped hands. Mom dug her nails into Esther's hand. It hurt, but not enough. She needed to really feel the pain. She needed to bleed.

As Meg cried, she whispered to herself—prayers and scolding and apologies—and for the first time since they spoke, it occurred to Esther what her sister must have seen, and her heart broke all over again.

When Mom spoke, her voice was low. Angry. "You'll both stay here tonight."

"I only live down the block, Mama," Meg said. "I'll be close. I'll—"

"No," Mom said. "I need my children under my roof."

Meg hesitated a beat, then nodded. "Okay. Yeah, that's—I can do that."

"Good girl," Mom said.

Esther pulled away, and when she looked at her sister, Meg avoided eye contact, focusing her gaze somewhere on the floor.

Mom stroked Esther's hair and Esther absently leaned into it, like a kitten.

"You two can sleep in the bigger room," Mom said to Esther.

The way the three of them had played musical rooms over the years—age and spats and nightmares making revolving doors of the upstairs—neither Meg nor her sisters could lay claim to any room with any real validity.

Except Claire, whose room would be just on the other side of a very thin wall, somehow too full and too empty at the same time.

"I can sleep on the couch," Meg offered before Esther had the chance.

Mom shook her head. "Nonsense. You'll have a bed. Won't take but two shakes."

She left Meg and Esther alone in the kitchen, Dad having disappeared. For a man who'd spent the better part of his adult life surrounded by women, he seemed to have a particular aversion to female emotion. When Esther was little, crying around Dad was a no-no. He'd leave the room, wiping his clothes and face like tears were contagious.

"Work," Meg said.

Esther frowned. "What?"

"He went to work." Her surprise must have shown, because Meg continued, "Your face is doing that crumpled thing."

Esther ignored the dig. "Dad went to work? Now?"

Meg shrugged. "He's Dad."

"His daughter just died."

"Is him staying home gonna change it?" Meg sat at the table—an avocado green and rusted metal relic they'd had since the dark ages—and started picking at the laminate. "You know how he is. He has to keep busy."

Esther made a noncommittal noise before going to the cabinet for a mug. The coffeepot was half-full and, thankfully, still warm.

"Do you ever think about that day?" Meg asked.

Esther paused for the briefest second, wrist-deep in the cabinet. "No," she lied. She poured a large cup of the strong coffee. Held it to her face to let the steam warm her nose.

"Claire did."

"Claire was—"

"Remember what she used to say? She said the darkness was coming."

Esther ignored the chill sliding down her back. Swallowed the too-hot coffee, burning her tongue.

Meg's voice cracked. "She said it's coming for all of us."

CHAPTER FOUR

CLAIRE

C laire was *starving.*

She hated skipping breakfast, especially when she knew there were waffles in the freezer, but when Esther had told her this was an *emergency* and they needed to go *right away,* Claire figured waffles could wait.

Usually, it was Meg standing behind the desk. It was half-rotted, like the rest of the building—the bones of an old warehouse, whose parking lot was now a Wash N' Fold—but they'd painted it blue at the beginning of the summer. Most times, Claire brought stickers to decorate it with, but in the rush to leave, she'd forgotten to grab her treasure box. Meg was the oldest, so she was the leader. She was the one who tapped the snow globe—a cheap, plastic souvenir from their first and only trip to Florida—and told them to come to order before they talked about Important Stuff, like why Dad hadn't gone to work in three days, what to name the German shepherd puppy that was always poking his nose through the fence, and how to avoid Uncle Joe at Thanksgiving.

Today, though, it was Esther who'd dragged them out here, *without breakfast,* and for what?

Meg sprawled on a beanbag chair, her long legs hanging spidery over the edge. In her lap was a small backpack which she unzipped to pull out a package of Pop-Tarts. She handed one to Claire.

"I thought we were out!" Claire said, gratefully taking the sugary confection. Cherry. Her favorite.

Meg winked, then turned to Esther. "Well? What was so important?"

Esther ignored her, tapping the snow globe with exaggerated ceremony. *Tap. Tap. Tap.* She raised it for a fourth, caught herself, and slowly set it back down. "This meeting will now come to order."

Meg rolled her eyes but smiled.

Claire bit off a large piece of Pop-Tart, tonguing the cherry goo that got caught in her teeth. They didn't get Pop-Tarts often, especially now that Dad was only working part-time. She tried to savor it, but she devoured it in only a couple of bites.

"There is an urgent matter to discuss," Esther said, "and it has to be dealt with before next month."

Claire frowned. She didn't want to think about next month. There were still three whole weeks of summer left before Meg would leave for college.

"Which is?" Meg asked.

Esther pointed at her. "Your stuff."

"I'm taking my stuff with me."

"Not all of it. I heard Mom tell you you could only bring a couple of boxes 'cause you're gonna have a roommate."

"So?"

"So I want to know what's happening with the stuff you're not taking."

"Nothing's *happening*, Essie. Jesus, you're acting like I'm dying or something. I'll be back sometimes."

Esther shook her head. "It's not right that it all just sits there and rots while you're away."

Meg sat up. "Why don't you just tell me what you want instead of getting all dramatic about it?"

"I'm not being dramatic."

"*An urgent matter to discuss*," Meg's voice went all high and mocking. "Dramatic."

Claire swallowed against the lump in her throat, a mix of chewed-up Pop-Tart and anxiety. "Why don't you just…not go?" she asked Meg. "Then you don't have to give away your stuff and Esther won't be dramatic and we can keep coming here and you can be in charge again."

"I can't just not go, Claire Bear," Meg said. "It's college."

"Yeah," Esther said, crossing her arms. "Meg can't *wait* to get away from us."

"That's not true."

Esther rolled her eyes. "Okay."

Meg looked at Claire. "It's not that I want to leave you guys. I just… I need to do this. Going to college means getting a job where I don't come home every day smelling like burnt plastic."

"You work at the Dairy Queen," Claire said. "You smell like waffle cones."

"You know what I mean."

Claire didn't, but she nodded anyway. She believed Meg when she said she wasn't leaving because of them, but that didn't change the fact that she *was* leaving.

Meg continued. "Indianapolis isn't far. Just two hours away. I'll visit all the time, okay? Promise." She turned back to Esther. "And no one's touching my stuff."

"What about your phone? You can't take that with you, right?" Esther asked.

Last year for Christmas, Meg had been given her own see-through phone. She didn't have her own line—too much money—but she could talk to her friends in private, and that was almost as good.

"The phone stays put," Meg said.

"But that's not fair!" Esther said. "I have friends too, you know."

"Quiet. Both of you."

Esther scoffed. "Pulling out the mom voice like you're grown or something."

The corners of Meg's mouth slowly dipped into a frown as she stared somewhere over Esther's shoulder. "I said hush."

Claire's stomach fluttered. "What is it?"

Claire shot a look at Esther, who'd snapped her mouth shut, looking hard in the same direction as Meg. Claire followed their gaze, heart jumping.

Movement behind one of the pillars about twenty feet away caught Claire's attention. Sometimes animals got in—the walls had huge holes; once they saw a bobcat prowling around the old offices, probably hunting the mice that lived behind the crumbling drywall—but this was no animal. Claire could see the person's shadow on the wall behind them.

"We know you're there," Meg called.

Esther came around the side of the desk, still holding the snow globe. She looked from Meg to the pillar and back, jaw working.

"You have five seconds to come out." Meg balled up her fist, but Claire could see her sister was shaking. "One. Two. Three—"

The shadow shrank as the spy—a boy!—ran toward the back of the warehouse, where a gap on the wall led to the street. Esther took off after him, her shoes making a sharp squeak on the concrete.

Meg made an exasperated sound and then bolted in the same direction. Claire, not wanting to be left alone with the shadows and the spiderwebs and the creaky ceiling, followed.

By the time she caught up with them, Esther had the boy face down on the grass. She sat on his back, pinning his arms to the ground.

"Why were you spying?" she demanded.

"I wasn't spying!" The boy writhed under her, his shirt riding up to expose large, yellowing bruises on his lower back. At first, he looked a little older than Claire, maybe ten or eleven, all gangly limbs, but then she caught a glimpse of a sparse shadow above his lip which meant he was probably older. Thirteen or fourteen. Esther's age. "Get off me or I'll—"

"Or you'll what?" Meg said. She nudged Esther's heel. "Come on. Let him up."

"He was spying," Esther said. "Who knows how long he'd been there?" To the boy, she asked, "Were you following us?"

"Yeah!" Claire added, not wanting to be left out.

Meg shot her a look before grabbing Esther by the elbows and jerking her up. Esther flailed, nearly catching Claire's chin with her fist.

"But my backpack! Remember last weekend I told you someone had gone through it and there was stuff missing?" Esther shot the boy a dark look. "I bet he did it."

The boy rolled over, but he seemed too scared to try to run. "I didn't take nothing."

"Wait." Meg dropped Esther, and she lunged at the boy. He flinched. "You're Donny, right?"

"You know him?" Esther asked.

"I know about him," Meg said. To Donny, she said, "You were the one they caught breaking into the cars at the plant, right?"

A light seemed to go on in Esther's head. "Yeah! Remember Dad was the one that caught him?"

Meg nodded. "He had to pick me up from work after. This little shit was still in the back seat." She narrowed her gaze at him. "Said it wasn't the first time either."

"Your dad's an asshole," Donny said, face burning.

Meg's expression tightened. "What'd you just say?"

He sat up, but one look from Esther seemed to keep him glued to the spot. She wasn't big, but neither was he.

"Well?" Meg prodded.

"See?" Esther said. "Told you. He definitely was the one who went through my backpack."

"What are we gonna do with him?" Meg said. She loomed over Donny like the pictures of Greek goddesses in one of Claire's books, a red halo of sunlight shining around her head. It would be hard when Meg was gone. Claire swallowed the thought before it could take over.

Meg squatted down next to him, a wicked smile on her face. "You like to steal from people, Donny? You think it's fun to take stuff from people who don't have much to begin with?"

Claire frowned. Took a careful step away from her sister. Ever since she found out she got into college, Meg's moods had bounced up and down. Her tongue had gotten sharper. Her temper shorter. Claire had thought Meg would be happy, even if Claire wasn't. But sometimes she heard Meg arguing with their parents in the kitchen. *Money*, Esther had told her once when she wandered out into the hallway too. *It's always about money.*

"No," Donny said, almost too quiet to hear.

"Then why'd you do it?" Esther asked, arms crossed over her chest.

"I didn't."

It was clear neither of her sisters believed him. Claire wanted to, though. He had a nice face, even if it was all scowly and a bit dirty around his eyebrows and mouth. She didn't know if he was the stealing type, but he definitely didn't look like the lying type. Besides, there was something about him that felt a little broken, like cracks in glass. Like the way Esther bit peoples' heads off when she got in trouble or hurt. Like the way Meg smiled sometimes, one corner of her mouth not quite lifting the same. Still, Finches stuck together, so Claire kept her mouth shut.

"What are you doing here watching us?" Meg asked.

Donny's cheeks looked like bruises. "I wasn't watching. Besides, it's a free country, ain't it?"

"Free country, all right," Esther said. "Free to whoop your ass."

Claire's eyes went wide. She'd never heard Esther cuss before.

Even Meg looked taken aback.

Esther leaned over Donny. "Go ahead and run. I'll catch you."

"You can try," he said, and his eyes seemed to go dark before narrowing back at Meg.

Maybe Claire was wrong. Maybe Donny *wasn't* nice.

Esther reared her fist back. "There's three of us and one a' you."

"What? You gonna hit me?" He glanced at Claire, almost like he was challenging her. She shrank back, stuffing her hands in her pockets to keep from reaching out for her sisters.

"Maybe," Esther said, but even Claire could hear the hesitation in her voice. Esther had never hit anyone. Not even Claire.

He seemed to consider her a second before leaning back on his elbows, sizing her up. Finally, he cocked his head. "What if I showed you something cool?"

Esther groaned. "Give me a break."

"Seriously. Unless you're too busy playing house or whatever."

Meg rolled her eyes. "Come on, Es. Let's go."

"I think we should see what it is," Claire said.

"Why?" Meg asked.

Because the way Donny was looking at her, it felt like they didn't have a choice. "Why not?" she said.

Looking at Esther for backup, Claire could tell her curiosity was getting the best of her. She worked her jaw, then looked up at Meg, who nodded once.

"Fine," Esther said. "But if this sucks…"

"Cool." He stood and glanced quickly back toward the warehouse before pointing toward the alley on the side of the parking lot. "This way."

Claire's fear melted into excitement as she followed a few steps behind her sisters. She'd hoped something like this would happen before Meg left. Well, not exactly like this. But *something*. Something big. Something that would stick in

Meg's memory like a signpost, so that when she got tired and lonely all the way out in Indianapolis, she could close her eyes and find her way back home.

"How much farther?" Esther asked after a couple of minutes.

"Yeah," Meg added. "It better be close."

Claire knew Meg was thinking about their bikes, left laying inside the warehouse. They weren't new—Claire's had been repainted three times, first white, then red, then a bright blue as it was passed from sister to sister—but that didn't mean they wouldn't get stolen at the first chance.

"It's close," Donny said. "Just on this next street."

He led them across the road and through a tangle of hydrangea bushes that'd spread from one house to the next. A shiver went down Claire's back as she imagined crossing the threshold into a world of talking animals and princesses and honeysuckle blossoms that gave good luck to those who ate them.

But there was no magic on the other side of the hydrangea gate, only another street with more houses and broken-up sidewalks. She was starting to doubt that Donny was taking them anywhere special, just biding time until he figured he could outrun Esther.

Finally, he stopped on the sidewalk in front of a house that looked a little like Claire's, except this one had a porch. The windows were blocked by iron bars, and the stone steps leading from the walkway up to the porch were crumbly. The lawn was patchy and brown. There had probably been a garden beneath the front windows at some point, but now it was all black dirt and spindly twigs like claws reaching out from below. She couldn't tell what color the house was supposed to be because of all the dirt and grime and peeling paint.

Still, it was just a house—and it definitely wasn't cool.

"Is this it?" Esther asked.

Donny nodded. "Isn't it great?"

"What's so great about it?" Meg asked. "There's a lot of houses like this around."

"You gotta go inside to see."

Esther crossed her arms, one eyebrow raised. Claire cast a look back toward the other side of the street. Was it brighter over there, or just her imagination? The trees on this side weren't thick enough to block out that much sun. She glanced back at the house and frowned at the few sprigs of green that seemed to reach away from the porch, toward the light.

It was one thing to find your way inside an abandoned warehouse or store and call it your own, but going inside someone's house was different. Wrong. Claire looked up at the windows, like big black eyes, and didn't like the idea of walking through rooms where people had slept. Had eaten. Had cried. Had maybe even died.

She could tell Esther didn't like it either. She kept shooting glances back the way they'd come.

Claire wrapped her arms around her middle, suddenly chilly despite the hot sun and dense air. It was hard not to feel like the house was watching her. Like it was holding its breath waiting for her to notice.

Donny went to the gate and unhitched the latch. The thing swung open with a horror-movie creak. He looked back, but none of them had moved. The corner of his mouth lifted. "You guys coming?" he asked. "Or are you too scared?"

"It's you that oughtta be scared," Esther said, all false bravado. "If it sucks in there, you're dead."

Meg chuckled. She followed Esther to the gate, looking back only when she seemed to realize Claire wasn't following. "C'mon, wee one."

Claire started to shake her head, but stopped herself. This was what she'd wanted, wasn't it? Something big and awesome? There could be treasure in the house. A magic lamp that granted wishes. But Claire didn't just read fairy tales. She was smart, had a reading level almost twice her age and sometimes the school librarian put books in her pile Claire might like—books about animals and bugs and history. She remembered reading about anglerfish with their glowing antennae that lured unsuspecting fish until they were too close to escape. There were snakes with skin the color of sand that hid in dunes, taking out their prey with one well-timed strike, and frogs whose colorful skin oozed poison.

What if this is just her putting on a pretty face? Claire thought. *What if what's inside is worse?*

Meg held out her hand; Claire took it. Meg's palm was clammy, but that was probably because it was so hot. Claire's shirt had started to stick to her back, and she could feel sweat along her hairline and behind her knees. Together, they went through the gate and up to the porch where Donny was bent over the doorknob.

"He's got a key," Esther told them. "Said he found it in the gap under the porch steps."

Meg frowned. "You're sure no one lives here?"

"I'm sure," Donny said. Then, as the locked clicked, "There we go."

Claire held her breath as he pushed the door open.

At first glance, the front room looked like any other ol' living room, except for all the rot and dust. There were patches on the walls where pictures had hung, and a brick fireplace in the corner. As Meg led her farther into the house, Claire smelled old garbage and rotting food. She covered her nose with the collar of her shirt, but it didn't help much.

"Stinks in here," Esther said.

"I doubt we're the only ones who've been in here," Meg said.

Esther looked at Donny, voice threatening, "If there's poop, or a dead animal…"

"There's none of that. Promise." He started toward the stairs. "Come on. The cool stuff's up here."

Claire watched Donny's face, the hollows in his cheeks making his eyes glow. She thought again of the anglerfish.

Donny was halfway up when Esther stopped, shaking her head. "I don't like this."

"Scared?" Meg waggled her eyebrows.

"No. Just not stupid. Those stairs are ancient."

"Donny went up fine."

"I guess."

"We're already here. Might as well take a look." Meg turned to Claire. "You good?"

Claire absolutely, definitely was not good. She nodded anyway.

Meg winked and started for the stairs. Esther and Claire followed.

The steps were mostly solid, but even under Claire's weight, they creaked something fierce. The carpet that covered them was torn and stained and coming up in places. More than once, the toe of her shoe got stuck and she barely caught herself on the railing, a whisker from biffing it.

Light shone through the uncovered windows, but the house seemed to swallow it, like the air was so dense, the house so hungry, the air couldn't make it past the front room. She glanced up and noticed writing on the wall, close to the ceiling: *I want to go home.* A chill snaked down her back as she followed the tail of the *e* in a jagged line down the wall, ending at a hole in the drywall. Skittering noises came from somewhere inside it.

"Holy crap."

Claire's gaze snapped up at Esther's voice and she realized she'd fallen behind. What felt like fingertips grazed the back of her neck and for a terrifying instant, she froze. The pulse in her ears blocked out any other sound. It got hot and the air got heavier, like a blanket had been thrown over her head.

Don't be a baby, she scolded herself, even as the phantom fingertips on her neck moved up to her head, scratching over her scalp.

"Don't move."

It was like she blinked and Donny was in front of her. His eyebrows furrowed as he looked at something on her head, hand raised. He took a deep breath, then she felt his hand graze her hair.

He let out a breath of relief. "Things are gettin' braver."

She followed his gaze to the stairs and spotted a black spider the size of a golf ball skittering toward the hole in the wall.

A spider. Not a ghost. Somehow it didn't make her feel any better.

A thought pushed through the revulsion. Donny hadn't killed it. He just…let it go. Her dad always said you could tell a person's goodness by how they treated animals. A spider was a kind of animal, wasn't it?

Claire clung to this, convincing herself that Donny wouldn't knowingly lead her and her sisters somewhere unsafe.

Donny nodded up to the landing, eyes shining. "Come see."

At the top of the stairs, she found Esther and Meg standing in the middle of a too-wide hallway. She blinked hard, suddenly dizzy, the corners of the hall where ceiling met wall going fuzzy, except when she saw them through the corner of her eye. The end of the hall seemed to extend slowly the longer she stood there, almost like a mirror trick, reflections bouncing off each other into forever.

Twenty or thirty doors of different shapes and sizes spread along both sides of the hallway. Some looked normal, like any one of them could have come out of her own house. Others didn't look like doors at all, more like gaps. Absences of light and space with a handle just visible in the darkness.

She tried to catch Meg's eye, but Meg was being slowly drawn toward a door directly in front of her that seemed to flicker in and out of existence, the flashes between here and gone again were yellow and orange, like fire.

"I feel sick," Esther muttered, and held out her hand to brace herself on the wall, changing her mind at the last second.

Claire realized if she looked at the floor, the dizziness faded—but then she looked up again, and the hallway had changed.

Where there were a bunch of doors, now there were only three.

She frowned, following the line of the ceiling, looking for tricks or mirrors or something, when she noticed a very slight gap between the ceiling and the wall. That was where the dizziness came from, she realized. The walls and ceiling wavered like they hung from strings. It was like being on a boat. Or on a bridge that dangled from somewhere she couldn't see. She planted her feet, suddenly unable to shake the feeling that they were going to fall.

"Weird, right?" Donny said, tone a little gloating.

"Weird," Meg said, cautiously stepping on a door in the middle of the floor. "This isn't real, right? Just a trick?"

Donny shrugged. "Open it and find out."

Esther tugged on an old bronze handle attached to a door at the far end of the hallway. "Why? What's inside?"

"Not telling."

"It's like I said then," Meg said. "They're tricks."

"Just open it," Donny said.

Claire, needing to be closer to her sisters, wandered deeper into the hallway, cautiously eyeing the doors as she went. One was intricately carved along the edges with vines and flowers, their petals stained red, while another looked flimsy, like if she leaned too hard on it, it would snap in half. A sharp pain rocketed up her leg and she realized she'd clipped her shin on a doorknob that only came up just above her knee. The door itself was a few inches shorter than her, the wood stained a brown so deep it was almost black. Gray water stains spread out from the hinges like storm clouds. Something in the middle of the door caught her attention, a crack in the wood. She pressed it, and with a soft click, a flap fell open revealing a key.

It looked like any old house key, except instead of a shiny silver or bronze, it was black and coated in what looked like soot that streaked her skin as she turned it over in her hand.

She heard Esther squeal, and when Claire turned, she saw Esther had a key of her own. She showed Meg how she found it, and soon Meg stopped in front of the biggest, widest door and pressed the center, and a key appeared in a little hatch just like it'd done for Claire.

"Maybe it's like one of those Victorian parlor games," Meg said, inspecting the key. "You know, like with the string? And there's a gift at the end."

Anglerfish, Claire thought.

"Have you already been in here?" Esther asked Donny.

"Not those doors," he said, catching Claire's eye.

His voice was calm, a little pushy maybe, but his hands were fists in his pockets. His jaw tight. Claire rolled the key over in her hand. It was still cold despite the heat of her skin.

"I don't know," Esther said, mirroring Claire's gesture.

"You don't know what?" Donny asked.

Esther shrugged. Then her head tilted, like she'd heard something. "Is there someone in there?" She asked, challenging. Then, turning to Meg. "It's an ambush, I bet. Him and his stupid friends."

"I don't *have* friends," Donny said.

"That supposed to make me feel sorry for you?"

"Look," Donny crossed his arms, his face a shade paler than before. "If you're afraid, just say that."

"I'm not—"

"It's cool. Really. I won't tell anyone."

"Esther—" Meg started.

"If there *is* someone in there, I swear to God…"

As their voices rose, the gap between the ceiling and the walls seemed to grow. Claire watched, unblinking, as the wobble rippled down the length of the wall, knocking loose patches of old paint and drywall.

"You find something?" Donny asked suddenly, drawing everyone's attention to Claire.

Claire hid her key behind her back, shaking her head.

"This is so stupid," Esther said.

"Like I said—" Donny leaned against the wall. Claire braced herself even though nothing happened. "—you can leave any time you want." The corner of his mouth lifted. "But I think you'll be alone if you do."

Claire followed his gaze to where Meg stood almost nose to wood with the door in front of her.

Meg looked at Esther, one eyebrow raised. "I will if you will."

"I dare you," Donny said.

No, Claire thought. *This is a bad idea.*

Claire's key scraped along the inside of her palm. It sounded like *shhhhh*.

"Open on three, okay?" Esther said.

Meg nodded, eyes shining.

"One. Two. Three!"

Both doors flew open, and Claire's sisters stepped inside, shutting the doors behind them.

Claire pulled her key from behind her back, catching Donny's eye. A look passed between them, and he smirked.

"I won't tell," he said.

Like the decision was already made. Like Claire was going to go through her door too.

She was scared, sure, but she was also curious. It hadn't sounded like anything bad had happened to her sisters on the other sides of their doors. And she kept coming back to what Meg said about parlor games. She wasn't sure what those were, but she liked the idea of finding a gift on the other side.

"Go on," Donny urged. "I'll be right here."

Something big and wonderful and memorable. It was exactly what she'd asked for. So why did she feel so afraid?

A voice seemed to bubble up from her belly. *Don't be such a baby.*

Body humming as little jolts of fear passed down her arms and legs, Claire got on her hands and knees because that was the only way she was going to get through the door, and then turned the handle. The dark was so thick on the other side that she took a sharp breath in to remind herself she wasn't drowning. It smelled like a basement, like woods inside of a basement, heady and damp and heavy. It smelled like lonely places.

She could feel Donny's eyes on her and her face flushed as she crawled deeper into the room. She must have kicked the door, because it quietly slid shut, the click like a finger snap. There were no windows or other doors that she could see, but no matter how many times she blinked, her eyes wouldn't adjust. She groped in every direction looking for another wall or the ceiling or the door she'd come through, but there was nothing.

Nothing except breathing. Hers? Or someone else's?

"Donny?"

Had he followed her in without her noticing?

"I'm not scared," she lied, "so you might as well stop."

The silence seemed to smile, amused.

A rush of air moved over her neck, pushing her hair aside, and her whole body trembled.

An open window, she thought. But where? And why was there no light? It was the middle of the day outside. There had to be some kind of light somewhere.

She sat back, her wrists aching, and reached up. Could she stand? Was there enough space? She kept her arms stretched out as she stood, shielding herself from walls that seemed to get closer each time she circled the room. She shuffled as she walked, hoping to hear the sound of her shoe hitting the key.

"Meg? Esther?" Claire walked blindly toward a wall and pressed her ear to it, hoping to hear her sisters calling for her, but the silence stretched like a rubber band. Even her own voice sounded wrong, too quiet, like trying to talk through a pillow.

Something pricked her hand and she jerked back, falling hard onto her backside. She bit her lip and tasted blood.

The sharp pain turned into a burning sensation that rippled up her arm, settling into her chest. She suddenly felt sleepy. She felt movement beneath the skin of her arms, like muscle twitches, but smoother.

The longer she was in the room, the less substantial she felt. The floor was nothing. The walls and air were nothing. She was nothing.

She sat down and the floor felt like wet sand. Like if she moved too much she would sink straight through.

She needed to get out of here.

Panic bubbled in her chest and a scream sat at the back of her throat. She tried to tell herself it was okay, that Donny knew she was here and if she didn't come out for a long time, he would simply open the door and she would be fine. But what if it'd locked behind her? What if without the key, Donny couldn't get inside?

She could die here, alone, in the dark.

You're not alone.

Claire froze. She couldn't tell if the voice had come from the room or inside her own head. The floor rumbled beneath her hands, almost like a purr. The dark seemed to undulate around her, stroking her skin and hair. She thought of the spider on the stairs, but this was different, like if water were solid. The dark bent softly against her arms and neck, velvety and thick. It made her skin crawl.

We're here with you. We'll always be with you.

Her voice crackled with tears. "Who are you?"

The darkness pulsed and then she felt the velvety touch move from her neck to her ears, to her nose. It climbed inside and slithered down her throat, viscous and sour. She felt sick, her belly heavy, like she'd swallowed too much water.

Muffled voices called to her from somewhere far away. She crawled toward them on shaky arms hoping, *wishing*, she would throw up, but the longer the darkness sat in her belly, the more comfortable it seemed to be there. It curled up, catlike, settling back against her spine. Finally, she heard Donny calling her name and she held onto the sound like a life raft until, groping, her hand touched wood.

The door fell open and the light hit her eyes like knives.

Several pairs of hands were on her, helping her, pulling her. She bit her lip to keep from screaming. When she thought maybe she could take it, she opened her eyes. The light didn't hurt so much now, but everything looked off. Meg and Esther were pale and seemed smaller somehow.

"You scared the shit out of us," Meg said, voice shaky.

"I was just…" Claire shook her head, her words all jumbled. "Sorry. There was a door."

"Yeah, screw the doors," Esther said, grabbing Claire's hand. "Come on. We're out of here."

"What happened?" Claire studied Esther, her tight lips, her pulse practically jumping out of the side of her neck. "What was in there?"

Esther ignored Claire, turning her steely gaze on Donny, who looked like a dog that'd been kicked. "Next time I see you, you're dead."

They slipped past Donny, Esther and Meg both practically running. They hustled back to the warehouse on either side of Claire. Meg stood almost too close, her hip bumping into Claire every couple of steps. She kept looking down at her and nodding, like she was worried she would disappear.

Thankfully, their bikes were exactly where they'd left them.

Meg mounted hers, then looked back, watching as Esther packed up her bag and swung it over her shoulder.

"What was in your rooms?" Claire asked. "In mine there was—"

"Nothing," Meg said, cutting her off. "There was nothing."

"Yeah," Esther said. "Nothing."

Yeah, Claire thought. *Mine too.*

The muscles in her belly rippled, making room.

Except, it seemed, Claire's *nothing* was coming home with them.

CHAPTER FIVE

MEG

NOW

I think I know how to get rid of the darkness."

Meg hadn't slept. It was hard enough being back in her old bedroom with its paper-thin walls and too-low ceiling. Hard enough that when she tried to summon silence, in the back of her head she was recounting every conversation she'd ever had with Claire, picking them apart with razor-sharp needles for the one hint, the moment when she could have turned everything around, if only she'd been paying attention. Her hands still itched with the feel of the fibrous rope, and when she closed her eyes, she saw Claire's grossly pale face, the bruises on her neck where the rope had squeezed.

Meg stared at the popcorn ceiling, counting the divots in the plaster from posters push-pinned and ripped down as her teenage tastes changed. She remembered her transition from obsessing over boy bands to girl rockers, all eyeliner and hair and attitude. She remembered folding up the NSYNC and Backstreet Boys posters and stuffing them into a drawer, only to find them rescued and re-pinned behind Claire's bed. It was always like that with Claire when they were growing up. When Esther would complain about getting Meg's hand-me-downs, Claire would patiently wait until she could claim them, too anxious to grow up, to be just like her big sister.

But Claire didn't end up like Meg. She was better. Smarter.

The summer before Meg went to college, Claire moved her bed to the wall between their rooms. Meg would wake up in middle of the night to soft tapping on the wall just above her head that wouldn't stop until she tapped back. I'm here, it said. Don't worry.

Now, laying in her childhood bed, she reached above her head and rested her hand against the cold wall. If she closed her eyes, she could almost feel a gentle tap. After a long time, she finally fell asleep.

In her nightmares she went back to that house, opened the door in that impossible hallway, and went inside knowing what she would see. What would be burned into the backs of her eyelids for the rest of her life.

She wondered if, when Esther slept, she saw it too.

The day of the funeral, Mom stacked boxes in front of the door to Claire's bedroom.

"Don't need looky-loos digging through her things," she'd said.

Meg wanted to tell her the looky-loos were already here. Meg's old bedroom shared a wall with Claire's, so she heard the middle-of-the-night footsteps, the door whispering open. The only one of them who hadn't gone in seemed to be Esther. Even after years and distance, Meg recognized her sister's hesitant footfalls creeping across the hallway, only to pause at the door a moment and then turn around. Every time Meg thought to bring it up, Esther changed the subject to flowers or prayer cards or parking at the funeral home.

Meg was wiping the living room floorboards at her mom's request when someone knocked on the door. It was too early for guests, and besides, everyone was supposed to meet at the funeral home, then come back to the house after. A quick look through the peephole revealed a boy who looked maybe twelve, with foppish blond hair. A Boy Scout, she figured. She opened the door to send him on his way, but she might as well have been invisible. He marched past her, calling out, "Mom!"

Esther emerged from the downstairs bathroom where she'd been on toilet duty. "Brandon? Where's your dad?"

Brandon? Meg's *nephew*, Brandon?

Ryan came through next, an *after* picture to Brandon's *before*, with the same blond hair and squashed nose. He carried a duffel bag over one shoulder and a garment bag over the other. He flashed Meg a quick wave.

"Did you bring his suit?" Esther asked Ryan.

He nodded, lifting the garment bag. "It's a little short in the arms but there wasn't any time to get another jacket."

Esther took the bag while planting a kiss on Brandon's forehead.

Meg watched the whole interaction with mounting discomfort. She felt like she was witnessing something intimate, not for her eyes. Esther the mom, Esther the wife.

Esther caught Meg watching, and her expression dipped before she plastered on a smile. "Go say hi to Auntie Meg," she said to Brandon.

Brandon dutifully crossed the room and opened his arms in front of Meg, head turned away. *Let's get this over with already.*

Meg bent down and hugged him, awkwardly, patting his back. Hard to believe this not-quite-child was the same toddler that'd chosen Meg's shins to smash with a Nerf bat. That was, what, a year ago? Two? Felt like it, anyway. She racked her brain for something to say. What did he like? Dinosaurs? All little boys liked dinosaurs, right? Except he wasn't a little boy anymore. Before she could come up with anything, the moment had passed and Brandon pulled away, not meeting her eyes as he trudged back to Esther.

"You okay?" she asked him, like hugging Meg was some sort of Herculean task.

Meg bristled, but then she caught a glimpse of his glassy eyes and realized whatever relationship, or lack thereof, she'd had with him, it paled in comparison to what he'd likely had with Claire. Her cheeks went hot with shame.

He nodded, but didn't look up from the floor. Esther looked up at Ryan with one of those micro-expressions only married couples could interpret.

Ryan squeezed Brandon's shoulder. "Let's go in the kitchen and see if Grandma has any of those yogurt things you like."

"He's big," Meg said when the boys left.

"Small for his age, actually." Esther leaned against the wall, arms crossed. "He got teased mercilessly about it at his last school. Not that any of his teachers gave a shit."

"Sorry. I didn't know."

Esther finally looked at her. "Of course not. How could you?"

Meg flinched.

Esther sighed. "I'm almost done in here. Think you can handle upstairs so I can get Brandon ready?"

"Yeah. Sure."

"Great. Supplies are in the hall cabinet."

Meg didn't tell her she knew where the supplies were. That she'd been in this house more often in the last month than Esther had in the last year. But the dynamic between them had shifted a long time ago. Meg was the eldest, but Esther was in charge.

Upstairs, she found a few rags and an old bottle of Windex she figured was enough for anything the bathroom could throw at her. Rather than clean the tub, she shut the curtain. No one needed to look in there anyway. She sprayed the toilet and the vanity and cabinet until all she could smell was ammonia, and then balled up the rag and threw it away. In the sink was a long, auburn hair, too long to be Esther's and too dark to be Meg's. Ridiculously, she was surprised to see it, like when Claire died, the rest of her would just…disappear.

She carefully lifted it off the bowl and then wrapped it tightly around her finger, until the tip turned deep red, then a sickly shade of purple. This was going to keep happening. She would always be finding pieces of Claire just when her mind found moments of relief. She unraveled the hair and dropped it in the toilet but didn't flush. *Let someone else be the one to send her away.*

Meg rode with her parents to the cemetery, alone in the back seat. Dad had the radio on and kept flipping between channels, none of the music the right background for their grief. Mom stared out the window, occasionally commenting in a low voice as she tapped her nails on the door:

The Addisons finally moved.

Fifty percent off at the Goodwill.

Grass looks good. Gettin' good rain this year.

They passed a street sign for Shady Glen Cemetery and they all went quiet. Mom's restless hands sank into her lap. Dad turned off the radio.

It was the worst sort of day for a funeral, all blue, cloudless skies. A Goldilocks sort of day, not too hot, not too cold. The kind of day that made it impossible to be in a bad mood because when you looked up and felt the sun on your face all you could imagine was possibility. *I could do anything today*, you'd think. And you would.

Gravel crunched under the tires like bones as they drove the circuitous route through the cemetery to the plot Esther had picked out.

"We got lucky," Esther had said. "It's right under a big oak tree. She'll have lots of shade. Lots of little critter visitors."

"She's not fucking Snow White," Meg had snipped. Esther had ignored her. Esther was good at ignoring her. But Esther didn't understand. Claire wouldn't have wanted to be in shadow. She would have wanted the sun.

Two rows of black folding chairs sat beside a casket perched on metal legs. They'd tried to cover up the gaping hole beneath it with green fabric, but the breeze shoved it to the side, revealing the dirt and the dark. A woman with big hair and a too-pink mouth waved from the head of the casket. The funeral director, likely—keeping watch while mourners arrived.

They parked, but no one moved to get out of the car until Esther and her family pulled up beside them. Other cars quickly followed. There were hugs and nods and *so sad*s. A blur of frowns and tears. Meg picked a chair at the end of one of the rows, too far to see Claire's face when they opened the casket, but close enough to see the gentle curve of her forehead, the brush of her auburn hair. Esther and her parents approached the casket, arms encircling each other for support. As they looked down, Dad nodded as if to say, *yes, that's her*. Tears fell silently down Esther's cheeks as she held up their mother, whose legs trembled.

Meg looked up, eyes burning, trying not to think of Claire disappearing down into the hole, into the lonely darkness she feared more than anything.

As the line of mourners moved in front of Claire's casket and took their seats, Meg felt eyes on her. She looked around, but everyone seemed occupied with their own grief, heads pressed together in hushed conversation. The funeral director stood over her parents, nodding and petting Mom's shoulder. Esther was wrapped around Brandon like a parachute, Ryan rubbing her back in small circles. No one seemed to be looking at Meg, but with every passing second, the feeling grew stronger. It was almost physical, an eerie pressure on her skin.

She sank down in her chair, trying to look without looking. She felt suddenly hot and uncomfortable, her sweater sticking under her arms and on her back. She told herself she was being ridiculous. Of course people were looking at her. Apart from being Claire's sister, she was the one who'd found her. A town this size, it wouldn't have stayed a secret for long. Still.

Movement in the corner of her eye drew her attention to the left, where the cemetery sprawled over gentle hills, spotted with trees and modest monuments and crumbling stone benches. At first, the figure seemed almost insubstantial, a wispy form rippling as a cloud passed over the sun. In the shadows, the figure—a woman—became whole. Her gray cardigan, ragged at the edges, dragged along the grass. Her long, auburn hair hung dead over her shoulders, and her feet were bare. Meg stopped breathing, unable to look away. The woman's face was a blank, eyes and mouth and nose nothing but flat pieces of flesh. She stared at Meg with no eyes, and Meg felt it, sharp and unyielding, straight through to her bones. Somewhere in the back of her mind, a baby screamed.

Then the sky wasn't the sky anymore, it was a crumbling ceiling. The trees were walls and they were closing in too fast, and when her hands balled into fists, she felt the bite of metal on her palm, and she knew without looking that it was a thin, bronze key.

A desperate thought cut through Meg's mind: *You're not real.*

The woman raised her arm in contradiction, reaching, clawing the air.

Meg rubbed her eyes and when she opened them, the woman had sunk to her hands and knees and was crawling toward her, cardigan billowing like storm clouds. Her hair tangled over her face, a stringy mask. Meg gripped the sides of her chair, a scream caught in her throat, unable to move or breathe.

Somewhere far away, it sounded like someone was calling her name, but she couldn't turn to look. If she looked away from the woman for one second, the slow, purposeful pace with which she crawled would quicken. She would blink and the woman would be on her.

The woman flung dirt and grass into the air as she clawed her way toward Meg. Meg's heart skipped and a soft whine escaped her body.

"Meg?"

The hand on her arm was like fire. Meg ripped away, crying out as her body finally came alive. She turned toward the sound of her name to see Ryan. He held his hand like it'd been burned, and his eyebrows stitched together in concern. Behind him, a sea of faces stared back—regular, normal faces, wide-eyed with confusion or fascination or both. Esther stood at the pulpit, the slip of paper in her hand hanging at her side, her lips set in a tight line.

The eulogies had begun and Meg hadn't noticed.

She fought to get her breathing under control, even as her chest ached with the force of her heart pounding. Her gaze swiveled back to the far side of the cemetery. The woman was gone.

But Meg was already half out of her seat and her legs trembled with the desire to run. She could sit and apologize and make excuses, but how long until the woman came back? No. She had to leave, as much for her sisters' sake as for hers. Claire would understand. Claire had known.

Meg slid through the row of bodies, muttering apologies as she hit knees and elbows and purses. She glanced back at Esther, who stared back unblinking, mouth agape. Mom yelled after her, but Meg waved her away. When she finally reached the end of the row she broke into a run. Wind whipped her already blurry eyes. Tears streamed across her temples and into her ears and she could barely see, but she made it to the car, only to realize her dad had the keys. She couldn't go back. She couldn't walk. So she let herself into the back seat where she slammed the locks down. She pulled her knees into her chest and buried her face in them, still seeing the woman's gray cardigan on the insides of her eyelids. The woman who looked like Claire.

CHAPTER SIX

ESTHER

NOW

For a long time after Meg ran off, no one said a word. Esther stood stock still, half in shock, half internally raging. Should she continue with her carefully written eulogy like nothing had happened or sit down and let someone more level-headed take over?

Just like Meg to make this about her, she thought.

After, it was all anyone could talk about. They'd had tact enough to whisper when they thought Esther wasn't listening, but she heard them all the same. It didn't matter that Claire lay dead not ten feet in front of them, or that the circumstances were horrendous enough. It was like the tragedy of Claire taking her own life was only validated by the fact that Meg had seen it.

Esther knew she wasn't being fair, but could she help it if she believed that if *she* had been the one Claire had called that night, Claire might still be alive?

The thought hardened her, and she continued with her eulogy, ignoring Meg, ignoring all of them. She caught a strange look from her husband, which she brushed off. Mom and Dad nodded as Esther described Claire's too-big heart, her kindness, which made her particularly suited for her work with social services.

"Claire was the best of us," Esther said through the lump in her throat. "She gave and gave and never asked for anything in return. She gave until she was empty, and didn't stop to fill herself back up again. I let her down. We all did." She paused, head down. Tears dripped onto the page, smearing the last of what she'd written. It didn't matter. She'd said enough. She turned to Claire, lifeless and plastic-looking despite the blush on her cheeks. *I love you*, she thought, hand pressed to her chest against a dull pain she knew would never leave.

More people had shown up to the house than to the service. The living room and kitchen were packed with faces she didn't recognize. At first Esther was annoyed. All these people content to eat the food and drink the booze without having ever paid their respects to Claire. Vultures. Leeches. But as she moved through the crowded living room and to the kitchen where her mother sat a sandwich on a plate for Brandon, part of her was grateful. Everyone was too busy with their plates and each other to offer awkward condolences. *I'm sorry* wasn't comforting; it was the sharp edge of a razor blade on a fresh wound.

In the kitchen, she studied the line of liquor bottles on the counter. It reminded her of a high school party, all cheap, generic booze, bottles half-full and probably stolen from somebody's parents' liquor cabinet. A bright green bottle of absinthe winked from the back of the row, next to a gallon of Smirnoff vodka. She bypassed both and reached for a bottle of no-name whiskey that, when she unscrewed the cap, smelled like pure ethanol. Esther wasn't a big drinker, usually. But today...

She poured several inches of the amber liquid into a plastic cup, and then topped it up with a can of Diet Coke. Her stomach clenched at the first sip, but she swallowed against it, a dare.

Ryan appeared from the basement with Dad's hand on his shoulder. When he finally extricated himself, he flashed Esther an apologetic smile.

"You okay?" he asked.

She nodded, burying her face in her drink. When she couldn't smell the booze, she caught the scent of something earthy and skunky. She frowned. "Is that pot?"

Ryan sniffed the air, frowning. "I don't smell anything."

"Where were you?"

"Your dad was showing me their new furnace and asking questions about warranties."

Esther looked up and spotted an old vent above the drop cabinets. When the house was renovated thirty or forty years ago, before her parents had bought it, they'd redone the heating, rendering dozens of vents all but useless. They didn't carry heat, but they did carry voices and smells from one end of the house to the other. She and her sisters used to play games where they'd talk into the vents and guess which room each other was in. Esther always lost.

Ryan followed her gaze. "Probably coming from upstairs. You want me to—"

"No. I'll handle it."

She shoved her way through the living room, waving off the few *I'm sorry*s lobbed at her like Ping-Pong balls, and started for the stairs. Her first thought was that a couple of teenagers probably crashed the gathering, thinking they'd get some free booze and then set up camp in one of the bedrooms upstairs, which made her think of Brandon. If her son was involved—no. One problem at a time. Brandon wasn't that kind of kid. But he'd been spending a lot of time with friends lately, and at the moment, Esther couldn't conjure their names or faces and wondered if she'd even met them or their parents. By the time she reached the landing, she was breathless with fear and frustration.

All of the doors were shut, but she followed the smell to the smaller bedroom, most recently Meg's. She pressed her ear to the door, but it was silent on the other side. She put her hand on the doorknob, expecting it to be locked, but it turned easily and when she swung the door open, she spotted Meg, cross-legged on the carpet, head tilted toward the open window. The stench was horrendous and a blue cloud of smoke hovered near the ceiling.

Meg didn't even look at her, taking a long drag from a joint pinched carefully between two fingers. She looked almost comical, lips pursed like she was blowing dandelion fluff. Her face was red and tear-stained, and the collar of her sweater was damp.

"So you're a pothead now?" Esther asked.

"Smoking pot doesn't make me a pothead," Meg said, voice low.

"Really? I kind of thought that was the only prerequisite."

"Must mean you're an alcoholic, then." Meg nodded at the drink in Esther's hand.

Esther ground her teeth as she took in the rest of the room. Someone— probably Meg—had covered the mirror above the dresser with a sheet.

"My son's here," Esther finally said.

"You think I should offer him a hit?" Then, finally looking at Esther, she rolled her eyes. "It was a joke."

"I didn't realize you were in the mood for jokes. The way you ran off earlier, I figured I'd find you up here curled into a ball or hiding under the bed. Guess that was just for show."

Meg only shook her head. She pulled a final hit and then ground the joint out on the windowsill before flicking it out the window. "There." She stood and brushed ashes from her pants. "Big bad weed is all gone. We done here?"

Esther closed the door, shutting them both in. "No. I don't think we are."

Meg seemed to brace herself, arms crossed and feet planted.

Esther sat her drink down on the bedside table and then tucked her hands into her pockets so Meg wouldn't see them shaking. "I just don't get it."

"Get what?"

"Why you?"

Meg opened her mouth, but before she could say anything, Esther plowed on.

"Of all the people in the world she could have called for help—" Esther rubbed her eyes with her knuckles until she saw spots. "—why did Claire call you?"

"I don't think she wanted help."

"Of course not. Why would the phone call a person makes before they kill themselves be a literal *call for help*?"

"I mean she didn't ask for it."

"Or she did, and you weren't listening. You weren't paying attention." *Like before,* she thought.

"I told you what she said."

The room felt suddenly too warm, the air like a wet blanket.

"Yeah. *The darkness.* She was depressed, Meg. She needed someone to pull her out of it, not feed her paranoid delusions."

Meg crossed the room in four quick steps, making Esther jump. Teeth bared, she stood almost nose to nose with Esther as she jabbed a sharp finger into her shoulder. "Why don't you say what you really want to say?"

Esther remembered a time when she might have backed down—back when she looked up to Meg, before their only conversations were about Meg needing a couple hundred dollars to fix her car, pay her rent, whatever. Not anymore. Esther straightened, meeting her sister's gaze eye to eye. "It's your fault she's dead."

The second it left her mouth she considered taking it back. But enough of a piece of her believed it, so she didn't even try. She braced herself, waiting for the backlash, her cheeks tingling in anticipation of a slap that never came.

Meg sighed, crossing her arms and then dropping them at her sides like she didn't know what to do with them. She shook her head, and when she finally looked back at Esther, there was a twisted smile on her face.

"You know what?" she said, grabbing Esther's cup from the end table. "You're probably right."

She swallowed the contents as a soft knock came from the door. Ryan peered in, frowning.

Meg stuck her hand up in an awkward wave as she flung the door the rest of the way open. She stuffed the empty cup into his hands. "Looks like your wife needs another drink."

Esther watched her walk down the hall, knuckles dragging along the chair rail, until Meg was out of sight.

"What was that about?" Ryan asked.

"I—nothing." Her gaze fixed on the sheet hanging over the mirror. The edge of the glass peeked through the bottom, but something about it looked off. With Ryan on her heels, she went to the dresser and pulled the sheet off the mirror.

"Jesus," Ryan muttered.

The glass was all but shattered, a series of spider-web cracks spreading across the mirror from the center, where it looked like it'd been smashed with something heavy. Esther's reflection in the shards was as jagged and disjointed as she felt. She covered the mirror back with the sheet, careful to curl the thing under so it would catch anything that fell, and then left the room, making sure to shut off the light and close the door tightly behind her.

Downstairs, there was no sign of Meg. Esther thought about asking her mother if Meg had left, but didn't want to field questions about why. The food was running out, but someone had made a liquor run which meant everyone would be lingering for a while yet. She found Brandon in the kitchen, his suit-front covered in crumbs. The cookie tray sat open beside the sink and she could tell, by the greenish tint of Brandon's face, he'd probably eaten his weight in chocolate chip.

"Grandma told me I could," he said when she started batting at his clothes.

I bet she did. "Where's Grandma now?"

Brandon shrugged.

"What about Grandpa?"

He shrugged again.

"Okay. You go to the bathroom and try and get some of this cookie off your shirt and I'll find them."

Brandon started toward the bathroom while Esther grudgingly ventured back into the living room fray. People were louder now, bolstered by booze and a shared anger at the injustice of young death. She wanted another drink, but Meg's comment about being an alcoholic—obviously untrue—clung to the back of her head like a sticker weed. As kids they'd said a lot of shit to each other in anger, but it almost never stuck long enough to really hurt. This time Esther had crossed a line. She glimpsed the cluster of framed photos of Claire on an end table and shoved down a pang of regret.

"Esther, there you are."

Esther looked around, finally spotting Uncle Bertram standing behind the couch. He cradled a glass of wine in one hand, waving her over with the other. She was surprised to see him here—not because they weren't close; Esther and her sisters always loved those few and far between visits when Bertram came bearing gifts from New York or Los Angeles, or whatever big city had been his home of the moment. Last she heard, he was in Europe, following a "friend" who'd been cast in the chorus of *The Phantom of the Opera*.

She slid easily under his arm as he planted a kiss on her cheek. "Auntie," she said, winking at their private joke.

He snorted. "I've missed you girls." Then his eyes glazed over and his jovial smile avalanched with pain. "I just can't believe it."

"I know."

"I saw Meg a few minutes ago. Poor thing was a mess."

Esther shifted uncomfortably. "We all are." Then, "Have you seen Mom and Dad?"

"Your mother went to lay down. Too much with all the people, I think, all of them whispers about her rotten luck. Like it's luck that's got anything to do with it. Not sure where Brian went, though. Probably wrist-deep in an engine or the gutters." Then, "I saw Brandon earlier. He's growing up to be—"

Esther had stopped listening.

The sound of a door slam had drawn her attention to the front of the room where a tall man with hunched shoulders and a mop of dark hair stood sheepishly beside a rack that practically bowed under the weight of dozens of bags and hats. She could only see part of his face, a sloping brow, a bristled cheek. She watched him walk hesitantly through a group of men toward the table of Claire's pictures, eyes darting like he was afraid of getting caught.

One of the men slapped his shoulder, making him jump. "It's Donny, right? Charlie's kid?"

The dark-haired man nodded, trying to wriggle out from under the man's hand like a worm caught on a hook. His gaze met Esther's for the briefest second. The circles under his eyes were so dark they were like bruises, and a long scratch marred the side of his neck. His arms were long and spindly, his hands curling in and out of fists.

A sharp ringing started in her ears, and then her mouth filled with the taste of metal. She stopped breathing and it was like the room began to vibrate. She felt the tremble through the floor, up her legs, where it settled in her stomach, making her feel sick. She flinched at the sound of cracking wood. She could smell something burning, too close.

"Esther?"

She barely heard Auntie's voice through the ringing in her ears, and when she finally forced herself to turn and face him, he frowned.

"Are you okay?" he asked. "You just went pale all of a sudden. Here." He led her around the side of the couch and made her sit. "Stay here. I'll get you some water."

The back of her head tingled, like she could feel Donny looking at her. Sizing her up. It was hard to breathe, and when she opened her mouth to call out for Ryan, all that came out was a strangled sigh. She needed to get out of there. She needed to hide.

She chewed the inside of her cheek until the pain woke up the rest of her body. She stood on shaky legs and shoved through bodies, ignoring people who called after her. She'd lost sight of the man, but she could feel him, still in the house. She found the basement door locked and there was no point in going to the backyard, which was completely fenced in. She hammered on the door of the downstairs bathroom only to find it occupied. She thought of bolting through the front door, but where would she go? Ryan had the keys. Where the *hell* was Ryan, anyway?

She ran, cursing the thunderous sound of her feet on the stairs, up and across the landing to the second bathroom. She ducked inside and locked the door behind her, and then stuffed a towel against the gap under it. *The smoke*, she thought, the ghost of the smell lingering in her nose.

Her mind flashed back to that day, in that house, and her legs crumpled beneath her.

No, she scolded herself, wiping away tears and snot. *It won't happen. Not today. Not ever.*

She recited the words over and over, a mantra, as she sat on the floor of the bathroom, huddled against the tub, and listened to the sound of footsteps in the hallway, on the stairs, waiting to see if today was the day she would die.

CHAPTER SEVEN

MEG

After her run-in with Esther upstairs, Meg almost left. She had her keys in her hand and everything, but Dad emerged from the basement just as she was headed for the door. Seeing the keys in her hand, he said he understood if it was too much and she needed to get out, but would she at least come back in a bit to help straighten up, if only so it didn't all fall on her mom's shoulders?

"Of course," she'd said. "I wasn't going anywhere. Just getting something out of my car."

He'd patted her shoulder, called her a good girl, and then disappeared back down into the basement.

So now she found herself in the backyard in a damp lawn chair pulled around to the side of the house where the fence cut in and an ancient oak tree with too many dipping bows cast a dark shadow over everything. This was where they'd buried Bear, she remembered. Bear had been the one and only dog her parents had allowed them to get. A thick-furred puppy with floppy, triangle ears, and a yip that sounded more duck than dog, he'd come from one of Dad's coworkers, free and just this side of feral. They only had him a couple of weeks before the undetected heartworms ruined his liver and kidneys. It was Claire who'd found him stiff and lifeless under the kitchen table.

Meg flexed her hand, still sore from the mirror. The shards hadn't broken the skin, but her knuckles were scratched up good, and each time she moved her fingers they stung. She'd been standing in the middle of the room, numb and anxious at the same time, when she saw the woman in the gray cardigan in the mirror. Her flat face was streaked with dirt—*grave dirt*, Meg had thought—and the tears in the shoulders of her cardigan were matted with what looked like blood. Trembling, Meg had lashed out. As her fist had made contact with the glass, she realized it wasn't the woman at all. It was her own reflection staring stupidly back at her.

She was clearly losing it.

Soon people started trickling out of the house, more condolences heaped onto her shoulders from the back door, half-hearted waves and deep frowns. The house seemed quiet when Ryan came into the yard, a sullen Brandon lurking behind him. Ryan stepped off the patio and into the middle of the yard where he looked around with his hands perched on his hips and his eyebrows deeply furrowed.

"Lose something?" Meg asked.

"Your sister."

"Ah."

"You didn't see her come out here, did you?"

If she had, Meg would have found anywhere else to be. "No."

"Bertram said she was looking a little freaked out. He went to get her water and when he came back, she was gone."

"Car still here?"

He nodded.

"Maybe it was just all the people. You know how she gets."

"Yeah," he said absently, still scanning the yard like she might appear from behind a tree. "It'll get worse now." He glanced at Brandon, who was busying himself with pulling weeds from between the concrete slabs of the patio. "I mean, it was already bad. But now it'll get really bad, and I don't know what to do about it."

"What do you mean?"

Ryan came toward her, arms crossed, and lowered his voice. "She doesn't sleep. She says she does, but I feel her get up in the middle of the night. Two, sometimes three times. She wanders around the house checking window and door locks. One time I found her passed out in the kitchen. She'd shoved the table against the back door and piled tubs of Christmas decorations from the basement on top of it. I left her there—shouldn't have, but I did—and when I got up in the morning, the mess was gone, and she acted like nothing had happened."

That *was* bad. But Esther had always been a little paranoid, hadn't she? No, not always, Meg reminded herself. Not until after *the house*. Meg pictured Esther hauling the table across the tile floor, sweat beading on her forehead, in her bare feet and pajamas. It was unsettling.

"I'm worried," Ryan continued. "I keep thinking one day I'm going to come home and find her hurt, or worse."

"I thought she was seeing someone," Meg said.

"She was. She stopped."

"When?"

He shrugged. "Could have been weeks or months ago. I wouldn't have found out if I hadn't realized the money wasn't coming out anymore." He sighed. "And now with Claire... I just—Can you maybe try talking to her?"

Meg laughed ruefully. "She doesn't want to talk to me."

"Why not?"

Meg ignored the question and stood. "Come on. I'll help you look."

Inside the house, Ryan went downstairs and Meg went up. She peered into her old bedroom just long enough to make sure Esther wasn't inside before closing the door again. She'd have to remember to deal with the mirror before her mom found it. The boxes in front of Claire's room looked untouched, but she pushed them aside anyway, and eased the door open, flinching at the creaky hinges.

It smelled like a library in Claire's room—all book pages and lavender and warmth. The bed was neatly made, her pillows stacked against the headboard and a quilt of patchwork Danish dolls folded at the foot. Meg ran her fingers along the edge of the quilt. They'd all gotten one for Christmas from their great-grandmother barely a year before she died. Meg had lost hers a long time ago, a hazard of constantly shuffling from couch to apartment and back again.

Other than the bed, there wasn't much furniture. A simple Ikea-style desk with a lamp on one side and a stack of library books on the other. Meg read the spines, frowning at the title on top: *Ariel and Other Poems* by Sylvia Plath. Behind the books were a few framed photographs—Claire and Brandon at the aquarium when he was maybe four or five, their parents in their very early twenties standing entwined in a park—and a corkboard of pinned ticket stubs and postcards. She opened one of the desk drawers and, hidden beneath a stack of what looked like bills or pay stubs, was a pair of tiny shoes, patent leather, with emerald bows on the buckles.

Baby shoes, never worn.

Even after more than twenty years, the patent leather was still shiny, the creases in the bows crisp. Meg slammed the drawer shut without touching them, no matter how badly she wanted to.

The rest of the room was tidy, save for a sweater tossed absently on the floor by the closet. Meg picked it up and held it to her face, inhaling Claire's scent, floral and fruity, before draping it carefully over the back of the desk chair. Anyone who walked in here would think Claire was the kind of person who had her shit together. That she was a woman who enjoyed her life and the people in it. When Meg looked at the photographs and the postcards and the brightly colored walls and bedspread, she saw a hard-fought war against the darkness that crept below the surface.

She leaned over the desk to get a better look and her foot hit something beneath it. A box. She nudged the chair out of the way to remove it and immediately wished she hadn't. Across the top was a label from the Portillo Family Funeral Home. Still, she couldn't stop herself from sliding her finger along the gap where a knife had already slashed through the tape. Couldn't help folding open the flaps, revealing a pair of red sneakers set carefully atop a pair of jeans and a gray cardigan. Heart hammering, she slipped her hand inside and stroked the fabric, thumb rubbing a cracked button. Something hard made her pause. Something in the jeans pocket. She should have let it be, but she couldn't. Without thinking, she reached inside the pocket and withdrew a small, black key, scratched to hell and flaking.

Meg stuffed the key into her pocket and quickly repacked the box before shoving it beneath the desk. A streak of black marred the edge of her finger that only smudged when she tried to wipe it away.

Remembering she was supposed to be looking for Esther, Meg left the room, carefully restacking the boxes outside the door. The only place she hadn't checked for Esther was the bathroom, but a quick glance showed no light under the door. Then she looked closer and realized a towel had been stuffed in the gap. A sharp pain pinched in her gut, even as she tried to tell herself there was a perfectly good reason for the towel, that it didn't mean anything.

She knocked on the door, and when no one answered, she banged harder. "Esther? Are you in there?"

No movement. No sound. She tried the handle, but it was locked.

"Esther! Open up!"

Panic building, she slammed her fist against the cheap particleboard so hard it almost cracked. She tried to imagine which window outside would lead to the bathroom, to calculate how long it would take for her to get her dad's ladder from the shed and climb up. If breaking the door down would be faster. She took two hesitant steps back, preparing to kick the door, when the handle jiggled.

She could hear someone struggling on the other side as the towel got caught beneath the door. Meg's pounding heart slowed, but barely.

The door finally opened to reveal Esther, flustered and red-faced, her slacks wrinkly. "What?" she demanded.

"Sorry, I—are you okay?"

"I'm fine."

Meg frowned, spotting a ball of dust and hair clinging to the hem of Esther's pants. "Auntie said you were freaked out about something."

"Auntie's being dramatic. I'm fine."

"Then why were you—"

"In the bathroom? None of your business."

"Ryan was worried."

"Ryan's just as dramatic as Auntie. I had a sick stomach, okay? I probably ate something off."

Meg didn't totally believe her, but pushing her any further would mean starting another fight and Meg didn't have the energy for it. "Okay."

"Okay."

She thought about what Ryan said and for a split second considered trying to talk to Esther, but the way she looked at Meg, all wild-eyed and daring, she knew there was no point. Something had spooked Esther, that much was obvious, but Meg had a snowball's chance in hell of prying it out of her. Instead, she gestured vaguely toward the living room.

"Pretty much everyone's left."

"Pretty much?" Esther peered pointlessly into the hallway.

"I think Auntie's still here. One of Dad's work friends was smoking in the backyard a few minutes ago."

"That's it?"

"I think so. Why?"

"Nothing." Esther moved past Meg, pausing a fraction of a second at the top of the stairs until Ryan came around the corner.

"Where were you?" he asked.

"Taking a massive shit, apparently," Meg said.

"Shut up," Esther said.

"Are you okay?" Ryan asked.

"Why does everyone keep asking me that? Yes. I'm fine. Can we please move on?"

"Sure." Ryan met Meg's eyes and gave her a *what the fuck* look that Meg returned.

The whole train of them went to the kitchen where they found Mom and Brandon packing up cold cuts and wilted lettuce.

Esther hugged Mom from behind. "I'm really sorry. We have to get going. Traffic."

Ryan frowned. "We can stay a bit. Help clean—" Esther cut him off with a look.

Mom nodded, struggling through a smile. "I wish you could stay a little longer, but I understand. You have lives and all that. I don't want to get in the way."

"Sorry," Esther said.

But Mom waved her off. "Just call me when you get home safe, okay?"

Esther promised.

They pulled Dad out of the basement for goodbyes, and he clung to Esther a second longer than usual. When it was Meg's turn, Esther embraced her loosely. When she pulled away, she opened her mouth to say something, but shook her head.

Meg could feel Ryan's eyes on her. She ignored it, putting his request out of her head. If Esther needed help, Meg wasn't the one who could give it to her.

"See you," Meg said.

"Sure," Esther said. "See you."

———————————

Meg finished packing up the leftovers while Mom scrubbed out the sink and mopped up sticky spots on the floor where people had spilled their drinks. They worked in silence, in a kind of celestial rhythm, with Meg's orbit circling, but not quite touching, her mother's. Soon the refrigerator was packed with casserole dishes and foil-wrapped plates, most of which would likely sit untouched until neighbors came looking for their Tupperware.

Dad came up from the basement just as they were finishing, glasses pushed up on his head, squinting at his cell phone. "Looks like Esther and them got home safe," he said.

"Thank Heaven for that," Mom said.

Mom slipped a damp hand through Meg's arm, like she could feel her start to pull toward the door. Toward home and quiet and alone, where she desperately wanted to be.

"It was a nice service," Mom said as she escorted Meg to the couch. They sat, and Mom stroked her arm. "All those flowers."

"Really nice," Meg said.

Dad followed, planting himself in his chair, cell phone still in his hand. If he wasn't in his basement tinkering, he was scrolling through Facebook, arguing with strangers on the internet about politics, whether he agreed with them or not. *It's his happy place*, Mom said once.

"Esther did a good job puttin' it all together," Dad said without looking up. "Real impressed."

"Yeah. She's a real gem," Meg said.

"You should be kind to your sister," Mom said, strained. "She's all you have left."

Meg sighed, head sinking back against the couch as she ignored childhood instincts. *Oh yeah? Well, Esther said...*

Mom settled deeper into the cushion. Still clinging to Meg's arm, she leaned against her shoulder. "Will you put something on? I can't bear this quiet."

Meg found the remote stuffed between the cushions, and then flicked through channels not really paying attention.

"Go back," Mom said. "*Antiques Roadshow*."

Meg obeyed, and then ticked up the volume before Dad could ask. On the television, an eager-looking woman in a Minnie Mouse T-shirt stood anxiously beside a man in a suit as he turned a pale-yellow vase upside down.

"People are so desperate to turn their trash into treasure," Dad mumbled.

"They're hopeful, Brian. That's all," Mom said.

Meg wondered if this was what it was like for Claire. Evenings spent on the couch with her parents, a prop to their lives. She never understood why Claire continued to live at home. She made decent money—enough to lend Meg a few hundred dollars when she asked—and she only had herself to support. She didn't know if Claire had ever had a boyfriend, or a girlfriend, if she went out with friends to happy hour or took trips. The ticket stubs and postcards on her corkboard had looked old, maybe hung for show to convince herself she was alive, that she had a life. Meg blinked away tears, shoulders sinking under the weight of new sadness.

Soon, gentle snores drifted up from where her mom's head lay heavy on her shoulder. Dad had drifted off too, his phone having dropped between his feet. Meg's whole left side had fallen asleep, but she didn't want to wake her mother so she slowly, gently, shifted just enough that her arm tingled with blood flow. She tried to focus on the show, but the appraisers' voices were low and careful, lullaby voices that made it hard to keep her eyes open. It'd been a long day, a long week, and maybe she would just close her eyes for a bit—

She startled awake. It felt like only seconds had gone by, but she could see through the kitchen window that it was dark outside, and the television had turned off. The only light came from Dad's table lamp, which cast an eerie glow across his empty chair. He must have gone up to bed, but Meg still felt Mom's weight on her.

She was cold, though, her skin like ice. Meg started to feel around for a blanket to put over her when she looked down, and instead of Mom's brown slippers, she saw bright-red sneakers. Claire's sneakers.

Her heart skipped and a painful tingle raced down the back of her head.

She squinted into the dark, trying to force the image to change, but the vivid red remained. Maybe all of last week had been some horrible nightmare. Maybe Claire was alive, and Meg had come over to visit and watch a movie, and they'd fallen asleep on the couch. Meg spun a dozen different stories in her head, but it only seemed to fuel the panic brewing in her belly. Her heart skittered in her chest as her gaze moved up Claire's body. Her legs were crossed delicately at the ankle, but her jeans were torn at the knees, revealing bluish skin. And the arm wrapped around Meg's was too thin, birdlike, her nails caked with mud. The tattered gray cardigan draped lazily over the side of the couch. Her head was turned down, blocking her face. The heady stench of dirt and rot wafted from Claire's hair. Meg swallowed hard as a roach wound its way through the strands.

The key in Meg's pocket dug painfully into her hip.

For a long time, Meg didn't move. She thought that if she closed her eyes, if she bit the inside of her cheek hard enough, she would wake up—really wake up—and Claire would be gone. But the longer she sat, the more solid Claire seemed to become. Her blackened fingers twitched and then began to caress Meg's skin. A violent shiver moved down Meg's back.

"You're not here," Meg said, voice barely above a whisper.

Claire sounded like she was gargling gravel. "Aren't I?"

This couldn't be real. *Wake up*, Meg ordered herself. *Wake up.*

"You snore. Did you know that?" Claire continued.

Meg nodded. Her mouth had gone dry, her tongue a dead thing.

"It's okay, though. I don't mind. I don't mind much of anything now."

"How can you be here?" Meg asked. "I don't understand."

"Aren't you happy? Don't you miss me?" There was a slight edge to Claire's voice. "Didn't you just *cry*?"

Her senses seemed to battle with one another. Logic demanded she realize this was a hallucination—a vivid, terrifying hallucination. But she could smell Claire. Beneath the rot and the dirt was her sister. She could *feel* her, the pressure on Meg's joints painful and throbbing—that *had* to mean it was real, right?

Did it matter?

"I *do* miss you."

Claire settled deeper into Meg's shoulder, and as she moved, Meg felt the bones in Claire's side shift too easily. "Good."

Skin crawling, Meg silently cried out for her parents to wake up. To find them and turn on the light. Even if this was Claire, even if she had somehow found her way back from the dead, there was something off. Claire wouldn't taunt and tease like this.

Or would she? Could death break your spirit the way it broke your body?

As though reading her mind, Claire giggled. "You know, it's funny. I thought by going to that house I was finally going to escape the darkness. But in those microseconds after my breath stopped and the light at the edges of everything faded, I realized that darkness is all there is. I'd walked right into the inky, sticky black of it." She giggled again, harsher. "Funny, right?"

"I'm sorry." Meg's voice cracked. "I'm sorry I didn't get there faster. I'm sorry after that first time I didn't just bring you home with me and lock you up and keep you safe. I'm sorry—"

Claire shushed her and it sounded like a coffin lid closing. She sat up, dragging her hair, dry and hay-like, across Meg's shoulder. Meg tried to look away, but once she caught a glimpse of Claire's face, the previously flat features changing now, taking shape, it was impossible to move. Her eyes bulged, blackened at the center and bloodshot. Her lips were crusted with mud at the edges, which flaked like snow as she spoke.

"Save your sorries. You're gonna need 'em," she said. Then, inching her face closer to Meg's, so close Meg could smell the pine of the casket, she said, "You know what's gonna happen."

Meg shook her head, eyes burning.

Claire nodded, and her neck made a squelching sound. "You saw it there in the house. You knew, but you ignored it. Can't ignore it now, can ya?" She picked up Meg's hand and held it to her face. Touching her skin was like touching the belly of a dead fish. "You're so warm." Then, squeezing Meg's hand, on the razor edge of pain, "Esther's next. She's gonna die, and it's gonna be your fault. It's always your fault."

Claire dug her black nails into Meg's hand. Meg screamed just as the skin broke.

CHAPTER EIGHT

MEG

S o? How's it going?"

Meg could barely hear her sister over the noise. Halloween was that weekend, and her dorm hall was awash with people in costume, fresh from their last classes, eager to get smashed and make stupid decisions. She would have locked herself in her room except that her roommate, DeeDee, had already claimed the room with her boyfriend for the third time this week. Seemed like they only detached for food and toilet breaks.

"Hold on," Meg said, clutching her phone to her chest.

Her parents had given it to her before she left on the condition that she promise to call at least once a week. It was an easy promise to keep. Mom found every reason to call in the evening—*just checking in* or *I found this gray T-shirt with Rogers's Bowling on it, do you want it?*—and sometimes in the morning, just before Meg's first class, to tell her to have a good day.

DeeDee said it was cute, which of course meant it wasn't, so after the first week or so Meg had started letting the calls go to voicemail. This, though, was the first time she'd heard from Esther since she left.

She ducked into the bathroom, which was miraculously quiet. "You there?"

"Yeah," Esther said. "Are you in the bathroom? You're all echoey."

"It's the only quiet spot."

"Okay. So. Everything's…good?"

Meg paced in front of the row of sinks, unable to keep still. She'd ingested more caffeine over the last month than she had in her entire life, and it had her jittery. She switched the phone to her other ear, buying time before she answered. She was going to class like she was supposed to and passing the ones that mattered. She ate when she remembered to and hydrated when her stomach started aching. Being DeeDee's roommate, she got invited to parties, only one of which she attended, and that was because DeeDee had tricked her, saying she just wanted some company getting food. *You need to get out more,* DeeDee had said. *You're starting to freak me out, and not just because you're being antisocial.*

Meg had nightmares, almost daily, and always the same one. She was back in the house, alone this time, and though she knew what she would find, knew in her bones she was in danger, she walked dutifully up the stairs and into the hall of doors. It was like she was trapped in her body, her mind screaming, begging to be let go, but her fingers still pressed the small mechanism at the center of her door—she'd come to think of it as hers, the way all of her faults and fears and anxieties were hers—and withdrew the key and waited for the door to open.

Some nights she was lucky.

Some nights she woke up before the rest of the memory played itself out. Before she saw it.

"Yeah." Meg croaked. "I'm good." Then, "Are you good?"

"Yeah. Totally."

Neither of them said anything, but Meg could feel the hall of doors hanging there between them. The thing they both constantly thought of but never said a word about. Even Claire had seemed to shut down in the days after. She spent almost a week in bed with a stomachache, only climbing out when Mom threatened to take her to the hospital.

Esther continued, breaking the silence, "Are you coming home for Thanksgiving?"

"I don't know."

"Why not?"

"I might have school stuff."

"Over Thanksgiving?"

"It's college. It's different."

She could almost hear Esther's eyes rolling. "Right."

"Since when do you care?"

"I don't. But Claire…"

Meg's chest ached. Claire had begged her not to go, saying something terrible would happen if she left. What Meg had wanted to tell her, what she wanted to tell Esther now, was that Claire had it backward—the terrible things would happen if she stayed.

"Claire will be okay," Meg finally said.

Esther made a noncommittal noise. Then, "I gotta go. Dad needs the phone."

"Tell everyone I said hi."

Esther threw out a half-hearted "'Kay," then hung up without saying goodbye.

It was fine, though. Let Esther be mad.

Better than dead, a voice whispered from the back of Meg's head.

"You coming?" DeeDee asked, one gloved hand perched on her hip. She was dressed as Felicity Shagwell to match her boyfriend's Austin Powers costume, blond hair piled high, and her dark eyes lined with too much white eyeliner. Her dress—*vintage*—was a size too small, squeezing her body like a sausage casing.

Meg, in a brief moment of optimism, had scrounged together a fairy costume made up of mostly dollar store finds—flimsy pink wings, craft glitter—but it was all still in the bag, stuffed under her bed.

"Nah. Not feeling too great," Meg said.

DeeDee paused, like she was deciding whether to try to convince Meg to come out anyway. She sighed, shaking her head. "It's that cafeteria food. I'm telling you, they put something in the meat."

DeeDee and her friends never ate in the cafeteria; they ate at the cafe down the street, all overpriced salads and *frites*.

"Yeah," Meg said. "Totally."

"You're sure you're not coming?"

Meg pulled her legs onto her bed, feeling the key in her pocket jab her thigh. "I'm sure."

"Suit yourself." DeeDee grabbed her bag and flashed her a quick peace sign. "Try not to puke anywhere, 'kay?"

Meg's stomach turned thinking of where she planned to go. What she planned to do. *No promises.*

———————————

The radio in her car didn't work, so she drove the two hours to Blacklick in silence. Speed traps littered the highway, flashing blue and red lights casting an eerie glow over the road. Meg wasn't worried, though. Not about the cops. She wasn't exactly in a hurry to get where she was going.

Every exit was another chance to turn around, another chance to go back to her dorm and slip on her ridiculous fairy costume and get hammered with DeeDee and her stupid friends—another chance to forget.

But the nightmares had gotten worse.

Used to be she got lucky. She would dream about the house with the hall of unusual doors, and in her dream, she would find herself at the bottom of the stairs, staring up into impenetrable darkness. She would take the first step and then jolt awake, just as something fat and slippery and undulating circled her arm. But every night for the past few weeks, she found herself one step further up the staircase, the metal tang of the air lingering on her tongue long after she woke.

Last night, she reached the top of the stairs. When she had woken up, sweaty and trembling, the little bronze key was clutched tightly in her hand.

Now, crossing the Blacklick town limit, she touched the outline of the key in her pocket. She should have thrown it away that day last summer, but she'd slipped it from drawer to box to dorm, only partly forgotten. They should never have followed that Donny kid. They should never have gone inside. A series of bad decisions had brought her, now, to Hill Street, where she parked her car across the road from the house.

A gaggle of trick-or-treaters bolted down the sidewalk, all giggles and sugar. Meg thought of Claire, probably wearing her pink Power Ranger costume (another Meg hand-me-down), and Esther grudgingly slipping a sheet over her head with eyeholes cut out. She wondered if they would come this far down the neighborhood. If they would take one look at the house and *run*.

She waited until the trick-or-treaters had turned the corner before climbing out of the car. She could still hear their laughter. Part of her wished they'd come back. As she approached the fence, she withdrew the key from her pocket. It was hot as she turned it over in her hand, the bronze sheen dull. It looked like any other house key, the teeth nearly identical to the one that matched the lock on her parents' front door. But part of the round head of it was cracked, a jagged bit of metal poking out that drew blood if she wasn't careful.

The fence creaked open before she could touch it, and as though pulled in by an unseen force, she crossed the yard to the porch, all the while telling herself that maybe this would end the nightmares for good. She would see whatever the house wanted her to see, and then it would be over. She could go back to her life. Back to forgetting.

The door, unlocked, opened easily. Meg stepped inside.

The foyer reminded her of an open mouth, the molding along the entrance archway like sharp teeth. She suppressed a shudder as she stepped across the threshold, over a damp, moldy rug, and started toward the stairs.

But movement in the corner of her eye made her turn. A hallway branched off deeper into the house, but it was too dark to see much farther than a few feet, the only light coming from the streetlamps through the windows.

Kids, she thought. Or people her age, hiding out in the dozens of abandoned properties to drunkenly paw at each other. The thought of getting caught by people like DeeDee and her friends almost made her leave, but then a car drove past, its headlights blinding as they flashed through the window. As the light brushed over the house, she caught a glimpse of the branching hallway, of a door near the end of it, with intricate spiral molding around the top and sides. Her door.

"Don't be stupid," she ordered aloud. Of course there would be a similar door. People designed their houses that way on purpose.

Except nothing in this house made sense. Nothing in this house was on purpose.

Clutching the key, she walked past the stairwell and toward the hallway, holding her breath.

It was hot on this side of the doorway, and the hall was uncomfortably narrow. She could feel the hot stink of air through the vents even though the shudder of a furnace was conspicuously absent. Sweat formed on her lip and hairline and she itched to peel off her jacket, but she didn't dare. She would put on a hundred more, she would smother herself, if it meant another layer between her and the house.

Finally, she stood in front of the door, her back pressed against the opposite wall. Was it just her or was it getting narrower? She glanced down at her feet, convinced she'd see them slipping across the floor as the wall pushed her forward.

This, she decided, was a mistake.

The last time she'd walked through the door, she'd expected something wonderful. How could she not? Unusual doors and mysterious keys were staples of her favorite childhood books. But instead of a gilded carriage or brightly lit lamp in the middle of a frosted wood, she'd been confronted with an empty room. What she'd *thought* was an empty room. It had only taken a moment for the temperature of the room to change, for Meg to feel someone else in there with her. Within seconds, the room became stifling, the air like a fist over her lungs. Sweat dripped down her face, burning her chapped lips. She smelled the heady stench of bodies mixed with booze and skunky pot. All of it together plucked a memory from the back of her mind that seemed to manifest around her. In the corner was her friend Krystal, her boyfriend's arm snaked around her neck. A bottle of vodka sat on the grass between them. Meg swallowed and she felt the burn of the alcohol down her throat. Krystal had turned to the boyfriend, a toothy grin on her face, and her lips moved without sound, but it didn't matter. Meg remembered exactly what she'd said that night that everything had changed. She remembered *everything*.

That first time last summer, she'd stood there watching it all play out in a kind of shocked stupor. It wasn't until she heard the baby crying that she'd started screaming.

Now, faced with the same door, she didn't linger on images of the house as an animal, the door moving through the house as if digested. Instead, she clung to the hope that this would settle her mind once and for all, that she would see that the door was just a door, the house was just a house, and anything she'd seen last summer was a vestige of heatstroke-induced hallucinations.

Before she could change her mind, Meg slipped the key into the lock and turned. The door opened, and she stepped inside.

Again, she walked into what looked at first glance to be a mostly empty room. It was different from before, though. Gone were the window and the tattered wallpaper. Now, the walls were bare and instead of a window at the far end of the room, there was a full-length mirror, the wood frame chipped and gouged. As she moved toward the mirror, she heard the door click shut behind her.

No, she thought. *Not again.*

Her breath came in quick, shallow bursts as she rushed to the door. She tried the handle, but it was like it'd locked from the outside. She closed her eyes, forehead pressed to the door.

Calm down. It's okay. It'll be over soon. Just don't look. Whatever you do, don't look.

"Meg?"

A chill snaked down Meg's body. *It's not Claire,* she told herself. *It can't be.*

"Meg! Please! No!"

Esther?

Almost against her will, Meg turned toward her sisters' voices. When she saw them, her whole body went cold.

Esther leaned against the wall, face pale. She sat in a pool of blood, holding a red-soaked rag against her belly. Meg's first instinct was to run to her, but her legs wouldn't obey, frozen in place by the image of Claire hanging by the neck from one of the rafters. Her lips and cheeks were blue, but her eyes were wide with surprise. She forced herself to take a step, but the movement made Claire's body shudder. Esther flinched, head turned away.

"Please," Esther begged. "Don't."

"What do you—" The rest of Meg's sentence was cut off by a flash from the mirror. She turned to see her reflection, not as she stood now, but streaked with blood, her expression wild, a gun in one hand, a rope in the other.

Meg stumbled backward. "No. I—I wouldn't. I would *never*."

Tears burning her eyes, she fumbled along the door for the handle. With her back to her sisters, she could feel the force of their stares. Worse, she could feel her own dead-eyed stare from the mirror.

Finally, the handle gave and she burst into the hallway, running headlong into the opposite wall. The whole house seemed to rattle with the force of it, but she barely felt the impact. She groped along the wall as she ran, choking on the smell of smoke and on her tears. Just before she reached the front door, she realized she was still holding the key. It had bitten into her palm, which was now streaked with dried blood. Snarling, she flung the key deep into the house and ran out the door, into the night, the sounds of her sisters' cries carrying after her.

CHAPTER NINE

ESTHER

*I*f I fall asleep now, I'll get a good six hours. I can function on six hours.

On five hours.

On four.

At two-thirty in the morning, Esther finally gave up on the idea of sleep. She went downstairs, flipping lights on as she walked through the living room and into the kitchen, where she poured herself a generous glass of wine. Glass in hand, she checked the window locks, the dead bolts on the front and back doors, and then went through the whole thing again because she told herself it would make her feel better. It didn't.

She sat at the counter where she had a clear view of both doors. The wine was gone, but she kept putting the glass to her lips, forgetting, as she considered grabbing a knife from the block, just in case. A car drove by, too slowly, its headlights flashing at the edges of the curtains. She tensed, half-standing, and mentally compiled all of the weapons at her immediate disposal—wineglass, knife block, coffeepot. She calculated the time it would take to get the back door unlocked, plotted the route she would take from the yard, through the gate, and around to the front where she'd hidden spare car keys deep inside a planter. Every time she walked through the plan, she was hit with a twinge of guilt. Ryan. Brandon. But then she reminded herself: he wouldn't be after her family. Just Esther.

It had taken the entire ride back to Chicago for her to make the connection. *Donny.* The kid who'd shown Esther and her sisters the house on that long-ago summer day. Could it be the same person? Donny wasn't exactly an uncommon name, especially in Blacklick, where boys' names were passed to each other like well-worn hand-me-downs. She tried to conjure the kid's face, but it had been more than twenty years and all she could definitively remember was a mop of dark hair and a square head that had seemed too big for his body. Still, it was too much of a coincidence not to consider.

Meg's voice kept coming back to her. *She said the darkness was coming for all of us.*

But Esther shook it off, calming herself by gently tapping her fingertip on the countertop—tap, tap, tap—then on the back of the couch—tap, tap, tap—small, syncopated touches that conjured a bubble of safety. She went through her routine once more, this time adding a check on the oven (off) and the flat iron she never used (unplugged, stored in the bathroom closet).

Esther didn't like coincidences. She didn't like the way they snuck up; the way they got brushed off as nothing.

Why had Claire chosen to end her life there of all places?

And why had Donny appeared back in their lives so soon after?

She remembered Claire had stayed friends with him for a little while when they were kids. Then something happened with his parents—Dad hadn't been specific about the details, but had warned Claire and Esther to keep their distance. As far as Esther knew, they hadn't had contact since then, so why had he shown up to the house?

For you, a voice in the back of her head whispered.

Preposterous. They were friends or something. Or maybe his dad had worked with Esther's dad at some point. Blacklick was tiny. Claustrophobic. Nobody needed a reason to insert themselves into their neighbors' lives. It just *happened*. Donny was no more a harbinger of doom than that fucking house had been a portent of the future.

She finally heard the car drive off and slid, shaking slightly, off the stool. She poured another glass of wine, which she drank greedily. She needed sleep, to put all of this away until she could look at it in the daylight, when her mind wasn't clouded by shadow and fear. She finished her wine and set the glass in the sink. Then she thought better of it and rinsed it, hiding it in the back of the cupboard. After the funeral, Ryan had treated her like a skittish kitten. She didn't want to give him another reason to worry.

She started for the stairs when a scratching noise broke the silence. She froze, hand on the banister. Had it come from upstairs? She thought about calling for Ryan, but didn't want to wake him in case—

There it was again, like nails on wood. She spun around, heart pounding. The door was locked. She'd checked it three times. She was okay. She was safe.

It's an animal, she thought. *A squirrel or a stray cat looking for warmth.*

She held her breath, waiting, listening.

This time, the scratch became a knock, soft and short, like the person doing the knocking knew she was there.

Every fiber of her being ordered her to go upstairs, to wake her husband and send him after the phantom knocker.

But what if there's no one there? What if I'm imagining it?

He's your husband. He loves you. He'll understand.

I can't stand the way he looks at me now.

Better to be safe. Better to hide.

She went back and forth in her head as the knock became a little louder, a little more insistent.

Ignore it.

What if it's an emergency?

Get Ryan.

I can't.

You're afraid.

I'm tired of being afraid.

Before she could stop herself, Esther crossed the foyer to the door, flinching with the creak of the floor underfoot. The knocking stopped just as she leaned toward the peephole. She held her breath and peered through.

The porch light was on, but the figure on the other side of the door was almost completely in shadow, like they couldn't be touched by the light. They stood statue-still, and for a long moment, Esther couldn't be sure her eyes weren't just seeing what she thought they ought to.

"Hello?" Her voice was quiet, barely above a whisper. "Who are you?"

The figure either ignored her or couldn't hear.

Get Ryan.

She patted the pocket of her robe for her phone, thinking she'd have 9-1-1 cued up and ready if anything went badly, then scolded herself when she realized she'd left it on her nightstand.

The stupidest thing she could do was open the door. She knew that. But she'd spent the better part of the last twenty years terrified of what she'd seen in that room, constantly looking over her shoulder, unable to sleep without seeing *him* in her nightmares.

Made brave by too much wine and exhaustion, she reached for the dead bolt, still watching the figure through the peephole. The lock clicked open, but the figure didn't move. She felt her heart racing in her throat, in her back, and in the tips of her fingers as she turned the handle, as she stepped back and opened the door.

Her stomach plummeted.

She didn't need to see his face to know it was *him*. Still draped in shadow, his chest rose and fell, his hands buried deep in jacket pockets.

It was like being disconnected from her body, her mind floating, carried away by terror. Her gaze fixed on his pocket, the distinctly gun-shaped weight in it, and her mouth went dry. She wanted to scream. To run. But the strings had been cut. She was frozen. Trapped.

"What do you want?" Esther asked, voice barely above a whisper.

The shadows around him rippled. Something wasn't right.

It was like being inside of one of her nightmares. The edges of her vision blurred, and when she tried to back farther into the house, her legs wouldn't move. She reached for the door, but it was like her arm was made of lead.

"Please," she begged. "What's happening? Why are you here?"

He withdrew his hands from his pockets. One of them held a gun.

The blood in her veins went cold.

No.

She felt the explosion more than she heard it. She stumbled back, her legs frightened back to life, and into the bureau where she knocked over a ceramic jug that shattered, spilling flowers and water everywhere. The shock of the crash dislodged the scream in her throat. She slipped and landed on her forearms on the jagged pieces, which tore into her skin. Blood pooled in the puddles of water and streaked her robe. She clutched her stomach where she was sure she'd been shot, but when she lifted her shirt, she found clean, unblemished skin.

Ryan thundered down the stairs, shouting something at her she couldn't hear. Her ears rang from the gunshot—what she'd been sure was an actual real gunshot in the moment, but now wasn't so sure. The figure had gone, the porch light casting a bright glow over everything where, just seconds before, there'd been almost complete darkness.

There's no one there. There had never been anyone there.

But as Ryan helped her to her feet, kicking the door shut as he looped an arm around her back, her nose wrinkled at the distinct smell of gunpowder.

Esther probably should have gotten stitches, but she hadn't wanted to wake Brandon. Thanks to his noise machine blasting a cacophony of rain and cricket sounds, he'd slept through the whole thing. Her arm stung like hell, and the gauze bandages weren't much against the blood that oozed every time she moved, but she managed to get the floor mopped and the ceramic shards tossed before Brandon was even out of bed. Ryan wasn't impressed.

"We should take you to get checked out," he said over the mouth of his coffee mug. He'd been brooding in the kitchen ever since she'd insisted on taking care of the mess herself.

She held up her arm, freshly bandaged. "What for? I'm fine."

"I'm not just talking about your arm."

Her face went hot. She knew he'd find out about her skipping out on therapy sooner or later, she'd just hoped it would be later. Ignoring his comment, she opened her laptop to log in for the day. Work had always been a good distraction for her. Being a project manager meant she had her irons in dozens of fires at a time—there wasn't enough time in the day to worry about things like phantom midnight visitors.

"Will you at least take a couple of days off?" he continued.

"I took time off," Esther said. "I need to work."

"One day isn't time."

"Two days," Esther corrected. "I'm sorry I scared you this morning, but I told you—it was a nightmare."

"You don't sleepwalk."

"Maybe I do now."

He sighed, setting his mug down. "We both know something has been going on with you. I was fine with you not talking to me about it because at least you were talking to someone. The paranoia is getting out of control. You hurt yourself."

"It's not paranoia if it's real," Esther snapped.

"If *what's* real?"

She didn't answer. She didn't know *how*.

He stood behind her, wrapping his arms around her shoulders. His weight felt good. Comforting. But she could feel how tense he was, how frustrated. He kissed the top of her head. "Take one more day. That's all I'm asking." When Esther started to protest, he shook his head. "No. Don't argue this time, okay? Your sister died. You've always been a strong person, but you don't need to be strong all the time. The nightmares and all that—it'll escalate if you don't check in with yourself."

He *had* been talking to her therapist. *Check in with yourself* was a favorite phrase of hers.

He continued, nodding at the laptop. "They'll survive one more day without you. I promise."

Of course they would survive. Esther's job as resident plate spinner wasn't all that complicated, but it was *hers*. Something she could control when the rest of the world felt so incredibly unpredictable. In her kitchen, at the counter, in her little digital world, she was in charge, and no one was coming for her. Did part of her want to curl up on the couch and cry until she was nothing but a husk? Yes. But cracking open that wall of darkness in the back of her head wouldn't bring her sister back. It wouldn't help her understand what was happening to her, or why.

But part of her wondered if he was right. Maybe by ignoring her pain she'd helped her nightmares manifest into something that had felt real.

And, *God*, had it felt real.

"Okay," she finally said, closing her laptop. "One more day."

Ryan went to work after making her promise to call him if anything like this morning happened again. She promised, locking the door behind him.

Except, without Ryan looking over her shoulder, she was tempted to work. With nothing to distract her, being alone in the house, in the quiet, made her hyper-aware of every creak and scratch and hiss. The heat kicked on and she jumped, thinking the air through the vents were whispers. She needed noise. She needed distraction.

After making another pot of coffee, she turned on the television, flipping through the cable channels they paid for but never watched, until she found the Food Network. She watched Rachael Ray get excited over EVOO and nutmeg for about an hour, which was almost twice as long as she could stand it, before grabbing her laptop. With *Iron Chef* blasting from the living room, Esther stood at the counter, her coffee quickly going cold as she opened her browser. She wouldn't work—she'd at least keep that promise—but in the sober light of day, she felt brave enough to do some digging into Donny.

If the past was coming for her, she was going to meet it prepared.

She didn't have much to go on. A face, a first name that was likely a nickname. Even if he was the kid from her childhood, there was no way to know if he still lived in Blacklick.

Claire would know, she thought.

A week ago, she could have sent her a quick text that Claire would have answered immediately because if Esther was asking, she would have figured it was important. Such a stupid, simple thing. An ache settled in Esther's chest as she realized she would always want to call or text her sister but would never be able to again. It wasn't right. It wasn't *fair*.

She opened Facebook and navigated to Claire's page. Her profile picture was at least a few years old. She stood in front of their parents' house on what was probably someone's birthday judging by the group shot, but Esther couldn't be sure whose. Esther hadn't gotten around to updating Claire's social media—Claire didn't have much of an internet presence, telling Esther once that digital interactions felt hollow—but it hadn't stopped people from posting condolences.

Sorry for your loss.

Claire was a sweetheart.

Wish we could have got to know you better.

Some people posted pictures, others posted kids' drawings, probably done by children Claire had served as caseworker for as they were shuffled between foster homes. A place like Blacklick, Esther could only imagine the things Claire had seen. People weren't just desperately poor—they were desperate. Less than a year ago, the governor had declared a state of emergency for the county because of how many people—how many *kids*—had died of fentanyl overdoses.

Esther scrolled and scrolled, looking for her sister's last post in the mass of wishes and clip-art flowers. She finally found it, posted a little over a month ago:

12:49 a.m. *Feeling relief tonight. I thought I wouldn't. Just goes to show.*

Before Esther could agonize over what it might mean, she glanced beneath the post itself.

Donny Lippman liked this.

She held her breath before clicking his name. The page refreshed with a profile for Donny Lippman. Almost every section was blank—probably marked private—but the minute she saw his profile picture, she knew.

She opened another tab and googled his name only to come up with pathetically few results. She found a Twitter profile with no picture, the last post from eight years ago, and a comment on a Reddit forum on combustible engines that sounded too formal to be someone from Blacklick. She tried searching his name in combination with Claire's, then, shaking, with her own, only to come up with nothing. Frustrated, she went back to Claire's Facebook page and scrolled through, hunting for any other instances where Donny had liked or commented on one of her posts. When she couldn't find anything, she went looking for Claire's Friends list, but the section was hidden behind privacy settings.

"What the hell, Claire," she muttered.

She spent what felt like hours standing at the counter, searching and finding nothing that would give her any answers as to why Donny would be commenting on Claire's midnight Facebook posts, why he would have shown up at her funeral. Why *his* face so closely resembled the apparition in the room that summer.

Her stomach was in knots, and a dull ache formed behind her eyes, which started to pound the longer she stared at her computer screen. Every time she clicked back to Donny's profile, she could have sworn he was the man in the doorway, his gun raised. Was it premonition or paranoia?

Finally, she forced herself to shut the laptop. Her headache was getting worse, and soon it would be a full-blown migraine. She grabbed an ice pack from the freezer and headed upstairs. She'd lay down for a little bit—just long enough for the worst of the pain to pass—then get back to finding Donny before Ryan got home. She told herself she'd explain it all to him because he deserved the truth, or as much of the truth as she was willing to give, but not until she could figure out how all the pieces fit together.

Exhaustion fell on her like a wave the minute her head hit the pillow. For once, she was too tired to be afraid.

It seemed like as soon as her eyes closed, she was startled awake. She lay there, still, eyes wide. Had it been a noise in the house? Or in a dream she couldn't seem to keep hold of? The cut on her arm throbbed; she must have been laying on it because a little blood had seeped through the gauze and onto her shirt. For a long time, she didn't move. Barely breathed. When she almost had herself convinced she could go back to sleep, a sound like a chair being pushed across the tile drifted up from downstairs. She froze, one hand on the side of the bed, ready to launch herself at whatever came through the door. She glanced quickly up at the clock on the wall. It was too early for Ryan or Brandon to be back, and no one she knew had a key to their house—a rule her in-laws had balked at. Could Ryan have given them a key behind her back? Even if he had, she couldn't think of a reason they would just walk in, unannounced.

She climbed slowly, slowly out of bed, flinching when the mattress creaked. Straining to hear any sound that came from downstairs, she crept across the room to her closet where she pushed aside her clothes to reveal a small, fireproof safe. They'd bought it when they bought the house, a place to store their important paperwork in case something terrible happened. Esther was the bookkeeper of the house, so Ryan never went into the safe, making it the perfect hiding place. She typed in the code and when the door popped open, she half-expected the gun not to be there. She'd bought it a little over a year ago, put it directly in the safe, and never handled it again. Part of her figured she'd get rid of it—she knew the statistics, that she was more likely to be killed by her own gun than someone else's—but still, she'd wanted to feel secure. More in control. Now, pulling it out of the safe, she didn't feel anything close to control. Only fear.

She held it gently at her side, finger as far away from the trigger as possible, as she moved carefully toward the bedroom door. Downstairs, she heard shuffling footsteps and a cabinet door opening. She peered down the stairs, but all she saw was the front door, very slightly ajar.

This is real, she thought, as though reassuring herself. *There is someone in my house.*

She gripped the gun a little tighter, and started toward the stairs.

She took them slowly, one at a time, feeling each stair out for the telltale creak that would alert the intruder to her presence. About halfway down, she slipped on someone's abandoned sock, her foot hitting the next stair too hard, with a loud thump. She froze. The movement deeper in the house stopped too. She held her breath, listening. She could almost feel the intruder doing the same.

How far into the house was he? Would she make it to the door in time if she ran now?

As her mind raced to come up with a plan, loud, clomping footsteps moved toward her. Her legs shook. She'd never make it out without him coming too close. She sat on the stair and held the gun up the way the man at the shop had showed her. Still, her hands trembled, and tears blurred her vision. She'd never fired the thing, didn't even know if she could, but she had to try.

When the intruder rounded the stairwell, his face came into full view. It was *him*, just as she'd seen him in her nightmares. His mouth opened in a wide O and a sharp sound made her ears ring. He reached for his pocket, one arm extended as if to slash at her, and a scream died in her throat. It was now or never. She didn't hesitate. She pulled the trigger, bracing for the kickback.

It never came.

The gun clicked but didn't fire. Her mouth fell open in surprise, and when she looked back at him, she felt sick.

It wasn't her nightmare at all.

It was Brandon.

He stood stock still with a bag of potato chips in one hand. His eyes were wide as saucers as he stared at the gun still pointed at him. His voice shook. "Mom?"

Like she'd just realized the thing was in her hand, she dropped it onto the stairs and reached out for her son. "I didn't—I thought—" She looked around, whole body trembling, lost. "There was someone. There was someone."

When she was finally able to pull herself to her feet, Brandon ran back the way he'd come. Esther followed, pleading and crying and apologizing, but he locked himself in the downstairs bathroom. She banged on the door, begging him to let her in, to let her explain, but she could hear him on the phone. That goddamned cell phone she'd insisted they get him when he started after school activities.

Ryan screeched into the driveway barely ten minutes later. Esther was on the couch, the gun in their closet on top of the safe because she'd been shaking too hard to get the PIN right. Ryan burst through the door, ignoring Esther at first, and headed straight for Brandon's bedroom.

This is it, she thought. *This is the moment my life falls apart.*

Ryan finally approached her. He stood in front of her, silent. She tensed under his gaze, unable to meet his eyes.

Just say it, she thought. *Put me out of my misery.*

"Brandon's worried about you," Ryan said.

Her head snapped up, and she frowned. This wasn't what she'd been expecting.

"Oh, don't worry," he said. "You'll hear just how pissed off I am, but right now, I need to know what happened, starting with why there is a gun in my house."

"Safety," she said, ashamed.

"Where is it now?"

"Upstairs."

He left her sitting there, and when he came back, he was holding the gun. She couldn't even look at it now.

"I guess I should be grateful you have no idea what you're doing." He turned the gun over, then set it on the coffee table. "The safety's still on."

"Why was Brandon even home?" Even to her own ears she sounded pathetic, childish, but she couldn't help it. "He isn't supposed to be getting off the bus for another hour."

Instead of answering, he went into the kitchen and returned with her cell phone. There were dozens of missed calls and text messages from Brandon.

They're sending us home early. Gas leak or something.

You awake?

Nvm. Tyler's mom's bringing me.

With every text, her heart sank further into her stomach, until it was like a rock pressing against her womb.

"You could have killed him," Ryan said. Calm, matter-of-fact. It was somehow worse than if he'd yelled.

"I know."

"What's happening, Esther? Why won't you talk to me?"

Tears burned her eyes. "I don't know."

It's Donny, she thought. *It's his fault.* She didn't know how or why, but she needed to pin the blame somewhere other than herself. She was a good woman, a good mother.

Bad girl, a voice whispered. *All your fault. All your fault, all over again.*

Later, Brandon emerged with a duffel bag slung over his shoulder. Esther hadn't moved from the couch, not sure she was welcome anywhere else in her own home.

"Where are you going?" she asked.

Brandon looked from her to Ryan, who was grabbing his keys from the hook.

"Brandon's staying at my parents' for a couple of days."

It was like a knife to the gut, but she nodded anyway.

"Are you coming back?" she asked Ryan.

He nodded. "In a bit."

"Okay." Then, when they were halfway out the door. "I love you."

Neither responded, the door closing behind them with a sickening finality.

CHAPTER TEN

MEG

I t was hard not to stare at the marks on her hand. The crescent-shaped scar was decades old, but Claire's nails had fit perfectly into it, like a mold.

It had never been like Claire to act out with violence, but the day Meg had left for college, Claire had clung to her, nails digging so deep into the back of Meg's hand that they drew blood. It'd taken Esther and their mother to pry her off.

Meg could still hear Claire begging, *Don't leave me.*

Claire's appearance last night—hallucination or not—seemed to be a reminder of all Meg's failures as a big sister.

Now, gripping the steering wheel with one hand, she rubbed the irritated skin around the scar, an itch prickling deep underneath, too deep to scratch. She didn't remember waking up from the nightmare of her dead sister, if it even was a nightmare. She told herself it had to be—if Claire could somehow come back, she wouldn't have come back *mean.*

Still, Meg couldn't seem to shake the cold from her neck and shoulder where Claire had laid her head.

She hadn't worked in a couple of days. Being a gig-worker had some perks—she got to choose her hours and take time off if she needed it without having to get approval from someone, but it also meant if she didn't work, she didn't get paid. Meg always seemed to be on the cusp of capital-b Broke, but lately it had been worse. They had raised the rent on her shitty one-bedroom apartment, again, and her ten-year-old car was constantly in need of expensive repair. After getting towed out of the ditch that night, she'd had to borrow money from her dad just to get it running. The bumper was held on with a bungee cord and duct tape held her side mirror to the door. Nobody in this town tipped, so Meg had to make do with what the delivery service apps paid, which wasn't enough.

But every time she told herself this wasn't meant to be her life, that she was capable of and deserved more than a car that constantly smelled like fried food and a checking account balance that never seemed to hit more than three figures, a small voice in the back of her head reminded her that she was wrong.

After a slow morning, she ventured out of Blacklick, toward more populous places with more disposable income, and managed to fill her afternoon with deliveries. Apart from the money, she was happy to have the distraction. The longer she spent in the daylight, upbeat music thumping from tinny speakers, the easier it was to put last night, and the image of Claire, broken and rotted, out of her head.

Around dinnertime, she started back toward her apartment. She hadn't eaten all day and was looking forward to spending some of her tip money on something that wasn't leftover cold cuts and macaroni salad. But as she pulled up to the parking lot, she spotted what looked like Esther's car idling in one of the visitor spaces. Meg thought about leaving before her sister saw her—Esther didn't show up out of nowhere for no reason, and Meg couldn't take any more bad news right now—but then she saw the driver. It was Ryan.

Claire whispered in the back of Meg's head, *Your fault.*

Her heart beat hard against her ribs, and she struggled to take a deep breath. She glanced up and thought she saw Claire's rotted smile in the rearview mirror.

He spotted her. Waved. Any chance of taking off before the bottom dropped out again was gone.

She shut off the engine as he approached the driver's side of her car but didn't get out.

"I was starting to think you weren't coming home," he said by way of greeting.

She frowned. "How long you been sitting there?"

He shrugged. Stuck his hands in his pockets. The bags under his eyes looked like bruises, and he kept chewing his bottom lip. He looked like shit.

Meg sat stiffly against her seat, bracing herself. "Esther's okay, right? That's not why you're here?"

He glanced up at the building, not meeting her eyes. "Can we go inside?"

Her stomach clenched. "Yeah. Sure."

The lock on the main security door to the building had been broken for months, but Meg made a show of turning her key anyway. Stalling. Ryan stood on the stoop, too close. He shifted his weight, hands stuffed tightly into his jacket pockets. She wished he would just tell her what had happened, but it was clear he was going to stay tight-lipped until they were upstairs.

Meg's apartment was on the third floor. Convenient in winter, when the tenants below her ran their heat, which rose to keep her apartment toasty. In the summer, though, it was like hellfire had settled over the place. Paint peeled off the hallway walls, littering the stained carpet like sad confetti. Several of the sconces were cracked or missing altogether, and some kid had been drawing increasingly graphic depictions of male genitalia on the floorboards. Ryan didn't seem to notice, his expression glazed, the look in his eyes somewhere far away.

There was a note on the door from the apartment manager, reminding her that windows left open in the winter could cause burst pipes, an expense she would be responsible for. She folded it up and stuck it in her pocket, casting one last glance at Ryan before letting them both inside.

It was small, with one bedroom just big enough to fit a double-sized bed and a three-drawer dresser. The door opened into the kitchen, a dingy room made dingier by the yellowing Formica countertops and laminate flooring that was peeling up in the corners. Ryan walked into the living room without being told and sat on the couch—Meg's only furniture apart from a coffee table she'd rescued from the dumpster which served as dining room table, desk, and vanity on those rare occasions that required mascara. She did her best to keep her apartment clean, but it was like the walls breathed dust and damp; the dirt was so packed into the carpet by dozens of tenants that no amount of vacuuming or scrubbing could lift the gray pallor from the place. She covered the walls with framed pictures she bought at thrift stores and garage sales. There was no rhyme or reason to their presence except that they were easier to look at than blank, white walls.

She set her bag on the counter and opened the refrigerator, grateful to see two beers among the sparse offerings. She popped them open, then brought them into the living room where she offered one to Ryan. He looked at the bottle for a long moment before finally taking it. Meg sat on the table and drank while Ryan stared at the carpet, beer untouched.

When her beer was half-gone, she finally broke the silence. "Esther's okay, right?"

"Define *okay*."

"Alive."

He nodded, and a small weight lifted from Meg's shoulders.

"Okay, so what happened? What's wrong? Is it Brandon?"

He shook his head, finally sipping from the bottle. When he looked up at her, new lines had formed under his eyes. "She bought a gun without me knowing. She almost shot Brandon because her paranoia is getting out of control."

Meg swallowed, tasting acid. "Jesus. Is Brandon okay?"

"Physically, yes. But he's freaked out. He's been worried about his mom for a while. I kept telling him everything was fine, that it would get better. He's staying with my parents for a bit."

"Doubt Esther took that news well."

He shook his head. "I don't know what to do anymore. I want to be supportive. I want to help, but she won't let me. She won't let anyone."

Meg nodded. "That's not new. She's been that way for as long as I can remember. She's always had this fierce independence. If Esther couldn't do it herself, she didn't trust anyone else to try."

"It's more than that. She's keeping secrets now. She hid a gun from me, for God's sake." He set the beer on the table and rubbed his face. "I just wish she would tell me what she's so afraid of."

Meg picked at the beer bottle label, letting the shreds fall to the floor. She didn't know Ryan that well, but she knew him well enough to expect another shoe to drop. "Not to sound like an asshole, but this doesn't seem like the kind of thing you wait all afternoon outside of my apartment to tell me." When he didn't immediately respond, she added, "Why didn't you just call?"

"I need to ask a favor."

"And you didn't want to give me the chance to hang up."

He nodded.

"You've been married to Esther for too long."

He smirked, but it quickly vanished. "I know things are strained between you two. I wouldn't have come if I'd thought there was another option."

It wasn't the first time Meg had been someone's last resort. It wouldn't be the last either.

He continued, "With Brandon out of the house and me going to work, I'm worried about Esther being alone."

Meg could already see where this was going. She finished her beer and started in on Ryan's. "You could take time off, couldn't you?"

Ryan was already shaking his head. "A few hours here and there, maybe. We're in the middle of several major deals with tight close dates."

"I think your wife takes priority."

"That's not fair. Of course she takes priority. That's why I'm here."

"Have you talked to my mom? She doesn't work. I'm sure she'd love to spend time with Esther."

"Esther would hate that worse than spending time with you."

Meg flinched. "Ouch."

"Sorry, it's just that I'm having a really hard time understanding the problem. It's not like you don't have time."

"I have a job."

Ryan opened his mouth, no doubt to say something shitty about her work, but was at least decent enough to stop himself. "Esther needs you, okay? She's the last person who would admit it, but she does. She was already on shaky ground, but it's like losing Claire put her over the edge."

"We're *all* mourning Claire."

"All the more reason for you two to work out whatever this bullshit is between you."

"It's not bullshit."

"Great. Good. Then do you mind spelling it out for me? Because I'm having a hard time figuring out why my wife, a woman who is physically, vehemently opposed to guns, would not only go behind my back to purchase one, but decide she needed to use it in our home." He stood, hands on his hips. "She's afraid, but she won't tell me what she's afraid of. And whatever it is, she doesn't trust me enough to protect her from it."

Meg scowled at the empty bottle in her hands. "Has Esther always liked this machismo garbage, or is it just for my benefit?"

For a long time neither of them said a word. Meg squirmed under his silent scrutiny, wishing for another beer or to go back twenty minutes and leave when she had the chance.

"You're right," he said finally. "I shouldn't have bothered."

"Sorry you wasted the gas," she said bitterly.

"Yeah, me too." He stormed toward the door, but before Meg could feel any relief that he was leaving, he paused and turned, flashing her a look that could curdle milk. "I always stuck up for you, you know. Every time Esther talked about cutting you off or reading you the riot act the next time you dared ask to borrow money, I told her she'd regret it. Maybe I was wrong then too." He sighed. "She's always been there for you. Now she needs you to be there for her. Why can't you just…look past whatever issues you two have? Just for a little while?"

Meg's eyes burned. She blinked back the tears before they could fall. "Ask her, then get back to me."

He shook his head and reached for the door. As he started into the hall, he said, "I thought you were a lot of things, Meg, but I didn't think heartless was one of them."

The door slammed shut behind him. Meg dropped the empty bottle onto the table to keep from throwing it.

———

Her phone pinged with potential deliveries for most of the evening, which she ignored. She only left the apartment after a third rummage through the cabinets revealed no forgotten bottles of booze, and even then, she walked the two blocks to the liquor store because she knew the moment she got in her car, she might actually consider giving in to Ryan's ask.

Back at her apartment, she drank her cheap, one-shot bottles straight, dumping the empties beside the couch. She stuffed her phone deep between the cushions because, with each shot, she came closer to reconsidering.

It wasn't her brother-in-law's fault that he didn't understand, but how was she supposed to explain her fear, her fervent belief that if she didn't keep her distance, some fatal mistake would cost Esther her life? He could think what he wanted, but Meg didn't live the way she did because she wanted to, or because she was heartless or unambitious. She deserved her shitty car and shittier apartment with its lifeless walls and mite-filled carpet. It wasn't sloth that had made her into what she was, it was penance.

Weighed down by self-pity and vodka, she lay on the floor of the living room and stared at the ceiling. The pinks and purples of twilight faded into night, casting shadows across the walls. She noticed a crack in the ceiling she was pretty sure hadn't been there before. She closed her eyes, part of her hoping the ceiling would collapse down on top of her. Somewhere in the building, a child wailed.

"He sounds hungry."

The sound of Claire's voice, craggy and hoarse, made Meg's heart skip, but she didn't dare open her eyes.

The floor creaked with heavy footsteps. A wisp of cold brushed over Meg's face, and when she finally forced herself to look, she saw Claire through the dark, sitting on the couch. Her hair was limp, and black mold covered most of her arms and neck. She leaned forward, elbows on her knees, hair dangling over Meg's face just close enough to touch the tip of her nose.

"You ever been that hungry?" Claire asked. "Starving so much your whole body feels empty and you just want to cry and cry?"

The combination of the booze and the sickly-sweet rot smell of Claire made Meg's head spin. When she finally found her voice, it tasted like acid. "Why are you here? What do you want?"

Claire pouted. "I thought you said you missed me."

"I do."

She grinned, teeth blackened. "I'm glad. It's good to be missed." Then, grin fading, "How bad do you think it hurts to starve? Do you just stop feeling it after a while? Like when you burn or drown?"

"I don't know."

Claire sat back and Meg gulped the air, desperate to get the rot out of her mouth, her lungs.

"How long do you think it would take for a baby to starve? A couple of days? A week?"

Meg tried to sit up, but Claire rested her foot on Meg's chest. Every time Meg tried to wriggle free, Claire pushed harder, until Meg could hear the fragile bones in Claire's ankle cracking.

"Well?" Claire probed.

Five days.

Meg shook her head. *No. Don't think about it.*

"You're right," Claire said. "Too morbid. Still."

She finally lifted her foot, allowing Meg to pull herself upright. Meg shoved herself away from the couch until her back was up against the coffee table. She didn't realize she'd been crying until she wiped her face, like she could rub this twisted echo of Claire out of existence.

"It's kind of funny, though," Claire continued, "if you think about it. Sometimes, you can do more damage by just sitting there, doing nothing."

"It's not *funny*," Meg said.

Claire frowned. "Isn't it? I supposed I can't tell the difference anymore."

"Sometimes all you can do is nothing," Meg said, almost to herself.

"Well—" Claire leaned over the side of the couch, scooping up the empty shot bottles, which she tossed into Meg's lap—"You would know."

Meg's face burned. She shoved away the bottles and then pulled her knees into her chest and leaned her head down, digging her nails into her shins just to feel the pain. At first, she couldn't figure out why Claire would torment her like this, but the longer she sank under the weight of Claire's judging gaze, the more she began to understand.

When she looked up again, Claire was gone. Meg crawled toward the couch—the sour rot smell lingering on the cushions—and dug around until she found her phone. It was almost dead. Eyes blurry, she sent a text to Ryan.

I'll do it.

The response was almost instant. She half-expected it to be something along the lines of *Fuck you*. Instead, he'd written: Tomorrow, 7 am. We'll tell her together.

Meg finished the one-shots, grateful for the haze, and climbed into bed with her clothes on. She was just drifting off when she realized the child in the hallway had gone quiet.

CHAPTER ELEVEN

CLAIRE

Sometimes it felt like worms wriggling around inside her. If Claire looked real hard, she could almost see the outlines of their bodies pressing against the skin of her arms and belly. Other times, it felt like clouds—hazy clouds covering her eyes and coating her mind. Thick, gray clouds hanging heavy and bloated in her chest. Angry, black clouds that shot lightning down her back. Sometimes it was empty and dark, like the room in the old house, and sometimes when she closed her eyes, all she could see was a blinding, white light. But as the days got shorter and colder, the emptiness and the dark lingered even after she opened her eyes in the morning, the nightmares left behind.

Today, the dark, twisty things inside her were heavy. It was the first day of winter break, so she didn't need to get out of bed, but she knew if she didn't soon, she would blink, and it would be dark again. Days slipped by like that sometimes. It was easier to be asleep than it was to be awake.

She rolled over and stared at the other side of the bedroom, where Esther's bed lay empty for the eleventh day in a row. Her blankets and stuff were still there, all tossed around like somebody had been sleeping in her bed, but Claire knew Esther had been sneaking out at night to go down the hall and sleep in Meg's room. Slowly, one item at a time, Esther had been moving her things into Meg's room, taking it over before Mom had the chance to object.

"What are you gonna do when Meg comes back and sees all your stuff in there?" Claire asked the first time she caught Esther doing it.

"Trust me," Esther had said, "Meg's not coming back." Then, like an afterthought, "I wouldn't."

Claire hoped that wasn't true. She missed Meg, missed the way she would drag Claire out of bed in the mornings before school, throwing Claire over her shoulder like a sack of potatoes. She missed the way Meg listened, instead of nodding and pretending to pay attention the way Esther did. As it got closer to Christmas, Claire went to sleep with her fingers and toes crossed, and whispered a prayer that Meg would change her mind and at least come home for a little while. If anyone knew what to do about the slippy days and the darkness in Claire's blood, it was her big sister. Meg never laughed when Claire told her about feeling heavy and weightless at the same time. Never called her a liar when Claire told her about the face in the dark when she woke up at night.

The Mickey Mouse clock on the wall told her it was past noon by the time Claire finally managed to get out of bed. She wrapped her blanket around her shoulders, which dragged the clothes and notebooks and Barbies behind her, leaving a trail from her bedroom to the kitchen.

Esther stood at the counter, finishing off what looked like a peanut butter and jelly sandwich. She spotted Claire and raised an eyebrow. "Look who finally rose from the dead."

Mom came through the back door and stomped snow onto the rug. Her cheeks were bright pink, and little crystals of white clung to her hat and collar. She carried a tangled mess of Christmas lights. She spotted Esther and frowned. "We have a table for that."

Esther shrugged. "I like it here better."

"Table," Mom said.

Esther groaned. Then, "I thought you said we weren't putting up lights this year."

One of Dad's rare proclamations—no Christmas lights, but they could put out the gingerbread men and the candy canes that didn't need to get plugged in if they wanted. He hadn't said outright, but Claire was old enough to know it wasn't good when Dad started coming home early half the week and staying home the other half.

"It's just a few," Mom said, defensive. "I want it to be nice for when your sister comes home."

"She's coming home?" Claire asked, struggling to keep the excitement out of her voice. "When?"

"Christmas Eve morning."

Claire did the math in her head. Three days.

"Cutting it close," Esther mumbled.

Mom shot her a look that could freeze water. Esther rolled her eyes and took her plate to the table where she flopped into a chair, no doubt annoyed that she'd have to go back to sleeping in their room, at least for a little while.

"Can I help?" Claire asked Mom.

"Think you can untangle this mess?"

Claire nodded.

Mom set the heap on the counter. "Then have at it."

Claire dropped her blanket on the floor and rushed to the kitchen where she plunged her hands wrist-deep into the ball of lights and cords. It was an impossible task untangling all the knots, and part of her knew she'd never finish, but at the moment it didn't matter because Meg was coming home, and just the thought of that was enough to lessen the weight in her arms and belly and chest, just a little, the darkness dissipated by bright, colorful lights.

The next two days passed in a whirlwind of decorating. Esther groaned and griped and complained every time Mom sent her into the attic for another bin of old garland and lights, but even she couldn't help smiling when it got dark and the lights glowed through the windows, making everything look and feel warm. Claire went grocery shopping with her mom, and they loaded up the cart with fixings and treats. Mom grimaced at the till, handing over a credit card before making Claire promise not to tell Dad how much it cost.

The night before Meg was supposed to come home, Claire realized she didn't have a present for her.

"She won't care," Esther said when Claire came to her, worried. "Not like she's gonna bring us presents."

Claire didn't mind that, but for some reason it felt important to give Meg *something* this year. She didn't have any money, though, so she would have to get creative. She thought about making Meg a card or drawing something, but Claire wasn't great at art and now that Meg was in college, she probably didn't want something as childish as a pathetic construction paper doodle. No, this had to be something *special*.

She remembered there were boxes of random stuff in the basement—things Mom had bought when times were good and garage sales were plentiful—but Dad didn't like any of them going down there without him, like they could get hurt just by looking at his workbench funny. So Claire waited until it was late, when she could hear Dad snoring through the wall and Esther had already snuck into Meg's room (bringing another drawer of clothes with her), and then she waited a little longer just to be sure.

Taking only a flashlight (which she'd stolen into her room from the junk drawer earlier that day), she crept downstairs in the dark, slow as a tortoise, using the handrail and the wall to guide her around the landing to the living room. Once she was sure no one upstairs would see the light, she clicked on the flashlight and went through the kitchen to the basement door. Claire hesitated, having never gone into the basement alone, let alone at night. Sometimes, when Esther was feeling mean, she would pretend to hear moaning or bumps in the night from down below, insisting their basement was haunted, and that it was why Dad spent so much time down there—because the ghost *made* him. Claire suspected none of it was true, but she held her breath as she listened closely for the sound of ghosts.

When she was mostly sure there was nothing waiting for her down below, Claire eased the door open and shined the light down the stairs. It barely broke through the darkness, but the only other lights were the bulb hanging in the center of the room, too high for her to reach, and the lamp on her dad's workbench, which was all the way on the other side of the basement. Heart hammering, she ran down the stairs, almost tripping at the last step, and headed for Dad's bench. The light from the flashlight bounced all over as she ran so she didn't see the bench before she collided with it. The force knocked the wind out of her, and she covered her mouth with her sleeve to muffle the sound of her cough as she struggled to catch her breath. She shined the flashlight over the bench until she found the lamp, which she clicked on. It wasn't much, but she laid the flashlight on the bench, pointed in the opposite direction, and the combined glow was just enough to see by.

On Dad's workbench were metal bits and doodads, a couple of empty Coke cans, and a package of sunflower seeds. Claire snatched a couple from the bag and sucked on the salty shells before cracking them between her teeth the way her dad had shown her. She spat the shells into the laundry sink, then studied the wall of boxes on the opposite side of the room. Some of them had already been pulled down and opened, *Christmas Stuff*, scribbled on their sides in black marker. Others had been heavily taped and stuffed way in the back, beneath layers of boxes of other holiday decorations, and tubs marked *To Donate*. It was the unmarked ones Claire wanted. No doubt she'd find some kind of treasure there.

But the bins and boxes of decorations were heavy. The ones she couldn't lift she shimmied from one stack to another, wincing every time something jingled or crashed in the boxes. She kept shooting worried glances at the stares, thinking she was one good thump away from getting caught. By the time she could finally access the boxes she wanted, she was sweating, and her pajamas were covered in dust.

She opened the first box with a pair of scissors she found on Dad's workbench and was immediately disappointed. Mom had probably just forgotten to label this one—it was full of gift bows and boxes and tags and ribbon. Claire pushed it to the side, thinking she'd come back to it once she found a gift worth wrapping. The second box was heavier, the tape thicker. She struggled to get the scissors through it, nipping her fingertip in the process. Finally, the flaps gave, and when she opened the box, she was hit with a smell like sour milk. She wrinkled her nose, thinking maybe a mouse or something had gotten in it, but then a flash of pink grabbed her attention.

It was a woven winter hat, barely big enough to fit over her fist, with a silky pom. There were books and albums and a plastic bag with a onesie tucked inside. When Claire opened the bag, the sour milk stench got worse. Holding her breath, she rolled it all up in a ball and stuffed it down into the corner of the box.

Baby stuff, she thought.

She pulled out one of the albums and flipped through it, pausing at pictures of her parents and sisters holding a baby wrapped in pink and yellow, a fuzzy mop of hair on her head. It was pretty clear to Claire that she was the baby in the pictures, but she didn't understand why Mom had them taped up in the basement. Claire had asked a couple of times for baby pictures, once for when she was Star of the Week at school and had to decorate a poster with pictures of herself, her family, and things she liked to share with her class. Mom had given her a couple of pictures from when she was four or five, but said she wasn't sure where her baby pictures were. Maybe she'd forgotten.

Toward the back of the album, Claire spotted a photograph of Meg sitting cross-legged on the couch, with baby Claire cradled in her lap. Meg smiled up at the camera with all of her teeth—rare for Meg, whose crooked bottom teeth had made her a closed-mouth smiler—and the longer Claire looked at it, the more she realized there was something different about Meg in the picture. Not just her smile, but the way she sat, open and happy. This had been a good day; one Meg would likely be glad to be reminded of.

Claire had found her gift.

She carefully lifted the film that kept the picture stuck to the page, and slowly peeled the picture away to keep it from ripping. On the back in slanted writing was a year: 1993.

Claire frowned. She was born in 1992. The baby in the picture didn't look big enough to be more than a month old, she thought, but couldn't be sure. She studied the picture again, this time more convinced that this baby was practically brand new. *Mom must have written the wrong year*, she thought.

With the photo held carefully in one hand, Claire sifted through the first box again, looking for the perfect box and ribbon to wrap it in. It really was the perfect gift. She couldn't wait to see Meg's face when she opened it.

Christmas Eve morning came and went, and Claire started to worry that Meg wasn't coming. Mom had started cooking dinner shortly after breakfast, peeling potatoes and slathering a large turkey in butter and salt and herbs. Every time Claire tried to ask about Meg, Mom sent her to the refrigerator for this or that ingredient, ignoring the question.

Esther hovered around the tree, pretending to adjust ornaments while she sized up the gifts sitting in small, neat piles at its base. All of the gifts had their names on them, *from Santa,* even though none of the Finch girls believed in Santa anymore. Claire had up until last year, when Esther, in a fit of meanness, showed Claire the box of unwrapped presents in their parents' closet after Claire had asked Esther for a stamp to send her letter to Santa.

Claire spotted her gift to Meg, sitting on top of the others in a box covered in penguins with glittery scarves, with a bright-red ribbon tied in a clumsy bow. She'd stuffed the box mostly full of tissue paper and sat the picture on top of the pile with a note: *I miss you.* Part of her was scared Meg wouldn't like it, and more than once, she considered taking it back and shoving it under her bed.

Esther nudged a crinkly package with her toe. "How many of these you figure are socks?"

Claire shrugged.

"Socks and underwear, for sure." She pointed to a smaller present. "That one's got potential, though."

Claire didn't much care about her presents. Besides the fact that she liked getting socks because they always had cute animals on them, or were the fuzzy kind that kept her feet super warm on nights when Dad wouldn't let them turn up the thermostat, Claire was more worried about Meg. She couldn't stop looking from the clock to the window, disappointed each time.

Finally, just as Mom announced that dinner was almost ready, headlights moved across the glass. Claire bolted for the door, throwing it open at the sound of a car door slamming. Meg wasn't halfway up the driveway before Claire ran at her, bare feet freezing on the concrete, and nearly knocked them both over with the force of her hug. Meg cackled and, dropping her backpack, threw Claire over her shoulder like she weighed nothing.

"You smell like syrup," Meg said.

"We had pancakes."

"Any left?"

Claire shook her head.

"Brat," Meg said, but she was smiling.

Mom met them at the door, still wearing one oven mitt. She swatted Claire's butt. "Come on now, get down. You're grown."

Meg dropped Claire onto the carpet, then went back for her backpack. Dad emerged from the basement, hands aflutter because they were letting the heat out, while Esther scowled from the couch. Mom lingered in the doorway, her expression almost sad, but flashed a smile when she caught Claire looking.

"Table needs forks and knives," Mom said. "And napkins."

Claire skipped into the kitchen to set the table, feeling lighter than she had in weeks.

At dinner, Meg ate like she was starving, which seemed to make Mom happy. She slid serving bowls of Stove Top stuffing and sweet peas across the table without being asked, and then served Meg the first slice of chocolate pie as she asked questions about college that Meg dodged by shoving more and more food in her mouth. Eventually, Mom gave up, and when everyone was finished eating, she packed up the leftovers which promised turkey soup, turkey sandwiches, and turkey omelets for the next several days.

Claire did her part helping to clear the table and put away the pots and pans as Esther washed them, but her whole body was practically buzzing. More than once, Esther jabbed her with a pot handle as soapy water dripped at their feet because Claire couldn't stop glancing over to the tree, at her perfectly imperfect bow. She dared to hope her gift would be enough to make Meg stay longer. Maybe forever.

Finally, Mom told them to sit around the tree. Esther's knees bounced as she eyeballed her small pile of gifts. Every year, she zoomed through the opening, leaving a pile of wrapping paper confetti, before sulking off to her room. Last year,

Claire saw how disappointed Mom had been, and so she'd opened her gifts with purposefully slow tears, and then fawned over every little thing until she coaxed Mom into a small smile. This year, though, Claire wasn't looking at Esther or her mom or even her own presents. She saw Meg's gaze go straight for the penguin box and her stomach clenched.

Mom turned on the radio and turned to the all-Christmas all the time station. A fuzzy version of "O Come, All Ye Faithful" warbled through the speakers.

Esther reached for the first present on her pile and Mom smacked her shoulder. "Wait 'til Dad comes with the camera."

Esther groaned. "We're not doing that thing where we go in shifts and you make us pose with everything, right?"

"I don't see why that's such a bad thing," Mom said.

"Better not," Meg said. "Esther might explode."

"Shut up," Esther said, hiding a smile.

Dad walked in and sank onto the couch with an exaggerated sigh. He held up the disposable Kodak at the ready. "Okay. Let the carnage begin."

Esther dove onto her pile like a cat on tuna, tearing into the largest from the pile. Claire pulled a present into her lap, but didn't open it, her gaze pulled to Meg, who'd bypassed the penguin box for something else. Claire caught her mother looking at her funny, so she turned back to her own pile and opened one of the smaller gifts. Inside was a pair of fuzzy socks with candy-cane stripes. She dutifully held them up to the camera, a too-wide smile pasted across her face.

Click.

Esther had already discarded her socks—knee-length and covered in cats— and was digging into the pile, shaking each present before choosing the next thing to open.

"Oh, cool!" Meg held up a leather journal, the spine striped in gold tones.

"So you can keep track of your schoolwork and such," Dad said.

"Or whatever you want," Mom added.

"It's great. Thanks."

Dad patted Mom's knee as she beamed.

Claire reached for a second gift, but a sparkle in the corner of her eye made her pause. Meg had pulled the penguin box into her lap and was carefully untying the ribbon.

Behind Claire, Mom whispered to Dad, "That from you?"

Claire took a deep breath to calm her thrumming heart.

Meg lifted the lid and, at first, smiled with her whole face. Then, as she continued to study the photo, her smile dipped. Her shoulders sank and she wobbled a little, the skin around her chin and eyes going a sickly sort of green.

"You okay?" Esther asked.

Meg quickly shoved the lid back on the box, stuffing the whole thing under her leg. "Eyes on your own paper, Finch."

Esther rolled her eyes. "Whatever."

Claire sank inward, tears dripping onto the gift in her lap. Meg had *hated* it. Did that mean Meg hated her?

She tried to distract herself by tearing into the gift, but her eyes were too blurry to see what it was. More socks, probably. She felt eyes on her and rubbed her face with the hem of her T-shirt, soaking it. In her lower back and ankles and chest, the coils of darkness wriggled and writhed.

Mom rubbed her shoulder. "Something wrong, honey?"

Claire shook her head and forced a smile that was almost painful to hold. "Nope. I'm just really happy."

"Weirdo," Esther said.

"Be nice," Mom scolded.

"I am nice." Esther squeezed Claire's knee. "She said she's happy."

Claire nodded, trying hard not to look at Meg, who wasn't paying attention to any of them. She stared into the tree, jaw clenched, wrapping the red ribbon tight around her finger.

Meg went to bed early, saying she was tired from the drive and the food. Claire wanted to ask her about the picture, but every time she thought she had the nerve to bring it up, the darkness slithered up around her throat, strangling the words before she could get them out.

Mom sent Esther and Claire to bed shortly after.

"But it's early!" Esther argued. "We're on break! It's not like we have school or anything."

But then Dad shot her a look and Esther saved the rest of her grumbling for when she and Claire were in their room with the door shut.

"Bet they wouldn't care if Meg wasn't here," she mumbled.

Claire didn't think Meg had anything to do with it, but she was too distracted to argue. She laid in bed and stared at the wall separating their rooms, like if she looked hard enough, she could see through to the other side, straight into Meg's mind. Claire tried to convince herself that it wasn't that Meg hated the picture, it was that Meg was so upset over leaving Claire that the reminder of how much she missed Claire was like a sharp cut.

No, the darkness said. *She hates you.*

Claire covered her face with her blanket, but the darkness was there too. It grew dense in her limbs and chest and burned at the back of her throat.

Don't worry, it said. *I'll hold you.*

She woke up the next morning just as the sun was coming up, the light streaming pink and orange through the curtains. Even before she was fully awake, a creeping sense of dread slogged its way down her throat and settled like a rock in her stomach. She peered through the faint light to where Esther snored lightly, still dead asleep, the covers bunched up around her neck. Claire quietly rolled out of bed and out into the hallway. Meg's bedroom door was shut, but something pulled Claire toward it. She pressed her ear against the door, but there was only silence on the other side. The wrong kind of silence. She carefully turned the knob and eased the door open, flinching when it creaked. The sunlight didn't reach these windows like it did Claire and Esther's room, so it took a minute for her eyes to adjust. When they did, she sank against the wall, fighting back tears.

The bed was empty.

Shaking, Claire rushed across the room and threw open the curtain, already knowing what she would see. Meg's car wasn't in the driveway.

Her sister was gone.

CHAPTER TWELVE

ESTHER

NOW

R yan didn't tell Esther where he'd gone after dropping Brandon at her in-laws', and Esther didn't ask. For now, it was enough that he had come home at all. She had expected another tirade, more digging, more questions, but when those didn't come either, she didn't know what to think. They moved around the house like planets in repelling orbits until, out of habit, Esther went into the kitchen to start dinner. She wasn't hungry and suspected Ryan wasn't either, but she itched for some sort of normal, something to help her forget that the morning had ever happened.

She thought about spaghetti—simple, easy—but the red of the marinara made her stomach twist. As she rifled through the cabinets and the refrigerator, everything she saw conjured vivid images of Brandon lying broken and bloody on the living room floor. Every cut of meat was like flesh. Every spice jar smelled like gunpowder.

In the end, she ordered Chinese food. When it arrived, she expected Ryan to take his carton of lo mein to the bedroom, but, to Esther's surprise, he sat opposite her at the counter, pulling a stool up from the other end. He ate mechanically, looking everywhere but at her. Esther barely touched her sesame chicken, stabbing it to shreds with a chopstick as her gaze followed Ryan's, hoping to catch his eye. If he couldn't forgive her—and she didn't blame him—couldn't he at least yell at her? Scold her? Threaten her with divorce? She could understand anger. Apathy was worse.

They'd just finished eating when his cell phone chimed. Esther recognized his text message tone and couldn't help leaning slightly toward him, trying to see who was on the other end. His shoulders seemed to relax as he read the text, a gesture that should have eased Esther's worry, but it only made her feel more tense. It felt like a decision had been made.

"Girlfriend?" Esther asked, thinking that falling into their usual banter might melt some of the ice between them, but her voice had come out too high, too panicky. She tried to smile when he finally looked up at her, but it dissolved, his expression somewhere between surprise and disgust.

Later, she would realize this had been the moment to open up, to lay everything bare. To tell her husband about that day so many years ago in the house with the strange doors, to go back to a night that was lodged in her mind like a piece of broken glass. This was the moment to tell him that she was afraid.

Instead, she shoved a piece of dry chicken into her mouth and chewed and chewed, swallowing the words along with the gristle.

Around nine o'clock, Ryan dragged a pillow and blanket out of the linen closet and set them on the couch.

Esther was heartbroken. Even during their worst fights, they always went up to the same bed. She could not, *would* not, believe that this was the thing that would end their marriage. Hoping that maybe she could annoy him into changing his mind, she lingered in the living room, pulling a book off the shelf and turning pages, unread, while he stared at his phone. But she was too anxious to sit still, so she swept (finding bits of glass left over from the night before), and then ran a rag over the dusty tops of the framed photos on the wall, lingering a moment on their wedding photo (Esther in white lace; Ryan in a fitted, navy suit with a marigold boutonniere).

She looked too happy in that photo. They both looked too happy. Maybe, if this was the thing that broke them, maybe she deserved it. Maybe she deserved worse for what she'd done.

Unable to look at the picture anymore, she turned to the windowsill and began to wipe. The porch light shone through the gap in the curtain. She paused, her attention caught on something sitting in the middle of the porch. Without thinking, she opened the door and looked down.

It was a key, the head flat, with large teeth on either side, the silver rusty.

"Something wrong?" Ryan called from the couch.

Esther snapped up the key and slipped it into her pocket. "No. Nothing."

Without another word, she bolted the door shut and went upstairs, the key burning in her pocket.

When she finally got up the nerve to come back down and tell Ryan goodnight, he was already under the blankets, eyes closed, either asleep or pretending to be. She said the words anyway, then went upstairs to lie down and wait for the nightmares to come.

———————————

She didn't sleep. Mostly she laid in bed and listened to the sound of Ryan's zombie-shuffle to the bathroom and the toilet flushing every couple of hours. Each time she tensed, hoping he might, in his half-asleep state, wander back into the bedroom with her, but she spent the entire night alone, hyperaware of the key sitting like a bomb in her underwear drawer. She shouldn't have brought it into her house. She should have thrown it into the street. *Too late now,* she thought.

The next morning, she got up and dressed, hoping to catch Ryan before he ran off to work. They couldn't dance around each other forever, and the longer he was left to stew, the less chance Esther had of taking control, of convincing him that she was fine and their son could come home and that she would never, ever betray his trust like that again. As she practiced mouthing a speech into the mirror, she almost had herself convinced.

Downstairs, she found Ryan in the kitchen. He was running late—usually he was gone by 7:30, and it was now 7:45—but he didn't seem to be in any kind of hurry. His coffee tumbler sat empty on the counter beside the coffeepot, a filter abandoned beside the jar of coffee grounds. His tie was around his neck, but not tied, his attention focused solely on his cell phone as he frantically typed.

"Something wrong?" Esther asked. A stupid question given, well, *everything,* but it was out before she could stop it.

He glanced up at her, a frustrated expression quickly smothered. "Work stuff," he said.

She didn't believe him but didn't push. She walked toward the counter and Ryan slid out of her way. Squashing the hurt, she finished making the pot of coffee, and then poured it into his travel mug with creamer and too much sugar, just the way he liked it. He'd shoved a carton of leftover Chinese food into his lunch bag. Esther added a fork, a napkin, and a package of the oatmeal cream cookies she pretended she bought for Brandon but were really for Ryan. Little things, but they added up to how much she loved her husband. She hoped he noticed. She hoped it would be enough to help them move past her mistake.

He was putting on his shoes—slowly, one eye on the door—when the doorbell rang.

Esther's first thought was Brandon. Anxious to see her son, she started toward the living room, but Ryan cut her off at the pass. One hand on the doorknob, he turned to Esther. "You should sit."

She frowned. "Why?"

"Please."

It was the pained look on his face that sent her to the couch. *The police,* she thought but quickly dismissed it. Ryan wouldn't.

When Ryan stepped aside and Meg walked in, it took a second for Esther's mind to make the connection. Meg never came to her house, mostly because she was never invited. And if she was, Meg was good at coming up with thinly veiled excuses not to come. There was no reason for her to show up out of the blue.

Except it wasn't out of the blue. Ryan stood sheepishly behind Meg, one hand hovering near the small of her back. A thousand thoughts rippled through Esther's mind, starting with the idea that Ryan could be having an affair with Meg. On some level it made a sick sort of sense, and the more she thought about it, the more her body loosened, lubricated by anger instead of weighed down by shame.

But then Ryan sat next to her on the couch, leaving Meg to stand awkwardly alone in the doorway.

"Hey," she said.

One syllable, and all the righteous anger dissipated. "Hey," Esther said. Then, "What are you doing here?"

Meg sighed, flashing Ryan an annoyed look. "I had really hoped you were kidding about the whole *tell her together* thing."

Esther looked at Ryan, who was studying his tie with great intensity. "Tell me what?" She turned back to Meg, who seemed to have found something equally as interesting on the rug. "Ryan? Meg? What's going on?"

He looked up, the corners of his mouth pulled down in strained determination. "I've been worried about you. You know that." He paused, and when Esther didn't fill the silence, he continued. "And after yesterday, whatever's going on in your head has obviously gotten worse. I blame myself, partly, for not realizing sooner that you'd stopped going to therapy, and then when I did find out, I didn't insist that you go back."

Insist. Esther tried to keep her expression neutral, but she spotted a twitch in his eyebrow that told her she'd failed. "That doesn't explain why Meg's here."

"She's here because I asked her to come. I can't be here all the time, and with Brandon staying at my parents', I thought—"

"You thought I needed a babysitter?" Esther looked from Ryan to Meg, incredulous. "Is that what this is?" She frowned at Meg. "You're here to *watch* me?"

Meg's face reddened.

Ryan pulled Esther's attention back. "You almost killed our son yesterday. Or have you already forgotten?"

Cowed, Esther shook her head.

"Until we can work out some sort of long-term solution, yes—Meg is doing us a favor by keeping an eye on you."

Esther shrank inward, humiliated. She'd made a mistake—a grave one, yes—but she was a grown woman. She could handle herself. She didn't need her big sister watching over her. Her only solace, and it was very, very small, was that Meg seemed to be just as uncomfortable with the situation as Esther.

Ryan continued, "We'll talk more when I get home, okay? Maybe between now and then you'll come up with something better." He kissed her forehead and stood, nodding at Meg as he passed.

"Or what?" Esther asked.

Ryan frowned. "What do you mean?"

"I mean what happens if I don't have another solution? Meg can't be my babysitter forever."

"Maybe that's a conversation you should have with Brandon," he said. "If you can't tell me why we've gotten to this point, maybe you can tell him." He looked at Meg. "Call me if anything happens."

Meg muttered, "Sure thing."

The door clicked shut behind Ryan and all Esther wanted to do was crawl into her bed and cry, but with Meg in the room, it was like a switch had been flipped, turning self-pity to jaw-clenching anger.

"Nice to know whose side you'd pick in the divorce," Esther said.

"I didn't pick anyone's side," Meg said.

"So he's paying you then, right? Figures. How much does my complete and utter humiliation go for these days?"

"He's not paying me. Is it so hard to imagine that I just care about you?"

Esther didn't believe her. Meg didn't do anything if it didn't directly benefit her somehow. Esther stood, starting for the kitchen. "I have to work."

"Go for it." Meg settled on the couch like she owned it. "I'll be here."

"Great."

"Great."

Esther stormed into the kitchen where her laptop sat charging on the counter. It occurred to her too late that she could probably have bribed Meg to leave and come back before Ryan returned from work, but she figured it probably wouldn't work anyway. Meg had walked in with a Big Sister aura. She would stay if she thought she was needed.

Esther opened her laptop, but instead of opening her email she clicked on the web browser. She navigated to Donny's Facebook page again, disappointed at the lack of update. She clicked on his picture tab and scrolled through the ones that were public. Each time she saw his face stretched wide in what looked to her like a wicked smile, a chill snaked down her back.

"Who's that?"

Esther jumped, nearly knocking her laptop off the counter. She spun around, blocking Meg's view of the screen. "You're spying now?"

Meg held up a bottle of water, one hand still on the refrigerator door. "I was thirsty."

"You could have asked."

"I didn't want to bother you." Then, looking over Esther's shoulder at the screen, "Donny Lippman? Why does that sound familiar?"

Esther had a mind to tell Meg to get out of her business, but there was something in her expression that made Esther pause. In the harsh kitchen light, the shadows under Meg's eyes were bruise-like against the paleness of the rest of her face.

"You look like shit," Esther said.

"I haven't been sleeping well," Meg said. "Don't change the subject. Who is he? A lover? I thought you had better taste. At least Ryan's employed."

Esther sighed, moving slightly out of the way as Meg leaned closer to the screen. "He was that kid. From that summer. Remember?"

Meg squinted at the screen. Then, expression darkening, nodded. "Why are you looking at his Facebook?"

"He was at Claire's funeral."

"What? Why?"

Esther shrugged.

"You're sure it was him?"

"I'm sure."

"Was Claire…friends with him or something?"

"I don't know." Esther scrolled through the page. "There's nothing here."

"That's because no one uses Facebook anymore." Meg nudged Esther aside and opened up another browser window. "There."

On the screen was an Instagram profile with what looked like a more recent picture of Donny, followed by pages and pages of other photos. His bio read: *God is good. Father is king. Family is all.*

"Yikes," Meg muttered.

Esther scrolled through the photos, most of which looked like they were taken in the same front yard—Donny grinning next to a truck, Donny holding a beer next to a fire, Donny curled around a woman who didn't look thrilled about it. Esther took a second look at that one to be sure it wasn't Claire.

"Looks like a winner," Meg said. Then, "He has kids?"

Esther clicked on a photo of Donny standing behind a little girl and boy, neither of whom looked older than four or five. He wore a button-down shirt and jeans, a too-wide tie dangling to his belt. His hands gripped their shoulders. The little girl was wincing, but the boy smiled dutifully. The caption read: *My kids are my LIFE and no one gonna take them from me over my dead body.*

In the corner of the photo, almost like he planted it, was the barrel of a rifle sticking out of the bed of the truck only a few feet away. Esther swallowed, her mouth suddenly dry.

"I don't see Claire in any of these. Do you?" Meg asked.

Esther shook her head.

"Thank Christ." Meg opened the water bottle and drank, eyes glued to the screen.

"But why was he there?" Esther asked. "It doesn't make sense."

"A friend of a friend. Or his parents. I don't know. Claire had a whole life. She knew people we didn't." Meg glanced back at the screen. "It's weird, though."

"It *is* weird." It wasn't validation, but it was close enough. Esther was *right* to be concerned.

When she looked back at Meg, she was looking at Esther, her expression unreadable.

"What?" Esther asked.

"We should talk about what happened."

"Ryan tell you to say that?"

Meg shook her head.

Esther closed her laptop—she was starting to feel Donny staring at her through the pictures—and went to the refrigerator where she studied the contents, not really seeing any of it. "I don't see the point."

"The point is that something is wrong. *Has* been wrong. And now with Claire... and I'm seeing these things, like—"

"What things?"

Meg ignored her. "I'm just saying. You can talk to me, you know. You're not alone."

Esther's mind flashed to the key, but quickly dismissed the thought. Telling Meg would only make it worse. Harder to bury. Harder to forget. "Sure."

"Seriously. Whatever it is. I won't judge you or anything."

"I'm not worried about being *judged*."

"What are you worried about, then?"

Everything. "Nothing."

"Something."

"Did this work with Claire?" Esther slammed the refrigerator door shut. Turned around and crossed her arms. "Did all the questions and platitudes make you feel better?"

"I didn't have to pry anything from her with a crowbar. We talked."

"Before or after you asked for a loan until payday?"

"I never borrowed money from Claire."

A lie. Esther and Claire didn't talk often, but they did talk. It was almost always about Meg.

"Sure, Meg. Tell yourself whatever you need to."

"If she ever did help me out, at least she never held it over my head."

"Because she was a pushover."

"Because she was my *sister*." Meg's voice caught. She cleared her throat. "We helped each other. She was there for me, and I was there for her when—"

She cut herself off, but Esther knew what she meant. When things got dark.

Esther stiffened. "What are you trying to say?"

"I'm saying—" She shook her head. Rubbed her face. "I don't know. I just—"

"I was there for her too, you know. I was there for *you*. Every time some job didn't work out or everything was just too much. A hundred here, two hundred there. No questions asked."

"If that's what this is about, fine." Meg dug her wallet from her pocket and pulled out a small wad of cash. Couldn't have been more than twenty dollars. She threw it onto the counter. "Take it." She whipped out her debit card and tossed that on the counter too. "No clue how much is left, but it's yours."

Esther's face reddened. "I don't want your money."

Meg shook her head, grabbed her water off the counter and started toward the living room. "I'll be in here. Try not to shoot anybody while you're *working*."

Esther muttered, "Bitch," before going back to the counter where she hid behind her laptop screen. She blinked back tears as she scrolled through Donny's Instagram, willing some kind of clue to jump out at her. Something to tell her why Donny was at Claire's funeral and what that meant for Esther's future. And for her past.

She glanced over the top of the screen, expecting to see Meg shooting a look right back, but Meg's gaze was fixed on the television. Esther started to say something, but then Meg wiped her eyes on the back of her arm and Esther sat back, silent.

CHAPTER THIRTEEN

MEG

Meg was climbing into her car when Ryan jogged up beside her. He'd been home less than five minutes, but Meg had no interest in sticking around longer than necessary. After the blowup that morning, she and Esther had spent the rest of the day in strained silence, only acknowledging each other when their respective boredom drove them both to the refrigerator. Meg was exhausted and just wanted to get home so she could let out the scream she'd been holding in the back of her throat.

"Hey," Ryan said. "Anything?"

"Well," Meg said, "She said a grand total of a hundred words, all of them sharpened to a point and aimed at me."

"Nothing about—"

"About Brandon? The gun? No." Meg rubbed her face. "Listen, it's like I told you, okay? Just because we're sisters doesn't mean we get along. We didn't braid each other's hair or swap boy stories or sneak into each other's rooms in the middle of the night just to talk."

"No. You rode bikes and explored broken places and depended on each other to get home safe." When Meg looked sharply down, he shrugged. "Esther used to talk about you a lot. And Claire. When we first moved out here, she'd drink a couple of glasses of wine and then tell me stories about the Midnight Society that met in the middle of the day, how you wouldn't let Esther hold the gavel that wasn't a gavel. She said she always threatened to stop going on the bike rides with you and Claire, but she wouldn't have stopped for anything."

Meg gripped the steering wheel, blinking away the sting in her eyes. She looked straight ahead at the house, gaze locking on a shadow in the living room window. At first, she thought it was Esther watching them, but the shadow was too dark, too dense, and the outline of the figure too thin. A car drove past, the headlights washing over the front of the house. She caught a flash of gray before the figure faded. She gritted her teeth against a chill.

Ryan continued, "Esther has always been a rough-around-the-edges kind of woman. I wouldn't change her for anything, truly, but I'm scared, Meg." Then, "You'll be here tomorrow, right? Same time?"

"She ever tell you about the house?" Meg asked, finally looking up at him.

He frowned. "Your parents' house?"

"Ask her about the house. Ask her what she saw behind the door."

Without another word, she started the car, drowning out Ryan's questions. Not that she could answer them anyway. Though she and Claire had talked about what Claire had seen, Esther never told. Meg suspected, though. And if she was right, it told her everything she needed to know about why Esther couldn't look at Meg without a sneer. Why she needed to get drunk before she could conjure good memories of their childhood together.

All Meg had ever tried to do was be a good sister, but she'd failed over and over. Two of her sisters had died because of her.

She pulled into the parking lot of her apartment building just as it was getting dark. As she approached the security door, she noticed a large box sitting on the stoop. She was surprised it hadn't been stolen—packages had a short shelf life out here in the open. Curiosity made her glance at the tag, looking for a name.

It was hers.

She frowned. She hadn't ordered anything and couldn't think of a reason anyone would have sent her a package. A mistake, maybe? There was only one way to find out. She hoisted the box onto her shoulder and carried it upstairs where she deposited it on the coffee table. She found a dull kitchen knife and slowly hacked through the tape until finally the flaps gave way.

Inside looked like a collection of junk—a notebook, a half-eaten bag of beef jerky, a baggie full of pens and pencils. She fished around looking for some clue as to what it was and where it all came from. Near the bottom of the box was a photo frame. Inside was the same picture of Claire and Brandon that'd been on Claire's desk in her bedroom. Meg sank down next to the coffee table, holding the frame to her chest. Had Mom packed up all of Claire's stuff? But why? That didn't make any sense.

She checked the outside of the box looking for a return address. She didn't recognize it, but a quick search on her phone told her it was a government building—Department of Human Services. Then it dawned on her. She'd been the one to call Claire's office to tell them what'd happened. She vaguely remembered giving them her address when they had asked where to send Claire's things. This must have been it.

Meg pulled everything out of the box, spreading it out around her, the photo still in her lap. She studied the contents, lingering on objects that surprised her—a bottle of vanilla scented body spray, a tiny ceramic elephant, a pink computer mouse featuring a cartoon flamingo and the words *be flamazing*. She picked up the body spray and spritzed the air, taking in a deep breath only to be disappointed. It smelled nothing like Claire.

The notebook turned out to be a datebook, with Claire's name written in tiny, precise letters on the inside cover. *If found, return to Claire Finch.* Meg flipped through to this month. The daily pages were mostly blank, save for a couple of innocuous notes—*milk; cancel HBO; Dad dentist*—but the monthly calendar was filled with tiny notations. Meg zeroed in on the twelfth, the day Claire died, where the date was encircled in a heavy red line. A lump formed in Meg's throat as she ran her finger over the line, and then tapped the days prior.

"When did you decide?" Meg wondered aloud. "How long did you sit with this?"

Another mark on the twelfth caught her attention. The scribbles were so small she barely made out the initials—DL.

The lump in her throat dropped to her stomach.

Donny Lippman.

Why would she make an appointment (a date?) to see someone on the day she'd planned to take her life? Was it some kind of last-ditch attempt? *Tell me why I should stay alive.* But if that were the case, why Donny? Based on what little she and Esther had found on his social media, he didn't seem like the kind of person Claire would have considered a friend, let alone a boyfriend.

But he was at the funeral. How did he find out? Who told him? Sure, he could have found out through friends or family—even if Claire had never spoken to Donny after that day years ago, there wasn't a family in Blacklick that wasn't three or four degrees of separation from another. But the longer Meg paged through the datebook, the more she saw his initials, the deeper a thought took root.

What if she hadn't just seen him that day? What if he'd been there with her?

What if he had killed her?

Meg took the datebook to Esther's house the following morning. Whatever vindictive feelings she'd been holding toward Esther took a back seat to the date book's contents. She wanted Esther to look through it, to see if she would come to the same shaky conclusion Meg had.

Ryan met her at the door, but instead of letting her in, he shuffled her back onto the porch, shutting the door behind him. He looked rough, bags on bags under his eyes and deep lines cut at the corners of his mouth, which pulled into a tight frown.

"I asked her," he said.

It took a moment for Meg to understand what he meant. She crossed her arms, trying to read the answer in his expression. "And?"

"She wouldn't say."

Meg didn't know if she was disappointed or relieved, but it was obvious Ryan was bothered. More so than yesterday. "Did something else happen?"

He shook his head. Lowered his voice. "She's breaking. It's like I can see it happening, but there's nothing I can do about it."

"Breaking? How?"

"She has these…rituals. Every night she checks all the locks, all the windows, sometimes twice, always in the same order."

"She's always done that," Meg argued, remembering Esther's rule of threes. Tap three times for good luck. Circle the block three times before putting her bike away for the night. And that was only what she saw. Meg figured there were more little rituals Esther went through when no one was looking. "It's just how she is."

He shook his head. "I get it, okay? We've been together almost fifteen years. Esther's eccentricities were…endearing. But early this morning I shut the bathroom cabinet door, then shut it again when it popped open. From the other room, I heard her tap the wall."

"Coincidence," Meg said. Though there's been a lot of that going around lately.

"Same in the kitchen. I shut the cabinet door, and she shut two others for no reason other than to make the sound." He sighed. "I can't go on like this."

"What are you saying?"

"I'm saying Brandon can't live with my parents forever. I don't want him to. He doesn't want to."

"But?"

"But who's to say something like this doesn't happen again? Whatever happened back then, it's eating away at her now and it's like she doesn't see it. Or doesn't want to. Next time it might be worse. Next time, she might pull the trigger."

"She wouldn't," Meg said.

Ryan stuck his fists in his pockets. "You don't know that. I have to protect my family."

"What does that even mean? Esther is your family."

"Exactly." He paused. "That's why I'm doing this. If you can't convince her to get help on her own, I'll have to do something about it."

Meg frowned. "Like what?"

But Ryan only shrugged. "Just do what you can."

Inside, Esther was in the kitchen. She glanced quickly over her shoulder, acknowledging Meg with a brief nod before turning back to the stove.

Ryan went ahead of Meg and kissed Esther's cheek. "See you tonight," he said.

"See you," Esther said.

He shot Meg a pointed look before he left. She didn't know whether she was more pissed that he'd essentially threatened her sister, or that he'd set the weight of it squarely in her lap.

"Hungry?" Esther asked.

Before Meg could answer, Esther had two plates on the counter and was heaping scrambled eggs onto each. She plopped a slice of slightly burnt toast on the yellow mound before passing a plate to Meg.

"Forks are in the drawer," Esther said.

Meg muttered, "Thanks," and went in search of cutlery. They both stood at the counter, silently shoveling gooey eggs into their mouths.

"Not quite done," Esther said as she swirled the eggs with her fork.

"Better than Dad's," Meg said.

Though their dad wasn't the cooking type, there had been some Sunday mornings when they were kids when Dad decided to make breakfast—board-stiff toast and eggs that bounced if they were dropped on the floor.

"True," Esther said.

Edible or not, Meg recognized the peace offering for what it was. She finished every bite.

"Working today?" Meg asked when the dishes had been rinsed and put into the dishwasher.

Esther nodded. "Why?"

Meg considered keeping the datebook to herself, but her suspicions had festered overnight, mixing with a familiar feeling of not having done enough. She couldn't let Claire down again.

"I want to show you something." Meg pulled the datebook out of her bag and set it on the counter between them. "It's Claire's."

Esther stared at the thing, frowning, hands folded tightly on the counter. "From Mom's house?"

"Her work. They sent me a box of her stuff yesterday."

Esther glanced past her like she expected to see the box materialize. "What was in it?"

"Pens. Pictures. This." Meg tapped the cover of the datebook, then slid it closer to Esther. "Have a flip through."

Meg twisted her hands in her lap, anxiously waiting for Esther to reach the page with Donny's initials. Would she come to the same conclusion Meg had? What would it mean? More importantly, what would they do about it?

She stopped when something fell out of the datebook, clinking loudly on the counter. The key from Claire's room. Meg frowned. That was impossible. She'd shoved the key into the back of her nightstand drawer, hadn't even looked at it since she brought it back from her parents' house.

Esther stared hard at it, barely breathing.

Neither of them made a move to touch it.

"Is that what I think it is?" Esther finally asked.

Meg nodded, carefully sliding the thing off the counter and slipping it into her pocket. It was hot to the touch, and left streaks of black on the counter.

Esther stared at the black marks before she continued through the book, finally pausing on this month. Meg knew the moment Esther saw the red circle because the wind seemed to go out of her. Her shoulders sank inward as she stared, unblinking. Then, her gaze narrowed and she frowned. "DL," Esther said. "Donny."

Meg nodded.

"Why would she be seeing Donny that day?"

"I don't know."

Esther paged back through the datebook, scanning no doubt for Donny's initials. "They're everywhere."

"Once a week. Sometimes twice."

"But why?"

"Work, maybe?"

Esther nodded, but her expression was all doubt.

"It feels off, right?" Meg asked.

"If she planned to—" Esther swallowed. "If that was the day, why meet with Donny?"

"Maybe she didn't."

"Maybe she did."

"Okay, and then what?"

Esther pushed away from the counter and paced between it and the sink. Each time she turned, her gaze landed on the datebook, the red circle like an eye staring out at them both. Meg watched Esther closely, studying the tightness of her jaw and the muscles in her neck.

"What is it?" Meg asked.

"Ryan asked me about the house last night."

Meg tried to sound surprised, failing miserably. "Oh?"

"Don't," Esther said. "Don't pretend."

"Sorry," she muttered.

"I was gonna read you the riot act when you got here, but now..." She picked up the datebook, thumb tracing the red circle. "Do you know why I never told you and Claire about what was in my room?"

Meg shook her head, breath held, scared to interrupt. Scared to let her keep going.

"Because I wanted it not to be real. I was afraid that if I said it out loud, it would be like busting that door open all over again. Like it could release—" She paused; took a shaky breath. "As I got older, I started to believe it was all just...stupid. Of course it wasn't real. But there was a voice in my head, whispering, warning me. Every time, I walk out that door almost believing it could be my last time. I'm scared. All the time. I keep saying I'm living cautiously, smartly. But the voice has only gotten louder. Clearer. And then Claire died and I just—" She shook her head. Sat uneasily on a stool. "And then I saw Donny at the funeral, and it was like staring down the barrel of a gun."

Meg's skin prickled. "Tell me."

Esther's voice softened to barely more than a whisper. She studied the counter as she spoke, fingers picking apart the corner of a coupon circular. "I didn't want to go in. That's the first thing. There was something...wrong about the whole house. You know how you walk into a place, and you think you're alone at first, but then it's like you can feel eyes in the back of your head?"

Meg nodded.

"It was like that. Like I could feel something else in the house with us. Someone. I don't know. I kept waiting for the feeling to pass and then you found your key and pushed me to find mine, and then, once it was in my hand, it was like I didn't have a choice. It sounds stupid saying it now, but by holding the key, by putting it in the lock, it was like the door owned me somehow."

She wanted to tell Esther she knew exactly what she was talking about, but kept quiet, hands wringing in her lap. She didn't want to stop Esther now that she had started.

Esther continued, "At first, the room was just a room. It was dark, and the floor was sticky. I kept peeling my feet up and flinching at the sound. I couldn't see much—the light from the window was sparse and mostly blocked by a big, old tree—but I could see writing on the walls. All different colors and sizes and handwriting. Some of the words had been scratched out and others written over. I stood practically with my nose to the drywall, but I couldn't read any of it. Then I started getting that prickly feeling again. That watching feeling." She took a shaky breath. "All I could think about was getting out of there. But it was like the words blurred together so much I couldn't even see where the walls ended anymore. I couldn't find the door. I started to panic. I screamed for you and pounded on the walls thinking you'd hear me from your room—but even if you did, there was no door. How were you supposed to get in? How could I get out?"

"I didn't hear you," Meg said. "I didn't hear anything."

"I was *screaming*. Maybe I'd made myself dizzy with it, but soon it was like the room wasn't even in that house anymore. I was *lost*. I finally made my way back to the center of the room, thinking if I calmed down, everything would right itself. But the second I caught my breath, a man with dark hair and a stubbly jaw and narrow shoulders came out of the dark. He was holding a gun, or what looked like a gun, pointed right at me. He didn't say a word, but somehow, I knew the words on the walls were his. The writing just above his head came into sharp focus and then I could hear him whispering them, over and over."

"What was it?"

"*You did this.*"

Meg stiffened. "What does that mean?"

Esther frowned, the coupon circular in shreds under her hands. A tic, Meg remembered, from their childhood. It meant Esther was about to lie to her, or at least not tell her the whole truth. "I don't know. He just kept saying it, over and over. His voice got higher and higher, like a CD sped up too fast. The gun trembled in his hand, and it was like I could *feel* the bullet in there. My skin itched, waiting for the bang. But then, somehow, I found the door. I couldn't get out of there fast enough. Nearly broke my ankle tripping over a dip in the floor." She finally looked up at Meg with haunted eyes. "Sometimes I felt like I'd brought him out with me, always there, hidden in the backs of my eyelids."

"And then Donny came to the funeral," Meg said, realizing. "You think it's him?"

"I *know* it is." Then, "If he's in Claire's datebook on this day..." She jabbed the red circled date. "There's a reason. There's a *link*, okay? Donny—*adult* Donny—was in that room that day, and he held a gun to my head. Who's to say he didn't do it to Claire too?"

There it was. Esther had come to the same conclusion as Meg. Claire had maybe been murdered. Meg thought hearing it from her sister—the steadfast one, the feet-on-the-ground one—would solidify the thought in her mind, but it had only planted more questions. The biggest of all: *why*?

Esther continued, "What if what I saw in the room wasn't me? I mean, what if I was seeing through Claire's eyes? What if I saw her death?" She stood, paced again. As she spoke, the words seemed to tumble out of her, conviction turning quickly to mania. "Maybe if I'd stayed in the room a little longer, I would have seen the end. Stopped it or—or at least seen enough that we wouldn't have thought that Claire would... What do we do? We have to *do* something."

Meg studied the red circle, willed it to twist and bend into something clearer.

An answer. She strained to remember every detail of that last phone call. Had there been some clue that someone else had been in the room with her? A shuffling sound or throat clearing? Had Claire sounded coached? Meg couldn't remember. The details blurred the harder she thought about it.

"Like what?" Meg finally asked.

Esther only shook her head as she opened her laptop.

"It doesn't make sense though, right?" Meg said. "Why would Donny *want* to kill her?"

"I don't know," Esther said.

"Wouldn't there have been clues? Something to make the cops think it wasn't suicide?"

"I don't *know*." Esther dug the heels of her palms into her eyes. "Why are you fighting this?"

Because it was too easy. Just like that, she was blameless, or at least less so.

But then, why was Claire haunting her? And why was Claire's key in the date-book when Meg knew she hadn't left it there?

Was it better that Claire's darkness had finally pulled her down so far that she couldn't get up again, or that Donny—or *someone*—had gone with her to that house and killed her? In some ways, Meg didn't think the answer mattered. Either way, Claire was gone and there was nothing they could do about it.

But the keys. That house. It meant something. Question was, what?

"Okay," Meg said. "What do we do?"

Esther turned the laptop around and joined Meg on the other side, their elbows fighting for space on the countertop. "We dig."

CHAPTER FOURTEEN

ESTHER

FEBRUARY 2001

Three inches of fresh, heavy snow soaked the sides of Esther's sneakers. No money for new boots this year, and she'd be damned if she was gonna be clomping around in Meg's old Walmart shit-kickers, so she doubled up on the socks and tucked the cuffs of her jeans as deep into the boots as they would go before setting off on her bike. The front wheel made a satisfying sloosh through the snow and the wet, but her arms and legs burned from shifting and tightening to keep herself upright. Wasn't too cold outside—above freezing, anyway—but by the time she got where she was going, she could feel the chapping of her cheeks and the back of her throat burned from huffing and puffing the chilly air.

For more than a year she'd been thinking about the house. The doors. The key that now sat snug in her coat pocket. And for more than a year, she didn't dare come down this way, afraid to see that it was there, that it was real. Or worse—that it wasn't.

But now she'd had enough.

Enough of the nightmares and the shadows. Enough of waking up sweating in the middle of the night to see Claire staring at her like it was Esther that needed hot milk and a blankie.

Screw that.

Esther had never backed down from a fight, and she wasn't about to start now.

She skidded to a stop on the sidewalk in front of the house, splashing mud. It was covered in the same thick layer of snow as everything else, but somehow it only made the house look more sinister. Icicles hung dripping from the porch roof like fangs.

A couple of houses down, some kids were rolling dirty snow into misshapen balls, probably for a snowman. They stopped when they spotted her. One of them shook their head while the others simply stared, jaws clamped tight. She wondered if any of them had been inside, if they also had keys they couldn't quite bring themselves to get rid of, kept hidden under old T-shirts. She doubted it. She couldn't explain it, but it had felt like the house had been waiting for Esther and her sisters. Eager, even. That was stupid, of course; it was just a weird house. Still. Fingertips feeling numb, she stuck her hands in her coat pockets. The key burned.

She could just leave it here. Throw the key in the snow and head back home. Try again to forget about it. It was tempting.

One of the kids whistled. When she turned, frowning, the tallest of the kids waved. "Wouldn't go in there if I were you," he shouted. "S'haunted."

"Bullshit," Esther yelled back.

The smaller kids tittered. A girl? Cussing? *Oooo.*

"It's true," the kid said. "My dad makes me take the garbage out and you can see the attic windows from my yard. I saw someone up there, just standing in the window. I couldn't see his eyes, but I knew he was watching me." He shivered. "You should go home. Play dress-up or whatever."

It was the dress-up comment that did it. Anger was like a fire hose against fear for Esther. She climbed off her bike, knocked the kickstand into place, and then flashed him the finger as she marched through the gate and up the path to the porch, followed by a chorus of *oooo*'s. But the righteous anger only carried her so far. The moment her foot touched the porch step, it was like it all drained out of her. She bit back a shiver.

She wished Meg was with her.

Not because Esther *missed* her or anything, but because Meg had a way of bringing out a fire in Esther, one she was never really able to conjure on her own. Meg poked all the soft places so Esther would know where they were, so she could learn how to protect them better.

But Meg couldn't even manage to stick around for twenty-four hours. Esther would never forget the way Claire's whole body seemed to cave in on itself when she realized Meg wasn't coming back.

"It's my fault," Claire had said, but wouldn't explain when Esther prodded.

Esther figured it had something to do with the picture Meg had been given. Esther never got a good look at it, but she saw the date on the back. Didn't take Sherlock Holmes to figure out what was probably on the other side. But that was Meg all over. Run away the second things get hard.

Screw Meg.

Esther took another step up the porch, feeling several pairs of eyes on her back, a silent dare. She almost turned around. What did she care what these idiots thought of her? But as her toe inched back toward the bottom step, she caught a glimpse of something on the side of the house, bright green against the white of the snow. She leaned on the rail to get a better look, and when she realized what it was, her lip curled into a sneer and her whole body felt engulfed.

Donny.

She remembered seeing him on that lime-green bike a couple of weeks ago, riding up and down her street like he didn't stick out like a sore thumb. At the time, she assumed he'd stolen it. The bike looked brand new and about six inches too short for him, his knees bunched up around his ears as he pedaled.

Haunted, my ass, she thought.

It was all Donny. Had to be. He was the one who'd brought them here. He'd probably planted the keys too. She couldn't immediately figure out how he'd managed to make her see what she'd seen, but it wasn't impossible. She'd been tormenting herself for more than a year over some stupid trick. And why? Because their dad had caught him stealing?

The fire in her belly bloomed, warming her all the way through, as she reached for the handle. She was going to kick his ass. For real this time.

Ready or not, here I come.

When she reached the door, it was already cracked open an inch. She nudged it the rest of the way with her shoe, half expecting Donny to jump out from behind a corner. But the room was empty. She took a tentative step inside.

"Hello?" she called. "I know you're in here. Might as well come out."

No sound. No movement. The place was eerily silent, the snow dampening even the white noise from outside. It was so quiet she could almost hear the rapid beating of her heart.

She placed a hand over her chest as if to calm it. "Donny! Come out!"

Finally, a sound from upstairs. A snicker?

Gotcha.

She started up the stairs, pausing to knock three times on the bottom post. But halfway up the stairwell, she heard another sound, someone knocking maybe, on the bottom level. She cast a quick look up at the landing in case Donny was messing with her, then followed the sound back downstairs and through the living room.

As she moved through the house, the ceiling creaked, like footsteps upstairs following her every move. She paused, testing it, and the creaking paused too. A chill snaked through her.

It's just Donny, she told herself.

But then another knock came from somewhere ahead. The kitchen, maybe.

She couldn't see directly into it, the dining room closed off by a wall with only a small, arched doorway. Her heart pounded, and she was struggling to keep her breathing under control. Anger cooled in her gut.

"Come out, asshole! I'm serious!"

Something flashed across the window to her right. She bolted across the room just in time to see Donny take off on his bike, jacket trailing from one arm. She banged on the window, but he didn't look back.

Coward.

Equal parts disappointed by not being able to confront Donny and relieved that she didn't have to spend another moment in this house, she turned toward the front door only to freeze mid-step.

The front door was gone.

No gap. No broken wood. Just *gone*, the wall stretching across the front of the house, wallpaper flaking and dust coating the chair rail, like it'd always been there.

Her first thought was, *No.*

Her second thought, a more rational thought, was that she'd gotten turned around. She'd only ever been in this house once, and it was a weird place, nothing where it belonged, so it made sense that she'd wandered deeper into the house than she realized.

She spun around, thinking—hoping—that when she did, she'd be met with the front door.

There was a door, all right.

In the arched doorway leading to the dining room, where five seconds ago there had been an opening big enough to see the whole room, was now a door. *Her* door, all knobby wood and rusted fittings. The key vibrated in her pocket. Almost absently, she reached toward the wall and started tapping her finger.

Tap. Tap.

Bang.

She jumped as something hit the door from the other side.

Donny, she thought.

But she had seen Donny ride away.

That didn't mean he hadn't circled the block and come in through the back door. But the *doors.*

Esther could barely breathe, her mind awash with white noise and the sound of her pounding heart. God, she was so stupid. What had made her think she could come back here and just…walk away?

"What do you want?" she asked, voice barely above a whisper.

The walls of the house seemed to expand and contract, like it was breathing. She thought of the icicle fangs outside and imagined fur along the roof and handrails that unfurled into claws. She thought of an alligator's wide-open mouth, and the fish too stupid to pay attention to where they were swimming.

She felt the heat of the key all the way through to her skin. She didn't have a choice.

"If I go in there," she said with more confidence than she felt, "you'll let me leave. Right?"

The house gave no response. It would have to be good enough.

She withdrew the key only to find it unnecessary. As she approached the door that shouldn't have existed, it swung wide, revealing a room so dark it hurt to look into. She told herself it would just be Donny in there. Donny and his stupid smirk—when she saw him, she was going to wail on him so hard he'd wish he'd never been born. Holding on to this thought, she swallowed a whimper and went inside.

While the rest of the house had been oddly warm, this room was freezing. The door shut behind her, and it was like being shut inside a cold locker. A few winters back, Dad talked about getting a job at a pig farm across the border in Illinois. Pay would have been better, but one look in the cold locker sent him hightailing it back to the plastics plant.

"There were pieces of 'em," he'd told Mom while Esther eavesdropped. "Just sittin' there. Heads starin' right through me."

For days, Esther hadn't been able to get the image out of her mind.

She took deep breaths to try and settle her heart. She thought she smelled the iron tang of blood.

Soon the cold seeped into her skin. It numbed her lips and ears, and she gritted her teeth to keep them from chattering. When, after a long time, nothing happened, she tried for the door only to realize it wasn't where it was supposed to be. She groped only to find flat wall. Panic rocketed through her as she moved along the wall, groping, but there was nothing. No door. No escape.

"Let me out!" she screamed.

Tried to scream.

Her lips moved and her throat burned, but no sound came out.

"Help! Please!"

Still nothing.

She banged on the walls with her fists. She kicked and scratched and wailed, but there was only silence. The room was a black hole, a vacuum for light and sound.

A tomb.

Icy tears dripped down her face as she fell against the wall. She sank onto the floor and drew her knees up to her chest. For a moment, she *knew* she was going to die there. But then her gaze fell on a shape in the dark. She couldn't *really* see it, but she knew it was there, the same way she knew her arm was attached without looking at it. She wasn't alone.

A scraping noise broke the dead silence, like nails on wood, and then the density of the room changed. She couldn't hear the figure's footsteps, but she could feel them. She felt its heat, and then, she felt its heady breath on her face.

Finally, an eerie yellow glow seemed to come from everywhere and nowhere. Her eyes ached as they adjusted and her first instinct was to close them, but the thing slowly coming into focus in front of her seemed to read her mind and dug its fingers into her eyelids, pinning them open.

It was *her*.

At first she thought it was a reflection, but then she realized the thing in front of her was another Esther: same short, dark hair, same downturned, gray eyes, same pursed mouth. As recognition washed over her, the other Esther's eyes shone.

Behind her, the room began to change. The walls moved slightly inward, the ratty wallpaper peeling away to reveal smooth, pink walls. Patches of carpet appeared on the floor, the edges dark like they'd been burned, and then the far corner where the wall met the floor rippled, but she could hardly make out what was coming out of it. Her eyes watered, still pinned open.

As though satisfied that she wouldn't look away, the other Esther released her eyes and leaned back.

She blinked furiously, wincing against the burn, and when her eyes finally cleared, she saw the rippling mirage of a crib.

It was like being transported back in time. Days flashed in front of her face like the pages of an amateur cartoon, black and white, except for a moment here and there in full color. The day Mom and Dad brought a new baby home, Esther confused as hell because they'd already had a baby—Claire—sleeping sound in her bassinet. Meg splay-legged on the floor, Claire curled between her knees like a kitten, and the new baby—Julie—cuddled against her chest.

The images fell away, leaving only the crib.

Instinct made Esther tap her finger against the floor, but the other Esther gripped her hands before she could tap the third—and most important—time. Panic built in her chest, knowing what would happen next.

A shadow emerged from the ceiling, humanoid but with spidery limbs. If it had a face, it was too muddled for her to see. Its long arms reached for the crib, for Julie.

Tap. Tap.

The other Esther leaned onto her hands, crushing them just as she managed to lift her finger for a third tap.

Her mother had called Esther's Rule of Threes an anxious tic. A self-soothing habit. It didn't mean anything bad would happen if she didn't finish her routine. Her tapping.

But the need to tap or knock or pat was like a bolt of lightning going through her. She didn't have control over it any more than she could control the flow of blood through her veins. When she tapped, the world turned as it should. When she tapped, everyone stayed safe.

She had only ever not finished the sequence twice.

Once, the morning Dad got laid off.

Once, the night Julie went missing.

Now, seeing it again, the shadowy figure reaching into the crib, Esther's body screamed.

The other Esther leaned over her shoulder and pressed her lips against Esther's ear. "Pitiful," she said in a voice identical to Esther's own. "It's almost like you wanted it to happen."

"I didn't," Esther murmured.

"Then fix it. Do the magic."

Esther struggled against the other Esther's grip, but she was too strong.

"See?" the other Esther said. "But you already knew that, didn't you? You know whose fault this was."

Esther bit her lip so hard it bled. Her fingers ached to tap, like it could magic her out of here, away from the other Esther, away from the memory of what had happened. She wrenched her head back, but the other Esther was stronger.

"Say it."

She shook her head, body racked with silent sobs.

The other Esther squeezed, nails cutting into Esther's hands. "*Say* it."

"Mine," Esther finally said, defeated. "It's my fault."

CHAPTER FIFTEEN
ESTHER
NOW

The browser window seemed to twitch under the strain of the dozens of open tabs, the result of Esther falling down rabbit hole after rabbit hole. After scrutinizing Donny's social media with a fine-toothed comb (again), she dug through his friends lists and followers and compared them to Claire's social media, looking for patterns. When that didn't pan out, she pulled up Google Maps and took a virtual Street View tour of the entire town, scrolling from house to house in search of the one that matched Donny's profile picture.

"You're not going to his house, right?" Meg asked as she watched over Esther's shoulder.

"I'm just looking," Esther said. For what, she didn't know.

Next, she looked up the websites for the two elementary schools in the district and scoured the pages for pictures that resembled Donny's kids in his profile picture.

"This feels illegal," Meg said.

"It's not," Esther said, though she had to admit this bit felt a little on the skeevy side. She couldn't shake the image of some pervert scrolling through the pictures like it was a menu.

But she pushed past the uncomfortable feeling and was rewarded. Toward the bottom of the home page was a collection of pictures of children, chalk in hand and tongues stuck out in concentration. In the uppermost right corner, a young girl in a faded yellow T-shirt and fraying shorts stood proudly behind a chalk drawing of a mermaid, its tail a florescent green.

"That looks like the same girl, right?" Esther asked.

Meg leaned over her shoulder, squinting. "Maybe?" Then, "Oh, wait. Look." She pointed to a caption in tiny print beneath the photo: *Melanie Lippman and her mermaid.* "How many Lippmans you figure are in Blacklick?"

Esther was already nodding. "It's her."

"Could be a niece."

"It's *her.*"

"Okay. So?"

"So it's *something.*" She wrote the name down and underlined it twice.

By lunchtime, they'd amassed an impressive list of *somethings*—some from further internet excavation, some from a brief phone call with their mother, who'd never met a piece of gossip she didn't like. They'd had to be careful, though. If Mom thought they were digging into Claire's death, she would shut down. Mom didn't like to dwell on bad times. "Once a thing happens, it happens," Mom always said. "You can't fix it. You can't change it. Leave it be."

Meg, being the better liar, told their mother a version of the truth—that they'd remembered him from childhood and were curious about what he was up to. Now, Meg assembled turkey and cheese sandwiches while Esther read through the list of findings, none of which seemed to have anything to do with Claire. At least, not directly.

"He drives a Ford. Or a Chevy. He likes guns." She shuddered. "His daughter is in fifth grade, or was when that picture was taken, and he's spent time in jail."

Meg handed Esther a paper plate. "Mom said 'in and out of jail.' *Spent time* implies he was in there for a while."

"Maybe he was." Esther took a bite of her sandwich, chewing thoughtfully. When she swallowed, she continued, "The point is the jail part. He could have a history of violence."

"Or DUIs."

"Mom said he's divorced. That the marriage was volatile."

"Mom's marriage is volatile. It doesn't mean anything."

Esther dropped her plate onto the counter hard enough for the sandwich to slide off. She didn't bother righting it. "Why are you so quick to defend him?"

"I'm not."

"You are."

"I just think we're jumping to a lot of conclusions really quickly." Meg peeled the crust off her sandwich, not meeting Esther's gaze. "What if we're wrong? What if we're digging into this shit, sifting through Claire's life, for nothing?"

"So what if we are?" Esther countered. "I'd rather be wrong and have done something, than be right and do nothing. Wouldn't you?"

After a long moment, Meg nodded.

"Good." Then, "Last thing. Mom said she's pretty sure he works with his dad at the car repair place over by the movie theater." She paused. "I think we should go there."

Meg frowned. "What do you mean *go there*? Like, confront him?"

"No, just...*go*. To look."

Esther didn't want to admit that she had her own doubts. Every time she looked at Donny's profile picture, she'd fixate on something small—a barely-there scar above his eyebrow, the curve of his earlobe—and think *maybe*. But then she reminded herself that the fact of his initials in Claire's datebook, and Esther's gut reaction on seeing him at the funeral, *had* to mean something. And then there was the house. Claire went there for a reason, and Donny was the one to show it to them in the first place all those years ago. Coincidence? Maybe. But Esther didn't put a whole lot of stock in coincidence. So she doubled down. Not only was he the man from her nightmares, but it was likely he'd murdered Claire, and Esther was going to prove it.

"Look?" Meg asked. "You mean *stalk*."

"Yes. I mean stalk." Esther took two quick bites of her sandwich, just enough to keep her stomach from complaining too loudly, and then threw the rest in the trash. "Grab a couple of Brandon's Gatorades out of the fridge."

Meg crossed her arms. "What makes you think I'm going with you?"

"Because I'm going, and Ryan is paying you to babysit me, remember?"

"He's not paying me to—"

"Megan Virginia Finch, if you do not get your shit and meet me at my car in two minutes, I swear on pain of death I will unearth the picture of that time at Kim Garnick's birthday when you let Cody Holder stick his tongue down your throat, and put it on a Christmas card."

It was a bluff, but one Esther knew would work. Back then he was just *Pockmark Holder*. Now, he was an Arena football player with a string of criminal charges from *grand larceny* to *improper contact with a minor* knocking around behind him like cans on a gravel road.

Meg's mouth dropped open. "You do not still have that picture."

"Care to test that theory?"

Meg looked hard at her for a moment, but Esther held her ground. She didn't know what she'd do if Meg called her bluff, apart from maybe knocking her over the head and dragging her caveman-style to the car. If Meg really put up a fight, Esther *could* go alone. Probably. But she really didn't want to.

Finally, Meg walked to the refrigerator and peered inside. "Red or blue?"

"Blue," Esther said, relieved. "No. Red. Leave the blues for Brandon. They're his favorite."

Grabbing her bag and laptop, Esther felt buoyed for the first time in months.

She wasn't cowering in her house. She was getting out. She was doing something. And by doing it, she might not only bring her sister's killer to justice, but she could end her nightmares for good. Brandon could come home, and her husband would forgive her, and life could move on. When Meg wasn't looking, she tapped the edge of the counter—tap, tap, tap—and let out a breath.

In the car, Meg stared stubbornly out the window as Esther drove.

"What's your problem?" Esther asked when she couldn't ignore it anymore.

"You could have stopped at *Virginia*."

Esther smirked. "I had to make sure."

They drove for most of the forty-minute trip in relative silence. Esther messed with the radio, jumping from station to station trying to avoid commercials, while Meg scrolled through her phone. More than once, she caught Meg looking at her out of the corner of her eye but didn't turn to meet her gaze. With every mile, Esther felt her resolve waning. A familiar voice in the back of her mind whispered to her the dangers she faced out here. It told her how stupid it was to go chasing after the man she believed would kill her. The voice sounded suspiciously like Meg's. She wondered if telling Meg what she'd seen in the house had been a mistake. For Esther, recounting the memory had only proven what she suspected when she saw Donny's initials in Claire's datebook. She thought it had had the opposite effect on Meg.

As they crossed the town limit, the *Welcome to Blacklick* sign cracked down the middle and covered in graffiti, Esther held her breath.

The movie theater—miraculously still in business—sat on the main drag, across from the town hall and police station, and in the same strip mall as a hair salon, a sandwich shop, and a dollar store. Across the small parking lot was Discount Auto Repair.

Esther parked as far from the building as she could while still having a clear view of the door. It was a small shop with one garage, the door hanging a little crooked on its tracks. The cinder block that made up the building was painted a garish blue that clashed with the mustard-yellow roof overhang. A sign above the building read *Help Wanted* and, beneath that, *Good, Honest Repair.*

"Mom could have been wrong, you know," Meg said, barely looking up from her phone.

Esther pointed to one of the only vehicles in the lot. "I bet that's his truck."

"Hard to tell without the arsenal in the back."

"Same rust spot above the wheel well."

Meg made a noncommittal noise.

"Must be important."

"What?"

"Whatever it is that's on your phone."

Meg sighed, tucking her phone beneath her leg. Esther caught a glimpse of what looked like a Facebook feed before Meg shoved it out of sight. Before phones became permanently attached to their hands, Meg would *pick*—at her nails, her hair, the stitching in the leather of the car seat—to avoid uncomfortable situations. Now she could just scroll into oblivion.

"So what do we do now?" Meg asked, petulant.

Esther settled into her seat, eyes on the garage door. "We wait."

They didn't have to wait long.

Donny strolled out of the garage carrying a disposable mat. The shirt of his mechanic uniform had come mostly untucked, waving behind him like a cape. His hair was wild, and his fingers were black with grease. Esther's body reacted instantly, skin pinching and heart hammering. Meg sank down in her seat, but Esther froze, eyes wide like a deer in headlights. She didn't breathe until he drove a run-down Oldsmobile, parked only a few spaces away from them, into the garage.

"One point for Mom," Meg muttered.

Esther nodded, her mouth dry. Her mind was racing, trying to outpace the voice in her head screaming *danger*. She told herself she was safe. They were in public. It was the middle of the day. He hadn't even noticed her.

Still, she kept her eyes glued to the garage door, waiting for him to come out again. For a long time, nothing happened. Meg shifted anxiously in her seat, occasionally checking her phone and muttering the time.

"I think we should go," Meg finally said. "He's working. I mean, we know for sure where he works now, like you wanted, but I don't think we're going to learn anything else."

Part of Esther agreed with her sister, but she still didn't want to leave. Not yet. She couldn't help feeling deflated. A million questions buzzed through her mind: Had Claire gotten her car repaired here? Was that what the marks in her datebook were for? Had the coroner noticed any black grease streaks anywhere on Claire's body? Staring at the garage door wasn't going to answer any of them; Meg was right.

She started the car and moved to put it in gear when Donny barreled out, face red and jaw clenched. Meg grabbed Esther by the collar and dragged her down so that she hovered below the dashboard. She heard an engine roar to life. Tires squealed, and she sat up in time to see Donny's truck fly past them toward the road. Without thinking, Esther stepped on the gas and followed.

"What are you doing?" Meg asked.

"Following him," Esther said.

Meg gripped the *oh-shit* handle as Esther turned too hard onto the road, hitting the curb. "Why?"

She didn't know. She just *acted*. "He looked pissed."

"Even more reason *not* to follow him. What if he sees?"

"He won't." Probably. The way he was driving, Esther had to run a couple of lights to keep up. He'd likely notice her soon if she didn't get pulled over first.

Meg held tight to the door and checked the hold on her seatbelt. "Don't kill us."

"I won't."

She followed him onto the highway, keeping a couple of car lengths between them. It wasn't exactly difficult; a glance at her speedometer told her she was going well over eighty. The steering wheel shook under her hands, and in her mind, she saw a terrifying flash of the tire hitting something in the road and sending them careening over the barrier. She white-knuckled the wheel and pressed harder on the gas.

He got off the highway after only a couple of exits. Esther followed, probably too closely, but once he hit the end of the off-ramp, he gunned it and she had to run the next light to keep from losing him.

"I'm gonna be sick," Meg muttered.

Esther shot her a look. "Do not puke in my car."

"Maybe slow down a little."

"I can't."

"You said yourself he looked pissed. Wherever he's going, you do not want to be there."

Esther ignored her, continuing to follow Donny through the next few lights until he finally turned onto a side street, and then into an office park. He parked in front of the corner building and Esther drove quickly past, hoping he wouldn't turn around.

"Oh," Meg said.

Esther parked several spaces away, finally turning to look at Meg. "What?"

Meg pointed. Esther followed her gaze to the door where Donny had gone in. In plain, block letters on the glass: *Department of Human Services*.

The pieces fell together slowly, then all at once.

Regular check-in meetings. A volatile marriage. The caption on his picture: *Ain't no one gonna take my kids from me.*

"Shit," Esther muttered.

"Yep," Meg said.

Esther sat back, still watching the door. "But this is it, isn't it? Proof." She looked at Meg, whose expression she couldn't read. "At least motive, then."

"Maybe," Meg said. "But if it's because of his kids, why would he think killing Claire would get them back?"

"Maybe he didn't. Maybe it was just a revenge thing."

"Okay, but then why would Claire agree to meet him at the old house?"

"She might not have. He could have followed."

"But if that's the case, then why did she go there? It was the middle of the night, Esther. She wouldn't have any reason to be there unless—"

Esther sat up straight in her seat, one hand on the wheel to keep herself still. Her whole body was buzzing. "I just know I'm right on this."

Suddenly the building door flew open. Donny came out barking at someone over his shoulder, his face flushed, fists clenched at his sides. A security guard stood in the doorway, arms crossed over a barrel chest. Donny continued to yell, spittle flying, but the security guard appeared unmoved. Esther quickly jabbed the window button, lowering it just enough that she could hear. But Donny must have heard the harsh thunk of the window movement because he turned toward them, lips parted in a sneer.

Heart hammering, Esther struggled to put the car in reverse, feeling his sharp gaze on her all the while. Meg sank low in her seat, hand over her face while Esther peeled out of the parking spot. Someone behind her honked but she kept going, unable to shake Donny's expression. He'd looked dead at her, and it was like living her nightmare. As she flew out of the parking lot, she kept her eyes on the road, knowing if she dared to look in her rearview mirror, she'd see Donny on the sidewalk, gun aimed.

She could almost hear the bang.

For a while, no one said anything about Meg taking off in the middle of the night. Esther was happy to get "her" room back, and though Mom seemed sad at first, she pushed her mouth up into a smile until it almost looked real. That first night, Claire tried to ask Mom about it, if Meg had said anything before she left, but Mom only said, "Hmm?" Pretending like she hadn't heard.

It was almost like Meg hadn't been there at all.

A few days later, Claire found the picture crumpled at the bottom of the small garbage can in Meg's bedroom. She tried to smooth it over her knee, but the thing had been crumpled and recrumpled so many times the creases cut like scratches through their faces. Part of her wanted to throw it away, to put it out of her mind and pretend like Mom did, but she decided to keep it, hidden in the back of her dresser drawer. It was a reminder that there was something wrong with her.

But it was hard to sleep knowing the picture was there. She lay awake, the black worms undulating beneath her skin as she listened to the rhythmic crinkle of the picture—*crack, crack, crack*—like the beating of a broken heart.

Tonight, Claire was wide awake. She'd tried squeezing her eyes shut, head buried beneath the pillow, but it was like her body refused to rest. She couldn't get comfortable with her arms constantly in the way, and the *crack, crack, crack* was worse than ever. If she paid too close attention, it got louder, sounding like it was coming from inside her own head. Finally, she threw off the blankets and crept out of her room into the dark hallway.

It was blessedly quiet, the only sound coming from the clock on the wall, a gentle ticking. She thought about dragging her blanket and pillow out here to sleep, but knew if Mom found her, she'd only send her back into her room. She thought maybe she'd get away with sleeping on the couch and started down the stairs only to start shivering the moment she left the warmth of the second floor. The second the snow started to melt, Dad had turned off the heat, telling them they could wear more clothes if they were that cold. Claire thought about going back for her blanket, but she figured once she got snuggled beneath the afghan draped over the back of the couch, she'd be fine.

She didn't notice the light right away. Once she saw the couch, all she could think about was sleep, but then she glanced toward the kitchen and saw the faint yellow light drifting from the direction of the basement door. All thought of sleep disappeared as curiosity pushed her toward the light.

The basement door was open barely a crack. She peered through the opening but only saw the stairs and the shaggy brown rug at the bottom. A shadow crossed the rug and she held her breath. Then came a strange hitching sound, like someone choking. She eased the door open a little wider, flinching at the creaky hinges. Whoever was in the basement didn't seem to notice. She took two careful steps down the stairs, crouching low, trying to see beneath the flimsy board that separated the stairs from the rest of the basement.

She recognized her dad's robe, the tie dangling behind him like a tail. He was sitting on the floor, the box where Claire had gotten the picture open in front of him. Her first thought was that she was going to be in trouble. She had tried to close it as best she could but couldn't find any tape and did a poor job of folding the flaps in on themselves. She'd buried it at the bottom of the stack, thinking no one would come looking for it. She was wrong.

The longer she watched her dad sift through the contents, she realized what the hitching, choking noise was. Dad was crying.

It was a strange thing, seeing her dad cry. Silly, but until now, she wasn't sure he was even capable of being sad.

Part of her wanted to go downstairs and comfort him, but she was frozen to the spot. Watching him felt wrong somehow. She wasn't supposed to see this. No one was.

Suddenly the crying stopped. Claire pressed herself against the stairs, willing her body to become invisible. She should have gotten up and ran. Even if he'd heard her, he wouldn't know it was Claire. But it was like her mind had been cut off from her body. Dad stood, and all Claire could see of him was from the hips down. He shifted his weight, the robe tie dragging, and then, quick as lightning, he snatched something from the box and threw it against the basement wall. The thing shattered, and for a moment, everything was still. Then Dad started toward the stairs.

Claire frantically crawled back into the kitchen. He'd be up the stairs before she had a chance to get to her bedroom, so she hid in the first place she could get to— the pantry. She squeezed herself beneath the bottom shelf, tucked tight against the used grocery bags and stacks of rust-eaten pans. In the kitchen, she heard her dad pause, could hear him breathing heavy from coming up the stairs. She held her breath, heart hammering in her chest. After what felt like a long time, she heard the creak of the stairs. Dust rained down from the pantry ceiling. He was going to his room. She inched the pantry door open and waited until she heard the gentle click of a door closing, then waited another minute before finally unfolding herself from beneath the shelf.

Maybe the box in the basement was like the room in that strange, crumbling house. Maybe that's where the darkness lived, where it waited, coiled into forgotten corners until someone like Claire disturbed it.

She needed to know what it was he'd thrown. She needed to know what it meant.

She crept down into the basement, now dark after her dad had turned off the light, using the faint glow of the streetlight through the high window to guide her to the wall of boxes, careful not to step on the pieces of whatever had shattered. She got on her hands and knees and scooped the shards she could find into a pile along with dust and nails from Dad's workbench, then carried all of it back upstairs to her bedroom. She laid the pieces out on her bed and spent most of the next hour trying to fit them together. By the time the sunrise peeked between her window blinds, she had a small corner of what looked like a ceramic Christmas ornament more or less assembled—half a snowman's head and what was probably supposed to be a snowbank. On the crisp white of the snowbank were hand-written letters: *lie*.

She couldn't figure out why someone would write "lie" on an ornament, and decided the rest of the word was still down in the basement. But Mom would be getting up soon, so any chance she had of finding the rest of the pieces would have to wait until tonight. She rolled the pieces up into a sheet of notebook paper and set it in her dresser drawer with the photo.

She crawled into bed and closed her eyes, suddenly very tired, *lie* inscribed on the insides of her eyelids.

Over the next several weeks, on nights when she couldn't sleep (which were most of them), she crept into the basement and hunted for the missing pieces of the broken ornament. Sometimes she found several. Sometimes none. Sometimes, she opened the box that'd made sadness come pouring out of her dad like rain and took one of the items with her. Soon she'd amassed a collection of what looked like random objects, which she kept in the same dresser drawer as the picture. Some nights she pulled them out and spread them across her bed like the pieces of a puzzle. Her favorite of them was a pair of dainty black patent leather shoes with white daisies on the toes, which she slipped onto the feet of a stuffed bear she'd had since she was a baby. The shoes made him look older and more worn out than before, but Claire liked the way they shone against his gray fur.

As time went on, she began to forget the shoes were even there and carried her bear around the house openly, a guard against the blackness still worming through her body. No one seemed to notice for a while. Then, after school, Claire came home to find Mom on the couch, holding the bear in her lap, tears dripping and wetting the bear's fur. She cradled it like a baby, rocking and soothing. It was like seeing Dad in the basement. Private, not for Claire's eyes.

She started toward the stairs when Mom finally looked up. Her expression twisted, despair turning to rage.

"Where did you find these?" Mom asked. Her voice was calm and sharp, like the razor edge of a knife.

"He's mine," Claire said stupidly.

Mom stood, the bear clutched in her fist by his neck. "You took them."

The shoes.

"I didn't take them." Claire blinked back tears. It was rare that she got in trouble because Esther and Meg got in enough trouble for all of them. "I found them."

"Found them." Mom's voice was barely above a whisper. Her arms started to shake, but still she held the bear outstretched, gaze fixed on the shoes.

"They were mine, right? When I was a baby?"

Mom dropped her arm, like her strings were cut. Something shifted in the room. It became crackly, like the moment before lightning strikes.

"I'm sorry. I didn't—They're just shoes, Mama, I didn't think it was—"

Mom crossed the room too fast for Claire to move out of the way. Mom slapped her, hard. They both startled at the sound. Claire was too surprised to cry, but she could feel her mother's stinging handprint on her cheek. For a brief second, Claire thought Mom would crumple—she didn't hit them, and always yelled at Dad when he spanked them—but it was like something broke in her mother. Still clutching the bear, Mom slapped Claire again, and again, hitting her face, her neck, her shoulder. Claire was frozen to the spot, hands up in defense. Tears streamed down both their faces and soon Mom was standing over her, Claire on the ground, curled up and choking. She stopped feeling the slaps after a while, only a white-hot burn across her skin.

Esther came in then, her bus from the high school only a few minutes behind Claire's. Claire heard the door open. Saw Esther's backpack drop only a few inches from her face.

"Mom?"

Mom's strength was waning, and the tears had blinded her to the point that she missed Claire more than she connected, but on her knees now, Mom had begun to hit with her closed fist, landing soft punches to Claire's arms and legs.

"Mom, what's happening?" Esther's voice sounded strange. Too high-pitched. Scared. "Mom, *stop.*"

Esther scrambled to cover Claire, taking the brunt of a few hits before Mom finally leaned back on her feet and pressed the bear to her face, agonized sobs muffled in the fur.

"Come on." Esther looped her arms beneath Claire's to help her up, but it was like Claire's arms and legs had been cut off.

Esther dragged her most of the way to the stairs. Then, wincing against the pain that came in waves now, Claire finally got her feet under her. She leaned on Esther all the way up the stairs into Claire's room where Esther let her fall onto the bed.

Claire groaned, the pain working its way up her middle and into her head, throbbing and stinging.

Esther closed the door, then stood in front of it, arms crossed. She watched the doorknob for a long time, barely breathing, as though waiting for it to turn. After a long time, she looked at Claire and frowned deeply, eyebrows furrowed, face pale. Her expression said what they were both thinking: Mom had never done that before.

"What was that about?" Esther asked.

Claire shook her head.

"Did you do something? Say something?"

"No."

"You're sure?"

Claire remembered the shoes. Hesitated. Nodded.

"Okay, well I guess just sit up here until she calms down. Maybe Dad's work is slowing down again. You know how she gets when that happens. On edge. Maybe she's—" Esther stopped, gaze drawn to Claire's open dresser drawer where the pom of a pink winter hat stuck out.

Esther pulled the hat out. Then, peering into the drawer, began pulling out the rest of the items—the broken ornament, the picture, a tiny felt elephant—frown deepening. "Shit," she muttered. She looked at Claire. "Where did you get all this stuff?"

Claire sat up, swallowing as a new, sharp pain zipped across her skull. "The basement."

"You need to put it all back." She glanced at the door. "Later. When Mom's not looking."

"Why?"

"How's your head?"

"It's just stuff."

"Yeah, but it's *her* stuff."

"Mom's?"

"No."

"Whose?"

Esther started gathering the items—*secrets*, as Claire had come to think of them—and wrapped them up in a T-shirt she found on the floor. She balled the whole thing up and stuffed it back in the drawer, which she closed. When she looked up at Claire, her expression was twisted in what looked like pain. "We don't talk about Julie," she said. "Ever."

Julie. Yes, that made sense. The *-lie* on the ornament. A little girl's hair barrette.

"Who's Julie?" Claire asked. "Why don't we talk about her?"

Esther sat on the floor, head resting against the dresser drawer that held the treasures. She closed her eyes and sighed. "Because she's dead."

CHAPTER SEVENTEEN

MEG

NOW

Meg was surprised the toolbox held her weight. The thing was cheap, the thin metal frame bending beneath her heel. She tried not to move, even as she started to wonder how she got here, wherever here was. All she knew was that she had to keep still. It was important.

But she was so tired, and her legs were so weak from running. She locked her knees to stay upright, until a woozy feeling forced her to stop.

It would be over soon. He promised.

She swayed slightly, listening to the whistle of the wind through a gap in the window frame. Her belly rumbled, but she ignored it. She wouldn't have to worry about food ever again.

Hurry, she thought.

Soon, a long-limbed shadow crossed the wall in front of her, its body lanky, the arms swinging like weights. Its legs ended in sharp points that teetered between the slats of wood on the floor.

No, she thought. *Not you.*

A coil of rope peeled away from the ceiling, two dimensional at first, then slowly, it took on body as it tied itself into a noose, which fell heavily onto her shoulders. Dangling somewhere near her chin was a key.

The shadow twitched and the rope tightened, burning her neck. The key pressed painfully against her throat, stinging, as the metal grew hot.

No. She changed her mind. This wasn't what she wanted. She reached for the rope, but another pair of hands clung to hers, holding them tight behind her back.

He's here.

She tried to call for help, but the rope was cutting into her throat. She felt blood trickle down her neck, and the edges of her vision were starting to go dark. Tears dripped down her face.

Behind her, someone laughed.

Meg's eyes shot open, heart hammering like she'd been running. Her skin was cold, but she could feel the sweat between her legs and on her back.

She started to sit up, but pressure on her side and belly kept her pinned to the mattress. An arm, skin mottled and split, circled her waist. Black-nailed fingers tapped a gentle rhythm against her belly.

"You were having a nightmare," Claire said. Her breath was like compost. She nuzzled her face into Meg's neck. It sent chills rocketing down Meg's body. "What was it about?"

"Nothing," Meg said.

Lips pressed against Meg's skin, Claire whispered, "Don't lie."

Meg closed her eyes, hoping this was part of the nightmare, that when she opened them, Claire—this dark, twisted version of her—would be gone. She should have known better. As Meg tried to wriggle out of her grip, Claire only pressed herself tighter against Meg, legs tangled and nails digging into her body.

"Remember that night when the sky turned green and the air was electric?" Claire asked. "I crawled into your bed, and you braided my hair until I fell asleep."

"I remember," Meg said.

It was the first and only tornado to rip through Blacklick. It'd taken a couple of houses and half the Walmart with it, too, far away to damage their house, but Meg stayed awake all night, trembling, listening to the whine and groan of the wind and rain. She'd been terrified, but with Claire lying there, needing her, Meg only just managed to keep from sobbing out of fear.

For a moment, neither of them spoke. Meg listened, not sure what it was she was listening for, until she realized Claire wasn't breathing.

She wouldn't be, of course, but the realization simultaneously made Meg incredibly sad and hyperaware of Claire's cold skin.

"Can I ask you something?" Meg asked.

"Mmhmm."

"Esther thinks…" She paused. "Esther thinks someone maybe killed you."

"That's not a question."

Meg held her breath, already regretting saying anything at all. If Claire had been murdered, did she even want to know?

Claire continued, "Someone who?"

Meg shrugged.

Claire was quiet for a long moment. Then she asked, "Would it make you feel better?"

"I don't know."

"You said *Esther thinks*. What do you think?"

"I think the only thing that matters is that you're gone."

"But I'm not gone." Claire pressed her forehead to the base of Meg's neck. There was a squelching, liquid noise, and then what sounded like Claire gagging. She leaned her chin against Meg's neck and something plopped, damp and heavy, down her face and onto the bed. A key. *Meg's* key. "I'm right here."

Meg could still feel the cool, papery dryness of Claire's skin on her neck when she arrived at Esther's house. Ryan shot her a meaningful look as she went inside, which she ignored. She'd agreed to keep an eye on Esther, to make sure she didn't do anything to hurt herself or anyone else, but she decided she wasn't going to be his spy. If he wanted answers, he needed to talk to his wife.

"Well," Ryan said, following her into the kitchen where Esther stood hunched over a bowl of cereal, "I guess I'll be going."

"Guess so," Meg said.

"Have a nice day," Esther added without looking up.

He hesitated, gaze jumping from Meg to Esther and back. He sighed and shook his head. "Thanks. You too."

As soon as his car passed the window, Esther dropped her spoon dramatically into her cereal bowl. "I thought he would never leave."

"Yeah." Meg opened the refrigerator, looking for something to get the taste of dirt out of her mouth.

She grabbed orange juice and poured a glass. As she drank, Esther stared at her expectantly.

"What?" Meg asked.

"We have to go to the police." When Meg didn't respond, Esther added, "About Donny."

"He gave you a dirty look, Es. Doesn't make him a criminal."

Esther frowned. "You know what I mean."

Meg took another sip of orange juice. It wasn't helping. Every breath in was like huffing the scent of an open grave.

It was one thing to poke around in Donny's social media, even to follow him, as stupid as that had been. But getting the police involved was something else. Something they couldn't take back.

She understood why Esther wanted to do it. Meg had come to the same instant conclusion Esther had. It made sense. Here was a guy with a history of violence who was meeting their sister, a woman who would have been responsible for removing his children from his care, and then she ends up dead. Open and shut, right? But then Meg heard Claire say it again in her head: *Would it make you feel better?*

Would it? Or were they looking for reasons to believe what'd happened to Claire wasn't their fault? That they couldn't have stopped it?

And the keys. Two now. She wanted to ask Esther if she still had hers, or if it had appeared to her somehow, like Claire's had. It was almost like the house was calling them back. But why? Did it have something to do with Claire's death?

Meg wanted to believe it wasn't a suicide just as badly as Esther did. More, maybe, because it was Meg who had gotten the phone call, and not for the first time. Meg, who should have known better. But something bothered her, and more than just the appearance of her dead sister in her bed at night. If she was real, wouldn't she have told Meg? If she wasn't, did that mean Meg's hallucinations, vivid as they were, were nothing more than a brain drowning in guilt?

"We can't just go in and accuse him of murder," Meg said finally. "They'll just brush it off."

Esther snatched the empty glass out of Meg's hand and brought it to the sink. "You don't know that." Then, "We'll show them the datebook. We'll *make* them listen. You'll see."

Meg could have refused to go with her. Esther was stubborn, but she was clearly still shaken from yesterday. She looked like she hadn't slept, the skin under her eyes loose and dark. If Meg refused, she was pretty confident Esther wouldn't go on her own. But a small part of her wanted to know. If they showed the police the book and they took it seriously, what would that mean?

It won't bring her back, a small voice whispered.

But didn't they owe it to Claire to pursue this? Was it why Claire kept appearing to her, why she seemed so angry? Meg tried to think rationally, too cognizant of the shaky ground Esther stood on when it came to her marriage, her family. Wasn't it Meg's job to look out for her? To keep her from making stupid mistakes if she could? But what if protecting Esther meant casting Claire aside? She couldn't choose. She didn't want to. Still. Her mother was right.

Esther was all she had left.

"Okay," Meg finally said. "We'll go."

Esther squeezed Meg's arm as she passed her on the way to the door, a smile tugging at the corners of her mouth. Meg startled at the gesture, unused to affection from Esther. They had been close, once. Maybe they could be again.

———————

They drove to the address on the business card one of the police officers had handed Meg that day and parked between two cruisers. One of them was occupied. The officer eyed Meg with what felt like an overabundance of suspicion, but then it might just have been annoyance at being disturbed on his break. For the first of what she figured would be a hundred times before they even reached the door, she wondered whether she should have given in so easily.

The officer at the desk handed them bond paperwork without looking up. "Fill these out. Only checks made out to Gary County will be accepted."

"Thanks," Esther pushed the papers back toward the officer, earning her a hard look. "We're not here for this. We need to see—" She shot a look at Meg.

Meg held out the card. "Officer Kingsolver?"

"He's not back from his lunch yet."

"We can wait," Esther said, all smiles.

"Could be a long lunch."

"We could come back—" Meg started.

"It's fine." Esther elbowed her in the ribs, smile so tight it looked painful. "No worries. We'll just be over here."

She dragged Meg away from the front desk toward a group of hard, blue chairs held in line and attached to one another by thick bars. Heaven forbid you forget for a moment where you were or who held the power. They chose a spot near the window where, Esther said, they would catch him walking up.

It didn't matter that Meg couldn't quite remember what he looked like, apart from an aggressive mustache, or that the police probably didn't use the front door to their own station. Esther couldn't be talked out of her plan. She pulled out her phone and started scrolling through screenshots, pointing out bits of cut-off images she thought were important.

"Pretty sure those are part of the address," Esther said, enlarging a blurry shot of Donny and his kids probably taken from his Facebook profile.

"You are not going to his house," Meg said.

"Who said anything about going? I just… It's important to find out everything we can." Esther nodded once, like she'd made a decision in that moment.

Meg didn't ask what it was. Wasn't sure she wanted to know.

After half an hour of waiting, Meg was working up the nerve to suggest to Esther they make an appointment, or at least come back another time, when she caught the desk officer looking at them. Another officer stood behind her, mumbling. She recognized him as the guy parked beside them in the cruiser, probably coming to tell them to move their car.

Good, Meg thought. *An excuse.*

But as he approached, hand already extended, she took in the slightly downturned eyes and mildly protruding incisor and realized—Officer Kingsolver had shaved.

"Ms. Finch," he said when she stood, taking his hand. "Again, let me just say how sorry I am for your loss."

"Thank you."

He nodded, but there was something lingering behind his eyes. Concern or suspicion or both. He turned to Esther and shook her hand as she introduced herself.

"I'm Meg's sister. *Claire's* sister."

"Lovely to meet you, ma'am." He raised an eyebrow at Meg. "So what can I help you ladies with?"

"I think it would be better if we spoke somewhere—" Esther nodded toward the door leading into the bowels of the station. "More private."

He cast a look around the empty waiting room, lingering on Meg's face. She struggled to keep her expression neutral. She may not have completely believed in the murder theory the way Esther did, but she didn't want to prejudice him against it right out of the gate.

"Sure," he said. "This way."

The walk from the waiting room to his office was surprisingly boring. Having spent hundreds of late nights propped on the couch with a bag of chips and the television for company, she'd expected to see a row of perps handcuffed and sitting on a bench, all hangdog expressions and booze breath. Instead, it looked more like the corporate offices where she used to temp, except with guns and badges.

He led them to a small desk toward the middle of a row of cubicles and snagged a couple of chairs from other desks for Meg and Esther. For a moment, no one spoke. Esther seemed to be studying Officer Kingsolver, looking for an angle. He appeared to be doing the same. Meg, on the other hand, was keenly aware of the curious eyes on them each time someone walked through the office. It didn't matter that she hadn't done anything wrong; it was hard to feel at ease around so many guns.

Officer Kingsolver gestured openly. "So."

Esther pulled the datebook out of her purse and held it protectively in her lap. He glanced at it quickly but didn't ask any questions.

"We're here about Claire," Esther said.

"Okay," he said. "Though I don't know that I can be of much help. Once the file is closed out on…something like this, we pass all the information and personal effects onto the funeral home and family. You know what I know at this point."

"I think we actually might know a bit more."

He raised an eyebrow. "Such as?"

Esther glanced quickly over at Meg, who tried to fix her face into something encouraging but was probably grimacing.

"We've come upon some information that leads us to believe Claire was actually murdered," Esther said.

Come upon some information. Jesus, she was laying it on thick. But Officer Kingsolver either didn't notice the effort or was kind enough to look past it.

"I see," he said. He nodded at the datebook. "Is that what you're referring to?"

Seemingly spurred on by his interest, Esther opened the datebook and leaned toward him as she flicked through the pages. "See these initials? They belong to Donny Lippman. We knew him when we were kids. He showed up to Claire's funeral and I knew something was off then because, from what I knew, they hadn't kept in touch. But then we figured out that she was likely instrumental in removing his kids from his care. A history of violence. Drinking too, probably. And look here—" She pointed to the twelfth. "—he's here on the day she… On that day. He was there. He killed her, I'm sure of it."

"Quite a few probablys and maybes in that," he said.

"He has motive," Esther said, frustration eking into her voice. "And opportunity."

"And means," Meg added, unable to watch her sister flounder. "That photo of the guns in his truck."

"Right!" Esther pulled out her phone and showed the officer the picture.

"Disturbing, I'll admit," he said, "But Claire wasn't shot."

"He's *violent*," Esther insisted. "Something happened to her in that house. She didn't do this to herself."

Officer Kingsolver looked at her for one long minute before turning to his computer. He booted up the thing and then clicked for a while until he found what he was looking for. "So it looks like we did speak to Mr. Lippman on the thirteenth at the behest of a Sarah Haig."

"Claire's boss," Meg said, remembering.

"And?" Esther asked.

"And according to Ms. Haig, Claire was working with Mr. Lippman to get his children *returned* to his care."

"Seriously?" Meg asked.

"That doesn't make sense," Esther said.

"Ms. Haig didn't think so either," he said. "Which, I assume, is why she pointed us in his direction. But Mr. Lippman appears to have had an alibi for that night." He sat back in his chair, shaking his head. "Look, I can't imagine what it feels like to lose someone this way. I've seen a lot, but thankfully never been too close. But there's no foul play here. I'm sorry."

Esther looked cracked in half. She held the datebook and her phone, mouth agape. Meg was just as floored. Why would Claire have been helping someone like him? Someone clearly unhinged?

"You're wrong," Esther said, shaking her head. "You're wrong."

Officer Kingsolver leaned forward, resting his elbows on his knees. His voice softened. "Have you spoken to anyone? Someone who can help in your time of grieving?"

Meg's face flashed hot. "She's fine."

He opened his mouth like he wanted to say something, but closed it just as quickly. He nodded. "Anything else I can help with?"

"No," Esther snipped. "You've been oh so helpful already."

She stood, knocking the chair over. An officer passing by shot Officer Kingsolver a look, but he shook his head, a gesture so quick Meg almost missed it. He followed them to the front with Esther quickening her pace. Her shoulders hitched and Meg figured she was trying to get out of there before the tears started.

"Take care," he said.

Meg ignored him. Esther turned around and, in a moment of blind rage, gave him the finger.

In the car, Esther leaned her head back against the seat. She didn't make a sound, but a few tears dripped down her cheeks, dotting her shirt collar. Meg rifled through the center console until she found a napkin, which she handed to Esther.

"Asshole," Esther muttered before dabbing at her eyes. "Did you hear the way he spoke to me? Like I was a fucking child."

Meg nodded but didn't really agree. He'd been gentle, not patronizing.

"And that bullshit about the alibi." She looked at Meg, but Meg must not have fixed her face in time because Esther's frown deepened. "You don't actually believe that, do you?"

Meg squirmed under Esther's scrutiny. "He *said* Donny had an alibi. Why would he lie?"

"No, he said he *appeared* to have an alibi."

"So?"

"So that means they didn't *actually* look into it. It means they found what they wanted to find so they could tie everything up in a neat little bow." She sniffed, turning the key so hard the engine ground. "This is fucking Blacklick, remember? Nobody cares about women like Claire. Women who don't get married and pop out babies at nineteen with the first pimple-faced jerk who tells her she's pretty and, heaven forbid, vote Democrat."

Meg didn't respond. They'd had a moment yesterday, something that felt like they were moving toward...not forgiveness exactly, but something close. Closure. She didn't want to ruin it.

But then she remembered Ryan's threat. Part of her didn't want to believe Ryan would follow through. What would Brandon say if his dad locked his mom away somewhere? It probably didn't matter. Ryan would come at every complaint with a shield of platitudes. *It's for the best. I'm doing this for Esther. I'm saving my family.* If Meg let Esther plow down this path of suspicion, how soon before she got herself hurt? Before she hurt someone else?

Esther hit the main road going too fast, fishtailing as her tires fought for purchase. Meg gripped the door, foot stomping the imaginary brake.

"Sorry," Esther mumbled. Then, after honking at a driver that cut her off, "We're gonna have to do this ourselves. You see that, right? We'll gather more evidence, stuff they can't ignore. We'll fucking arrest Donny ourselves if that's what it takes."

"Let it go, Es."

"Excuse me?"

"It's like he said, okay? Donny had an alibi. And it makes sense that he would come to her funeral if she was helping him to—"

Esther turned too quickly into a McDonald's parking lot, hitting the curb hard. Meg bounced in her seat, which made her bite her tongue. She tasted blood.

Esther hit the button to unlock the doors. "Get out."

"I'm not hungry."

"Get the *fuck* out."

Meg looked hard at her sister, but she refused to meet her gaze. Esther's chin trembled, nails digging into the leather of the steering wheel.

"Look, we can talk about this, okay? I just don't want you doing anything you'll regret."

"The only thing I regret is telling you anything in confidence." She finally looked at Meg, cheeks blazing. "You don't care about anything other than yourself."

"That's not true. I care about you. I'm worried—"

Esther laughed. "Sure. So worried, like my husband is worried, right?" Her lips pulled into a tight frown. "Get out of my car. Now."

Meg obeyed, not wanting to stoke the fire, but held onto the open door. "My car's at your house."

"I'll have it towed." Esther leaned over the center and grabbed the door, pulling it shut, and then hit the locks before Meg could get to the handle. She peeled out, nearly clipping Meg with her bumper. Even as Esther hit the gas, flying down the road toward the highway, Meg thought she would come back. They'd had some real blow ups in the past, but never anything so bad that Esther had left Meg stranded. So she went inside the McDonald's to wait.

Her optimism lasted less than an hour. She tried texting Esther, calling, but every attempt to get hold of her went unanswered.

Fucked that up, didn't you? Meg thought.

She just hoped Esther had gone home and not to do something incredibly stupid. She started to text Ryan, only to delete it. If he asked, she'd make up some excuse about an emergency that necessitated leaving her car. She had no idea what that would be but prayed it would come to her soon.

Tomorrow, she would make Esther see sense. Once Esther had time to sleep on it, to move past the anger.

Meg ordered a burger and fries and started the long walk to her apartment, phone tucked carefully into her back pocket. Maybe Esther would call. Maybe Meg hadn't screwed up everything all over again. Esther was all she had left. She couldn't lose her like she'd lost Claire.

Like she'd lost Julie.

CHAPTER EIGHTEEN

ESTHER

Esther got as far as the highway before she thought about turning around. It was what her son would have called a *dick move*, leaving Meg at the McDonald's with no car. But the betrayal she felt, knowing her sister wasn't on her side, was total. Sure, they weren't as close as they used to be, but they were blood. Didn't that count for anything?

She could almost hear Ryan asking if she would have done the same for Meg. *Yes*, she thought emphatically. *She would have.*

When your sister tells you something is real and true, you believe them, a moral obligation Meg had never subscribed to, especially when it came to Esther. Growing up, if something was missing from Meg's room, Meg didn't hesitate to blame Esther. If something was broken, it was Esther's fault. If Meg got blamed for something she hadn't done, Esther was the one who would pay for it. Esther, being the middle child, was a born scapegoat.

She should have known she couldn't count on Meg, that she was on her own. If she was going to prove Donny had murdered Claire, she was going to do it *her* way.

At the next exit, she turned around and headed back to Blacklick, where she parked at a gas station. She scrolled through her phone until she found the picture she was looking for—the bronze address numbers, barely visible behind Donny. After messing with the photo settings, she could just make them out: 1053. Or 1058. She scowled at the screen. Even if she had the exact number, it wasn't much to go on. A quick Google search pulled up half a dozen addresses in a ten-mile radius that could have been a match. She ground her teeth, growing more and more frustrated. She cycled through a litany of reasons why she would never be able to solve this, and then hung the blame on the necks of Meg, Officer Kingsolver, Ryan, and then finally herself. It was criminally unjust that Esther would be the only person who wanted this, but was the least equipped. Like her teachers used to say, all potential but none of the follow-through.

"No. Stop." Esther set her phone in the cupholder and, after clicking the locks, closed her eyes and took a deep breath. "You can do this."

Her time with her therapist hadn't been a total wash. She'd seemed almost excited when Esther told her about her performance anxiety, that she dreaded the idea of anyone needing her because she wouldn't be able to deliver. She was stupid, incapable, and folded under pressure.

"Compartmentalize," the therapist had told her. "Separate your knowledge into what you do and do not know. What you can and cannot do. Focus first on what you have, and then analyze it for its use."

"Like MacGyver," Esther had said.

"Yes. Like MacGyver."

Back to her phone, she ignored what she didn't know (everything) and focused on what she did: she knew Donny lived at a house in Blacklick, whose address was 1053 or 1058. She knew there were seven or eight houses within the town limit that shared that numerical portion of the address. She knew (vaguely) what the house looked like. So how could she use those pieces individually or together to find what she needed?

When it came to her, she could have kicked herself for not thinking of it sooner.

Google Street View.

She'd tried it before, unsuccessfully, with Meg looking over her shoulder, but now she could focus.

Seven or eight houses weren't a lot, so she searched each of them individually in Street View until she found one that closely resembled the front of the house in Donny's picture. The siding was the right color—a little more worse for wear in Donny's picture—and the address numbers hung in the right spot. The eve over the front door sloped at the right angle, and the large pine tree to the left of the building stood tall in both images.

She'd found it.

"I am MacGyver," she said, and set her navigator for the address.

As she pulled onto the street, she felt her bravery waning. Apart from the image of the gun collection itching like a rash at the back of her mind, the first house she passed had a flagpole mounted in the middle of the yard, a *Trump 2020* banner hanging flaccidly from the top. These people didn't like outsiders poking around in their business. Esther may have grown up in Blacklick, but she was a Chicagoan now, and it showed.

The first time she drove past the house, she didn't slow. The big black truck wasn't in the driveway, but the curtains were wide open in the front window, so she could clearly see a woman walk past. His wife? Ex-wife? She remembered her mother saying their relationship was tumultuous, but that could have meant anything. She wished there was a way to know if Donny still lived here, but even she wasn't that adept at internet sleuthing.

By the third drive-by, she knew she needed to decide whether to investigate further or leave. Mr. *Trump 2020* had poked his head out the front door more than once, giving her the full blast of his jowly scowl.

Taking a small measure of comfort from the assumption that Donny wasn't the type to be anywhere his beloved truck was not, Esther finally parked in the street in front of the house. The lawn was patchy and yellow. A child's bike lay abandoned next to the cracked driveway, not far from a beach bucket and shovel covered in mud. The mailbox leaned at a precarious angle, propped up by a stack of two-by-fours that were water-logged and dotted with mold.

Okay, so she was here. Now what?

She went back to her phone, pulling up Donny's Facebook page again, looking for direction. She scrolled through his pictures, pausing on a photo of Donny and a woman who looked like the one in the window. Their heads were bent together, a couple of light beers on the table between them. *My love*, he'd captioned it. According to the tag, the woman's name was Tara.

"Excuse me!"

Esther jumped, nearly dropping her phone. The woman—Tara, maybe; her hair was lighter out here in the sunlight—shouted from the stoop. She clung to the door as she leaned over the steps.

"You can't just sit here," the woman yelled. "This is my property."

Esther's first instinct was to take off. As an adult, she'd never been great at confrontation, especially with women whose whole personality was *I will fight you*.

But Esther knew herself. If she drove away now, she would never come back. She was Claire's last hope. She couldn't give up.

Swallowing her nerves, she grabbed her bag—a large, black thing that more resembled a briefcase than a purse—and tried to fix her face into something non-threatening. She climbed out and left the car doors unlocked. Usually a major no-no, but she wanted to be able to make a quick getaway if it came to it.

Esther flashed her an *I'm a professional* smile as she slowly circled around the front of the car, mind whizzing through cover stories.

"It's Tara, right?" she asked, flushing with relief when Tara's ears seemed to perk up.

"Yeah. So?" Tara said.

"I'm Esther." She paused, pissed at herself for not using a fake name.

Tara looked Esther up and down, probably drawing her own conclusions. She tossed a look into the house, then shut the door. She crossed her arms. "Donny ain't here."

Esther bit the inside of her cheek to hide her relief. "I'm not here to see—"

"Yes y'are. Figured it was only a matter of time before they sent someone else out." She softened slightly. "Claire was okay, though. I was sorry to hear about her."

"Thank you," Esther said. Part of her worried Tara knew exactly who she was, but how could she? She picked apart Tara's words. *Before they sent someone else out.* Oh! Tara must have assumed Esther was with the county, with Claire's department. She could use this. Maybe. She figured Tara had had more than enough experience with people like Claire, the way she eyed Esther up, suspicion and fear vying for superiority in her stance; she'd be able to pick out a fake at a hundred paces. Esther would have to be careful. "I'm sure you won't mind if I have a quick look around." She tried to sound authoritative, but her hands were shaking.

For a second it looked like Tara might refuse. Esther didn't know what she'd do at that point. Run?

But Tara's shoulders sunk as she sighed, moving out of the way of the door. "Make it quick. I have a shift."

Wearing a tight smile, Esther approached the stoop, careful not to touch Tara as she slid past her into the house. The door slammed shut behind her, making her jump.

Tara moved in front of her, a smirk playing on her lips. "Sorry."

"No problem." Esther cleared her throat, unsure where to begin. She was being given access to Donny's house, access she would not get again, so she needed to be on the lookout for clues. But she couldn't *look* with Tara staring at her the whole time. "I'm sure you have things to do. No need to linger on my account."

"I'm fine," Tara said.

Of course she was.

Esther grinned. "Great." She went deeper into the living room where piles of laundry took up most of the couch. A torn leather recliner sat at an odd angle near the fireplace, a men's hoodie draped over the back.

"It's mine," Tara said, defensively, as she followed Esther's gaze. "I mean, it was Donny's, but he gave it to me."

Tara crossed the room and grabbed the hoodie, wrapping it up in a bundle in her arms. Her body was stiff, expression neutral, but Esther recognized the look in her eyes. She was afraid.

Esther put her hand up, a gesture meant to calm a skittish animal. "Listen, I'm not here to cause problems for you, okay? I'm sure you've been through a lot."

Tara nodded.

"But you can understand where I'm coming from too, right?"

"No. I really can't." She dropped the hoodie on the couch pile. "You people ruined our lives. My kids get scared when they see a strange car drive up now. They think you're gonna come take them away again."

"No one's taking anyone away," Esther said, then immediately regretted it. She couldn't make this woman any promises. "If I could just get a look around…"

"Like I told you. Donny's not here. He moved out, just like you all told him to. Now I'm here alone with kids up my ass about when their daddy's coming home and why they gotta have macaroni and cheese for the third night in a row." She rubbed her nose. "I work *hard*. Put in double shifts up at Uncle Frankie's all the time. Best bartender they got. I didn't sign up to be a single mom and now 'cause of one accident we been ripped apart."

"Accident?" Esther asked, nonchalant as possible.

Tara's gaze narrowed. "You don't know?"

Esther shrugged in a way she hoped was noncommittal. "I try not to make snap judgments based on what's in a file. I'd like to hear it from you, if that's okay."

Some of the tension released from Tara's shoulders, even as she sized Esther up. She wasn't the kind of person to trust easy, but Esther saw she'd won points by asking Tara for her point of view. Tara probably figured she'd been railroaded by the government, that if she could just be heard, her life could get back to normal.

"Let's sit," Esther added, gesturing to the small dining room table just outside the kitchen.

"Sure," Tara said. "Okay."

Esther followed her to the table, eyes sweeping the room. Nothing really jumped out at her as significant, except for a couple of pictures hung unevenly on the wall. She recognized Melanie, the girl from the school photo, in a pink and purple set of overalls, hair in pigtails. There was a picture of Donny and Tara—the same one from his Facebook profile—and one that made her stop. She'd know that bucktoothed smile anywhere. The picture was of Claire. In it, she was twelve, maybe thirteen, the year before she finally got braces. An older boy (man?) had his arm around her shoulder. She didn't recognize him, but she would have bet money that it was Donny. He was wearing that same self-satisfied smirk she remembered from that day when it all started. He would have been, what, nineteen in this picture? Esther bit back her disgust, but she must have been frowning too hard. She finally turned to the table where she caught Tara looking at her with a curious expression.

"Something wrong?" she asked.

"I…" Should she mention Claire? Would that give her away? "Just appreciating your pictures. I can…tell there's love here."

Tara nodded. "So much love."

Shaken, Esther joined Tara at the table, keeping her back to the wall and giving herself a clear view of the front door. Tara looked at her expectantly. Esther cursed

herself for not having a notebook or anything in her bag. She thought about recording the conversation on her phone, but figured it was more likely to make Tara clam
up than anything else.

She smiled warmly. "So. Let's pretend I haven't read your family's file. What is
it you want me to know?" Before Tara could begin, Esther added, "Let's start with
the accident."

Tara sat back in the chair, legs crossed, and began picking at a cuticle. "He's
not a bad guy, you know. He's done some stupid stuff, but who hasn't, right? The
important thing is that his heart's in the right place. He wouldn't hurt a fly. Not on
purpose."

Esther's skin tingled.

Tara continued. "Our girl, Melanie, she gets these night terrors. Big, scary bad-
dies that come at her in the middle of the night, and she wakes up screaming loud
enough to wake the dead. Made me jump out of my skin the first time I heard it.
Been happening since she was a little thing. She says the worst ones are when she
wakes up and feels hands around her throat and she can't breathe. She says it's like
the night is choking her." Tara shivered. "This time, though, it was like she couldn't
wake up. Donny had gone in after her—he's better at this stuff than me—and then I
heard a thump and when I went in, she was on the ground, blood on her forehead."

Esther leaned ever so slightly over the table, the image flashing in graphic detail
in her mind. "What happened?"

"She got away from him. He was holding her, trying to keep her from hurting
herself, but when she's in these night terrors, she's strong. Plowed right into the
corner of the wall where it juts out next to her closet. Cracked her skull."

"But you didn't see it?" Esther asked. "You weren't there. Right?"

Tara frowned. "Donny told me what happened. I believe him."

"Sure. Why wouldn't you?"

"Exactly."

Esther tucked her hands under the table, visibly shaking. She didn't know how to keep the conversation going, or if she even wanted to. She imagined Donny holding on to his child as she writhed, terrified. Him getting frustrated or angry. Or maybe *he* was the nightmare. Maybe it was Donny that crept into his daughter's room every night and put his hands around her neck and *squeezed*...

"Doctors didn't see it that way, though," Tara continued. "They pegged him right away. There was an *investigation*." Her eyes flicked suspiciously over Esther. "But you know all that."

Esther made another noncommittal noise. Everything seemed to point to Donny being involved in Claire's death. But if what Officer Kingsolver had said was true about Claire trying to help him, then why would he do it? And then there was that picture. Were they friends? Lovers? (Please, no.) Did their relationship have anything to do with it?

"And Cl—Ms. Finch got involved?" Esther asked, looking quickly at the clock on the wall. Ryan would be home soon.

"Not right away. Some other old bitch with an ax to grind. Hated Donny from the start. Claire came later."

"How come?"

"Luck, probably. I don't think they knew about their history."

"What history is that?"

"Don't think I should tell you."

"Why not?"

"'Cause it might look bad."

"She's dead," Esther said, struggling to keep the wobble out of her voice.

"Not for her. For Donny."

There was a struggle playing out on Tara's face. She wanted to protect Donny, would probably say anything to get him back into her house with their kids, but Esther noticed each time Tara mentioned Claire, an edge crept into her voice.

"Were they...a couple?" Esther asked.

"No," Tara said, too loud. "They were just...close."

"You didn't like that."

"It didn't matter. It was before me."

Esther studied Tara's twisted mouth and tense shoulders. It seemed to matter a lot.

Tara crossed her arms, tossing a look up at the clock. "You got any more questions? Like I said before, I have a shift. I need to get ready."

This was getting away from Esther too quickly. "So they were friends?"

"Kind of."

"What does that mean?"

Tara threw her hands up, exasperated. "It means I don't know!" She sighed. "It seemed like they were in their own little world sometimes. I didn't pry because I figured it meant all this"—she waved dismissively at Esther—"would go away and we could get on with our lives. But then they took my children and wouldn't let me have them back until Donny moved out." Her voice caught. "I wondered if it was all an act, like she was pretending to get close to him so she could break apart our family."

"Claire wouldn't do that," Esther said.

"How would you know?"

"We...worked together for a long time. I know her."

"Not like Donny knew her. She *did* something to him," Tara said, as though the thought had just occurred to her. Then, "He came home late one night—before they made him move—and when he crawled into bed beside me, he was like ice even though it was barely sixty degrees outside. Shivering. I thought he was sick or something, but when I tried to get him some pills and water, he dragged me down and held me so tight I could barely breathe. His heart was hammering against my back. I thought he was going to die. He said the darkness had got inside him again. He said *she* wanted more."

A chill ran down Esther's back. "She, who?"

Tara shrugged.

"Claire?"

Tara shrugged again. "He'd never said nothing like that until Claire came around. I'm not saying Donny's perfect, but something happened to him. He's a good man. I just want him to come home."

So much for Tara's ambivalence toward Claire. Maybe she figured now that Claire was dead, she could pin Donny's behavior on her. It wasn't like she could defend herself.

Esther's mouth was cotton. This hadn't gone at all like she'd imagined. And seeing that picture of Donny and Claire—she was a kid—conjured all kinds of horrifying images of the two of them together. She croaked, "I appreciate your time." She started to stand. "If I have more questions—"

"You can call," Tara said firmly. "The department has my number."

"Of course." Esther managed a weak smile before she made her way to the door.

She cast one last look at the photo of Claire and Donny on the wall. *The darkness had got inside him.* Claire used to say stuff like that, back when they were kids, and their imaginations were greater than their sense. Except Claire had never stopped saying it, had she? Esther had just stopped listening.

Even as Esther started to wonder if she'd gone down the wrong path, the image of Donny's daughter's head hitting the corner of the wall brought her roaring back. He was violent, volatile, and the darkness had him. He'd said so himself. Maybe Tara knew and she was lying to herself, like she'd lied to herself about her daughter's "accident."

She turned to Tara, who was following at her heels, urging her toward the door. "I really appreciate you talking with me today. I know what you've been through is hard."

Tara raised an eyebrow, like she didn't believe Esther could possibly know.

"My son…" Esther was surprised by the sudden welling of tears. It'd been two days since she'd seen her son. She missed him terribly. "I made a mistake, and it cost me. But I'm working hard to fix it, as I know you are."

Tara seemed to soften a little. Her crossed arms loosened.

"I get it," Esther continued. Then, as she was walking out, "Talk soon."

"Sure," Tara said. "Yeah."

Esther just managed to keep it together as she walked to her car, started the engine, and drove down the block. Once she was out of sight of the house, she pulled over, tears threatening to bubble over. She took out her phone and texted Brandon: How are things? I miss you.

The little dots that showed her son was typing flashed for what felt like ages, but then they disappeared. No response.

She started to blame Ryan's parents. They'd always been kind and accepting of her, but would they poison her son against her?

No, she decided. She deserved the silence. She'd fucked up.

But when she solved this, when Donny was finally arrested and they all saw what she had, they would forgive her—Ryan, Brandon, *and* Claire.

CHAPTER NINETEEN

CLAIRE

JULY 2001

It was like their house was haunted and Claire had never realized until now. The cool air that drifted up from the basement through the old vents was ghost breath, and the places on the walls where the paint was discolored, pictures removed but the nails still embedded in the plaster, were the shadows of the ghosts' reach.

Mom shuffled through rooms almost blending into the walls, flicking off lights as she went, until they were all bathed in darkness. She sniped at Esther and Claire if either of them dared to turn on a lamp. "You pay the electric bill?" she asked, not bothering to wait for a response.

Esther shrugged it off. *Lean times.* "Spaghetti month and sixty-second showers are coming next," she said. "You'll see."

But Claire knew the truth. She'd unearthed Julie's ghost and now it was all Mom could see. All she *wanted* to see.

Sometimes Claire followed Mom through the house, invisible, holding her breath. But Mom only ever walked. Sometimes she paused and stared, eyes focused somewhere in the middle of the room on something—some*one*—Claire couldn't see. At night, she fell asleep to the swish-swish sound of Mom's slippers, drag-ging across the wood floor as she paced. Sometimes, Mom's agonized cries drifted through the vents, all the way up into Claire's bedroom, a constant refrain.

Toward the end of July, overtime hours opened up at the plant. Dad worked every hour his body would allow, even as Mom's midnight wanderings got worse. Even Esther, who could sleep through the end of the world, eventually made her way back into their bedroom, claiming it was too hot in Meg's. But Esther laid awake, just as Claire did, the *swish, swish, swish*, like nails scratching down their necks.

One night, Claire was jolted awake by the sound of a crash. At first, she thought it was a holdover from her dream. In it, she'd been deep underground, the darkness taking bites out of her arms and legs, little by little. She couldn't see it but could feel the weight of her flesh leaving her body. But then Esther sat up, eyes wide and glassy in the near dark of their bedroom.

"What the heck was that?" Esther whispered.

"Don't know."

For a long time, they sat there in the quiet, listening to each other breathe, to the gentle ticking of the clock on the wall. Then came another crash—this one sounded distinctly like broken glass—and Mom's screams.

Esther bolted out of her bed and into Claire's. Her body trembled even as she told Claire not to worry.

They held each other, Claire soothed by the sound of her dad's calm, author-itative voice, even if she couldn't tell what he was saying. Eventually, they heard footsteps on the stairs, followed by hitching, racking sobs. Mom was crying.

"That stupid picture," Esther muttered, then crawled out of Claire's bed and into her own without another word.

Just as Claire was falling asleep, her gaze drifted over to the window, cracked open to let in a breeze. She couldn't tell if it was a dream or if she was still awake when she saw the face in the glass, mouth cut into a wicked grin.

The next day, Dad told them they were going to spend a long weekend with Auntie.

"Bert needs some help around the house," he said. "I told him you both were willing and able."

"Great," Esther said, annoyed.

Claire, however, was excited. She loved Auntie, but more than that, Auntie wasn't as tight-lipped as her parents and Esther. If someone was going to tell her anything about Julie, it would be Auntie.

Auntie lived in a bigger small town about half an hour away from Blacklick. *Too big to be narrow-minded, too small to be pretentious* was the way he described it. Claire wasn't entirely sure what that meant, but she liked that it was a place where Auntie seemed to be happy, and that it had two different ice cream places instead of just one, which meant they could try something different each time they visited.

The ride into town was quiet, however, and no one was in the mood for ice cream. There was a fresh scratch on Dad's cheek neither Claire nor Esther had been brave enough to ask about, and when they left that morning, Mom had stayed locked in her bedroom.

Auntie's house was small, the two houses on either side of it towering over his like the monoliths from *The Neverending Story*. Claire didn't like walking between them, always feeling eyes staring down at her from the upper windows. The garden was more of a wildflower meadow, colorful flowers mixing with weeds and ferns, creeping farther and farther into the lawn every year, the bright reds and purples stark against the blue siding of the house. On the door, which was a cheery, canary yellow, was a twine and birch wreath, decorated with bright orange buds. The sign hanging from the bottom read: *Hello, Summer!*

Surely, Claire thought, the darkness couldn't follow her here.

Dad parked in the driveway but didn't shut off the engine. He never went inside if he could help it. "When we get home," he said, "I want you to clean your stuff out of Meg's room." He looked at Esther, whose mouth was open, a complaint on the tip of her tongue. "Nuh-uh. Don't want to hear it. All of it out. Meg's moving back and she'll want her room the way she had it."

"Meg's coming home?" Claire asked.

"It's her home too," Dad said, on the verge of yelling. "She's got every right to live there for as long as she wants. Now go on. I got to get to work."

Claire's face burned as she silently climbed out of the car, backpack hanging from her shoulder.

"What's up his butt?" Esther whispered as they approached the door.

Auntie met them at the door with hugs and smiles, a bright blue scarf wrapped around his neck despite the warmth. Claire remembered he called it a talisman, a tool against evil and bad energy. Maybe what Claire needed was a talisman. She put it on her mental list of things to ask him about.

Inside, the house smelled like sugar cookies. A large, candy-white candle burned in the center of the dining room table atop a checkered tablecloth. The couch was laden with piles of pillows and blankets for sleeping and fort-making, and a stack of Disney VHSs sat on the mantel beside the television.

Auntie took their backpacks and put them in the second bedroom where no one slept, because it had no bed, just bins and bins of colored yarn and beads. Back in the living room, he clapped his hands once. "Okay, we've got movies and popcorn and frozen pizza, cookie mix, some embroidery kits, scrapbook supplies... you name it, we're doing it."

Esther grinned innocently. "Arson?"

Auntie pretended to consider it. "Maybe after the embroidery."

They made pizza, which Claire picked at, and then settled down on the couch to watch *The Little Mermaid*. Usually, this movie would be enough to lift her out of a funk—*The Little Mermaid* was Claire's favorite—but all she could think about was her dad yelling at her as they got out of the car, and Mom locked away in her bedroom like some banished princess.

It was all her fault. By digging through those boxes and unearthing that picture, she'd released the ghosts. She'd let the darkness in, let it spread through them all. She'd *seen* it, even in Esther, though her sister didn't seem to notice. Claire had seen it moving beneath Esther's skin, slithering around her throat and down her arms, making her hands twitch and her fingers tap.

And now Meg was coming home and there was nothing Claire could do to save her from it.

After the movie, Esther went into the kitchen licking her lips at the thought of chocolate chip cookies. Claire expected Auntie to follow; as much as he catered to their needs for sugar and snacks, he wasn't keen on messes. Esther wouldn't wait for directions before covering the kitchen in cookie mix. But Auntie stayed on the couch, looking at but not really watching the end credits.

"Penny for your thoughts?" he asked. "Or a dollar, I suppose. Inflation and all that."

Claire shrugged.

"Whatever it is, you don't have to tell me, but I couldn't help noticing you didn't sing along." He bopped on the couch, doing a poor impression of Sebastian as he sang "Under the Sea." He smiled, but it quickly fell. "Are you okay?"

What would he say if she told him about the house? About the dark things that clung to her, that ate her from the inside out? She wondered if he would brush it off, tell her all about her wild imagination, and then make sure her parents knew they were playing in abandoned buildings. She could already hear the tirades. Esther and Meg would get in trouble. No, Claire couldn't do that.

But she had *questions*, and Auntie almost always had answers.

"I'm okay," Claire said. She struggled to keep eye contact, afraid she'd chicken out. She pinched the skin under her knee. The dark things liked the pain. It distracted them. "But I found something, and now I want to know."

"Know what, dear?"

She took a deep breath. "About Julie."

Apart from a slight twitch in his eyebrow, Auntie's expression remained neutral. He seemed to be deciding something, probably whether or not to lie. He glanced over his shoulder toward the kitchen. "Think you can keep from burning my kitchen down, Esther?"

Esther gave him a thumbs-up, a slick of chocolate on the tip.

"I may regret this," he muttered. Then he met Claire's gaze. "Come on. Let's go see the ladies."

The ladies were the starlings that took up residence in the oak tree in his backyard. Auntie thought of them as his companions, and installed a large, intricately carved birdbath with a fountain in the center. He hung feeders from every branch and kept them fully stocked in organic, fiber-rich birdseed.

"They're getting fat," Auntie said, pointing out a particularly plump starling as she sat contentedly on a thin branch.

"Healthy," Claire said.

Auntie nodded. "Very, very healthy." Then, "I'm not exactly sure where to start."

"The beginning?"

"Good idea."

He sat on the stone bench beside the birdbath, and Claire joined him. She wished he would say something, anything, before Esther came looking for them and he changed his mind, but he seemed lost in the ladies as they dove from the oak to the bath, flicking water as they ascended.

Finally, he spoke. "You ever heard that saying, *Time heals all wounds*?"

Claire nodded.

"Well, it might be true for some, but for most of us, time doesn't heal anything. Just buries it. Makes the edges dull. Even a dull knife can cut if you push hard enough." He played with the fringe of his scarf, wrapping it around his fingers. "I'm guessing your mother is in one of her dark spots? Locked in the room? Moody?"

The darkness got her. *Claire's* darkness. "Yeah."

"I think if they'd found the person who did it, she would have had an easier time of it. You put a box in the ground and expect to call it closure. Really, it's just a Band-Aid." He rubbed his face. "Sorry. The beginning." He sighed. "I guess there isn't a whole lot to the story when you have to put words to it. Julie was born very shortly after you. Less than a year. People took to calling you Irish twins."

"What does that mean?" Claire asked.

"Another conversation for another day."

"Okay."

Auntie continued, "It was hard. Your parents were making it work with the three of you, even if they had to stretch a nickel to make a dime more often than not. Then Julie was born, and even though they were one foot in the poor house, a fourth daughter was a blessing." He smirked. "I thought Brian was going to drop dead of a heart attack when he found out, but then she came and the look on his face… He loves you girls. So much." His smile faded. "Sometimes I really think you saved them. Meg and Esther were old enough they could have got by without attention. Wouldn't have been good for them, Lord knows, but they would have survived just fine. But you were still a baby. You needed them, so they put all their focus onto you."

Claire felt the worms wriggling in her belly. "What happened to her?"

"She just…disappeared one night. Your dad was at work and your mom had to run to a friend's. Her son had a wicked fever, and the pharmacy wasn't open that late. She was gone twenty minutes. You all were asleep when someone walked in, took her, and walked right out with no one the wiser."

"And no one knows who did it?"

He shook his head. "The police were all over Meg, though. All but accused her of lying about sleeping through a break-in. Didn't help that the door was unlocked."

"Mom never leaves the door unlocked," Claire said.

Auntie nodded. "I know."

"Maybe she made a mistake that time."

"Maybe. Probably." He patted her knee. "I don't think Meg did anything wrong. Or Esther for that matter. It's just one of those tragic things. Could've happened to anyone."

"Esther said Julie died."

"She did. They found her just abandoned somewhere, poor thing."

Claire frowned. "So then how did she die?"

An argument seemed to play out on his face. Finally, he settled on, "I don't know." Then, "No one really knows. I mean, they know how, just not the why or the who." He shook his head. "Sorry, pet, but it's not a conversation for little girls. You don't want to know."

Yes, I do.

The back door slammed open, making both of them jump. Esther waved. "Uh—I think the oven is smoking? A little?"

"She'll kill us all," Auntie muttered, not without a little admiration.

Their conversation clearly over, they both started for the kitchen, Claire walking a little slower to take in what she could of the outside, the bright sun and the clear breeze. In her belly, the worms burrowed and writhed, almost like they were afraid. Maybe because now, Claire knew how to get rid of the darkness for good.

All she had to do was find who killed Julie.

CHAPTER TWENTY

MEG

By the time Meg got to her apartment, it was near dark and her stomach gurgled, protests against the burger and constant movement. She'd be lucky if she didn't puke. Her legs were jelly and her feet thrummed, achy and sweaty. She needed to work out more. Or lay off the junk food. Or stop pissing her sister off.

Meg should have kept her mouth shut. Nodded along and dealt with the consequences later. It was her tried-and-true strategy, one that had seen her through things far worse than an argument with Esther. She tried calling Esther multiple times—there was the matter of her car sitting in Chicago to be dealt with—but Esther never picked up. She also didn't dismiss it, sending the call straight to voicemail, which Meg took as a good sign. Maybe Esther wasn't answering because she hadn't seen the calls.

Right.

Ryan had texted twice, but Meg was too scared to read them. Either Esther had done something bad, in which case Meg would get the full blame, or it wasn't important, and Meg ignoring it wouldn't make a difference.

As she fought with her keys at the main door, she heard what sounded like a crying cat. She looked around, behind the bushes that had long shed their foliage and behind the huge crack in the concrete steps. Nothing. She figured it must have been coming from one of her neighbors' windows, a fat house cat mewing at the scent of grease and salt. Except it came back louder, more insistent, and from the direction of the line of garages at the edge of the lot.

Nights had been getting colder; the days cloudier. Meg wasn't an animal person per se, but the thought of coming across a cat carcass—and she would be the one to find it, on an already shitty day, because that was how the universe worked—was enough to pull her toward the garages. She held out a cold french fry, waving it around like a soggy magic wand.

"Here, kitty, kitty," Meg cooed.

She made kissy noises as she crept around the side of the first garage, not wanting to startle it. She wasn't planning to bring it inside. She didn't have any food or a litter box or a car or money to get them, but she could at least give it her leftovers.

The mewing sounded farther away now. She followed the sound, dropping pieces of french fry as she went, like Hansel and Gretel's breadcrumbs. If she didn't find the cat in the next few minutes, she'd leave the food and hope the cat found it. But as she reached the midpoint of the line of garages, the mewing became something else. It stretched and sharpened. Long mews became hitched cries. Her body knew it before her mind. She froze, skin prickling, and held her breath.

Not a cat. A baby.

Abandoning the bag, she followed the sound, jiggling the door of each garage she passed, all of which were locked. The sound seemed to move with her, getting farther with each garage she passed. She thought about calling the police, but there was still part of her that clung to the idea that it was a cat. She'd had a long day. Her mind was frazzled and her stomach was sick. She just needed to find it, put her fears at ease, then get directly into bed. As she reached the end of the row, the crying turned to whimpers. Somehow that was worse. It sounded like despair.

Meg found the last garage open a crack at the bottom. On her hands and knees, she stuck her ear against the opening. The whimpering was clearer here. It was a baby, and they were trapped in someone's fucking garage.

She tried to lift the door, but the mechanism was stuck. That was the way with most of these garages: doors dented and wheel tracks bent from idiots driving into them and a property manager too cheap to care. The harder she pulled up on the door, the louder the baby's cries grew. The sound was like an electric wire wrapped around her neck and arms. She trembled, panicked, as she threw all her weight into pulling the door up, only for it to remain stuck fast.

She should call the police. They had those battering ram things, right? At the very least they'd force the property manager to open it with the spare key.

But the moment she took her hands off the door, the whimpers turned to cries of pain. She had to get inside there, now.

She squatted, stomach rumbling and sick, and gripped the door just under the gap. She took three deep breaths and then pulled, a growl rumbling deep in her chest. Her back and knees burned but the wheels jumped, no more than an inch, but it was enough that she could get a better grip. Finally, the door gave and she shoved it the rest of the way open.

The stench of rot rolled over her, making her eyes water. Wood slats on either side looked one good storm away from crumbling, and in the corner was a pile of black garbage bags. Meg said a quick prayer that the baby wasn't in one of them.

But then she spotted it, a bundle of blue and yellow blankets tucked against the wall beneath a Grateful Dead poster. A tiny hand protruded from the blankets, fist red and trembling. Meg took a step forward, then froze when she saw the pajamas.

Fuzzy red and white, candy-cane striped with little strawberries around the wrist.

Meg knew if she looked closer, she'd see a patch of blond hair and a birthmark in the shape of a star at her temple.

Julie.

But it was impossible. If Julie was alive (which she *wasn't*), she would be almost thirty by now. Claire's age, almost.

For a moment, Meg let herself imagine it. All those family holidays with another seat at the table. Another voice during their Midnight Society rides. Would Julie have been strong and outspoken like Esther? Caring and bright like Claire? Would she have grown up to get married, stay in town, maybe have her own kids? Would she have done something brave like move to another country where she would collect trinkets she'd send to Meg to make her laugh?

A hundred thousand possible lives. All of them gone in a blink.

Tears blurred Meg's vision as she slowly walked toward the bundle. She bent down and scooped up the baby, her own sobs caught in her chest. But the baby felt wrong. Too light. She rubbed her arm across her eyes to clear them, and when she looked down at the bundle in her arms, the blankets were tattered and faded. The baby wasn't a baby at all—it was a doll, one eye missing, hair crudely chopped. The arms had come dislocated from the sockets and dangled in their cloth coverings.

Movement in the shadowy corner startled her, making her drop the doll. It landed on the concrete with a sickening crack.

Tears still streaming down her face, Meg ran from the lot. The baby's soft, hiccuping cries followed her, barely audible above Meg's pounding heart.

———————————

Even with all the lights on in her apartment, it was too dark. Meg hated this time of year, when the days got shorter, and the night moved in before it was welcome. It took hours for the sound of the baby's cries to stop echoing around in her head, which made the sloshing in her stomach worse. She spent a long time just sitting in the bathroom on the cool floor, head resting against the wall. She remembered being little and having a bug, how her mom would coo over her.

"You'll feel better once you get it all out," Mom told her.

She wished the same was true now, that she could just purge the anxiety, the guilt, and flush it away. Instead, it sat there, a rock in her belly.

Without her car, she was trapped in the apartment and needed a distraction. Her television was useless—the couple next door had finally put a password on their internet so she couldn't access Netflix. She had a couple of DVDs but had sold her DVD player last month for twenty bucks to a college kid who didn't know any better. She turned to Claire's datebook.

She practically had the thing memorized by now, but still she paged through the thing, glossing over any mention of Donny. She lingered on the individual curve of every *e*, on the way Claire always crossed her *t*'s without picking up the pen. She wanted to find meaning in the mundane, and found herself picking apart the two-item grocery lists and appointment times like they were riddles.

If this were a movie, Claire would have left some kind of code, something to point Meg in the direction of a stalker, some enemy who wished her dead. But this wasn't a movie, and Meg was having trouble holding on to the murder theory. Maybe it was the way Esther had run with it, like a dog with a bone, or the fact that Claire was *Claire*—kind and quiet and incapable of making enemies.

Kind and quiet people get murdered every day.

Even when Esther wasn't here, she was still arguing with Meg.

Claire was depressed. That was a fact no one could argue, but every time Meg started to accept that Claire would take her own life, it was like Meg's mind glitched. Maybe if she was on the outside looking in, she could accept what made sense on a logical level: Claire had been suffering from severe depression for a long time. She was taking medication, but not always. It simply became too much.

But why at the house?

Where did Donny come in, if at all?

There was a piece missing somewhere. Meg wasn't going to find it in Claire's work life.

Her dad picked up on the second ring. "Everything okay?"

Meg's face reddened. Seemed the only times she spoke to her parents were during disasters. "Yeah, no, everything's fine. I just—are you still at work?"

"Just got home."

Which meant he was anxious to eat dinner, to get in the shower and try to relax before he had to get up in the morning and face the day all over again.

"Think you could pick me up? My car's at Esther's—starter issue—and I've got some of Claire's stuff. Figured Mom would want to have a look."

"Uh, sure. Yeah." He sighed. "Let me just get my shoes back on."

She could have walked. Even though her feet were barking after her earlier hike from McDonald's, her parents' place was only a mile or so away. But Dad was observant. If he'd noticed something off with Claire, or if she'd said something or given some clue that made her suicide make sense, the only way she could get him to tell her was if Mom wasn't around.

The second she got in the passenger seat, it was like she was transported back to the day he picked her up from college, a failure.

He wasn't an easy man to read, but that day, the trunk and back seat fit to bursting with her stuff, the disappointment had radiated off him like heat.

When he had finally spoken that day, it was like needles in her skin. "This was your shot, Megan. You were gonna *do* things. You were gonna *prove*—" He'd bit off the last of his sentence, but Meg knew what he was going to say. She was going to prove to her mother that she wasn't a failure. That she was *responsible*. That she could be trusted.

She didn't tell him that it wasn't the work, or even her grades that were the problem, though they had slipped enough that the school served her with an academic dismissal before the end of the year. It was that every time someone looked at her for too long, she felt them probing through to the heart of her. They saw her for what she really was—a liar. After a while, she'd stopped going to classes altogether, unable to face anyone. She slept, and when she couldn't sleep, she listened to her roommate anxiously turn the pages of the books Meg was supposed to be reading, her grainy indie-rock mixtape on an endless loop.

Now, with those memories circling the drain of her mind, she couldn't bring herself to ask about Claire, or to say anything at all.

At her parents' house, Dad kicked off his shoes and headed straight for the kitchen. Meg followed, and when she caught Mom's eye, she offered an apologetic smile and a wave.

It took Mom a moment to return the smile. "Hungry?"

Meg shook her head. "I ate."

"Good." Mom's gaze fell to the table. "Dad said you had something to show me?"

"Let's eat first," Dad said, already digging into a pile of mashed potatoes.

Mom sat, not bothering to hide her disappointment. She glanced up briefly as Meg set the datebook and a few other small things on the counter.

"Just gonna run to the restroom," Meg said.

Neither of her parents acknowledged her.

She told herself she didn't need to sneak around behind her parents' back to look through Claire's things, but part of her was still ashamed, so she opened and closed the bathroom door before creeping across the hall to Claire's room. The boxes from the funeral were gone, leaving the doorway clear. She hesitated, listening for movement downstairs. Satisfied, she eased the door open and slipped inside, shutting it behind her.

It didn't look much different from when she was here for the funeral. The mirror she'd broken had been removed, and the bed was made. Meg was overcome with the urge to climb into it, to slip beneath the covers and inhale Claire's scent, but she didn't have time to linger. She went straight for the desk and began rooting through the drawers.

Pens and loose paper. A polished chunk of clear quartz. A deck of cards and baggie of shells, still grainy with sand. With every object Meg pulled out of the drawers she grew more and more anxious. The answer was here. It had to be, because if it wasn't, then there *was* no answer. And Meg could not handle that. The last item she pulled from the top drawer was the collection of Sylvia Plath poems she'd found during the funeral. She almost cast it aside too, but then something caught her attention—a page sticking out a fraction of an inch too far. She flipped to the page to find a printed article stuffed inside. She zeroed in on the headline—*Historical Society Petition Halts Development*—just as the bedroom door swung open.

"What are you doing in here?" Mom asked.

Meg stuffed the book back in the desk, deftly slipping the article into her pocket. "Nothing, I—I just wanted to see."

But Mom wasn't listening. She quickly went to the desk where she replaced everything back in the drawers with shaky hands. "You shouldn't be in here."

"I'm sorry." Meg felt the accusation keenly. *You* shouldn't be in here. *You*, the one who should have saved your sister.

Meg started toward the door, only for Mom to grab her by the wrist, nails digging into skin. She forced Meg to look at her, the bags under her eyes, bloodshot and unblinking, the fleck of potato stuck in a crease at the corner of her mouth.

"He's not here now," Mom said, voice trembling and anxious. "You can tell me what happened to Claire."

"I don't—"

Mom squeezed. A drop of blood oozed from the place her nail cut Meg's skin. "No. Just tell me. I deserve to know. I deserve…" Her voice broke. "Please."

Meg put her hand over her mom's and gently pried away her grip. "I don't know." This time, she wasn't lying.

The night Julie disappeared, Meg was nearly twelve years old and pretty responsible for her age. She kept her room (mostly) clean and she did her homework
and chores without being asked (except when *Sailor Moon* was on). As the eldest,
it was her job to set an example for the littles by following the rules. All this her
mom explained as she hauled on her coat and slipped her feet (sans socks) into
snow boots.

"What are they?" Mom asked.

Meg rolled her eyes. "I know the rules."

"Great. Out loud, please."

Meg wore two sweaters over her pajamas because her bedroom was the coldest
in the house. Down here in the living room, she was sweating. Though she was
pleased that she would get to stay up—it was already well past her normal nine
o'clock bedtime—she was a little scared. She'd babysat her sisters before, but Dad
was always home, just napping between shifts.

"Megan," Mom snapped. "The rules. Now."

"No oven, no stove, no microwave," Meg began. "It's okay to pick up the phone,
but if someone asks for you or Dad, I tell them you're in the shower and you'll call
them back."

"Unless it's Grandma, then you can tell her where I am," Mom said. "Go on."

"Don't open the door for anyone."

"Anyone," Mom emphasized. "I don't care if the police are banging down the
door. You don't open that door. Got it?"

"Yes, ma'am."

Boots on and coat buttoned, Mom reached for the doorknob. "I'm trusting
you, Meg. This is a big deal."

Meg's stomach clenched. "Okay."

"I'll be gone an hour at the most."

"Okay."

Mom hesitated. Cast a look back at the kitchen, at the phone.

Scared or not, Meg realized this was an opportunity to prove herself. If she could get through the next hour with no mess-ups, Mom might let her start babysitting for real, and not just her sisters. She could start earning her own money, maybe enough to get her own pair of pearly-white K-Swiss sneakers everyone wore at school.

"If Julie wakes up—" Mom started.

"Formula's in the cabinet. One scoop, fill the water up to the eight line. Shake it up. Burp her after." Meg grinned.

Mom returned the smile. "Looks like you've got everything handled."

"It'll be fine," Meg said. "I promise."

She stood at the window until Mom's headlights disappeared down the street. They'd gotten almost a foot of snow over the last couple of hours, and she could already hear the plows groaning along, shoving the muddy slush. Maybe tomorrow she and Esther would take their plastic sleds out. Meg's had a crack along the side, but a few strips of duct tape would do the trick.

She thought about watching TV, but couldn't remember if that was part of the rules too. Mom had a thing about late-night TV. Said it was inappropriate. Even if Mom wouldn't find out, all Meg had to do was picture those K-Swiss sneakers, the logo clean and glittery. Instead, she went into the kitchen where she pulled down the formula and a clean bottle, just in case.

Five minutes down. Only fifty-five to go.

The temptation of the television was almost too much. Meg had the remote in her hand and was just teetering into convincing herself she could get away with ten minutes of TV without doing damage, when a knock on the door made her jump. She dropped the remote, which landed with a hard crack on the glass coffee table.

"Shit," she muttered as she studied the table for damage, face reddening at the curse. A small indiscretion she allowed herself to prove she wasn't the goody-goody Esther accused her of being.

The knock came again, louder this time. Meg stared at the door, frozen.

Mom wouldn't have knocked. She had her key. She never forgot her key. And even if she had, she would have announced herself so Meg knew it was okay to open the door. Meg glanced at the clock—ten-thirty. There was no reason for anyone to be knocking on their door this late at night.

Unless it was the police.

What if there'd been an accident? The roads were icy, and Mom was in a hurry. She could have taken a corner too hard and slid into a snowbank or a sign or a building or—

Bang, bang, bang.

Whoever it was, they weren't going away. If they knocked any louder, Julie would definitely wake up, and though Meg had had a hand in bottle-feeding and burping Claire, Mom had always been around to direct her. The confidence she'd exuded before Mom left seemed to drain out of her.

She crept slowly toward the door, and then, up on tiptoes, peered through the peephole and frowned.

Krystal, a girl from school, stomped her feet against the cold, arms crossed tight across her chest. She was in Meg's homeroom, and they'd talked a couple of times, but they weren't really friends. So why was she standing outside Meg's house this late at night?

Maybe she was in trouble. Maybe something bad had happened.

Sure is smiley for being in trouble, Meg thought, but figured it was a force of habit. Esther broke out into giggles when she was in it deep, which only ever made it worse on her.

Meg reached for the doorknob but hesitated. The rules. But would Mom want

Meg to just…leave Krystal out there in the cold? Probably not, if only because she'd hear it from Krystal's mom later. Casting a quick glance toward the stairs— Esther was still in her room—she opened the door.

Krystal's bright pink coat looked medicinal under the porch light. Her hair hung down over her shoulders, which she tucked behind her ear as she flashed Meg a toothy smile. "Hey."

"Hey."

"Nice PJs."

Meg looked down. They were her pajamas from last Christmas, covered in snowmen and candy canes. She hadn't realized how small they'd gotten, hugging her crotch too tight and stopping about three inches above her ankle. Her face burned. "Thanks." Then, "My mom's not home." *Why did I say that?* "I mean—I can't really let you in or play or anything." *Play? God, shut up, Meg.*

Krystal shrugged. "That's fine. I just need you to open up the back gate."

That was definitely against the rules. If Mom found out, she'd be buried out back in full view of the gate she wasn't supposed to touch.

"Why?" Meg asked.

"Alex was messing around and threw something over the fence." She thumbed over her shoulder and Meg saw three other kids, none of whom she recognized, doing a bad job of hiding that they were laughing at her.

"What is it? I'll go get it."

Krystal shook her head as she took a step toward the open door. "I know where it went. I can be in and out superfast."

Every second Meg stood there talking to Krystal was a second closer to when her mom would come home and catch her. A second closer to being in real trouble. To hearing her mom say, "I'm not mad; I'm just disappointed." Just thinking about it gave her a stomachache. But there was a reason Krystal wasn't telling her what it was, which meant it was the kind of thing that, if Mom or Dad found it before Meg did, she would be stuck answering questions that would also get her in trouble.

"Fine," Meg said. "But you've got, like, five seconds."

"Awesome. You're the best."

Meg hoped it was too dark for Krystal to see her blush. "K. I'll meet you back there. Just cut through the hedge."

Meg cast a quick look up toward the bedrooms, crossing her fingers that her sisters were still asleep, and would stay that way until she got back.

She slipped on her jacket and stuck her sockless feet into her boots. They were still damp—she'd discovered a hole toward the bottom when she was walking back from the bus stop but hadn't told her mom about it. Yet. She'd wait until Friday. Dad's payday.

In the backyard, she could already hear Krystal and her friends outside the gate. She silently willed them to be quiet. Mom wasn't friends with any of their neighbors, but that didn't mean she wouldn't listen if they told her about a bunch of kids lingering outside their yard. Meg's heart pounded as she fought with the rusty lock. *They'll get whatever it is they're here for, and then they'll leave. It'll be fine.*

But when she finally got the lock off and eased the gate open and Krystal and her friends poured through to the backyard, she knew she'd made a mistake.

"It's so dark back here," Krystal said. "Spooky."

"You scared?" one of the boys asked.

"Shut up, Alex." Krystal wandered deeper into the yard.

"Where is it?" Meg asked. "The thing you need?"

"Around here somewhere," Krystal said.

Alex and the other boy—Meg didn't know his name—followed behind Krystal. Alex shoved the other one into a tree, then took off toward the shed when the other boy tried to retaliate. Krystal giggled, but Meg was hovering dangerously close to full-on panic. She heard a car slow down, and her heart jumped into her throat.

"Just tell me what it is and I'll help you look," Meg said, struggling to keep her voice calm.

"It's—ope!" Krystal pulled a small bottle from her pocket. She flashed Meg the label. Vodka. "Here it is!"

"Hey! Not without us!" Alex and the other boy trotted over, their hair mussed and dirt streaking their faces.

Meg was so screwed.

"Hey, slow down, Krystal," the other boy said. "Donny's gonna get pissed if you hand him an empty bottle back."

Krystal shot him a look that could melt ice.

The other boy withered.

Alex snatched the bottle out of her hand and took a sip, hiding a grimace behind his elbow. Then he caught Meg looking and offered her the bottle. "You want some?"

She started to shake her head, but the look on Krystal's face stopped her, lip curled and eyes penetrating. She expected Meg to say no, was gleefully anticipating it. But in her expression was a dare.

Meg barely knew these kids, but she knew their type. If she said no, it would only give them more reason to linger, to taunt and tease and make Meg's night as miserable as possible because it was fun. The only way to get them out of her yard was to give in.

Silencing the voice that told her Mom would catch her, that she was as good as dead, she snatched the bottle out of Alex's hand and tipped the mouth against her lips. She only let a few drops in, but it was like setting her mouth on fire. She shuddered as she passed the bottle back.

Krystal raised an eyebrow.

"Shitty," Meg said, choking back a cough. She almost added, *My dad's is better*, but didn't want to risk tempting them into the house.

The other boy snorted.

"Since when do you drink?" Krystal asked.

Meg shrugged.

"I knew there was something about you," Alex said, eyes suddenly hungry. "Something mysterious."

Krystal's face burned. "She's not mysterious."

"Nope. Just bored," Meg said, mimicking something she'd heard one of the older girls in the neighborhood say once.

"I hear that," the other boy said.

Sensing her chance, Meg ran her hand through her hair in what she hoped was a nonchalant gesture. "Y'all should go. My mom'll be back soon, and she'll have all our heads if she catches us."

The boys shot each other a look.

Krystal, at first, looked unmoved. Then her expression softened. "I'll walk you in."

Meg hesitated, then nodded. Arguing would only delay their leaving. "Sure."

The boys went back out through the gate—Meg would need to remember to lock it again—while Krystal strode up toward the house, Meg hot on her heels.

At the door, Meg blocked the way, a panicked smile on her face. "Thanks."

Krystal grinned. "No problem." Then she pushed past Meg, through the door and into the kitchen. "Nice place," she said, too loud.

Meg flinched, waiting for the telltale wail of Claire or Julie upstairs. Claire had been sleeping through the night for ages, but Julie was a light sleeper. The wrong sound would send her bawling.

She thought she heard movement upstairs. A frantic sort of shuffle. Had Mom already come home? Had Julie started crying and Meg hadn't heard it? Her whole body went hot as she made a beeline for the stairs, already coming up with excuses. She was in the bathroom and had only just heard the crying. She'd been investigating a weird noise in the backyard (without going outside).

Krystal followed, but Meg barely noticed her, too worried about the trouble she was about to be in.

Upstairs, Claire and Esther's door was shut, and when Meg pressed her ear to it, she didn't hear any sound. Julie slept in their parents' room. When Mom had left, the door had been open a crack, just enough that Meg could hear Julie if she woke up. Now, the door was wide open.

Mom must have come in and heard Julie crying. She would have come barreling up the stairs wondering where the hell Meg had been. Meg slowly made her way to the room, mind going around in circles as she tried to come up with an excuse Mom would believe. But when she finally went inside, Mom wasn't there. Relieved, Meg went to Julie's bassinet. Just to see her. Just to set her mind at east.

But the bassinet was empty. Julie was gone.

Meg stopped breathing.

There had to be a good reason. Mom came back and got her, deciding she didn't trust Meg after all.

Krystal appeared beside her. She took one look at the bassinet and froze.

"This can't be happening," Meg said.

Krystal mumbled something, but Meg couldn't hear it over the ringing in her ears. She'd been outside for five minutes. Ten, tops. This wasn't possible.

She bolted downstairs and threw open the front door, silently begging her mom's car to be there. She didn't care about getting in trouble anymore, as long as it meant Julie was with their mother. As long as it meant that the worst hadn't happened.

But there was no car in the driveway. There was nothing but snow and cold and the dark.

Mom came home shortly after. All Meg could tell her was that Julie was gone. The police were called and when they asked Meg what happened, she told them some bullshit lie about noise outside that she went to investigate. About seeing someone by the window just before Mom came home, but that she didn't get a look at their face and didn't go outside to look because it was against the rules.

The police told her she did the right thing.

But Meg knew better. She was a coward and a liar, and the way Mom looked at her from then on, she thought so too.

———————

Now, back at the apartment, Claire was waiting.

Meg knew she would be. How could she not, with the memory of that night burning bright and angry in her mind?

Meg found her on the living room floor, on her side, ear pressed to the ground. The skin around her nail beds and eyes had begun to peel away, too dry and too wet at the same time. The corner of her mouth had been eaten away, and when she grinned, all Meg saw were black teeth and gray gums.

"Come listen," she said.

Meg crossed the room in silence and laid down next to her sister, facing her, close enough that she could smell the mud on her breath.

She giggled and it sounded like wind through gravestones. "They're fighting. Can you hear it?"

Meg nodded.

"She's a liar, for sure. And he knows it." She tucked her hair behind her ear, revealing a star-shaped birthmark on her temple. "Funny to think how their lives would be so different if she'd told the truth. I'd bet money he looks at her and she's not even the same person anymore."

Meg forced herself to catch Claire's eye—Claire, whose outsides now reflected Meg's insides, all black and grotesque and wrong—and stopped breathing when Claire's gaze locked on hers.

"Do you want to know?" Claire asked.

Meg tried to shake her head, but she was frozen, just like that night.

"Do you want to know what it's like to find yourself alone in the cold, in the dark?"

"Please," Meg whispered.

Claire rolled toward her, hands reaching for her throat. Meg tried to claw free, but Claire's hands were like a vise, squeezing until Meg couldn't breathe and she felt her pulse in her temples, a frantic thump that made the light go dark at the edges of her vision.

And with each beat, a flash of memory.

A bottle of shitty vodka.

The empty bassinet.

Claire's red shoes.

A room in a house that seemed made up of Meg's failures. Her guilt.

The darkness that had clung to them, to Claire and Esther and Meg, had seeped into their skin and was slowly, slowly consuming them from the inside out.

"It won't be long now," Claire whispered. "Soon you'll see what I saw. Soon she'll come for you too."

CHAPTER TWENTY-ONE

ESTHER

NOW

E sther cursed under her breath when she saw Ryan's car in the driveway. She was hoping she'd beat him home, that she'd have enough time to come up with a reason for being gone, for Meg's car to still be parked on the street. But her skin was humming from her interaction with Tara, and her mind was a swarm of bees. Claire's relationship with Donny was another question atop a mountain of speculation and mystery, but it just proved that there was another possibility for motive. Maybe the reason Donny had killed her had nothing to do with his kids and everything to do with this *friendship*, or whatever it was. The key, maybe, was the darkness Tara mentioned, the darkness Claire had tried to talk to Esther about, that Esther had dismissed as stress or typical seasonal depression because Esther couldn't bear to see it for what it was.

She imagined Donny listening to Claire describe it, imagined him leaning into it, stroking it, choking and clinging to it. *Misery loves company.* Maybe he thought himself too much of a coward to listen to his own demons, so he gave a voice to Claire's. Maybe he made the darkness real enough to...

Esther rubbed away frustrated tears as her phone pinged with a new text.

It was Ryan.

We need to talk.

It wasn't a coincidence that the text came now. He was watching her.

Keep it together, Es, she thought.

He couldn't possibly know where she'd been, so she could say anything, and he wouldn't have a reason to contradict her. Unless Meg had talked to him. She wouldn't, though. Meg hated conflict.

Esther couldn't linger knowing Ryan was watching, scrutinizing her actions and expressions, so she shouldered her bag and walked purposefully for the door. She wouldn't even mention the text. If he asked, she'd claim she hadn't seen it yet, that she doesn't read texts while she's in the car, parked or not. Safety and responsibility were her two priorities.

She was barely through the door when he pounced.

"Where have you been?"

She blanked. "Shopping."

Ryan raised an eyebrow. "Where are the bags?"

Esther matched his haughty tone. "You can shop without buying anything."

"Where's Meg?"

"She went home."

"Without her car?"

"I dropped her off." Not totally a lie.

"Why?"

"Why all the questions?" She nudged past him to give the redness in her face a chance to cool. "And why are you home early?"

"Why does it matter?"

"Because I'm not in the door two seconds before you're jumping down my throat." Pain started in the back of her head, radiating forward. "I'm not a child, Ryan, and I'm tired of being treated like one."

His tone sharpened. "Have you talked to your therapist?"

"Why?"

"Because your son wants to come home, Esther. He wants to sleep in his own bed and get on the bus with his friends and not live out of a duffel bag."

"So bring him home!"

"It doesn't work that way."

The pain was getting worse. She rubbed her face, damp with tears. "Just say what it is you really want to say, Ryan."

His lips were set in a tight line, but in his eyes, he looked defeated. "I just want our family back. I want things to be normal."

"And it's my fault that they're not, right? That's what you're saying?"

"Your paranoia has gotten out of control. I didn't say anything because I thought you were getting help. I thought there was a process and if I was patient, you would—"

"Get fixed?"

He didn't say anything. He didn't have to.

"My sister is dead, Ryan. I'm sorry if I can't immediately be okay with that."

"I'm not saying—"

"You don't understand. And you never will because you don't bother to ask. You don't care. You just want your 'crazy wife' to chill out."

Esther almost thought she'd managed to turn the tables, but then something changed in his expression, and she knew it was over.

"Yes," he said. "I want my crazy wife to chill out. Because if she doesn't, she does something stupid, like buy a gun and keep it in our home without telling me, and then almost kill our child because she was too proud or too stupid to realize she needed help."

"I don't need—"

"I didn't want to do this, but I don't think I have a choice." He took her hands, which were cold and clammy. "Here's what you can do. You can either continue down this path and pretty much guarantee you'll alienate both me and Brandon, knowing you can only push someone so much until they're too far to come back."

Esther's stomach dropped. "You're leaving me?"

"Or," Ryan continued, "you can get help. Real help, this time. And with time and trust, we can get back to where we were. We can be better."

"What does that mean? *Real help*?"

He pulled her into the kitchen where his briefcase sat on the counter beside a pile of mail. In the pile was a brochure, brightly colored and glossy, which he handed to her. *Betty Ford Rehabilitation Center* was printed bold and bright across the center, surrounded by images of women laughing and walking and drinking coffee.

Esther didn't understand. Rehab? She wasn't an addict. "What is this?"

"It's a center for mental and physical rehabilitation. People go there for a more personal care experience."

He sounded like an infomercial.

"The doctors there are some of the best in the state," he continued. "They specialize in anxiety disorders. Phobias. There's around-the-clock care and good food and—"

"Wait." She couldn't believe what she was hearing. No. It was worse. She *could* believe it, and she felt the betrayal all the way to her bones. "You want to lock me up?"

"It's voluntary. And you can leave whenever you want. It's all in the brochure, babe."

"I can't believe you would do this to me."

"I'm not doing anything. You put us here, so you have to get us out."

"By committing myself."

"By committing yourself to getting better. Prove to me, and to Brandon, that this paranoia isn't you."

She felt sick. "It's not paranoia. You just don't get it."

"Help me, then!" He snatched the brochure out of her hands. "Lord knows I've been trying to help you, but it's gotten me nowhere. All you give me is—"

"Claire was murdered."

It got his attention, which was part of the point, but once it was out of her mouth, Esther couldn't take it back.

Ryan dropped his arms to his sides. "When did you—did the police say something?"

Esther hesitated barely a second, just long enough to consider lying. She knew the truth, even if the police weren't convinced of it yet. But it didn't matter how firm her beliefs were, she could see the suspicion on Ryan's face. More than a decade of marriage meant she could read his expressions like a book, the same way he could read hers.

"Esther," he said, a warning, "what did the police say?"

She tried to maintain eye contact, but she felt him scrutinizing every eyebrow twitch, every blink and intake of breath. She dropped her gaze to the floor. "I showed them evidence. There was motive. There was—"

Ryan sighed and it was like a punch to the solar plexus. She knew this would happen. She knew he wouldn't take her side. He'd already decided that she was broken. *Maybe*, a small voice whispered, *he's right.*

"See, Es? This is what I'm talking about." He set the brochure on the counter. Smoothed it out. "You need help."

"What I need is for people to believe me." She rubbed her eyes, but the tears were coming hard now and no matter what she did she couldn't see. "I'm not crazy. I know what I saw!"

The last seemed to come out of her mouth without her even speaking. She shook her head and waved in front of her face, like she could dissipate the words before they landed.

"What do you mean?" Ryan asked. "Saw what?"

"Nothing," she snapped. Then, seeing the brochure on the counter, her shoulders sank. She didn't have the words anymore. And it didn't matter because no matter what she said Ryan would use it as a reason to send her to that place and nothing would ever be normal again. She would resent him, and he would be suspicious of her, and Brandon would creep through the house avoiding them both until he was old enough that he could move away and move on and never look back.

It wasn't fair.

Why did no one *ever* believe her?

When Esther thought of the night Julie disappeared, she pictured a row of dominoes that started in her science class.

They were supposed to be taking a test on force and motion, a subject Esther was iffy with. She was iffy with most of the topics in science and had gone into class that morning feeling sick.

During the test, she was halfway through before she noticed the tapping. Every few seconds, someone made three sharp, quick taps—*taptaptap*—and then muffled giggles drifted around the room. It'd taken too long to realize they were making fun of her, of her absent-minded *tap, tap, tap* before she wrote an answer.

Every night, before she went to bed, it was her routine to check the lock on her window, to look under the beds and in her closet, leaving each task with a tap, tap, tap. But that night, she forced herself into bed without her checks, without her taps, hearing her classmates' giggles and taunts every time her finger twitched.

The night Julie was taken, before Mom came home and the screaming had chilled her to her core and everything changed forever, Esther woke up from a dream about hundreds of fingers jabbing at her forehead—tap, tap, tap—and saw someone, all wild hair and spidery limbs, like something conjured from one of her nightmares, outside her window. He skulked behind the tree in the front yard, a poor attempt at hiding, and when he turned toward the window, their eyes met. Esther dove beneath her blanket and imagined him walking up to her window, his face pressed against the glass, his breath fogging it. But when she finally got up the nerve to look, there was no one in the window, or in the yard. He, whoever *he* was, was gone.

Still, she wanted to be sure, so she quietly crawled out of bed and eased open the door, but voices coming from the hallway made her pause. Peering into the dark, she saw Mom's bedroom door open and two shadows in the room. She caught a flash of Meg's pajamas in the sparse light and figured it was her and Mom, but then the whispers got louder, shakier. Meg was afraid.

A tap on the window ripped Esther's attention away from the hallway. Her heart pounded as she inched toward Claire's crib where Claire still slept, dead to the world. She lowered the side and climbed in beside her, eyes fixed on the window where too many shadows conjured shapes that may or may not have been there. She didn't see the figure's face, but she could feel him there, watching her.

It seemed like a century passed, and then the screaming came.

Julie was gone.

The police came and poked through their rooms and minds. Esther couldn't seem to focus, trying to make sense of what she was told—that Mom had gone to get medicine for a friend, that something had happened, but Meg had been in the bathroom and didn't see anything, that they'd been alone all night—and what Esther had seen.

While the police spoke in hushed tones to Mom and Dad, who'd rushed home from work, Esther grabbed Meg's arm and pulled her away.

"What?" Meg snapped.

"I saw you in Mom's room," Esther said. "There was someone else in there and it wasn't Mom. Too short."

A complicated series of expressions passed over Meg's face, from surprise to angst to rage. "I was in the bathroom," she said. "You didn't see anything."

"I did, though. What happened? Where's Julie?"

Meg grabbed her arm just above the wrist and squeezed. "You were probably sleepwalking. You do that a lot, you know."

"I don't—"

"Remember last weekend? You woke up in the kitchen with peanut butter all over your hand."

Esther frowned. Had she? She didn't even like peanut butter.

"And at Auntie's you were dancing with his ficus for like an hour before he could finally convince you to go back to bed."

She didn't remember that, either, but why would Meg make it up? It was true Esther didn't sleep well, and almost always woke up tired... Had the figure in the window actually been a nightmare? Had it bled into reality?

"You can tell me all about it later," Meg said, visibly calmer, "but right now the cops need facts, not your...craziness."

"I'm not crazy," Esther said, but Meg wasn't listening anymore. Still clinging to Esther's arm, she was watching the police and her parents, breathing like she'd been running.

"It'll be okay," Meg said, almost to herself. "They'll find her, and everything will be okay."

But it wasn't. And it was all Esther's fault. If she hadn't broken her routine, if she hadn't worried so much about what those idiot kids in her stupid class had thought, Julie wouldn't have disappeared.

Esther slept on the couch. It was stupid and clichéd, but she couldn't bring herself to sleep in the same bed as the man who would lock her up rather than listen to her. The next morning, she woke up to find the brochure displayed prominently on the coffee table, alongside a cold cup of coffee and a banana. She threw the lot in the garbage, mug and all, and dressed, not sure what her next step should be, but knowing she couldn't just sit here. Maybe she'd visit Tara again. Get her out of the house. There was something Tara wasn't telling her; maybe it was feeling Donny there, in their house, that had made her keep quiet. Esther would explain that she knew how hard it was to believe terrible things about the people you loved, but when the evidence was plain and clear and left on the coffee table for you to see the moment you opened your eyes, belief didn't matter.

Fuck Ryan and his ultimatums. And while she was at it, fuck Meg for not supporting Esther in this one thing, for never supporting her when it wasn't convenient. Esther didn't need either of them. She was intelligent and capable and not paranoid and when the truth finally came to light, they would finally see how wrong they were. They would beg for forgiveness. They would grovel. And Claire would rest easy.

She approached the front door ready to take on the day, but stopped when she noticed the dead bolt hadn't been locked. She struggled to quash the too-familiar pricklings of dread working their way up her chest. She was alive. She was safe. But the door had been unlocked for who knew how long while Esther had been vulnerable. She didn't want to believe Ryan hadn't locked the door on purpose, but it was like she didn't know her husband anymore. Was this some kind of childish, retaliatory act?

She steeled herself. Told herself it didn't matter. Nothing had happened. Nothing *would* happen, because she was on top of it.

When she opened the door, something flew at her. She jumped, a scream caught in her throat. Her heart was still hammering when she realized it was a piece of folded paper. She cursed whatever solicitor decided to shove a flier through her door, but then she unfolded the paper and her whole body went cold.

I will only warn you once. Stay away from my family.

There was no signature, but Esther knew who it was from. Tara must have told Donny about her visit. Stupid of Esther not to give a fake name. Of course he would make the connection. And now he knew where she lived. But how? She'd moved away from Blacklick a long time ago. She knew homeowner information was public record, but how would he know where to look? Unless Claire had said something.

She took a step back into the house, the door still hanging open. Part of her wanted to slam it shut, lock it tight, and crawl under her covers until Ryan came home. She could show him the note, prove she wasn't paranoid like he thought, but then she realized Ryan's mind was made up. He would accuse her of writing the note herself. He would add it to his pile of reasons she needed to be sent away.

No. She had to handle this herself.

Trembling, she ran to her car and, once inside, locked the doors and turned the key so hard the engine screamed in protest. She hit the gas and flew out of the driveway without looking. Her body functioned on autopilot, her mind ordering itself away.

Years ago, she'd moved to Chicago to make herself feel safer. But now she knew it didn't matter where she was—Donny would have found her one way or the other. So for the second time in as many days, Esther headed back to Blacklick.

CHAPTER TWENTY-TWO

CLAIRE

SEPTEMBER 2007

Every day after school, Claire walked the three blocks to the county library where the woman behind the counter knew Claire by face and subject matter. Though she frowned as she set up the microfiche and unlocked the door to the records room, thinking Claire's search too morbid for a *nice young girl* like her, she dutifully left Claire to it, never pestering or prodding, though more than once she left a stack of more suitable volumes outside the small room: The Baby-Sitters Club series, *An Abundance of Katherines,* Harry Potter. Claire always checked out at least one of these, if only to make sure she would always have access to the records room (and to discourage any passing fancy to inform Claire's parents of her research sessions). Though she'd only ever told the woman behind the desk that she was looking for articles about her family, it wouldn't take a genius to put two and two together. The older she got, the smaller and more claustrophobic Blacklick became. She understood now why Meg had left, why coming back had turned her inside out.

In the small, private room, Claire set down her backpack and withdrew a note-book full of pencil scribbles and printouts. A yellow sticky note marked where the first article she found was taped to a notebook page:

LATE-NIGHT KIDNAPPING SHAKES
LOCAL COMMUNITY

At approximately eleven p.m. Thursday evening, Julie Finch, three months old, was kidnapped from her home. Though her mother, Annette, was out at the time, the three other Finch children were present, though none claim to have seen the person responsible.

Police are asking for any and all tips, which can be directed to the station or anonymously through the tip line.

Though the article had been printed on the front page of the local paper, it was barely more than a few inches long. She'd almost missed it during her first search. In her subsequent visits she'd found a few other articles, never more than a paragraph or so, all more or less stating the same thing: No leads, tips can be directed, the family requests privacy, etc.

A second article was taped to another page in her notebook, this one just as brief as the first. Claire had highlighted a few lines: *The baby was found deceased in an abandoned house not far from where the family lives. Details regarding cause of death have not been released to the public.* No leads, tips can be directed, the family requests privacy, blah blah all over again.

Without clues, everyone seemed to give up.

Claire wouldn't make the same mistake.

Today, she decided to change up her search. She had scoured every page of every newspaper in the county looking for any mention of a kidnapping or babies found abandoned. It didn't make sense to Claire that this was a one-and-done deal. There hadn't been anyone with a specific grudge against her family that she knew of, but given the time frame, Claire couldn't discount the idea that they had been targeted. What were the odds that someone with an itch to take a baby just happened to be walking by? There had to have been others, which meant there had to be a pattern.

But three full reels later, she'd found nothing. As she was loading a fourth, she noticed a shadow on the wall in front of her. She forgot sometimes that three of the room's walls were actually windows, and sometimes people got nosy, lingering behind her, squinting as they tried to read over her shoulder. They all got bored eventually. But halfway through the fourth reel, the shadow hadn't moved. The librarian, she thought. She plastered on her sweetest, most good-girl smile and swiveled in her seat.

It wasn't the librarian. It was a guy with a buzz cut. He wore a WWF T-shirt that was frayed along the hem and cargo shorts that sagged above bruised, skinny knees. She startled, thinking she'd been staring too hard, too long, but then she realized the guy wasn't even looking at her. He was looking somewhere past her, at something on—or in—the shadowy wall. He looked familiar—a kid from school, maybe, but he looked too old to be in high school. She couldn't think of his name, or where she might have seen him. A muscle twitched in his cheek, and then he met her gaze, and his face bloomed red.

She started to wave, but he turned without a word, heading for the row of DVDs.

She went back to her work, but every so often she felt eyes on the back of her head and soon it was impossible to focus on anything else. She read and re-read the same article three or four times before deciding to give up. It was getting close to dinnertime anyway, and she didn't want her mom getting suspicious. So she dutifully packed away the microfiche and the reels and made sure to lock the records room from the inside before turning out the light. Out of habit, she grabbed the first book off the stack left outside the study room and made a beeline for the checkout desk.

The guy followed.

"I didn't peg you for a Harry Potter nerd," he said.

She set the book on the counter and handed the woman—not the nosy librarian, a volunteer who kept one eye on the door like she couldn't wait to pounce on someone trying to steal books—her library card. "I'm not."

"Then why are you checking out the book?"

"It's complicated."

"You don't have to be ashamed, you know. Harry Potter's kind of cool. In its own way."

The woman raised her eyebrow, the universal female signal for *this guy giving you trouble?* Claire subtly shook her head. The woman shrugged, checked out the book, and handed it back with a receipt. "Due next Friday."

"Thanks." Claire tucked the book under her arm and headed for the door. The boy was hot on her heels.

"More of a *Sandman* guy, myself," he said. Then, "So is this an act or do you really not remember me?"

She stopped and turned, frowning. "Should I?"

"I don't know." His face reddened again. "I remember you, though."

Maybe it was the way he held himself, like there was something perched on his back, weighing him down. Or maybe it was the half-smile that, if she ignored the buzz cut and the darkness in his eyes, seemed kind of sweet. Lost. It came back to her slowly, and then all at once. The house. The door. The room with the blackness that still lived in her belly. And the boy who had brought her there.

"Donny, right?" she asked.

His smile brightened. "Yup."

"Why were you watching me?"

He fixed his gaze on a crack in the sidewalk. "I wasn't."

"You were staring into the room."

"I wasn't looking at you."

"What were you looking at?"

His voice softened. "Nothing."

"Something."

He was quiet for a long time. When he finally looked up, the shadows under his eyes had darkened. "You wouldn't understand."

Something told her she would. "Try me."

Crossing his arms, he looked everywhere but at her. He looked up where the clouds had cleared and suppressed a shiver. "You know the hottest time of day and the sun is just blasting and you can see that little shimmer above the asphalt? When it's so fucking hot you could cook an egg on the sidewalk?"

Claire nodded.

"I got scars on my back from laying on the street on days like that. My skin sizzled." He lifted his T-shirt to reveal shiny patches of skin alongside fist-shaped bruises. "Could've cooked myself to death and I still wouldn't have felt it. It's like—" He shook his head, like he was trying to jiggle the words loose. "Everything is just cold and blank and boring and the only time I really feel something is when I'm afraid. When I see—" He cut off the last of it, rubbing his face with his hands. "It's like it's looking at me." He laughed ruefully. "What's that saying? The abyss stares back or something like that? I wasn't looking at *you*. I was looking at the abyss."

The abyss. The blackness. It was all the same, Claire figured. She wondered if pieces of it had broken off and wriggled inside him too. Because she knew what he meant. The cold and blank and boring.

He continued, "What were you looking at in there, anyway?"

Her knee-jerk reaction was to tell him to fuck off, but he'd cut himself open a little for her just now. It was only fair that she did the same. "Newspaper articles."

"For like a project or something?"

She could have lied and that would have been the end of it. But she'd been keeping her search secret from everyone. It was a lot to carry. Too much, sometimes.

She didn't have to look at her watch to know she was already pushing it for time. She started toward the sidewalk. Without being told, he followed.

"I'm looking for someone," she said.

"Someone special?"

She didn't like the hopeful lilt to his voice. "My sister died when she was a baby. Someone took her and killed her and I'm going to find him."

"Oh." Then, "When was this?"

"Long time ago."

"Then why do you care?"

Anger rippled through her. "Excuse me?"

He put his hands up, defensive. "Sorry. It's just—if it was a long time ago, then why does it matter?"

"Because it hurt my family and it's still hurting them, even if they won't admit it." She adjusted her hold on her bag. "Someone has to pay."

"Will it make the hurt stop if they do?"

She shrugged.

They walked for a while in silence, Claire listening to their rhythmic shuffle-steps. There were things she wanted to ask him—why that house, why that room, if he'd known what was inside and if he'd felt what she had when they crossed the threshold—but every time she felt the words bubble at the back of her throat, she swallowed them whole. Esther said it was childish, still thinking the darkness inside her came from that house. That Claire was just depressed. But Claire knew better.

At the crosswalk, Donny jabbed the button that would turn the light. He nodded at the tiny strip mall on the other side. "You want a pop or something?"

Claire shook her head. "I need to get home."

"Right. Okay." He shifted his weight. "You coming back tomorrow?"

"Yeah."

"Maybe I'll see you."

"Maybe."

He smiled, and when the light turned, he started across the street. Claire briefly lingered, and when he looked back, she turned back the other way. It was the wrong way, but her insides had gotten cold and hard and heavy. She needed to get home.

Anglerfish, she remembered, the image of a younger Donny's crooked smile crossing her mind, and walked a little faster.

CHAPTER TWENTY-THREE

MEG

NOW

Meg woke up on the bathroom floor with hair in her mouth and a blinding headache. She tasted vomit. Her arm had gone numb and when she finally forced herself to sit up, head spinning, painful tingles rocketed down to her fingertips. A small, empty bottle of cheap whiskey lay next to the toilet. She didn't know where it came from, and for the sake of what was left of her sanity, she didn't speculate.

She leaned against the wall, head tipped back. It would be easy to blame the booze. Healthy, even.

No, Meg decided. It was the product of her own fucked up mind, her guilt manifested as this woman, half in the grave and seething with resentment. She didn't dare imagine what might come next. Could it get any worse?

Her stomach growled, but the thought of eating anything brought with it the taste of bile. She stood on shaky legs and leaned over the sink. A stream of drool dripped from her lip as she fought the urge to vomit.

Get it out, she thought. *Get all the bad out.*

She turned on the faucet and as soon as the scent of the water hit her nose she started to gag. What came out wasn't bile or fluid, but a deluge of leaves and dirt, great clumps of it tangled with long, brown hair. Snot dripped and her eyes watered, muscles strained with the effort. Her heart pounded, and when it all finally stopped coming, she closed her mouth only to feel grounds of dirt between her teeth. Fighting against a second wave, she cupped water from the faucet into her mouth, which she swished around her mouth and then spit. She did this three or four times before she could make herself swallow without worrying it would come back up.

She splashed her face, letting the water drip down her chin and neck, and then caught her reflection in the mirror. She looked almost as bad as she felt, her cheek scarred with the tile grout and the skin around her eyes bruise-purple. Her lips were torn from chewing them in her sleep, and a bit of crusted blood flaked from the corner of her mouth.

The nightmares were getting worse, bleeding into the dark and making her question her grip on reality. Could a person die from guilt?

She splashed more water on her face, and then went into the kitchen in search of some crackers or sandwich bread, something to calm the burbling in her stomach. On the counter she found a lukewarm glass of water—a gift from past-her—and next to it, Claire's datebook. Sticking out of the pages was a slip of paper.

The article she'd found in Claire's room.

HISTORICAL SOCIETY PETITION
HALTS DEVELOPMENT

Meg took the glass of water and the article into the living room, where she sat on the couch and read.

A petition filed with the Gary County Historical Society has slowed the timeline for one Indiana developer, whose plan to revitalize a three-mile radius surrounding Blacklick's downtown area was put on hold this week. But Marcus Forton, President of IDP Partners, isn't deterred.

"You see these all the time. People get caught up in the nostalgia. But Blacklick is ready for a facelift, and I think once these unsafe properties are replaced with new, modern homes and shopping centers, it'll mean more for the community."

The petition centers around one property, located at the edge of the proposed demolition and rebuild, whose history is murky, at least according to Forton.

"These forties houses are a dime a dozen," he said. "Part of that mid- and postwar boom. Hill Street is one of the oldest in the community, but its history lies with its people, not with a crumbling house."

The original filer of the petition could not be reached for comment.

Meg's mind was still sluggish from the booze, from the nightmare, so she had to read the article twice before she could make any connections. *Hill Street.* She sipped the water, wincing at its metallic tang. *It couldn't be.*

She found her phone under the couch, the battery just clinging to life. Google wasn't any help. The Historical Society's website was down for maintenance, and any other searches only brought up the article she'd already read. Nothing about the house or the person who'd filed the petition.

It had to be the house. Why else would Claire have had the article tucked away in her things? Had she been the one to file the petition? If so, why? And did it have anything to do with why she'd gone back to the house in the end?

Every answer seemed to spawn a hundred questions. Her memory was useless as she tried to conjure their last conversation, every word summoning the image of Claire's dangling red shoes.

She needed to talk to someone who wasn't Esther. Someone on the outside looking in.

Meg tucked the article back into the datebook, which she packed into a small messenger bag along with bottles of Tums and Tylenol. Then she plugged in her phone to suck up as much juice as possible while she figured out how she was going to get any answers with her car still trapped at Esther's.

She tried calling her sister, but the line went to voicemail each time, so she texted her: I have a lead. Call me.

She let her phone charge for an hour, while she forced herself to eat a slice of bread and finish the glass of water. Still nothing from Esther, so she called her parents' house, hoping she could convince her dad to bring her to Esther's.

Mom picked up on the third ring.

"Dad around?" Meg asked.

"He's at work," Mom said. *Duh.*

"Oh." Meg paused. "When will he be home?"

"Late, I assume. They're short-staffed." Then, "Did you need something?"

The last thing she wanted was to be alone in the car with her mother. It wasn't that they didn't get along—she couldn't remember the last time she'd fought with her mother—but that night took up space between them, like a wall made up of everything they didn't say to each other. She didn't want to talk about being accosted in the bedroom. Didn't want to talk about Claire or the house or anything until she knew more. It would be easier to tell her no, and then spend more money she didn't have on a Lyft. But she'd gone almost a week without working now and rent was coming up due.

"A ride," Meg said finally. "To Esther's. My car is there."

"Why is your car at Esther's?"

Her mind flailed. "I went with her to an appointment and she dropped me off at my apartment after. We didn't really think about it."

"Mm." Mom sighed. "Okay, well, I guess I have some time. I'll be there in a few minutes."

"Thanks," Meg said, but Mom had already hung up.

Meg was waiting on the stoop when Mom pulled up, having changed and wrestled her hair into something masquerading as clean and presentable. She didn't want any questions, not that Mom would ask. But the *looks* would come, and with them new waves of anxiety.

She got in the car and buckled, cradling the messenger bag in her lap. Mom glanced at it, eyebrow raised, but didn't say anything. Her hair was pinned back, but she wore mascara and blush, unusual for Mom, but especially in the middle of a weekday.

Neither said hello, but Mom turned up the radio slightly, a country music station, as if to discourage small talk. Meg looked out the window and caught her reflection in the side mirror. Claire stared back, hovering just behind her, eyes dark, one rotted hand resting behind Meg's shoulder on the seat.

Meg forced herself to look away, focusing instead on her fingernails as she picked at her skin.

"What kind of appointment was it?" Mom asked as they started out on the highway.

"Hmm?"

"You said you and Esther went to an appointment together. What was it?"

Meg's cheeks flashed hot. "Oh, uh, hair appointment."

Mom turned to look at her and, studying Meg's hair, frowned.

"Esther's appointment. I just went with."

Mom nodded. "Glad you two are getting along."

"Yeah."

Mom's grip on the wheel tightened. She glanced up at the rearview mirror, a sigh working its way up.

Claire's breath blew cold and damp on the back of Meg's neck.

Meg's stomach ached and her jaw clenched. *Don't ask,* she begged silently. *Please don't ask.*

Because there was no satisfying answer she'd be able to give.

But as quickly as the moment had come, it passed. Mom sank into her seat, shoulders hunched. And when Meg chanced a glance in the side mirror, Claire was gone.

They spent the rest of the ride in silence, eyes fixed on the road ahead. When they pulled into Esther's driveway, Meg was relieved to see her sister's car gone. Maybe seeing that Meg's car was gone would make Esther respond to her later, but it probably wouldn't. No one held grudges quite like Esther.

"Thanks," Meg said and started to climb out of the car.

Mom grabbed her elbow, both of them startled by the force of it. Still, Mom clung on.

"What did you take?" she asked.

"Take?"

"From Claire's room." Mom let go of Meg's elbow, but it didn't matter. She was pinned by Mom's stare. "I saw you take something."

Tell her. For once, tell her.

"I—nothing. I was just looking."

"Megan. Please."

Part of Meg wanted to rip herself open, to spill everything all over the both of them—Claire, Esther's obsession with Donny, the datebook...but finding the article, didn't mean anything. Not yet. If it'd given Meg hope—and *oh,* did it give her hope—it was fragile. If it broke, if it all came to nothing except having to accept that their sister had died and there was nothing they could have done to stop it, she wanted to keep that pain for herself. She couldn't, *wouldn't*, give it to her mother to carry.

Meg eased out the door without looking back. "Thanks for the ride," she said.

"Meg. Wait." The driver door slammed, and Meg turned to see her mother standing beside the car, fingers tangled in front of her. "Just—I need to know."

Meg's whole body went cold. *No*, she thought. *I can't do this now.*

Mom took a cautious step toward her. "Why there? Why that...that *place*?" Before Meg could answer, Mom continued. "It's just... We tried so hard to shield you three from it. We thought if you didn't know, then you could forget. You could move on." Her voice cracked. "But somehow, she found out, and I'm scared that's what did it. That's what made her do it."

"What are you talking about? That Claire found out what?"

Mom shook her head.

"Mom. Tell me."

Tears dripped down her mother's face, and her shoulders sagged like the effort of keeping herself standing was too much. "That house? It's where they found her." She started to tremble. "It's where they found Julie."

Meg drove, not really paying attention to anything except her heart in her throat. The house stood at the back of her mind, door wide, a great gaping maw. It was at the center of everything. Julie had died in the same place Claire had, the same place where Meg, Esther, and Claire had been on the last day of the last good summer they ever had. In a lot of ways, it was where their friendship had died too. But *why*? Deep down, she knew the answer would be there, but she couldn't bring herself to go back. Not yet.

If she went back now, the house would surely eat her alive.

Instead, she found herself back in the police station parking lot. Now that she knew where he liked to take lunch, she kept an eye peeled for Officer Kingsolver, mustachioed or otherwise, but the place was pretty empty. *Probably a shooting somewhere*, she thought, her mind too eager to find dark places to go. *Or a War on Drugs convention.*

The second she cut the engine, she thought about leaving. Thanks to Esther's mouth, Meg doubted Officer Kingsolver would give her the time of day. And even if he did, who was to say there was anything else to share? But Meg needed someone to talk at. Someone to sit there and listen and nod and then tell her she was wrong and to just go home.

The lobby smelled like old food and bleach. An older couple sat in the corner chairs, knees touching but the rest of their bodies turned away, like the effort of being next to each other was too much. The woman was shaking her head as she scribbled on a clipboard. The man leaned forward, elbows resting on his knees, gaze fixed on a point somewhere only he could see. She recognized the look of someone trying very hard to keep it together.

Meg met the reception officer's gaze and offered a weak smile. "Hi," she said, approaching the desk. "Me again."

The reception officer raised an eyebrow. If she recognized Meg, she wasn't showing it.

"I need to see Officer Kingsolver. Again." Then, when the reception officer didn't blink, "Please."

The reception officer slid a card under the glass. "Call this number. If you have information pertaining to a current case, you can leave a message and Officer Kingsolver will receive it. If you have information pertaining to a closed case, or anything else, you can send an email to the address at the bottom."

She almost took the card. But then she felt cold fingers lace through hers, and she knew Claire was with her. She remembered what Claire had said to her in the beginning, that Esther was next and it was going to be Meg's fault. She couldn't give up.

"Is he in the office today?" Meg asked, sliding the card back toward the reception officer. "I can wait if he's out on a call, or in a meeting or whatever. Really, it's no trouble."

"Problem?" Another officer approached from somewhere, arms perched on his hips.

"No problem," the reception office said, still looking at Meg. "Right?"

Jesus. "I'm just looking to speak with Officer Kingsolver about my sister's case. I'm not here to make trouble."

"Officer Kingsolver will get your message if you call—"

"It's fine. I'm here." Officer Kingsolver walked up to the desk carrying a coffee in one hand and a folder in the other. "Let her back. Won't take long."

The reception officer's eyes shot daggers. "Suit yourself."

She hit a button and the door clicked open. Meg hustled through, careful not to lock eyes with anyone as she followed Officer Kingsolver back to his desk.

He sat with a grunt and wiggled his mouse to wake up his computer. Meg sat just as a screen saver of two gap-toothed children flashed across the monitor.

"Your kids?" she asked.

"Yep," he said, not looking at her.

"Cute."

"Thanks." He glanced at his watch before finally turning toward her. "Not to be rude, but let's get down to the point, okay? It's like I told your sister, we've spoken to Mr. Lippman at length and we have no reason to suspect—"

"I'm not here about that."

He raised an eyebrow.

"Well, I am, but not like that. I don't think—" She hesitated. She didn't know what she thought. "I was just hoping I could get some more information from you."

"Like?"

"Like if there was anything out of place in the house where Claire—" She swallowed, ignoring the dangling red shoes in her periphery. "If anyone noticed anything weird."

"Define weird."

"I don't know. Just…weird."

He tilted his head slightly, like a dog that's heard a whistle. "Why are you asking?"

She got the sense that if she told him anything glib, he would dismiss her and this would have been a waste. But she also didn't want him to look at her like he'd looked at Esther, like some delusional woman too wrapped up in her emotions to see anything clearly. *Something* was wrong. Whether it was a big something or a little something didn't matter.

She had carefully folded the article from Claire's room and placed it in her wallet. She took it out and handed it to him.

He read it quickly. His mouth dipped into a small frown. "The place must have meant a lot to her."

Meg shook her head. "No. It meant the opposite of a lot." When he didn't respond, she continued. "We all went there when we were kids. Me, Esther, and Claire. It was…frightening. I still don't quite understand what happened, but I know that after, none of us ever wanted to go back." *And Julie,* she thought. *What if this was about Julie?* "And before that, our youngest sister, Julie, was taken. She died and they found her there. But Mom didn't tell us—didn't tell *me*—until recently. I don't know if Claire knew."

"A place doesn't have to have *good* memories to mean something to us," he said gently.

"Look, I understand, okay? I know what it looks like from your position. I see it. But you weren't there when it—" She rubbed her face. "I'm just looking for something. I don't know what. Just…anything."

He looked at her for what felt like a long time, tapping the article against the desk. Finally, he sighed and stood. "Wait here."

When he returned several minutes later, he was carrying another folder. He dropped it on the desk in front of her, but didn't sit.

"What's this?" she asked.

"You know what a Freedom of Information request is?"

She shook her head.

"Google it. Fill out a form. It won't go anywhere, but there will be a record, which is the important thing."

"I don't understand. What is that?"

"A gift," he said. "Process usually takes several days. Weeks. And that's if someone's bothered to look at your request. Luckily, I know a guy."

She opened the folder and scanned the first page. It was the police report.

"Everything I know about your sister's...incident...is in that folder. Copies, of course."

"Why?" Meg asked.

He raised an eyebrow.

"Why give it to me? I'm sure it's a risk for you."

"Fill out the form. Okay?"

Too tempted to go through it all here, she closed the folder and clutched it to her chest. "Thank you." Then, "Can I ask another favor?"

"I suppose."

She nodded to the article. "Would you be able to find out who filed that petition?"

"Probably. Why?"

"I don't know," she said honestly.

He took a moment before nodding. "I'll see what I can do. No promises though."

"Right." She stood, shook his hand. "Thanks."

"Sure. And Meg? Be careful, okay?" He pointed to the folder. "Some doors, once you open them, they stay that way."

CHAPTER TWENTY-FOUR

CLAIRE

AUGUST 2012

I told you, Donny, I'm not interested. Not like that."

"Okay, but listen." Donny paced in front of Claire's car—a 1995 Chevy Malibu she inherited from Esther when she saved up enough for something that didn't clang when you stopped—hands running through his wild hair. "We make *sense*, Finch. We *match*."

Claire leaned against the hood of the car, paper cup sweating in her hand. The few sips of the milkshake she'd managed to get down had already curdled in her belly. She hadn't touched her burger or fries, a fact that would have riled her mother to no end not just because of the waste of money, but because Claire herself was wasting away. She needed to eat more. She knew that, but the dark things inside her had grown fat with her failures, taking up what little space she had.

"Just because something makes sense," she said, "doesn't make it right."

"It's because I'm old, isn't it?"

It came out as a joke, but it wasn't. Not really.

Sure, Claire was nineteen, almost twenty, now, an adult with a car and a bank account, but she wasn't always, and this wasn't the first time that Donny, seven years her senior, had tried to kiss her.

She tossed her milkshake and lunch in the trash. "I think I'm gonna go."

"Wait. No. Sorry." He cut her off on the way to the driver's side of the car and grabbed her shoulders. "You're right. I shouldn't have—it was stupid. I'll figure it out. Eventually." He smiled and it looked odd on his face, like he was mimicking an expression he'd seen someone else make. "Come on. Show me the article you found."

Claire regretted telling him about it the moment it had left her mouth, but after years of nothing, it was hard to keep a lead to herself. She'd found it on a rare day that she could do her searching alone, without Donny lingering nearby. She'd been going through a reel she found by chance, misplaced in the library's microfiche cabinet when she came across a headline that made her pause. About halfway through the article was a quote from a girl named Krystal, who'd claimed to have been one of Meg's friends, saying she was "shocked and saddened" by what had happened. It wasn't much, but the odd choice of words for a girl who couldn't have been older than thirteen at the time had made Claire wonder.

"I found something," she'd told Donny. "A clue. Or not. I'm not sure."

He'd insisted on taking her to lunch at the Dairy Queen to celebrate. For once, she was excited. But the longer the printout sat in her back pocket, the more she doubted.

"It's probably nothing," she said as she unfolded the printout.

He took it from her and leaned against the driver's side door, eyes darting across the page. His expression remained maddeningly neutral. "Huh," he said finally.

Her stomach sank. "See? I told you. It's nothing, probably." She paused. "It's weird, though, right? I've never heard Meg mention anyone named Krystal, but she had to have known Meg to be quoted like that. Did you know her?"

"No," he said. "No idea." Then, "What were you gonna do with this?"

Claire shrugged. "I don't know. Maybe try to find her. See if she remembered anything, or if Meg had ever said anything to her about it." Claire was scraping the bottom of the barrel now and she knew it, but every time she thought about giving up, she could feel the darkness inside her undulate, like it was excited. "But that's a dumb idea, obviously."

Donny was still staring at the page, eyes unmoving. His jaw clenched, like he was thinking too hard. When he finally looked up, the tension seemed to drain from his face. "I have an idea. Give me your keys."

She unclipped her keys from her belt loop, but hesitated before handing them over. "Where are we going?"

He rolled his eyes. "C'mon. Just trust me, okay?"

There were times that Donny creeped her out. Like when he talked about their darkness, when he looked at her like he was hungry, or sick, or both. But sometimes, like now, she remembered that he could be sweet when he wanted to be. That when the rest of her family shut her out, he was there to listen, to encourage her at the times she felt the most lost or useless. Sometimes, she remembered that first day they met, and her first instinct that told her he was, at his core, a good guy.

"I trust you," she said, and handed him the keys.

They didn't go far.

At the edge of town was a subdivision, half-built, with yards still more dirt than grass, the houses too tall and too boxy, all of them the same soft, gray color. When they first broke ground last year, Dad said it was developers coming in and thinking they could civilize the people of Blacklick, like they were all dumb hicks who didn't know any better. Then the money ran out and the development stopped mid-plan because those same dumb hicks took one look at their cookie-cutter houses with too much plastic, set them up next to the exorbitant price tag, and decided they weren't interested, thank you very much.

Except a few families had moved in. Young, wide-eyed couples who took one look at progress and got weak in the knees.

Claire couldn't figure out why Donny would want to bring her here, unless he thought wallowing in The Establishment's failure would make her feel better. It wouldn't.

He pulled up alongside the curb in front of the third house, distinguished from the others only by a tall flagpole at the center of the yard, the trinity of flag patriotism flapping in the breeze: America, POW, Indiana. A chalk drawing took up the whole driveway, but rain and shuffling footprints muddled the image.

"Can't promise she's home," Donny said, "but it's worth a shot."

"Who?" Claire asked.

"Krystal Clark. I think she's actually Krystal Beaumont now, but…" He shrugged, his face scrunched like he'd tasted something sour.

Claire frowned. "I thought you said you didn't know her."

"Hmm?"

"Earlier, when I asked, you said you had no idea."

"Must've misunderstood." He shut off the ignition and pocketed the keys. "C'mon. Let's see where this goes."

Claire hesitated. He wanted to talk to Krystal? Now? She didn't even know what she would ask. She wasn't ready.

But Donny was halfway up the path now and it wasn't that she didn't trust Donny, but whatever information Krystal had—if anything—she didn't want to hear secondhand. She needed to see Krystal's face when she talked about that night.

Smoothing her T-shirt, she jogged to catch up with Donny, and then walked a half-step behind him the rest of the way, instinctively hanging back when he jabbed the doorbell. The sound must have set off a dog; deep, bellowing howls came from inside, followed by someone yelling.

Finally, the door opened. The woman—Krystal, presumably—looked like she was pushing thirty and not happy about it. Her hair was striped with thick highlights, and her eyes were ringed with black eyeliner that only drew attention to the creases at the corners. She wore a tight T-shirt that said *Pink* across the chest, and shorts that squeezed her thighs. She was barefoot, her toenails a bright coral.

"Hey, Krystal." Donny flashed a smile. "How's things?"

Krystal looked from Donny to Claire and back again, her expression morphing from annoyance to forced neutrality. "Donny. Hi."

"This is Claire Finch."

Claire waved.

Krystal's gaze was fixed on Donny. "What do you want?"

"Can we come inside? Claire has some stuff she'd like to ask."

"Unless you're busy, or..." Claire absently glanced past Krystal into the house. Krystal caught the look and shut the door a few inches.

"Yeah," Donny said. "Unless you're busy."

Claire could tell she was tempted to turn them away. Desperate to, actually. Every time a sound came from somewhere in the house, she flinched. Claire knew she should put her out of her misery, apologize for interrupting her life, and leave. But the darkness was awake now, and it was hungry.

She smiled. "Won't take long. Promise."

Krystal sagged. "Fine." She nudged the door open a little wider. "Follow me."

Donny followed directly after, leaving Claire to close the door behind them. The foyer wall was covered in framed pictures of two children, smiling like they were in pain, perched in increasingly awkward positions against JCPenney enchanted forest backdrops. Krystal led them down the hall and through the kitchen, where a Crock-Pot bubbled on the counter, and into a small den. Floor-to-ceiling wood paneling and animal pelts—this was her husband's space.

"Nice place," Donny said. He caught Claire's eye and raised his eyebrows.

"Yeah," Claire said. "Really nice."

"It's Tate's office. My husband," Krystal said, emphasizing husband. "He's a contractor."

"Hunter?" Donny asked, nodding at the fox pelt displayed awkwardly beside a flat-screen television.

"Yep."

"Cool."

Krystal sat in the only chair in the room, leaving Donny and Claire to stand. Claire stuck her hands in her pockets, not really sure what to do with them. She looked to Donny, waiting—hoping—he would break the tension somehow. But he seemed to be enjoying himself, wandering the room, handling Krystal's husband's things.

It took a long time for Krystal to peel her gaze away from Donny and land on Claire. "So? You have questions? About what?" She squinted. "I don't even know you."

"Right. I know." Claire pulled the printout from her pocket.

"Go on," Donny said, suddenly beside her. "Show her."

Claire handed over the printout, which Krystal unfolded and read as the color drained from her face.

"Her baby sister," Donny said unnecessarily.

"I got that," Krystal said. Then, looking at Claire. "Sorry."

Claire nodded, accepting the printout back. "It says in there that you were Meg's friend."

"Oh. Yeah. We were friends."

"I don't ever remember seeing you guys hang out."

"It was a school thing."

"Right."

"Sorry—what is this?" Krystal sat back in the chair, arms crossed tight over her chest. "Are you accusing me of something? Because I wasn't even there when it happened, okay? Some guy was knocking on doors when I was a kid asking if anyone knew the Finch family. He had a camera and said I was pretty." She shrugged. Her gaze flicked to Donny, almost too fast for Claire to catch. "I said what he wanted to hear."

"Why do you keep looking at him?" Claire asked.

Krystal blanched. "Huh?"

"You keep looking at Donny. Did he call you or something?" She turned to Donny. "What is this?"

He smirked. "Maybe she just likes me."

"I do not like you," Krystal snapped.

"Then what the fuck?" Claire snatched the article out of Krystal's hands. "Is this even real?"

"Whoa, hold on." Donny grabbed her arms. Held her still. "You showed that to me, remember?"

Krystal stood. "Y'all need to leave. Tate will be home soon."

"Jealous type?" Donny goaded.

Krystal's face reddened. Then, after several deep breaths, she turned to Claire, voice lowered. "I get it, okay? I really do. But all you're doing is hurting yourself. There's no point in digging up the past, is there?"

"I dunno," Donny said. "No statute of limitations on murder, right?"

Krystal shook her head.

"Or accessory to murder, I suspect."

Claire shoved him away. "Stop it." Then, turning to Krystal, "Were you there? Did you see anything? Hear anything?"

Krystal clutched the edge of the desk. "No. I wasn't there."

Maybe it was time to give up.

She stormed out of the house, knocking one of the JCPenney pictures off the wall. Donny followed, and when she reached the car, he grabbed her arms, studying her face with a creeping intensity.

"I know that look," he said.

Claire scowled. She just wanted to go home, to be alone in the dark and maybe bleed some of the darkness out.

"Let's go. I want to show you something."

She started to argue—she was tired of his surprises—but he was already heading for the driver's seat. He had the keys, so there would be no coaxing him out, and anyway, she was too wrung out to fight. She flopped into the passenger seat and leaned back, arm draped over her eyes.

Maybe we'll wreck, she thought hopefully. *Maybe it'll all end right now.*

Donny set his hand on her thigh. It was warm and clammy, but she didn't shove it aside. Instead, she pretended to sleep. She must have actually been tired, though, because it didn't take long for her breathing to slow, for the darkness to take over.

When she woke up what felt like seconds later, she looked over to see Donny staring at her.

"Sorry," he said, smiling. "You looked peaceful."

Claire sat up and rubbed the sleep out of her eyes. Her back ached from being bent a weird way, and her arm had fallen asleep.

It was dusk, the sky an ashy pink. The last remaining vestiges of the sun glared off the hood of a car that had seen better days. The wheel wells were rusted near to dust, the tires sad and flat. To the right, she spotted a trailer perched up on blocks, the hitch a vulgar protrusion, surrounded by overgrown grass and weeds.

"Where are we?" she asked.

"My house," Donny said. "My parents aren't home. I figured we could talk."

"Talk about what?"

Donny smiled again, a wait-and-see smile. "Come on."

Driven by curiosity—she'd never seen Donny's place before, never heard him talk about it—she followed him to the door, which opened with a loud creak. Inside, the only light came from the hood above the stove, a tiny thing nestled between a fold-out table and a tall, narrow cabinet. A saucepan sat on one of the burners, the inside crusted with what looked like spaghetti sauce. The table was covered in a film of dust and grease, and the carpet *squished* when she walked. The whole place smelled like cigarettes.

"Sorry about that." Donny gestured to the floor. "Mom wasn't paying attention and overflowed the sink last night. I dried up what I could."

She suppressed a shiver as dampness eked into her shoes. "It's fine." Then, "You wanted to show me something?"

He nodded. "My room's back here."

She followed him through the living room, eyes darting from the stained, beige couch to the paneled walls, smoke-stained yellow near the ceiling. On the walls were a couple of framed pictures, but she didn't pause long enough to get a good look at them.

The first thing she noticed about Donny's room was the darkness. Every wall was covered in posters—metal bands, movies—and the window was blocked by a thin, black sheet that hung from thumbtacks in the ceiling. He flicked on a lamp, and the bloodred shade cast an eerie glow over the room. But it was otherwise tidy, tidier than the rest of the trailer. His bed was rumply, but made, and the only thing on the floor was a small, stuffed ostrich, which he kicked beneath the desk.

He gestured to the bed. "Sit."

Something inside told her not to. The feeling was sharp and fleeting, batted away by what she thought was logic. Donny could be a creep sometimes, but all guys were creeps. He'd been there for her forever, wasting his free time at the library with her when she knew he'd rather be doing anything else.

So she sat.

"Something to drink?" he asked, then went to his closet where he burrowed around in a basket before returning with a half-empty bottle of whiskey. "I wait until they're almost empty, then steal them from my Dad's room. He figures he finished it and goes out for another." He snorted, but it came out forced. "I can get ice too, if you want."

"No thanks."

Donny shrugged and took a long swig straight from the bottle. When he looked back at her, his eyes sparkled.

"Good?" Claire asked.

"Terrible, actually, but I don't care."

She smirked.

"You sure you don't want some?"

"No. I need to get home soon."

At the mention of Claire leaving, Donny's smile vanished. He sat on the bed beside her, still gripping the bottle by the neck. She worried he was going to put his hand on her thigh again, but he seemed to be making a concerted effort not to touch her, inching toward the edge of the bed, his feet turned slightly away.

"I'm sorry today didn't go the way you wanted it to," he said.

"Yeah." Claire studied her hands, picking at her cuticles to keep the tears from welling again.

"Nothing really seems to go the way you want it to, huh?"

The comment caught her off guard. She wouldn't have said *nothing* went the way she wanted it to. Sure, she ended up at the community college rather than Indiana University like she'd planned, but college was college. And, yeah, she'd seemed to hit every dead end there was to hit in her search for Julie, but she hadn't gone into it thinking it would be easy. She also hadn't thought it would be this hard. This *hopeless*.

He continued, "I used to play this game when I was little. I'd wake up in the morning, usually from my mom and dad fighting on the other side of the wall, and stay perfectly still until I could come up with ten reasons to get out of bed. It could be anything. Dumb stuff. Like knowing Mom would be working late enough that I could probably watch a rerun of *Teenage Mutant Ninja Turtles* before she got home and started yellin.'" He sniffed. "Once I got my ten reasons, I got out of bed and went through the day. Then I'd do it all over again the next day, and the next. Eventually ten reasons got to be too hard, so I made up new rules for the game. I only needed five reasons, or three." He wiped his nose with the back of his hand. He met her gaze, eyes glistening. "You ever do anything like that?"

Her first instinct was to lie. She'd never told anyone, not even Donny, about the little ways she tricked herself into getting through the day. Admitting that just existing was a chore seemed like a failure. But something about him made her want to tell. What was it he'd said? Her darkness speaking to his darkness? She could almost feel the vibrations of it in her chest, a thumping bass line.

Before she could respond, he nodded, like she didn't have to. He sighed. "I'm down to one reason. One fucking reason and you know what? I'm tired. And I know you're tired too."

He stood. The fatted darkness in her belly wriggled.

"How long before that one reason isn't enough?" he continued. "What then?"

"I don't know," Claire croaked.

He took another swig from the bottle. "I do." He went to the table next to his bed, blocking her view as he rummaged through a drawer. He turned and started toward her, one hand behind his back. "Remember when I said we match?"

She nodded, trying to look anywhere but in the direction of his hidden hand.

"I truly meant that. And I know you see it too. And the worst part is that you don't care. You don't even feel it because you're so numb to it all." He sat next to her and set the bottle down, and then took her hand, stroking it with his thumb. "Julie was your one thing, one reason to get out of bed, but now you have nothing, just like I have nothing."

Tears burned the corners of Claire's eyes. She didn't have nothing, did she? She had her family. School. But family and school were dim and gray in her mind.

Family meant existing in the solar system of her house, orbits moving toward but never crossing each other. She couldn't remember the last time her mother had said something of substance to her. And school? Well, it was school. She went, she took tests, but it never seemed to mean anything to her. The middle of her first semester, her dad had pulled her aside and said, "These are going to be the best years of your life." She'd cried herself to sleep after that.

"I have nothing," Claire said, barely a whisper.

Donny nodded. "Yes."

Tears streamed down her face. Her body seemed to weigh a thousand pounds. She sank inward, feeling only Donny's tightening grip on her arm.

"We're gonna fix it," he said. "Together."

Inside, the darkness writhed and twisted. It filled her, bloated her, made her mind hazy and her eyes droopy. She watched Donny turn her arm over so that the delicate skin of her inner forearm faced them. Her gaze narrowed on a smattering of freckles. For a second, they looked like they formed a star.

"We'll go together," Donny said, but his voice sounded far away.

Claire started to speak, but the darkness climbed up her throat, choking her vocal chords. If she opened her mouth, Donny would see it there, stroking her tongue. She felt the darkness clutch her lungs as she breathed, felt it cradling her heart with every beat.

Let go, it seemed to say. *Let us take you.*

If not for the blood, she might have given in.

It took too long for the image to pierce the haze in her mind. Dripping red, the flash of a knife. The haze cleared and she saw Donny clutching what looked like a small hunting knife, his head thrown back in a mix of pain and ecstasy. The skin on the arm that gripped hers was cut, and blood ran from his wrist onto her leg.

We'll go together.

A sharp pain pinched the back of her head.

He met her gaze and smiled, his eyes clouded and sleepy. "Your turn."

The darkness purred.

Like being in that place between sleep and awake, it took the knife's sharp tip pricking her skin to push Claire into motion. She ripped her arm out of his grip before he could cut any further, clutching her arm to her chest as she stood. Her heart hammered, the fog clearing, and she finally felt the sting from the small cut.

He inched forward on the bed and she flinched. "What are you doing?"

"You said—"

She shook her head. "No. No, I don't want this. I want to go home."

"Claire—"

The darkness bubbled in her belly. She tasted it, acidic, in the back of her throat. Already the fog was threatening to take over once again. She couldn't stay here. She couldn't look at him. At the blood.

She ran.

CHAPTER TWENTY-FIVE

ESTHER

NOW

For most of the drive, Esther didn't have a plan. Running on a cocktail of terror and indignation and adrenaline, she weaved through traffic, her mind drifting back to the note before she could rip it back. Her first instinct was to go back to Tara, to accost and accuse, but no doubt Donny had told her exactly who Esther was, so Esther likely wouldn't even get through the door. Her next thought was to go to Meg, but after Esther had abandoned her at that McDonald's she would be anything but sympathetic. Maybe Ryan had already spoken to her about the facility. Maybe he'd recruit Meg to convince Esther to check herself in. Fat chance of that.

She couldn't go to the police, either, not without implicating herself in impersonating a government official.

There was only one place she could think of where someone might actually listen.

She half expected to see Donny's truck in the human services parking lot but was greatly relieved to see it almost empty. Still, she parked a ways down, closer to a cluster of doctors' offices in the same office park, just in case.

Inside, the waiting room was very beige, with carpet that seemed to blend into the walls, except where Kool-Aid stains spotted the floor. In the corner was a plastic children's table and chairs, the top covered in crayon marks. Behind it was a bin filled with colorful toys and a shelf of Little Golden books. A small television above it played *Blue's Clues* with the sound off.

"Can I help you?" The woman at the reception desk waved from behind a thick pane of glass. As Esther approached, her smile brightened. "Do you have an appointment with your worker?"

"No, actually."

The woman's smile wavered.

"My name's Esther. My sister was Claire Finch. I was hoping to speak with her supervisor, or someone who worked with her."

The tension fell out of the woman's shoulders. "Oh, God. Yeah, I heard, obviously. I'm so sorry for your loss."

"Thanks."

"Can I ask what you need to speak to her supervisor about?" She smiled apologetically.

Esther matched her smile, tooth for tooth. "I'd prefer it to be private, if that's okay."

The woman raised her eyebrow as she nodded. "Of course. I'll see if she's available."

She slid a cover over the speaker hole before picking up the phone. Esther studied the woman's face for clues as to what she was saying, but the woman had mostly turned away. A habit, Esther supposed, from dealing with parents like Donny. Finally, she set the phone down and slid back the cover. "Go ahead and take a seat. Sarah will be out in a few."

Esther thanked her and sat, brain whirring. Part of her thought what she was planning to do was drastic and, maybe, wrong. But what other choice did she have? Donny had threatened her, and while the police and her husband might not have believed her, there was a chance this Sarah person would, especially if she knew Donny's background. Esther had to hope it would be enough to get someone looking in his direction. And even if it didn't directly result in his arrest, maybe it would bring out his guilt, *his darkness* as Tara called it, and he would confess. To everything.

"Esther?"

A woman poked her head out of the doorway beside the reception window. Sarah, presumably. Her smile was wide, but her eyes were cautious behind thin-framed glasses. She looked younger than Esther had anticipated, in a rainbow-patterned cardigan and black jeans.

Esther stood. "That's me." She held out her hand to shake, but Sarah had crossed the room in two large steps, arms open, and was embracing Esther before she could stop it.

"I am so sorry about Claire," Sarah said into Esther's shoulder. "She was a real sweetheart. The kids loved her."

"Truly," Esther said, extricating herself. "Thanks."

"Katelynn said you had something you needed to talk to me about?"

Esther shot a glance at the reception window, where the woman—Katelynn—watched unabashedly. "I do."

"Okay, no problem. Let's head back to my office."

Sarah led her through the door, past a tall counter that corralled reception and a small kitchenette. "Water? Coffee?"

Esther shook her head.

"You sure?" Then, "I'm right around the corner here."

Sarah's office door hung open, decorated in childish drawings of people and houses and trees. A printed sign at the center read: *All Are Welcome Here.* Inside the office was more of the same, scribble-slashed coloring pages and construction paper chains clung to every available surface. A table in the corner displayed an impressive collection of tiny succulents in a rainbow of colors.

Instead of sitting behind her desk, Sarah sat in one of the two chairs on the opposite side, and then gestured for Esther to take the other. Esther hesitated, wishing for the barrier of the desk between them. Without it, she felt vulnerable. That, she decided, was probably the point.

"You know," Sarah said, "I'm actually really glad you're here. Claire used to talk about you all the time, so it's a real pleasure to meet you."

Esther was taken aback. "Really?"

Sarah nodded. "Your other sister too. Meg, I think? And your husband and Brandon, of course. Real cute kid. How old is he now?"

"Twelve."

"Oof. Tough age. Doing well, though?"

"Yes. He's doing great. We're all doing really great."

Sarah's smile didn't budge, almost like it was painted on. "That's good to hear."

A moment of heavy silence passed. Esther tried not to fidget, but the longer Sarah quietly smiled at her, the more uncomfortable she became. She thought of Tara being dragged in here over and over again just to be told her family would have to split up, that her life was being upended again. As bristly as Tara was, Esther felt kind of bad for her. For what Esther was about to do.

"So," Sarah said, finally breaking the silence. "You had something you wanted to talk to me about?"

Esther nodded as she tried to gather her thoughts. How much should she tell Sarah? "It's about Donny Lippman. I think he was one of Claire's—" Clients? Subjects?

Sarah raised an eyebrow, but her expression otherwise remained maddeningly neutral. "Oh. Do you know him?"

"Yes. I mean, no, not really. We...hung out once or twice when we were kids."

"Mm. Yes, I think I remember Claire mentioning that." Then, "Forgive me, but how do you know about Donny as it pertains to this department? Our cases are confidential, as I'm sure you understand."

"Right. Obviously. Claire never mentioned anything to us. But we saw a few notes in her datebook, the one your office sent to Meg? We saw his name. Blacklick is a small town, so there were already rumors, I guess. We put two and two together."

"We?"

"Me and Meg."

"I see."

The conversation was already getting away from Esther. "It's none of my business, obviously. And I don't want to be a bother, but Claire was my sister, and I know she cared very deeply about her work, so when I learned... I couldn't just let it go. Plus, I'm a mother. You understand."

"When you learned...what exactly?"

Sarah hadn't pulled out a notebook or pulled up Donny's file as they spoke. She looked almost passive, distracted. Her mind on other, more important cases. Maybe this was a bad idea. But Esther was already ankle-deep in it. Nothing to do but wade through.

"I have reason to believe—" God, she sounded like some daytime cop drama. "—that Donny is living back at home. With his kids." When Sarah didn't react, she added, "Whom he is suspected of abusing."

For the first time, Sarah's expression seemed to crack, her smile less welcoming, more placating. "I see."

Esther should have left it at that, but the silence that followed those two words was like ants crawling up her legs. "As I said, none of my business, but I loved my sister very much and being here, telling you what I know, feels like a way to connect to her. I think it's what she would have wanted."

Sarah nodded and stood. The painted-on smile was back. "Yes, well, I do appreciate you coming in. Like most government arms we are stretched thin, so knowing there are others out there with the best interest of the children of the community at heart definitely helps."

She offered her hand, but Esther only stared at it. "That's it?"

"I'm sorry?"

"I just told you that a dangerous man is back living with his children despite a direct order not to, and you look…bored."

"I assure you, all tips given to human services are taken seriously. We will follow up if and when we decide it is necessary."

"If." Esther scowled, struggling to keep the frustration, the fear, out of her voice. "Someone is going to get hurt, maybe die."

Someone already has, she wanted to add.

"As I said," Sarah said, "I very much appreciate you coming in. If you have any other information to share, please feel free to come back."

Esther stood, shaking Sarah's hand limply. "Sure. Thanks."

Sarah followed Esther back toward the reception area, and she couldn't help but feel like she was being escorted out. Just another busybody with too much time on her hands.

They weren't going to do anything. *No one* was going to do anything. Esther had failed.

"Listen." Sarah paused just before the reception desk and lowered her voice. "I get it. It's hard to find closure with these types of things, but I can promise you you're not going to find it this way."

"Right," Esther said. "Thanks."

"I mean it." Sarah crossed her arms, gaze flicking up toward the reception desk where Samantha was on the phone, fingers flying over her keyboard. "I really shouldn't be telling you this, but it sounds like you might need to hear it."

Esther stiffened. "Okay."

"Claire was struggling. Had been for quite a while. Running late or missing appointments with families altogether. She missed a court appearance about two weeks ago, which forced a continuance that meant someone who should very much have been in jail was not. He went back to the house where his children were still recovering from his last fit of rage. There was a standoff with police, which ended…poorly."

Esther felt her body go cold. "But the children were okay, right?"

Sarah shook her head. "Look, I'm not saying Claire died because of this. But I am saying that she was carrying more than any of us could have realized. She cared about you, and it's clear you care very much about her, but the best thing to do, I think, is to remember her however you can while the world continues to spin around you. You'll catch up eventually."

———————

A line of cars blocked most of the entrance to the cemetery. On a hill to the right, a sea of black. Esther eased her car past the line, looking for an empty lane to turn off. But she was only half paying attention and didn't see the woman trying to cross in front of her until the last second. She slammed on her brakes, heart in her throat. The woman continued across the road, head bent, as though she hadn't noticed Esther coming at all. Or had hoped Esther wouldn't be so quick on the brake pedal. As she waited for the woman to reach the other side, she glanced up at the funeral on the hill. She hoped whoever they were mourning had died in an *absolute* way. Illness or an accident. Something conclusive. Something boring.

Claire's supervisor had seen straight through Esther. She wondered if Officer Kingsolver had spoken to her after Esther had her fit at the police station. She wouldn't have been surprised. Now she couldn't stop thinking about what Sarah had said, couldn't stop envisioning Claire, bereft after hearing about what her inaction had caused, deciding that it was all just too much…

She continued down the narrow, winding road until she spotted the large oak tree that marked where Claire had been buried.

The walk from the car to Claire's grave was cold, the wind too biting for autumn. She thought about going back to her car to grab a sweater out of the back seat, but, if she went back now, there was nothing to stop her from just getting in the car and leaving. So she walked on, arms wrapped tightly around her middle and head dipped low against the wind.

What would you do if you knew something? Something that could hurt people?

As Esther approached the small headstone, Claire Elizabeth Finch, Beloved Daughter, their last ever conversation swirled through her mind, a tempest of words and regret.

It was odd for Claire to call, let alone to call first thing in the morning. That should have been Esther's first clue. Instead, she'd been distracted by granola bars and turkey sandwiches, by Brandon's aimless search for his school ID, by a coffee maker that decided to shut off mid-pour, by Ryan, who couldn't seem to get through a morning without turning her kitchen inside out.

"Sorry—" Esther had mashed her finger down on the brew button, phone pinned between her ear and shoulder. "—who's hurting people?"

"No," Claire said, exasperated, "just—pretend you know something—"

"Har har."

"—and it's a big, big something. And if you told people about it, it would hurt them. Do you tell?"

"No," Esther said. "Definitely not."

"But if you don't, it might be worse."

Esther had glimpsed her husband, then, blowing a kiss from the front door. She said, half-jokingly, "Ryan's not cheating on me, is he?"

"It's not about Ryan."

"Is it about Meg? Did something happen?"

"Meg's fine. I think."

"Okay." Esther poured the dregs of the coffeepot into a mug, frowning at the grounds floating on top. As she struggled to fish them out with a spoon, she said, "You're a grown up. Just use your best judgment."

Claire's voice hitched. "I need help, Es. I don't know what to do."

Esther had sighed, already thinking about her morning meetings and the overflow of emails she'd been ignoring since the day before. She just needed to get a handle on her day, then she could be useful. She loved her sister, but maybe she babied her too much. For someone who dealt with people in crisis all day, Claire was exceptionally bad at dealing with her own. Solving her problems for her wouldn't help.

"Listen," Esther said as she booted up her computer. "I've got a chaotic morning. I think you should take some time, think on the issue, and then call me tonight and we can talk about it more, okay? And, hey, you might not even need to! I bet you'll figure it out. You're smart like that."

Claire was silent for a long moment. At first, Esther thought she'd hung up. Then, Claire said, barely above a whisper, "Sure."

Claire never did call back.

Now, as Esther stood just to the side of her sister's grave, unable to set foot on the ground just above where Claire was buried, she realized how colossally she'd failed. As a human and as a sister.

I need help, Es.

It wasn't like Esther didn't know Claire had issues. She'd seen the scars and heard the clatter each time she banged on the bathroom door, the breathless fear of getting caught with the razor blade again. But Esther always wrote it off as just something teenagers did. Even Esther had, once, taken one of Mom's good kitchen knives to the basement, a rare afternoon when no one was home, and slid the knife along the inside of her forearm. It was a small cut—a scratch, really, that hadn't even broken the skin—but Esther had expected to feel something from it. Some cosmic understanding of her anger and fear, but all she felt was a sting. She'd never done it again.

But none of that mattered because *Claire hadn't killed herself.* It was Donny who had taken Claire away from Esther. She had to believe that, because if she didn't, if she was *wrong*…

She curled in on herself, no longer feeling the cold, but an all-consuming numbness. She sank down onto her knees and leaned forward, her head resting on the cool, rough headstone.

Even if human services visited Tara and Donny's house, all they would find was a pissed-off Tara and a few photographs on the wall. They would dismiss Esther as nosy and dramatic, and nothing would change. Everyone—the police, human services, even her own family—seemed to have put Claire's death firmly in the past. If there was anything Esther could have done, it seemed to be too late.

She always seemed to be a breath too late.

Next to Claire's headstone was a marker you couldn't see unless you were looking for it, the grass overgrown and creeping across the bronze, slowly dragging it down. Only the *-lie* and *Fi-* were visible through the creepers.

They hadn't had a ceremony for Julie. Too painful. Too final. The marker was a formality, ignored, and then forgotten. It was easier to just pretend Julie had never existed.

Over the years, Esther had convinced herself it wouldn't have made a difference whether she'd told Mom and Dad what she'd seen, even after days of recording herself on her tape recorder snoring peacefully all night, every night. Esther didn't sleepwalk. Never had. Because what had she seen, really? Meg and some girl. A girlfriend, maybe, though Esther had never asked. Meg hadn't come out yet and would have been sneaking around still, so it made sense. The figure in the yard had probably been a neighbor looking for his dog. They were always running off and digging in the gladiolas on the Finch property. So she'd kept quiet.

Now, though, Esther started to wonder if that had been a mistake.

Two sisters, gone because Esther kept quiet. Because she didn't want to *look*. Because she was too worried about herself, about everyone looking at her and only seeing the behavior—the paranoia and the routines—and never *her*.

She glanced down at Claire's grave, at the loose dirt and roots, and without thinking, plunged her hands into the mound. The heady scent drifted upward, the soil cool and grainy between her fingers. She scraped her nails along pebbles until it hurt, and then chewed the inside of her cheek because it didn't hurt enough.

What she would give to go back in time, to that phone call on a busy morning.

"Say something," Esther whispered through clenched teeth, the thing she should have said that day. "I don't care if it kills them to hear it, say something and for God's sake, save yourself. Please."

Tears blurred as she burrowed deeper into the loose dirt, a sob caught painfully in her chest. Up to her elbows now, the soil was colder than the air and bit sharply at her skin. She could feel her nails bending back with the force of her digging, but it was like something primal, wordless, had bubbled up from her belly and invaded her limbs, so she dug and dug until, finally, her fingers brushed something soft. She froze, bent forward at an awkward angle. A twitch at the tip of her fingers sent shivers up her arms.

Worms, she thought, as the twitch became a writhe that moved slowly up her fingers and the backs of her hands. But when she tried to pull her arms out of the dirt, the writhing stilled and something gripped her wrists. Panic seized and she yanked back. Something popped in her shoulder, but the grip held, icy and sharp, and moved, spiderlike, up her arms. She watched, unable to breathe, as the ground just beneath her face pulsed with movement. A scream died in her throat. The earth shifted, the grip up to her elbows now and pulling, and as they broke the surface of the grave, Esther felt the world tilt, teetering on the edge of consciousness.

The fingers, deformed and streaked with mud, clung to her skin like knives. Blood wept from scratches along her wrists, pooling around the hand that held her. It wasn't until she noticed the ring—a cheap, bubblegum machine turquoise that Brandon had given to Claire when he was little—that Esther finally screamed.

It couldn't be.

But there was the ruffled edge of the ugly blouse their mother had picked out.

And there was the scar on the side of her hand from when Claire tried to jump a wobbly ramp on her bike.

Esther tried to contort her body to get her legs beneath her, but the grip on her arms was too tight, her chest too close to the ground. Her breath came in short, hot bursts as she fought to free herself. And then the ground seemed to split. Dirt caved in at the crack as it grew wider. Worms and fat, black flies wriggled loose from the soil. A line of small, brown roaches crept up Esther's arm, stealing her breath. Then different movement at the base of the crack snatched her attention. Dirt fell away to reveal a pair of lips, pale and cracked, the teeth behind them black and rotted. Whispery breath like wind through a dead tree drifted upward, and pulled by the sound, Esther leaned closer to it.

"I need your help, Es."

A guttural noise escaped Esther's lips as the dirt continued to fall away, revealing more and more of Claire's face, eaten by bugs and rot, until finally Esther couldn't stand it. Her body trembled and her stomach heaved and all she could do was scream and scream.

Behind her, harried voices invaded the fog around her head. Someone grabbed her shoulders, and she stiffened like she'd been shocked.

"Should we call an ambulance?"

"Don't be dramatic, Lisa."

"I'm the dramatic one?"

Like flies in her ears, the voices flitted in and out, but it didn't matter because all she could see was Claire's face, her cloudy eyes, a tear in her nostril that wept black.

"Hush now, hun. I know. I know."

Slowly the owner of the coddling voice eased Esther back onto her heels. Though her eyes told her Claire still had a grip on her arms, as she leaned back, she felt the grip fall away. She gasped, her breath restored, and when she looked down at the grave, the dirt was disturbed, but the crack—and Claire—were gone.

CHAPTER TWENTY-SIX

CLAIRE

OCTOBER 2012

Claire didn't hate working as a server. It took up the time in the evening when she would otherwise be at home, alone in her room, dwelling, and there was a certain satisfaction that came with leaving work with money in her pocket that other jobs couldn't give her. She made enough to cover what scholarships didn't pay for at the community college, and on good nights, she slipped a little cash into her parents' clothes pockets for them to discover later.

After a while, she developed a routine. School, work, home, repeat. It was nice. Even when she couldn't sleep because of the way the darkness plucked at her muscles and filled her lungs, when she looked too hard at the knives in the block on the counter, she could count on her routine to get her through.

Until today.

It had been slow for a Friday. A couple of tables on top of her regulars. She didn't make much, but it was nice to have a low-key night every once in a while. She'd closed out her tabs and had started on her side work by nine o'clock. She was refilling tubs of blue cheese dressing when the bartender, an older woman named Josie, tapped her on the shoulder.

"Some guy at the bar is asking for you," she said.

Claire's first instinct was that it was her dad, who would only have come to her work if there was something wrong. She abandoned the dressing and followed the bartender to the front. There was only one person at the bar.

Donny.

He spotted her and grinned beneath at least three days' worth of patchy beard. "Claire. Hi."

She froze, hand instinctively covering the place on her arm where he'd pressed the tip of a knife only weeks ago.

He patted the stool next to him. "Come. Sit."

"I'm working," she said.

"After, then." He nudged his empty beer bottle forward. "Me and Josie'll just keep each other company for a bit."

Claire waited for Josie to catch her eye, to understand the panic on her face, but either Josie hadn't noticed or didn't care. It was Claire's own fault. She didn't exactly alienate the girls at work, but she hadn't made it a point to get close to any of them either. No drinks after her shift. No inside jokes about the regulars. School. Work. Home. Repeat.

"Take your time," Donny said, pulling her attention back to him. "I'll be right here."

Back at the walk-in, Claire dragged her feet, wasting time. She thought about taking off through the back door, but she remembered the only access point to the street was blocked by the dumpster, the rest closed off by a tall, concrete wall.

Once her side work was done and she was cashed out, she paused in front of the back door. *Fuck it*, she thought, and went out into the dark.

She'd been right, of course. In the glow of the streetlight just outside the concrete wall, she could see the dumpster taking up the whole of the only gap in the wall. She thought about climbing—her work sneakers were nonslip, after all—but the dumpster was full and the idea of climbing through a week's worth of old food made her head spin.

If she were Meg, she would have marched right back into the dining room and made enough of a scene for him to leave. If she were Esther, she would have called the police, or her dad, or someone to handle it on her behalf. But Claire wasn't her sisters. She hadn't been smart enough or determined enough to get out of Blacklick the second she turned eighteen.

She was trapped.

Just go inside, she thought. *Call Meg. Call Dad. Call anyone.*

As she started back toward the door, she spotted a small gap between the side of the dumpster and the wall. The last time it had been slid back, someone had shoved it off-center. It wasn't much room, but Claire was small-ish. If she sucked in her belly and didn't think too hard about it, she might make it.

She jogged toward the dumpster and then held her breath as she squeezed inch by inch through the gap. The wall scraped painfully at the backs of her arms and her apron got caught on a metal piece jutting out of the dumpster, but just as the panic started to set in, she thrust through to the other side.

She'd have to circle the building to get to her car, which meant walking by the windows of the restaurant, but if Donny was still at the bar, it was unlikely he'd see her. Still, she jogged the whole way only to stop a few feet short, heart hammering.

Donny leaned on the hood of her car, phone in hand. He must have heard her curse under her breath, because he looked up and grinned in that knowing way.

"Finished?" he asked.

She clutched her folded apron and server book to her chest. "You need to leave."

"I will. But not before I say what I came to say."

She should have confronted him in the restaurant, with other people around. Out here, the parking lot was nearly empty, and the streetlights didn't do much to make her feel any safer. He'd tried to kill her. What could he possibly have to say to her?

She fumbled her phone out of her bag, held it up so he could see. "You have about ten seconds to get off my car before I call the cops."

"C'mon, Claire Bear. Don't be like that."

She started to dial.

"Okay! Okay. Just—hang on a sec. Let me apologize. Please."

"Five seconds."

"Christ." He rubbed his face. "Right. Okay. So I'm sorry. Obviously. And I know that doesn't cut it. I know that, all right? I'm not really a words kind of person. I just—" He closed his eyes. Took a breath. "I know you know what it feels like when it gets you. It just wraps itself around your throat and your lungs and squeezes."

Her breath caught and she coughed. *Don't*, she willed the darkness. *Don't*.

"But I'm getting help," he continued. "I'm figuring it out."

"Good for you."

"I'm serious!"

"Two seconds."

"Can't you forgive me? Please?"

She didn't want to. She shouldn't. "Will it get you off my car and away from my job?"

He nodded.

"Fine. Forgiven. Now leave."

For a brief second, she thought he might challenge her. She could only keep herself from trembling for so long, could only hold up this shallow veneer of confidence another moment or two. Finally, thankfully, he shoved off the hood and backed onto a mulch-covered median. Still too close. But she didn't have a choice. She marched to the car, breath coming in short, shallow bursts, and climbed into the car feeling his eyes on the back of her neck.

As she drove away, she refused to look in the rearview mirror, knowing she'd see him standing there, watching.

Several days passed in which Claire walked into work expecting to see Donny waiting at the bar, but he was, thankfully, never there. By the next weekend, she almost had herself convinced she could fall back into her routine. School, work, home, repeat. But seeing Donny had stirred something inside her, something she thought she had shoved down deep enough that it couldn't wriggle its way out. As time went on and her focus drifted away from school and work, she began to realize what burying her head in her routine and forgetting about Julie had done.

The darkness inside her sisters and parents had been allowed to fester, to spread its tendrils through their veins, braiding itself around their muscles and burrowing deep in their bones. Meg came over one afternoon to have Dad look at her car and Claire saw the spidery reach of the darkness in the corners of Meg's eyes. And all because Claire had infected them with it. She brought the darkness into their house and then fed it by opening the box of Julie's things.

Her limbs grew heavier, her mind hazier. She opened her eyes every morning disappointed at having woken up at all. But the routine had saved her once. Maybe it would save her again. School, work, home, repeat.

Except her body seemed to have forgotten all concept of time. At night she lay awake, staring at the ceiling, trying to ignore the finger-like shadows creeping over her neck. Mornings, she relied on the threat of academic dismissal if she missed too many classes to pry her out of bed. She took pills to sleep and drank enough coffee to cause an ulcer to wake up and for a while, she functioned.

Tonight, though, the pills weren't working. As the darkness whispered to take

THROUGH THE MIDNIGHT DOOR   283

more, to take the whole bottle, she lay stone still, humming to herself to drown out the sound. *This is it*, the darkness cooed. *This is the end.*

She shook her head. Bunched the blanket in her fists. It was so fucking cold in here, but she was sweating. She closed her eyes. Tried not to think about exactly how many pills were left in the bottle, to wonder if it was enough. She threw off the blankets and stood, heart beating so hard she could feel it in her throat and behind her eyes. She would get rid of the pills, then she could sleep.

You need the pills to sleep.

Fuck the pills.

She pulled the bottle out of her drawer and decided she would flush them down the toilet. She hesitated at her bedroom door, spinning the bottle in her hand. What if Mom or Dad heard her? What if they came to check on her and saw what she was doing? What would they think?

The window. She would toss the bottle out the window and hope she wouldn't be able to find it again in the morning.

She made a beeline for the window, threw open the curtains, and screamed.

A shadow lurked below in the yard, and when it spotted her, it ran toward the house. Frozen, Claire's gaze darted to the lock, grateful that some of Esther's quirks had rubbed off on her. But then the shadow moved into the light and fear turned to surprise, and then frustration.

Donny waved from beneath the glow of the security light.

Trembling from the burst of adrenaline, she opened the window. Before he could say a word, she hissed, "Leave me alone."

"Wait. Please." He stood on tiptoe, his voice barely audible. "Are you okay?"

"I'm fine."

"Because I got this feeling, so I came over to check."

"In the middle of the night?"

He shrugged. Smiled.

"Go home, Donny."

"What's that?"

She hadn't realized the pill bottle was in the same hand that'd pushed the window open. She threw it back to her bed. "None of your business."

"Look, I know you're mad at me, but I'm worried about you. Can you please come down? So we can talk?"

Her first reaction was to tell him to fuck off, but once she'd done that, what did the rest of her night look like? Staring at the ceiling and hoping she had the willpower to ignore the pills screaming at her from her bed? He'd said he was getting help. Maybe it was working. Maybe she could get help too.

"Okay," she said. "One minute."

She quickly dressed and slipped on a pair of sneakers, and then crept downstairs and out into the front yard where she found Donny standing next to a car parked on the street.

"Are we going somewhere?" she asked.

"Only if you want. I figured we could just sit."

She imagined her dad waking up to use the bathroom, seeing the security light on and coming out to check. "No. We can go."

He smiled. "Good."

She didn't pay attention while he drove. She rested her head against the cool window, eyes closed, listening to the gentle hum of the tires on the road. She didn't open her eyes until the car stopped and he shut off the engine. When she realized where they were, she chewed the inside of her cheek to keep from crying.

They were parked in front of the house where the darkness came from.

"Take me home," she said. "Take me home now."

"Give me ten minutes and if you want to throttle me, I won't stop you. But I bet by the end of it, you'll thank me."

"Why would I ever thank you for bringing me here? This is where—" She bit off the last of her thought. "I can't."

"Remember how I told you I was getting help?" He nodded at the house. "It's here. I swear." Then, "I'll show you."

Somehow the house looked less menacing at night. It looked like it belonged among the dark and the shadows and the eerie silence, like it was sleeping. But anything that was asleep could be woken up.

Donny took the keys out of the ignition, got out and rounded the car where he opened Claire's door and offered his hand. "I'm begging you, Claire. Let me help you."

"Why?"

"Because you're like me. I saw it that first day we met. You're more than other people. You just need to see it for yourself."

His words meant nothing, but she couldn't keep denying that no one looked at her the way he did, like he could see through to her deepest, hidden part. No one else bothered.

She took his hand and let him lead her into the house.

It was exactly as she remembered, down to the patterns of dust on the handrail leading up to the hall of doors. The place was like a mausoleum, the ancient furniture like crypts, and the molding fixtures like totems, guides into the afterlife. Dust swirled around her legs, stroking and caressing, and the walls seemed to shudder with her careful touch, as though breathed into life by her presence.

"She likes you," Donny said.

Was he talking to Claire, or the house?

They paused at the top of the stairs, where the hall of doors was just visible in the moonlight shining through a cracked window. Donny squeezed her hand.

"Do you remember which one is yours?" he asked.

"This is ridiculous," Claire said, voice barely above a whisper. "It's just an old house."

"I remember," he said, ignoring her. He pulled her toward the hall, pausing in front of a dark, wooden door that looked smaller than she remembered.

She started to argue that she couldn't go in, not because she was scared (and she was), but because she didn't have the key. Except the moment she opened her mouth, she felt something sharp scrape along her throat. She gagged, tasting bile and metal, and braced herself on the wall as Donny rubbed her back. Something hard scraped across her tongue and then fell out of her mouth onto the floor with a heavy clink.

The key.

She shook her head, trying to back away, wiping spit from her mouth. But Donny still held her hand and kept her pinned to the spot as he picked up the key.

He held it out to her. "Trust me."

But Claire refused to take it. She didn't trust him. She didn't trust anyone. The only solid, steadfast thing in her life had always been the darkness, and it was waiting for her on the other side of a flimsy bit of wood. She pulled back, fighting against his grip, but he was stronger. He looped his arm around her neck and kissed her cheek as he dragged her by the throat toward the door.

"It's okay," he cooed as she fought, as she choked. "You'll see."

She scratched at his arms, drawing blood, but he didn't seem to feel it. Every time she managed to get her feet beneath her he tightened his arm around her throat and pulled, knocking her off balance.

It didn't make sense that he was this strong, that she was so weak after months of carrying trays full of heavy plates and glasses at the restaurant. It was like there was something about being here, about the house that changed him. Changed her.

He pinned her against the wall as he opened the door, and then shoved her inside, locking it behind her.

The dark was crushing. She gasped for air, drowning in it, as she crawled back toward what she hoped was the door. Too weak to stand, she banged her fist on the door, begging to be let out.

The darkness slithered through her body, making her head spin. Inky black shadows twisted in the corners of her eyes, so she squeezed them shut, but somehow, she could still see them, like the room lived inside her head. Back against the door, she pulled her knees up to her chest as the shadows peeled away from the wall.

Don't touch it. Mustn't touch it.

The shadow's long, spidery limbs prodded the spaces between the wood slats in the floor, testing, until finally it emerged solid as smoke from the wall. A scream died in Claire's throat.

"Do you see?"

Donny's voice came from everywhere and nowhere. Claire clawed at the door, barely feeling the pain as a shard of wood lodged beneath her nail.

Soon the creaking sound of the shadow creature's movements was drowned out by a mournful whimper. At first, Claire thought it was her own, but she held her breath and the sound carried, fearful and heavy. The shadow bent over a shape slowly coming into focus at the other end of the room.

It can't be, she thought.

She started to crawl forward, but the moment the shadow creature noticed, it pinned her back to the door, its sharp limb digging painfully into her shoulder. Two more limbs like pincers grew out of its back, and she followed its hollow-eyed gaze to the space just ahead where a second figure appeared, legs splayed, head hanging.

She didn't have to see their faces to know who they were.

It was Meg lying still against the wall. It was Esther drooped over in a pool of sticky black liquid.

Claire's stomach rolled. "They're dead." Her whole body began to tremble, then her muscles locked, strangled by the darkness. "They're dead!"

The shadow creature leaned down close to Meg, like it was smelling her. Like it was going to devour her.

As the darkness inside her squeezed tighter, Claire realized that it was a piece of this shadow creature that lived inside her. It was darkness. It was sadness. It was loss. She'd brought it home and let it infect her sisters and it was killing them right in front of her.

Donny's voice came through the door. "You can change it."

"I can't," Claire whimpered.

"Don't you feel her? Don't you feel her love?"

The darkness wrapped around her heart and the pain was extraordinary. Was this love?

A third figure emerged from the shadows, and Claire immediately recognized herself despite the bubbling skin and too-wide eyes. The shadow creature turned its attention away from Meg and toward the Claire figure. It licked the false-her's cheek and Claire felt it, rough and stingy.

"Tell her what you want," Donny said. "Show her."

"I can't."

"You can."

How could she, when she couldn't breathe, couldn't think, couldn't move? When the thing she wanted was impossible?

"Tell her," Donny urged.

Claire opened her mouth and no words came out, only a strangled sigh. She closed her eyes and wished for the end. For the beginning. For everything at once. She saw the darkness hovering like a storm cloud over her family's house, grown from their collective grief on the night Julie died. She saw them all breathing it, saw it stick to their lungs and throats. Maybe she hadn't been the first to bring the darkness to their home, but she had shaken it awake. Made it remember. Made it hungry.

I want to go back, she thought.

The shadow creature twitched.

I want to go back and rip that night out of time. I want all the days that should have come after. I want to look at Meg and Esther and see them whole, cracks filled and the light back behind their eyes. I want the life I was supposed to have. I want my heart back. My lungs. My body.

As her thoughts spun wild in her mind, the scene before her changed. Slowly at first, then all at once the darkness split, falling away like torn fabric to reveal a different room in a different house she almost didn't recognize. Meg and Esther sat across from each other, alive, light warming their faces. In their laps were two girls, mirror images of each other, no more than two or three years old. Meg and Esther helped them roll a shiny red ball back and forth, each of the smaller girls giggling each time the ball tapped their bare feet.

"Kick the ball, Claire!" Meg said. "Kick!"

Esther nuzzled into the neck of the other girl. "Julie, Julie bo-boolie, banana fana fo fulie," she sang, then tickled her belly until Julie squealed.

Yes, she thought. *This is right. This is what was meant to be.*

This is what is, a voice whispered.

Yes, Claire thought. *This is what is.*

If she stayed perfectly still, Claire almost couldn't feel the shadow creature's limb in her shoulder. She almost couldn't feel anything.

CHAPTER TWENTY-SEVEN

MEG

NOW

Police report in hand, Meg felt like she was on the cusp of...something. Like taking the first step toward the ledge, anxious to see what lay below. She hoped Officer Kingsolver would be able to find out who had filed the paperwork with the historical society, knowing—*hoping*—that somehow it would make everything clear.

She didn't even leave the parking lot before opening the police report. Seeing the words "apparent suicide" dashed off the way someone would write *milk* on a grocery list was jarring enough that she didn't know if she even wanted to continue. But she pressed on, somehow imagining she was somewhere else, some*one* else, reading the rest of the report like it'd happened to someone she didn't know.

She skimmed the parts that described the state of Claire's body, swallowing against the nausea, and focused on the parts that described the state of the room. It was short, barely a few lines, with a list of items the reporting officer concluded were out of place: small toolbox, trash bin (empty), stool, gas can (full).

Stool? Gas can?

She paged through the report looking for more, but gasped when she was met with photos. Close-ups of Claire's face and neck, of her hands limp at her sides. Meg threw the folder onto the passenger seat and braced herself on the wheel, waiting for the world to stop spinning. She chased away the disturbing images by focusing on the stool and the gas can.

Why would Claire stand on the toolbox when there was already a stool in the room? But she pushed the suspicion away as quickly as it had come. The stool was rickety or broken or in her distress she hadn't even seen it. All plausible.

But the gas can?

Again, maybe it was already there. Some kids planning a little Friday-night arson. But why leave it there before doing the deed? Had Claire disturbed them somehow? Wouldn't they have just chased her away? Or maybe it wasn't kids at all. Maybe the reporting officer only thought there was gas in it—maybe it was water, or piss. They'd found worse when they were kids and abandoned houses were their playgrounds.

It could have meant nothing or everything, but she wouldn't be able to figure it out on her own.

She needed Esther.

Meg was relieved to see Esther's car in the driveway. Esther still wasn't returning her calls or texts, so ambushing Esther at her house was the only way Meg figured she'd be able to get her to listen. Police report tucked protectively in her bag, she went to the door and knocked. For a long time, no one answered. She tried the doorbell, smashing it repeatedly until finally the door opened.

Meg's breath caught.

Esther stood on the threshold, her face a worrying shade of gray. Claire—or the thing masquerading as Claire—clung to her middle, arms with flaking skin wrapped tight around Esther's belly. Claire's chin rested on Esther's shoulder and glared at Meg with cloudy eyes. When she smiled, her mouth looked painted black.

Meg tried to ignore Claire, focusing on Esther's eyes, which seemed to go in and out of focus. "Are you okay?"

Esther made a noncommittal noise as she began to lean on the door frame. The clink of glass pulled Meg's attention down. An empty wineglass hung precariously in Esther's hand.

She was drunk.

Biting back a shiver, Meg gently pressed Esther's shoulders, pushing her into the house. "Come on. Let's get some coffee in you."

Esther grumbled and turned, sliding out of Claire's grasp. But Claire's hand lingered near Esther's, their fingers tangling. Together, they went to the couch, where Esther sank into the cushion and Claire sprawled out, head resting on her lap. Esther began to stroke Claire's hair, but with the kind of absent motion that made Meg think Esther didn't even realize she was doing it. Claire purred and nuzzled, and as she burrowed her face into Esther's leg, Meg flinched at the crinkle of her papery skin.

In the kitchen, she found an empty wine bottle in the sink. A second opened bottle sat on the counter beside a smattering of bloodred droplets. A fruit fly hovered above the mouth. Meg dumped the wine and set both bottles in the sink to drain before attempting to clean the counter mess. Futile, of course. The wine had already saturated the butcher block.

She glanced into the living room to make sure Esther hadn't moved, then started on the coffee, all the while *feeling* Claire's presence. Part of her tried to rationalize it, mind churning up from deep recesses words like *shared hallucination*. Another part, a quieter, more shameful part, knew better. She thought of the night she woke up on the bathroom floor, hungover despite not knowing how or when she'd gotten drunk, thought of her dead sister being there to hold her, and how her touch seemed to stir something inside her. Something dark and ugly and hungry.

Claire only ever seemed to appear when Meg was at her lowest. Like Claire, or the thing inside her—inside them—was feeding on her guilt. Her shame. Her sadness.

She poured two cups of coffee, black, and brought them into the living room. Esther hadn't moved. Her hand still rested on Claire's head, fingers tangled in her hair. Meg sat the cup on the coffee table in front of Esther, a slow blink her only acknowledgment. Was this what Esther's darkness looked like? Complete dissociation? Her hair hung limp around her face, half-damp, and mascara was smudged around her eyes. It was jarring to see her this way, the opposite of put together. Esther started to reach for the coffee, but Claire nudged her arm a hair to the right, toward the empty wineglass. Esther picked it up and sipped the air, frowning.

"Es?" Meg asked, ignoring Claire's cloudy-eyed stare. "What happened? What's wrong?"

Esther blinked, and then looked at Meg, eyebrows furrowed, like she'd only just noticed her.

"Es."

Esther's shoulders dipped and her head fell back against the couch. "He's gonna lock me up." Her words slurred heavily. *He's gonnnnna lock me up.*

Meg stood and grabbed the wineglass from her, shivering when Claire's hand caressed her knee. She carefully handed Esther the coffee. "Drink."

Esther nodded, but didn't bring the mug to her lips.

"Who's going to lock you up?"

"Ryan." The name came out strangled. "He thinks I'm seeing things." Then, "Cause I probably am." Tears welled, and as they dripped, Claire fingered one off her cheek and stuck it in her mouth.

"No, he doesn't. Es, what *happened*?"

"I need another drink."

Meg shook her head. "No booze. Coffee. Talk."

When Esther finally looked up at her, Meg's insides ached at the despair she saw on her sister's face. "I did a dumb thing. A bad thing. And now they'll know and they'll tell and they'll lock me up and I'll never see Brandon again."

Meg's stomach churned, fearing the worst. "What thing?"

"Doesn't matter. I lied and they didn't believe me and it's all over." Esther dropped the wineglass, which thudded on the rug. "I just wanna go to sleep. Just sleep forever."

Claire's eyes brightened, and she stroked Esther's shoulder, which twitched under her touch. Esther seemed to notice Claire and her eyes went wide, then, like a curtain being shut, her expression glazed over and her head dipped.

"Here." She set her coffee on the table, then grabbed Esther's arms and pulled. "Come on. Stand. You can do it."

But Claire was like a mountain on top of her. "Leave her," Claire crooned.

Meg ignored her and pulled harder, putting all of her weight into lifting Esther off the couch. "I swear to God, Esther, if you don't get off this fucking couch right now…"

But Esther was oblivious, content to melt into the fabric of the couch under the weight of their dead sister. Both of them.

Meg was tempted to let her. To *join* her. How easy would it have been to bury the voice in her head telling her to dig, to prod, to worry that something was very, profoundly wrong, and sink beneath a comforting blanket of numbness? Too easy. Her dad had always told them that if they ended up in a car accident to go limp. *That's how the drunk drivers survive it.* Steeling yourself caused damage. But giving in? Give in and you just might walk away.

Esther always was the smarter one.

Meg dropped her arms and took a weak step back. Claire curled around Esther's middle, arms like creeping vines, as Esther's head dipped forward like a puppet with her strings cut. Meg felt a stab of jealousy, remembering how Julie had clung to her just yesterday. It had *hurt*, but even the hurt was better than nothing.

She left them and went into the kitchen where she looked for the half-empty bottle of wine she was sure was on the counter. Unable to find it, she opened another. She didn't bother with a glass. Instead, she tipped the bottle against her lips and drank greedily, the wine burning her throat. She had a lot of catching up to do. When she finally came up for air, her tongue grazed something caught in her teeth. She dug it out with her fingernail and when she examined the thing, her stomach lurched. It was a fruit fly.

Nausea surged through her and she ran for the bathroom, abandoning the bottle in the sink. She kneeled in front of the toilet and gagged into the bowl, a line of red saliva dripping from her mouth. She didn't puke, but she couldn't stop gagging, couldn't stop feeling the fly in her teeth. Her whole body ached, every muscle contracted. Her eyes watered and burned until finally she staggered to her feet. Leaning against the vanity, she scooped water from the sink into her mouth. She rinsed and rinsed, unable to swallow, until she could run her tongue along her teeth without gagging. Face and collar damp, she sank to the floor where she leaned her head against the wall.

She suddenly realized how dark it was in the bathroom and couldn't remember if she'd bothered to turn on the light on her way in. The glow from the living room lamp cut beneath the door in jagged shards of yellow, which Meg ran her fingers through, imagining she could feel the heat of it. The room started to spin and she leaned into it, rolling her head against the wall. *Go limp*, she thought, ignoring the cotton mouth, the cramp in her belly. *Give in.*

A soft knock on the door slowed the spin to a gentle roll. She eyed the gap beneath the door, but saw no shadowy feet. *Claire*, she thought almost smugly.

"I don't need you," Meg muttered. "I can sink all on my own." Julie may have been Meg's first albatross, but Claire clung just as tightly, just as heavily.

Knock, knock.

But thoughts of Claire also brought thoughts of the house. Of the million questions and the answers prodding her, sharp and biting but too quick to catch. She rubbed hard at her eyes, trying to force the image out of her head, but it only seemed to saturate the sharp lines of the house, only filled her head with flashes of memory, of moments begging to connect.

"No. Please."

At first, she thought the words came out of her mouth, but her tongue was all but stuck to the roof of her mouth, and her throat was dry and craggy. But then another sound, like a strangled mouse, broke through the fog. Meg stood on shaky legs and, leaning against the door, pressed her ear to it. All she heard were muffled sounds, footsteps and whimpers, but none of it sounded right. She held her breath and listened, barely able to hear over the sound of her own pounding heart. It was like she could feel the change on the other side of the door. Something was different. Something was wrong.

One hand braced against the door frame, she turned the knob with agonizing slowness, wincing at the almost inaudible creak of the mechanism. She eased the door open just enough to see through, but all she could see was the far side of the dining room and the kitchen. On the wall were two shadows.

"Please." Esther's voice. Strained, begging.

When the other voice spoke, it sent ripples of fear up Meg's arms. "Beggin' don't work. See, we tried that in the beginning, when they first came for my kids. You shoulda seen Tara on her knees just bawlin'. I never seen anybody as low as that. 'Til now, I guess."

Meg held her breath. It was Donny.

She inched her head out, trying to see into the living room where their voices came from, but a loud bang, like a fist on wood, pushed her back.

"This time it was almost worse," Donny continued. "They waited 'til it was my day for supervised visitation. Waited 'til Tara brought my kids to that sad little room with toys for babies, broken toys, and bullshit smiling suns all over the walls before they sprung it. They got a tip, they said, that me and Tara'd broken the habitation agreement, which meant they had the right to take our kids away. Again."

His voice was getting closer. Meg shut the door until there was only a crack to see through. It was just enough to see Esther inching backward into the dining room. To see Donny only a few feet away, gun dangling at his side.

Ice shot through her veins. Meg couldn't feel her body anymore, couldn't breathe. She blinked and it was like being transported back to that night, frozen in fear. She'd lost Julie that night. Would she lose Esther now too? Blinking back tears, she carefully patted her pockets looking for her phone, only to realize it was in her bag, all the way on the other side of the living room. Ryan should have been home now, she thought, but there wasn't a clock that she could see so she had no idea what time it was, or if Ryan had already been home and left Esther the way Meg had found her. Broken.

"I'll do anything," Esther said. Her gaze flicked to the gun and her expression caved. "I have a son."

"Oh, I know," Donny said. "Maybe I'll go see him instead. Then you can see how it feels."

The sound that came out of Esther was like a knife to Meg's guts. "No."

Donny chuckled. "See? That's the difference between you and me. I wouldn't involve your kids. That's cruel." He sniffed. "I just wish I knew why you felt like you needed to stick your nose in my business. I knew it was you right away, the second your name came out of Tara's mouth. As they were explainin' how the kids would be going to a temporary foster home and that we could send along clothes, Tara was just shakin' her head and sayin' how it was her fault. You believe that? She thought it was her fault. She said, 'This wouldn't have happened if I hadn't let that new caseworker in the house. I knew I shoulda told her to mind her fucking business.' Then the social services lady gave her a funny look 'cause, come to find out, there wasn't no new caseworker. Or there was, but she hadn't gotten around to a home visit yet. Tara told us the woman's name was Esther and I'll be damned if I didn't put two and two together faster'n anything."

I did a bad thing, Esther had said.

Esther leaned against the dining room table, legs visibly trembling. Tears dripped down her face. "I'm sorry. I'll tell them. I'll call and tell them I lied and it'll all go away. I swear." Then, almost to herself, "I didn't mean it. I don't want to die. I don't."

"You can't fix nothin'," Donny said. "Claire tried and look where it got her. I got that darkness in me, same as her, real as the blood that runs through it. Thanks to you, everyone's gonna see it. They were never gonna give my kids back, but at least now they'll have a reason. Least now it'll make sense."

He raised the gun and pointed it at Esther's chest.

Time seemed to slow and speed up at the same time.

Are you going to let this happen again?

The voice was in Meg's head, but it sounded like Claire.

Esther glanced toward Meg. Their gazes met and Esther's eyes widened. Behind her, Claire lingered in the shadow of the window, arms clasped around her middle. And in her mind's eye, Meg saw Claire climbing up onto a toolbox, pulling the noose made of old bedsheets around her neck. Fire burned the length of Meg's body.

She ran, not feeling, only seeing, a singular focus to get to Esther the thing that kept her legs moving. Just as her arms encircled Esther's shoulders, the world exploded behind her. The pain was instant and extraordinary, and when she looked over, her arm was limp at her side.

Esther screamed as they fell, Meg breaking most of their fall with her hip, and then all Meg heard was sharp ringing, all she felt was fire, then cold, then nothing at all. Fog closed in at the corners of her vision and the last thing she saw before her world went black was Claire as she kneeled beside her. Something like a smile broke the sagging skin and she leaned forward, kissing Meg's forehead.

CHAPTER TWENTY-EIGHT

CLAIRE

After a while, Claire's grades began to slip. Not so much that they threatened to kick her out, but enough that a couple of her teachers pulled her aside to make sure she was okay.

Door's always open.

If you ever need anything.

Her boss at the restaurant wasn't as understanding.

"There's a bunch of kids kicking down my door to play bartender," he told her when she walked in late for the third shift in a row. "Don't think you're not replaceable."

She might have quit on the spot if she cared at all, but she didn't, and so she dutifully worked her shift, served her tables and collected her tips, and left without another word. She would be late again and he would maybe fire her, or maybe he wouldn't, but she would cross that bridge when she got to it.

If she got to it.

That was the thing about living two lives. She could dip her toe in or slide whole beneath the surface. She could walk away and never look back.

Every spare moment was spent at what she started to think of as the sisters house. Sometimes with Donny, but mostly without, especially after he met Tara, and she ended up pregnant.

That was how he put it. Ended up. Like it had just happened, with no plausible explanation.

At first, she was tormented by the spindly shadow creature, lurking in the corners of her vision, too solid for the beatific scenes in front of her to play out in a way that she could disappear into them. But as the days passed, she discovered that if she gave in—just a little—if she let the shadow creature take small bites out of her, enough to sate him, he would leave her be for a while.

She barely noticed the missing pieces.

She could watch her sisters—all of them—play and grow and love, all in that dark little room.

It didn't matter that every moment spent in that room was a hundred moments outside. It didn't matter that some days she didn't remember to eat or drink. Nothing mattered except time in that room with her sisters.

Years passed in a blink. She graduated by the skin of her teeth with a degree in social work, and got a job with the human services office. She didn't hate the job, and sometimes fell into it the way she'd fallen into the house. But then, during a home visit, she would see little girls, sisters, pushing each other on a trampoline or dumping piles of leaves in each other's hair to the soundtrack of raucous giggling, and Claire would be drawn back into the sisters room for hours or days.

The excuses came easily. She was sick, or her parents were sick, or she was needed to care for her nephew. Suspension loomed on the horizon, but social work was largely thankless and underpaid. There wasn't anyone else clamoring for her job this time.

And, surprisingly, she liked it. It was a little sick and a little selfish, but it was nice to know she wasn't alone in the darkness.

It also came in handy, it seemed. She hadn't heard from Donny in almost a year when he called her in the middle of the night, anxious. Panicky. There'd been an accident, he said. Not his fault. And now they were taking his kids away.

"Tara's beside herself," he said.

She couldn't help picturing two Taras, side by side, holding hands.

Me too, she'd wanted to say.

Jennifer and Kyle Laurie were good people.

It was what they told the triage nurse at the hospital, what they murmured to the doctor who examined their four-month-old daughter, who they'd brought into the ER, presenting with lumps on the head and weak limbs.

It was what they told the charge nurse when she told them they were putting their daughter in an air-evac to Indianapolis, where a bigger hospital with a better-staffed pediatric unit waited to treat her.

Good people. The words kept jumping out at Claire as she read the file. Good people weren't accused of lying. Good people weren't investigated by her office. Except, sometimes they were.

According to the file, the baby had suffered a subdural hematoma. It would heal on its own, and eventually, she would be fine. The mother, according to the notes, had been inconsolable. And the father…well, that was for Claire to investigate.

A home visit was scheduled for the afternoon. The father, Kyle, had a documented history of violence, and a decision needed to be made regarding their other children, whether they would be taken into care while the rest of the system worked itself out. It was Claire's job to speak to the parents, write her report, and make her recommendation.

She never made it to the Lauries' house.

As she was leaving the office, she got a text from Donny.

They're gonna tear it down.

She forgot all about the Lauries and their child, blinded by panic. She drove to the sisters house and burst into the upstairs room where the shadow creature was waiting for his tithe, which she gladly gave. She didn't feel it anymore, anyway. She didn't feel much of anything.

———————————

Jennifer and Kyle Laurie were not good people.

Claire found out about the standoff and subsequent shooting during dinner. Dad came home harried and uninterested in Mom's Crock-Pot chicken and dumplings, parking himself on the couch with the television on.

Kyle's brother worked with Dad at the plant. At shift's end, the brother's cell phone was practically on fire with missed calls and texts. Dad told the brother to forget tomorrow, that he'd cover for him. Then he came home and turned on the news.

Kyle told the police as they surrounded his home, guns drawn, that if anyone was going to break up his family, it would be him. The police didn't move fast enough to save his eldest, a twelve-year-old named Corrie, but Jennifer and their toddler and the baby, still at the hospital in Indiana, survived. If that was what you wanted to call it.

Logically, Claire knew there was nothing she could have done. Even if she had made her appointment, even if she had seen something in the house that made her recommend removal of the children, it wouldn't have happened for twenty-four hours, minimum. Even if, after all that, they came for the kids, Kyle Laurie wouldn't have let them go without a fight. If anything, she might have saved them by removing the immediate threat—her.

But she had missed the appointment because of the sisters house. How many more would she miss? How much more heartbreak would she cause?

Then she remembered Donny's text, and part of her was relieved. They would tear the sisters house down and it wouldn't matter anymore. She would carry her darkness the way she always had. Nothing would change.

Except the darkness was heavier now, and there was less of her to carry it, the strongest bits of her long devoured by the shadow creature. And worse, it seemed to have grown in Meg and Esther too. And the harder Claire thought about it, the more she feared that they were all connected, that every time she'd given the shadow creature a piece of herself, she'd given him a piece of her sisters too. They were all linked, with the house at the center of it. It was eating them alive, and Claire had selfishly let it happen. She was killing them all.

Days passed with no word on the demolition. Claire locked herself in her room to keep from visiting the house, to keep what was left of herself intact. Then she found the article in one of Dad's newspapers. The historical society was getting in the way. Even if they lost, it would be months, maybe years, before work could continue and then what? Could Claire keep herself together that long? Could she protect Meg and Esther?

The answer, of course, was no.

She spent every day in bed, tear-soaked and tired. Nights she sat by the window, watching the dark, ignoring Donny's calls.

I have to do something, she'd texted him. *This has to stop.*

She expected him to argue. To try to reason with her for the sake of the house.

After a long time, he responded: Do what you feel is right.

She couldn't help but smirk. Donny had called her bluff. There was no right anymore.

Now, she sat on the floor of her bedroom, back against the foot of her bed. The room was awash with light—her ceiling light, the desk lamp, even the flashlight on her phone. She'd stuffed a towel beneath the door to keep it all in, but every time she blinked a little more darkness seemed to creep in from the window, shadows spreading their fingers along the wall from somewhere behind the drapes.

She knew he was out there. The shadow creature. She could feel the darkness inside her reaching out to him, the pieces of him he left inside her when he nibbled and chewed.

As long as the house stood, he would be able to find her. He would devour her—he would devour her sisters—one way or another.

She knew what she had to do.

I t was too hot in the waiting room. Too many bodies. Seven bodies. Three plus three plus one. Esther couldn't stop looking at the *one*, an older man who kept chewing the dirt under his fingernails, silently urging him to leave, to restore the threes balance. Ryan's arm around Esther's shoulders was suffocating, but she was too scared to find out what would happen if he let go.

Meg had been shot, and it was Esther's fault.

Across from her, a woman stared at Esther, gaze moving between her face and chest. A streak of blood cut across her shirt. It was in the creases of her fingers and under her nails. The EMT who'd taped the cut on her eyebrow had offered to clean her up, but Esther refused. She needed to see it there, like Meg's blood was somehow a sign that Meg would live.

If Ryan hadn't come home, she might not have.

The moments after Donny shot the gun blurred in Esther's mind. The blood was stark, coloring the seconds between knocking her head on the side of the table and Ryan clutching her face. There'd been screaming, the echo of it still lingering in the back of Esther's head. They'd fallen hard, Meg's hand pressed to her chest, her breath coming too shallow, too fast. Donny had frozen and then stumbled back. He'd turned to run and—

"Donny," Esther said under her breath.

"They're looking for him," Ryan said. "They'll find him. I promise. He can't have gone far. He's not going to hurt you."

Esther nodded, vaguely remembering the police cars. Ryan had come home just as they'd hit the ground. Esther would be forever grateful that he didn't blink, didn't stop to ask what was going on. Because of him, Meg might live.

Esther glanced at the clock. Meg had been in surgery for two hours and twenty-two minutes. For two-thousand, one hundred and thirty breaths. "Why aren't they done yet?"

"It's probably a good thing," Ryan said.

Two-thousand, one hundred and thirty-one. "Or she's not waking up." Four years ago, Ryan had to have his gallbladder removed. What was supposed to have been a routine surgery turned into the worst six hours of Esther's life. The organ had been folded with scar tissue, difficult to remove, and at the end of it all they struggled to get him to wake up from the anesthesia. She'd known she was going to lose Ryan that day, just like she knew now that she was going to lose Meg.

Ryan squeezed her. "Babe. It's going to be okay. I promise." Then, "I owe you an apology."

She turned to face him, saw his expression was haggard, lips pinned up in a forced smile. "For what?"

His gaze drifted toward the cut on her eyebrow, the blood on her shirt. "I almost lost you today. I am so sorry I wasn't there."

"Mrs. Peterson?"

She turned toward the voice. A woman in surgical scrubs offered a weak smile she couldn't read. Esther stood too quickly, feeling the room spin. She tapped the button of her coat as she held her breath. *Tap, tap, tap.* Ryan held her arm until she steadied herself. "Is Meg okay?"

"She should be coming out of anesthesia shortly. She would have been luckier if the bullet had gone through, but we were able to locate it in her shoulder and remove it without further damage. She'll be in pain for a while as the muscles heal, but she'll be okay."

"Can I see her?"

The doctor nodded. "I'll walk you back."

Ryan started to follow, but a sharp look from Esther pushed him back into his seat. She needed to see Meg alone. To explain. To apologize. She couldn't do that with Ryan hovering over her shoulder.

The doctor led her through the triage area to a large hallway, mostly blocked off by a nurses' station where a gaggle of them stood huddled together over someone's phone. One of them caught her looking and raised an eyebrow, as if daring her to say something about it.

"She'll be groggy," the doctor said as she paused outside a closed door, "so don't be worried if she drifts in and out. That's normal."

Esther nodded, gaze fixed on the door. After a long moment, she held her breath and went inside.

Meg's face was ashen. The sight of it made Esther's stomach drop. She looked dead. But the monitor beside her beeped with a steady heart rate and she could see Meg's chest rise and fall with each breath. Bandages on her shoulder stuck out from beneath the hospital gown. A couple of drops of dried blood dotted her neck. Esther pulled a chair close, careful to avoid the IV and oxygen lines. She wanted to reach for Meg's hand, but something stopped her. Guilt, maybe. This was supposed to have been her.

An hour or so passed. Every once in a while, Meg's eyes fluttered open. They seemed to focus on Esther for a second before closing again. Ryan talked his way back and dropped off Meg's bag. He'd be back, he said. Brandon had called. He wanted to come home. But any relief she might have felt that her son was coming back was dampened by the thought that she'd almost lost Meg thanks to her own selfish stupidity. Ryan had been right. Her paranoia had almost gotten Meg killed.

More time passed and Esther went to the bathroom to pee and splash water on her face. She thought about going to the parking lot for some air, or to call her parents, but she couldn't bring herself to worry them. Not yet. Not until she was sure Meg would be okay. When she went back to the room to peek in on Meg, she saw her sister was finally awake.

Meg's eyes were bloodshot, her face only slightly less pale than when Esther had first come in.

Esther sat, blinking back tears. "You look like shit."

Meg frowned, and for a second, Esther thought she would drift off again. But Meg looked at her, eyebrow raised, and said, voice craggy, "You should see the other guy." Then, frowning, "What happened? Did Donny—"

"They're looking for him. They'll get him." Esther struggled to keep from staring at the bandages. "Ryan came home. Called the ambulance." Then, "You shouldn't have done that. You shouldn't have got in the way."

"Yeah, I'm maybe regretting it a little."

Esther nodded, tears burning.

"I'm kidding, Es. You're my sister. I would do it again."

"It's my fault. I went to Claire's supervisor and told her I thought Donny was living at home. I was there, Meg. There were pictures of them together on the walls and it didn't make any sense. I panicked. I just wanted someone to look at him, to watch him long enough to slip up. But now…" She shook her head. "I fucked up."

Meg tried to sit up, but when she moved her face contorted in pain.

Esther stood, hand hovering over the nurse call button. "What are you doing?"

"Smacking you. Come closer. It hurts to reach." Meg sank back against the pillow, eyebrows furrowed. "You went to his house? Why?"

"I don't know. I thought…" Esther rubbed her face. "I thought maybe I'd find something there."

"Like a written confession laid out on the kitchen counter?"

"Something like that."

"And?"

"And nothing. There were pictures on the wall of them, from a long time ago. Claire looked so young. I didn't realize they were friends."

"Why would they be friends?"

Esther shrugged. "It doesn't matter." Then, picking at the edge of the thin blanket, "I should have just accepted it from the beginning. Claire's gone and that's it. There's nothing else."

It hurt to say out loud, the thing that'd been worrying at the edges of her heart for days. It was easier to believe that Claire had been murdered, that Claire had been *taken* from her, than that Claire had simply left while—and maybe because—Esther hadn't been paying attention.

"What about the datebook?" Meg asked.

"What about it? It's a datebook. It doesn't mean anything, right? I mean, if she was working on Donny's case then maybe those were days she'd planned to drive by his house to check on the kids? Or there were meetings about him or his kids or any number of things." Esther wiped her eyes with her sleeve. "You were right. I couldn't let it go and you got hurt. You almost died."

Meg groped around her bed and, finding the remote, adjusted the bed so she was sitting up. She glanced from Esther to the floor. "That my bag?"

Esther nodded.

"Hand it to me. Before you go falling on your sword, you should see something." Esther set the bag on the bed and Meg dug through one-handed until she found what she was looking for. She held up a plain folder, *Claire Finch* written in sharpie on the tab.

"Is that—"

"Yes," Meg said. "There's pictures, so just…be careful, I guess. And an article." She paused. "You remember a while back, that developer guy came in all blustery about reshaping the future of Blacklick?"

Esther nodded.

"He was going to tear down entire neighborhoods, until someone got cheeky with the historical society." She shifted uncomfortably. "Someone's trying to save the house."

Esther frowned. "You think Claire—"

"I don't know what to think," Meg said.

"Why would someone want to save that house? It's…" She didn't have to finish. Meg knew.

"I don't know. But it's in the middle of everything. Always has been."

"What does that mean?"

"Did Mom ever tell you about Julie? About what happened after?"

Esther shook her head. She didn't like where this conversation was going. She wanted to leave. She started counting the pieces of medical equipment. So many fours and sevens. No threes. She needed threes.

Meg continued, "It was that house. They found her there."

Esther's stomach rolled. "That's not right. That can't be right."

"Why would Mom lie?"

"Why wouldn't she?"

Meg shook her head. "Not about this."

"Okay, so, what? You think that's what this is about? You think Claire knew what happened that night?"

Meg's expression suddenly went blank. Her back stiffened. "What do you mean?"

"Don't." Esther slapped the folder down, barely missing Meg's leg. "Please don't do that right now. You know what I'm talking about."

"Bad time?"

They both looked up to see a nurse smiling from the doorway. Esther hadn't heard the door open.

The nurse didn't wait for a response before tending to Meg, checking her bandage and her lines. "How's the pain?" she asked Meg.

"Hurts," Meg said.

The nurse tapped on the keyboard next to the heart monitor. "On a scale of one to ten?"

Meg tried to grab the folder, but Esther was faster. She slipped it into her purse as the nurse made some adjustments to the saline drip.

"Scale of one to ten?" she repeated when Meg hadn't answered.

"Ten," Meg said.

The nurse raised her eyebrow, but didn't argue. "I'll have the doctor check in on you."

"How long do you think you'll need to keep her?" Esther asked.

"At least overnight," the nurse said. "Just want to make sure we don't see any infection."

"Hurts," Meg said, weakly. "Think you could send that doctor in soon?"

The nurse smiled and it was like a raised middle finger. "You bet."

"Smooth," Esther said. "She doesn't think you're a drug seeker at all."

"I was shot," Meg said. Then, "You should go home."

"Because you don't want to talk about this?"

"Because I need to rest." Her voice broke. "Please. Just go, okay?"

Esther didn't want to leave. She wanted to hash this out now, to dig up the bodies of their shared past, but once the doctor came with the pain meds, Meg would be out like a light, which, Esther figured, was the plan.

"Fine," Esther said. "I'll be back tomorrow to help you check out."

Meg shrank back against the pillow, the relief palpable in her expression. "Can't wait."

When Ryan picked her up, Esther was disappointed to see he'd come alone.

"Where's Brandon?" she asked as she climbed into the car, hoping he hadn't changed his mind about coming home.

"On his way home. My parents will wait with him until we get there."

Esther's heart dropped. As hopeful as she was to have her son back under her own roof, Donny was still out there. He could come back.

Ryan seemed to read the worry on her face. He nodded. "I know. But I would just feel safer with him near us. I know it sounds stupid…"

"It doesn't sound stupid," Esther said.

He put his hand over hers and squeezed. Esther blinked back tears.

"Is Meg doing okay?" he asked.

"They're keeping her overnight in case of infection."

He nodded. "Smart." Then, "We don't have to stay at the house tonight. If you're worried."

"It's fine."

"I just don't want you to be scared."

"I'm not scared," Esther said, and for the first time in a while, she almost meant it.

At home, she didn't bother with taking off her shoes or dropping off her bag before she went upstairs, leaving Ryan to handle his parents. She found Brandon in his room, hilariously enormous headphones cupping his ears as he sprawled across his bed, XBox controller in hand. The sound coming from the headphones was so loud she could hear every word from the doorway.

On your left.

There's like six coming this way.

What's the matter? Can't handle it?

Your mom couldn't handle it when I—

"Oops," Brandon muttered as his character blew a hole in another character's chest. "Friendly fire. My bad."

Several people chuckled through the headphones.

She didn't like that Brandon played these kinds of games, always worried that the Blog Post Karens were right about video games and real-life violence, but it was moments like this that filled her with a sense of wonder. Brandon was a good kid. And while a lot of it was his innate goodness, his desire to see other people succeed where others only wanted to tear people down, Esther hoped she'd had a small hand in it too.

She didn't bother announcing her presence. She fell on the bed beside him and wrapped his head in a hug so tight the headphones dug painfully into her shoulder. Brandon squirmed and could easily have freed himself, but instead let her hold him for as long as she wanted. He didn't look up at the screen until a blast echoed through the headphones, and on the screen, his character crumpled in a smoking heap.

"Sorry," Esther said.

Brandon shrugged, nudging the headphones off his head. "S'okay. They were being weird anyway."

Though it pained her to do it, she finally let him go and sat up, waiting for him to look at her. When he did, she felt the same beautiful, terrible pain she had that day in the delivery room. *Look at this beautiful creature,* she thought. *He is a wonder in spite of me.*

"How was Grandma's?" she asked.

He shrugged again. "Fine, I guess." Then, "How's aunt Meg?"

"She's good! I mean, she's okay. She's recovering." Then, when Brandon looked like he might crumple, "The doctor said she's going to be fine. She can go home tomorrow." She studied his expression, his eyebrows furrowed tight. "What did Dad tell you?"

"Aunt Meg got hurt. That she was in the hospital."

Esther nodded, relieved. "Yes. But like I said, she's fine."

"It's not—" He huffed, picking at a button on his controller. "It's not like Aunt Claire, right?"

"Not at all. It was an…accident. That's it."

"Okay."

"Okay."

He finally looked up at her. "Are you okay?"

She smiled to keep the tears that burned her eyes from falling. "I'm fine, sweetie. Everything is good." She kissed his forehead even though she knew he hated it. "I'm glad you're home."

He smirked. "Thanks."

The only thing that made her leave his bedroom was knowing he would still be there when she shut the door. Her son was *home*, which meant everything would be okay now.

Downstairs, she heard Ryan in the kitchen. She started in that direction, but froze when she passed the dining room and saw the blood on the rug. Had Brandon seen it? She shoved the chairs aside and pulled up the rug, which she rolled up and dragged toward the back door. They'd dump it with the trash in the morning.

She went to the kitchen thinking about dinner, Mom-mode back in full force, but she found Ryan standing oddly still at the sink. She walked up beside him and saw what he was looking at—three empty bottles of wine discarded in the sink, the red dregs of it lingering around the drain and spotting the counter beside it.

Ryan's jaw worked, eyebrows furrowed.

Esther felt like she ought to say something, but she couldn't think of anything that wouldn't set him off. His grandfather was a drunk and an asshole, so though he never said anything when Esther imbibed, she always felt his eyes on her, judging.

He turned on the faucet and let the water run. "I don't get it."

"Don't get what?" she asked carefully.

"This was your solution to me telling you that you needed help?"

"You didn't tell me I needed help. You gave me an ultimatum. You were going to send me away."

He ripped a towel off the oven handle and ran it under the water before furiously scrubbing at the stain on the counter. "You called him Donny, right? Like you know him."

"No. I mean, yes."

"Which is it?"

"I knew him. When we were kids. We all did."

"And? Esther, people don't just shoot people for no reason."

Esther took a shaky step back. "What exactly are you implying?"

"I don't know. I just…want you to make it make sense. I know you and Meg are going through a lot right now, but it just seems like this hole you're in, you just keep digging deeper and deeper. I don't know how to help you, if I can help you, and it scares the shit out of me."

It felt like the world was spinning. Five minutes ago, everything was fine, they were moving forward. Now it was like Ryan was blaming her for what happened. The worst part was that he wasn't wrong.

So she shut off the water, took the rag out of his hand, and told him everything. *Almost* everything.

She told him about the datebook and Donny's obsession with guns. She told him how she'd seen Donny at the funeral, his odd behavior and the fact that Claire had seemed to hide their friendship from her sisters. Then she told him about going to his house and lying about who she was. She told him how everything she found out seemed to point to the fact that Claire had been murdered, but no one seemed to care. And then she told him about her desperate act at the social services office.

"He had to know it was me," she said, unable to look her husband in the eye. "So he came, and I opened the door because—"

"—because you were drunk," Ryan snapped.

Esther nodded meekly. "Meg was here, though I don't remember her coming in. I was just so..." She struggled to find the words, but nothing came. "Claire was my sister. I couldn't just let it go." She wrung the rag around her fingers. "It's like I can feel her arms around my neck, like when we were little, and Mom took us to the pool at the Y. I could barely swim but that didn't stop her from clinging on. I must have half-drowned a hundred times in one summer, but it didn't matter because she trusted me to keep her head above water."

"Honey, Claire's dead. You can't save her."

"I'm not trying to save her. I'm trying—"

"No." He gripped her arms, too tight. "Look at me."

Esther obeyed.

"You have to let this go. For our sake. For Brandon's. Please, I am begging you to just live your life."

She nodded, even as the feel of arms around her neck tightened, even as she struggled to stand under the weight of it, even as she choked.

Later, they ate macaroni and cheese in the living room—despite the clean floor, Esther swore she could see the blood where it had seeped through the carpet to the wood—in the glow of the television. The food tasted like nothing. Brandon was absorbed by the screen, but Ryan kept sneaking glances at Esther that she pretended not to notice. She ate. She laughed when Brandon laughed. She cleared plates when they'd finished eating and washed the dishes slowly, by hand, under screaming hot water. Ryan had offered, kindly, but she needed to keep herself occupied. She showered and followed her husband to bed where they had awkward makeup sex that left her feeling emptier and lonelier than when she'd been sleeping on the couch alone.

Ryan fell asleep shortly after, and Esther tried to do the same.

She tried. Truly and actually. Because despite what her husband might have thought, her family was everything to her. What he didn't understand, though, was that her family wasn't limited to her husband and son.

So when she was sure Ryan was sleeping, and at two in the morning when she heard the telltale ding-dong of her son's television shutting down, she crept downstairs, grabbed the file from her bag and brought it to the bathroom, where she sat on the toilet and read under harsh, yellow light.

CHAPTER THIRTY

MEG

She told herself it was the drugs that made the shadows twist in the middle of the night, that made Claire appear at the foot of the bed, a crooked smile on what was left of her face. She climbed spiderlike over the edge and crawled up Meg's body until they were face to rotted face. Meg tried to slither out from beneath her, but Claire held the edges of the blanket down, too tight for what little strength the morphine had left behind. Meg started to call for help, but Claire stuffed a corner of the blanket into her mouth.

"Hush now," Claire murmured. "You'll wake the baby."

Meg swallowed, tasting metal, as the soft light above the door flickered and died. She turned her head to look and the world followed at half-pace, spinning as she struggled to focus. Her head pounded and her heart stammered, and it was like someone had stuffed cotton over her face and in her ears. She couldn't hear. Couldn't breathe.

As her eyes adjusted to the dark, another figure emerged from the shadows, swaying as it stepped out of the sticky blackness, cradling something in its arms.

"You don't think babies can get scared, right? Because what do they know?"

Claire said. Her breath scraped Meg's cheek, thick and rough as a cat's tongue. "But they know when they're in danger. They can smell it." She nuzzled Meg's neck. "You can smell it too, can't you? He *reeks*."

Tears dripped down the sides of Meg's face, pooling in her ears.

"Was this how it felt?" Claire asked. "Did you feel like someone was holding you to the spot? Was someone—" She shoved the blanket deeper into Meg's mouth, making her gag. "—choking you so much you couldn't possibly have stopped him?"

Meg nodded frantically, expression begging Claire to take the blanket out. Mucus slid down the back of her throat and blocked her nose. She could feel her pulse in her temples, in her eyes, as her body fought desperately for air.

"Liar," Claire said.

The light flickered again, and the figure turned to face Meg. A scream died in her throat as she followed the length of the figure's arms to the baby it held, to the star-shaped birthmark on its temple.

"You could have saved me," Claire said.

Meg nodded.

"But you didn't."

Meg shook her head. The movement made the room tilt.

Claire covered the blanket in Meg's mouth with her hand and pressed. "Let's play a game, big sister." She caressed her cheek on Meg's. "I'll hide. You seek."

Just as the corners of Meg's vision darkened and her chest heaved, the weight lifted, and her arms were free. She rolled over and pulled the blanket out of her mouth, splashing the bed in a stream of drool. She coughed so hard her ears popped and she tasted bile, but after a long moment she was able to take shallow, measured breaths. The lights were back. Claire and the shadow figure, with its long, sharp limbs and hollow eyes, were gone.

No. Not gone. *Hiding.*

The next time the nurse came to check on her for pain, Meg lied. "I'm at maybe a one or two," she said. "I'm feeling much better. But could I just get a couple Tylenol?"

The nurse changed her bandage, nodding in a way that could have meant the wound was looking good or her arm was moments from falling off, and then helped her to the bathroom.

"Try to poop," the nurse said. "Can't let you leave if you don't."

Meg wasn't entirely sure she wanted to leave. At least here she had a big red button at her disposal. One push and someone would be on the way to rescue her from her nightmares. At home, she would be alone. But she couldn't stay here forever. No doubt they'd heard back from the insurance company where Meg hadn't been paying premiums in more than six months and were anxious to free up her bed for a paying customer. So she did as she was told, though it took longer and hurt more than she'd thought.

When she emerged from the bathroom, she found Esther sitting on the edge of the bed. Esther looked rough, like she hadn't slept. Meg figured that was partly her fault.

"Hey," Meg said.

Esther offered a weak smile. "Hey." Then, "I come in peace. Just here to help you check out. Give you a ride home."

"How do you know I didn't already call Mom?"

Esther's smile widened. "Did you?"

"Of course not."

"Okay then."

Meg walked to the bed, massaging her bicep. Her shoulder hurt like hell. The Tylenol was a joke. Maybe she'd take more. Maybe she'd take the whole bottle.

Esther stood, leaving space for Meg to crawl back into bed. There was a chair right behind her, but she seemed content to stand. She wrung her hands, realized she was doing it, and stuffed them into her pockets.

"Something on your mind?" Meg asked, already regretting it. She knew what Esther wanted to talk about, but Meg wasn't ready. Didn't know if she'd ever be ready.

"Brandon came home last night."

"You don't look happy about it."

"I was. Am. I missed him."

"So what's the problem?"

The door opened, followed by a too-chipper, "Knock, knock."

The nurse carried a packet of paperwork and a pair of folded scrubs, which she sat on the chair beside the bed. It took a moment for Meg to connect the dots. Her clothes were probably covered in blood, and she couldn't walk out in her hospital gown.

"Did we have success?" the nurse asked.

Meg nodded.

"Excellent. I'll get the doctor to sign off and walk you through some basic after care. You'll want to change—" She nodded to the scrubs. "Your shoes are in the bureau."

"Thanks," Meg said.

"It was a pleasure," the nurse said before taking her leave.

"What'd you do to her?" Esther asked.

"Nothing. She's always like that." Then, "Can you help?"

Esther gingerly helped her undo her hospital gown and put on the scrubs, which were a size too big. Meg used a hair-tie to bunch up the waistband. It wasn't pretty, but they'd stay up. As promised, the doctor visited and walked her through how to change the bandage and what to use to clean the wound, and told her to make an appointment with her primary care doctor for follow-ups. Meg thanked him, though they both knew there was no chance of follow-up. She'd keep it clean and covered and dodge the medical bills until they gave up on her. She was already drowning in debt, what was a little more?

They wheeled Meg out to Esther's car. Policy, the orderly said, when Meg insisted she could walk.

In the car, Esther was silent. Stupidly, Meg thought maybe Esther had decided to drop the subject altogether. She had her son to think about, that ridiculous ultimatum Ryan had proposed… They would both just let it go and pretend they never found Claire's datebook and if Claire found her way into Meg's nightmares again, well, she'd wait her out too. Claire couldn't haunt her forever.

Out of the parking lot now, Esther glanced at Meg and shut off the radio. "I read the file."

Meg laughed ruefully. "Smart. Wait until I'm trapped in the car."

"You're not trapped," Esther said, like Meg could just roll out at the next red light.

"Well?"

"You didn't read it?"

Meg gazed out the window. "I skimmed."

"Well, I read the whole thing, cover to cover." She paused. "We need to talk about that night."

"No. We don't."

"You obviously thought so. You brought the file to my house, remember?"

"I changed my mind."

"Why?"

Meg ground her teeth. In the corner of her eye, she saw a shadow flick across the side mirror. "Pull over. I'll walk."

"Why are you so selfish?" Esther sped up, swerving around a merging car. "Why do you refuse to just—"

"You almost hit that guy." Meg glanced over her shoulder. "And that was my exit."

"I don't care, Meg. I'll fucking drive forever if that's what it takes for you to tell the truth for once."

Meg's stomach twisted in knots and tears burned her eyes.

Esther continued, "You know Ryan told me to let it go. He said Claire was dead and that I needed to leave it be." She shook her head. "I can't do that, just like I know you can't. Claire was our sister, just like Julie was our sister. We failed Julie. You're telling me you're willing to fail Claire too?"

No. She wasn't. But how was Meg supposed to explain? How was she supposed to make Esther understand that it wasn't selfishness that kept a moment of childish weakness buried deep? It was fear. Meg felt Julie's loss every day, like a burr caught between her ribs. But as long as it stayed beneath the surface, it couldn't attach itself to anyone else. By keeping her guilt and fear folded up under her skin, she got to keep Claire and Esther, because they didn't know exactly how worthless she was as a human being. As a sister. They may have kept each other at arm's length for one reason or another, but arm's length was still within reach. If one of them fell, she could still catch them.

Except that wasn't true anymore. Claire had fallen as far as someone could and Meg hadn't caught her. Yesterday, maybe, she would have said it was because she hadn't been quick enough or strong enough or good enough to save her sister. She glanced in the side mirror and caught Julie's reflection, blurry at the edge, and knew that wasn't true. Julie—Meg's guilt at having done nothing to save her—was like a vise around her arms. She'd never stood a chance. Until now.

"You were right." Meg said, leaning her head against the window. "That night, when you said you saw me in the bedroom with someone."

"Who?"

"Some kid from school. Krystal. I didn't really know her that well."

Esther frowned but stayed silent.

"She just...showed up out of nowhere with some other kids. She told me they'd accidentally thrown something into the yard and wanted to get it. They had a bottle of vodka. I drank some." Tears burned her eyes. "I fucked up. I had never fucked up so hard in my life, and by the time I realized Julie was gone it was too late. I panicked. I told myself that this kind of shit happened to other people, that they'd find Julie in an hour, and no one would have to know. I prayed—I swore I would never leave any of you alone ever again if they found Julie safe."

Esther reached across and squeezed Meg's arm, which only made the tears run faster.

"I'm sorry I called you a liar," Meg said. "I'm sorry I didn't do anything to help because I was too scared, too selfish. I thought everything would be okay, but it wasn't."

"I'm sorry too."

Meg frowned. "What for?"

"For getting you shot, for starters."

The corner of Meg's mouth lifted. "Forgiven."

"And for lying. Or, at least, not telling you everything I knew."

"What do you mean?"

"I saw something that night too."

Meg's whole body went cold. "What?"

"At the time, even with everything going on, I didn't think it was important. Weird shit happened around us all the time. Wasn't even a day or two before it happened that Dad found one of the neighbors passed out drunk in the backyard because he'd walked home from the bar and slinked through the wrong back gate."

"Es..."

"Do you remember that? Mom had a fit."

"Esther!"

She flinched. "Sorry. I just—what I mean to say is that it wasn't important..."

She shook her head, eyes reddening. "Something outside my window woke me up that night. I was freaked out, but I looked because, like I said, weird stuff was always happening, and I saw this…thing creeping around in the yard."

Pieces started to come together in Meg's mind, but it only made her feel worse. "Who do you think it was?"

"I don't know," Esther said. "It was too big to be a person. The limbs too long and sharp." Then, "Claire used to ask about that night. I tried to get her to leave it be, but you know Claire. She had a way of making you tell her anything she wanted to know."

"What'd you tell her?"

"An abridged version of the truth. I was worried for a long time that she'd say something to Mom, that Mom would end up back in that dark place again. But it was like Claire let it go so I put it out of my head too." Esther reached behind the seat and pulled out the file, setting it in Meg's lap. "I know we're right. I know there's something wrong about what happened to Claire. What happened to Julie."

Meg nodded, mouth dry.

"I've had enough of secrets and half-truths, Meg. I'm just so fucking tired." She rubbed her face. Sighed. "Krystal was a bully."

"You knew her?"

"She made me her object of torment for a while in middle school. Back then I didn't understand why she hated me so much. I think I get it now." She paused, frown deepening. She opened her mouth to continue, but shook her head.

"What is it?"

Esther's gaze fell to her hands.

"Es."

When Esther finally spoke, her voice was barely above a whisper. "Sometimes I think Claire was right. About the darkness. Sometimes I feel like I can see it." Her voice broke. "But why us? That's what I keep coming back to, over and over again. Why did it choose us?"

Meg started to feel sick. "What if it didn't?"

"What do you mean?"

Meg's stomach lurched as her body went hot and cold at the same time. They were so stupid. They couldn't have been this stupid. She grabbed the door, eyes squeezed shut against the wave of nausea moving through her. "Pull over."

"I can't. There's—"

"Pull. Over."

Esther cursed as she crossed over two lanes of traffic to the shoulder. She slowed, and before the car was fully stopped, Meg had the door open. She tumbled out onto the grass, barely able to get her feet beneath her. Her shoulder hit the side of the car as she tried to balance herself, and a sharp pain ripped down her arm and across her chest. She fell, knees digging into the dirt. She gagged as Esther rounded the car, but nothing came up.

"Jesus." Esther sank down next to her. Rubbed her back. "Are you okay? Is it your arm?"

Meg shook her head, groaning as it made the world spin. Every time she blinked, she saw Julie, saw pieces of her fall away only for Claire to gather them up, swaddled in her arms. "She's dead," Meg spat. "They're both dead and that's it."

"So does that mean we forget them? Does that mean we let slide whatever happened to them because it's just too hard to deal with?" Tears choked Esther's voice. "This is our fault, Meg. We have to fix it."

"We can't."

"We can." She crawled around in front of Meg, forced her to look at her. "Together, okay? Please."

Everything was numbness and everything was pain. Meg ached in every inch of her being as the door she kept locked tight against the past broke open. She thought she could live with knowing what she'd done, taking her punishment day in and day out, however it decided to present itself. But some part of her had to have known it couldn't last forever. That sooner or later she would have to face it.

Meg nodded as she reached for Esther's hands. "Okay. Together." She stood and let Esther help her back into the car. Her shoulder throbbed and the pain behind her eyes had grown sharper.

Back in the car, she pulled her phone out to give her hands something to do and noticed she had a missed call from a number she didn't recognize, and a new voicemail. As Esther slowly pulled back into traffic, Meg tapped in her pass code and listened. It was Officer Kingsolver. He had some news on the historical society petition.

When it was finished, she listened again.

"We have to go back," Meg said.

"Back where? The hospital?"

"No. The house. We have to go back to the house."

Esther paled. "Why?"

"Do you trust me?"

"Yes."

"Then drive."

CHAPTER THIRTY-ONE

CLAIRE

HER LAST NIGHT

The house tried to expel her from the beginning. Doors locked where there was no lock to speak of, and the wooden frames of windows swelled until they were stuck fast, as if the house had taken a deep, daring breath.

It had been a mistake to call Meg. She wouldn't understand. She would try to stop Claire, and who knew if Claire would ever be brave enough to try again. But it had been a moment of weakness, of loneliness. A childish part of her had thought Meg would understand, would maybe even help. Now she had to hurry.

A square of light from the streetlamp illuminated a path of crumbling brick to a side door. It was cracked open an inch, forgotten, lost in the light. The hinges shrieked a warning as she pushed the door open and made her way inside.

The shadow creature was waiting at the top of the stairs, legs dangling spider-like over the rail. He would try to stop her, to devour her before she had the chance to do what she came to do.

Go ahead and try, she thought. *There's nothing left.*

She started up the stairs, even as the ceiling bulged and the walls trembled, and a deep groan like she'd never heard before rumbled out of the vents.

Claire would end the darkness, or she would die trying.

CHAPTER THIRTY-TWO

ESTHER

NOW

It reminded Esther of a movie she saw once. A young man tormented as a boy by his father returns home against his will, expecting to see this towering, brute of a man only to find that his father had withered with age, his muscles shrunken and his toothy, hungry grin reduced to an empty hole for shoveling in soft foods. The father was hardly intimidating, but the fear was still there, like an extra bone growing across the young man's rib cage he never noticed until someone or something poked just the right spot.

The house was like that.

Even as a kid, Esther had been good at compartmentalizing. After that day, after being trapped in the room and shown what she then believed to be her future, she did what she could to lock the memory, and the house, away. She never talked about it. Never thought about it, if she could help it. But sometimes, on the school bus or in the car with her parents, they'd drive past the street, and without realizing why until after, her body tensed and she held her breath, and she felt cold for hours after.

Now, standing in front of the house she felt the same shiver travel down her back and settle between her shoulders.

"Someone walk over your grave?" Meg asked.

"Not funny," Esther said. Then, "What are we even doing here?"

"It was Donny." Meg looked at her. "The historical society petition. He filed it."

"You think there's something inside he wants to protect."

"Or hide."

Esther swallowed. "Do you think Claire—"

"I don't know. All I know is that it all started here with Julie. This is the center of the black hole."

Esther sighed and, starting toward the gate said, "Let's do this, then."

Meg put her hand out. "Me first."

Esther's first instinct was to fight, but she let herself feel grateful instead. She followed, hyperaware of every creak of the wood porch under her feet, of every whistle of wind through the branches of the tree in the yard. She studied the ground on either side of the crumbling stone path from the sidewalk to the porch. The grass and weeds closest to the house had rotted, and fingers of the rot spread out into the rest of the yard, like death was seeping from somewhere inside.

Meg hesitated at the door, gaze fixed on a window to the left.

"What is it?" Esther asked.

"Nothing," Meg said, but her face had gone pale. "Just being here. I don't like it."

Esther grabbed her hand and held it tight. Meg worked her jaw, then nodded once.

The door opened too easily, like the house had been waiting for them. Like it was welcoming them home.

The front room was trashed. Someone had dragged in an old mattress, which was stuffed against the wall and covered in food garbage—chip bags and beer bottles and take-out containers. A pile of cigarette butts sat under the window.

"You smell that?" Meg asked.

"At least it's not hot out. It would be worse."

Meg seemed to just notice the mattress. "No, not that. It's like…" She took a few steps deeper into the room, sniffing the air. "Like gas?"

All Esther could smell was old food and body odor. Her stomach turned thinking about how many bodies had laid on that mattress in varying states of undress. Then, with startling clarity, it occurred to her what a stupid idea this was.

She lowered her voice. "What if they're still here?" She nodded at the abandoned food. "Squatters or whatever?"

Meg shook her head. "That's not squatters. That's partiers. They've already slunk back to whatever daytime lives they lead. Probably be back tonight, though, so we shouldn't linger for long."

Esther agreed, but not for the same reasons. From the moment she'd walked through the door she'd felt a kind of static on her skin, like fingertips hovering just over the surface.

They both turned toward the stairs.

"Race you," Meg said, but neither of them moved.

"It's just a house," Esther said.

Meg's gaze drifted somewhere to the right of the stairs, lingering before finally facing Esther. "Right. Just a house."

But as they started toward the stairs, beneath the veneer of vandalism and neglect, Esther saw hints of what the house had been. Things she'd noticed as a kid but hadn't realized what they meant. Idyllic furnishings and decor that conjured images of *I Love Lucy* and *Leave it to Beaver*. Ceilings set too low. Fist-shaped gouges in the walls.

The stairs groaned underfoot. Esther leaned hard on the banister, terrified the wood would give and she'd go crashing through it. Meg held her hand, running the other along the wall where words had been carved into the plaster, almost all of it illegible.

Meg flinched and dropped Esther's hand. Her face paled.

"Meg?" Esther asked. "You okay?"

"I'm going," Meg whispered.

"We can take it slow. Does it hurt?"

But Meg didn't seem to be listening to her. She shook her head, gaze fixed on a spot in front of her. "I don't want to see."

Chills snaked down Esther's body. There was nothing there. But if she turned just so, if she looked out of the corner of her eye...

A crash from somewhere downstairs made her jump. A lingering partier? Or something worse?

"Come on." Esther grabbed Meg's arm and climbed the rest of the way to the landing, knocking her hip on the banister at the top.

Meg's face was contorted in pain, but when Esther tried to look at her shoulder, Meg shoved her away.

Esther thought maybe this was too much for Meg. Esther kept forgetting that it was Meg who'd found Claire. Meg who was probably seeing her now, reliving it in painful detail. Esther wondered if this had been a bad idea. If they should leave.

But then she saw the doors.

Where downstairs it had been torn apart, the hall of doors looked exactly as it had when she was a kid. Her gaze immediately fell on her door, the one made of reddish wood, with chips all along the bottom. Meg crossed the hall to a door that hung open a few inches.

"I know," she said to no one. "I remember."

But Esther was drawn toward her cherrywood door, unable to look away from the light coming from the gap under it. She blinked, and in the split second between she thought she saw the flicker of a shadow, like footsteps moving through the light. A sharp tang filled the air, making her nose burn and her eyes water.

"I smell it," she said. "The gas."

The floor creaked behind her, and when she started to turn, she saw something big and heavy coming at her out of the corner of her eye, but she was too slow to avoid it. Pain rocketed through her jaw and down her neck and she could taste blood. Then something covered her mouth and the sharp tang became almost sweet. Panic surged. She struggled, nails digging into flesh, but soon she felt weak, her muscles gave, and fog clouded her vision. Where was Meg? Esther tried to scream, but the rag was jammed into her mouth the moment she opened it.

"Shh. There we go. Easy does it," a voice whispered.

She had the vague sensation of being lowered, and then everything went dark.

Sometime later, Esther couldn't tell if her eyes were open or closed. If she was asleep or awake. She was vaguely aware of movement somewhere ahead of her, but it was like trying to spot a black fish in a sea of ink. Her head felt like it was split open, and she could feel her pulse behind her eyes and in the back of her throat. She leaned painfully against something sharp—a corner, maybe—but when she tried to right herself, a wave of nausea moved through her, making her mouth water.

Her wrists burned and her shoulders ached from having been wrenched behind her. She couldn't feel her fingers, but when she pulled, she could feel something scrape her skin. Rope, maybe. She squinted into the dark, looking for some sign of Meg, but all she could see was the drowning blackness. It disoriented her, even more than whatever bleach cocktail had been shoved over her face. She could still smell the dregs of it.

"Meg?" The dark seemed to swallow her voice. "Are you okay?"

"Meg's gone."

The sound of Donny's voice was like a cold knife scraping down her back.

She fought to keep the tremor out of her voice. "What the hell do you mean gone?"

Silence.

"What have you done with—" Words died in her mouth as something sharp bit into her shoulder, pinning her to the wall behind. The pain was extraordinary. She struggled to breathe, the air in front of her face now hot and putrid, like some rotted thing dangled in front of her. Then she felt a pinch, a *bite*, at her collarbone. Every muscle went weak, and in her mind flashed a memory—the night Julie was taken, the shadow outside her window.

The darkness is coming for us all.

"Don't struggle," Donny said. "That'll only make it hurt. She doesn't hurt you if she doesn't have to." She could almost hear his smirk. "I'd say you'll learn to like it, but we won't be here that long."

She. Esther's first thought was Tara, that she and Donny were on some fucked-up Bonnie-and-Clyde kick, that if someone turned on the lights, she'd see Tara on the other end of the knife twisting in Esther's shoulder. But there were some things a body knew without the eyes having seen it. Whoever *she* was, it wasn't a woman on the other end of this pain.

For the first time in her life, Esther didn't think about the numbers. She didn't count her breaths or the seconds between streaks of shooting pain. All she could think about was Meg. Donny was lying to her. Meg was here. She was alive, and they were going to get out together.

"Did Claire like it?" Esther asked.

She didn't need the answer. Didn't want it. But she wanted Donny distracted, hoping she had a better chance against the darkness without being outnumbered.

"I tried to help Claire," he said, voice carrying from somewhere else in the room now. Like he was pacing.

The bonds were too tight, and every time Esther tried to pull one of her hands free, they only seemed to get tighter. Her right arm had gone numb, and even in the pitch black, the corners of her vision started to fog. Panic flickered in her chest.

She struggled to get control, to take deep, measured breaths, but she could feel the darkness bubbling under her skin, gripping her muscles and filling her lungs. With her body under attack, her mind reached a sick clarity—Meg was dead, and Esther was next.

A glow suddenly grew from the other side of the room, illuminating a tiny patch of floor. In the center of it lay Meg, body bent, and neck twisted too far to be natural. Blood pooled under her open mouth.

Esther screamed.

When Donny spoke again, it was in reverence. "She shows you things. The future, the past. What could be. What should be. It's beautiful if you think about it."

A mirage, Esther thought, Donny's words barely sinking in. But she couldn't stop staring at the blood, at the horrifying twist to Meg's body.

Donny continued, "Unless you fight it. She can be generous. I learned that after a while. If you give in to the darkness, just a little, she gives you a little in return." He sighed quietly. "She gives you relief."

The grip on Esther's throat strengthened. She tried to pull away, but there was nowhere to go.

"Fight, and she's forced to paralyze you." Donny's voice was inches from Esther's ear. "She'll thread herself between your ribs and squeeze. She'll show you your worst nightmares. You'll be numb with it." Then, "I only wish I could see what you see." He laughed. "It's me, isn't it? You're terrified of me."

A sound distracted her, just for a moment. A tapping. Tap-tap-tap. One, two, three. She tried to ignore it, but the more she pushed it away, the louder the sound became.

"Fuck you," she said. To Donny. To the incessant tapping.

"What did I just tell you? Fighting will make it worse. But I suppose you don't know how to do anything else, do you?"

Esther hissed as new pain shot through to her back. "You don't know anything about me."

"I know everything about you." The floors creaked with Donny's footsteps. "I've been watching you for almost your whole life, Esther. I've been watching all of you."

A chill snaked down her body. "Bullshit."

Tap-tap-tap. One, two, three.

"And it's not even because you're special," Donny spat. "It's because your curtains were open."

Somewhere beneath the darkness, Esther heard a groan. "Meg?"

"No!" Donny slapped her so hard she saw stars. "You're listening to me now."

The pain lingered for only a second. Meg was alive. That was all that mattered. Esther had to get to her.

The thing in her shoulder hitched, and for a second the room filled with dim light, like she'd finally opened her eyes. She spotted Meg in a crumpled heap only a few feet away. There was no blood, and her chest rose and fell with jerking breaths. Donny stood in the center of the room, bruises under his eyes, flexing his hand. In the corner of her eye was a shadow she didn't dare look directly at. She still felt the pain in her shoulder, and she was still pinned to the wall, but the weight on her chest was a hair lighter.

Donny caught her watching him and his gaze narrowed. Darkness closed in around the edges of her vision, but she discovered if she focused on Meg, if she believed they would get out of there alive, the light remained.

Donny crouched down in front of her, eyes darting toward the shadows and then back again. He cocked his head and then gripped her chin and turned her face slightly, as though studying her. "S'gonna leave a mark," he said with a hint of pride. Then his expression fell. "I could never understand, as much as your mouth got you in trouble, why your dad never hit you. Not once. Even when you deserved it." He dropped his grip and stood. "If you'd have lived with my dad, you probably wouldn't have made it to ten." He nodded at Meg. "Her, neither."

"How boring," Esther said, voice quavering. "Daddy issues."

Tap-tap-tap. One, two, three.

Where was it coming from? A shadow seemed to linger in the corner of her eye, disappearing the moment she tried to look at it. She caught the ghost of a scent—lavender—and her breath caught.

"He beat me real good one night. Pretty sure he broke something. Not like my mom would've taken me to the hospital or anything. So I went for a walk. I must've walked for an hour before I saw your house, all lit up from the inside. Everyone else's curtains were closed, but yours were wide open, like you dared someone to look. So I did. And you know what I saw?" He didn't wait for Esther to answer. "You were all just sitting there in the middle of the living room—you and Meg and your parents and the babies—stacking blocks and knocking them down again, laughing and shit, like it was the craziest thing. Like you'd invented fun or something." He shook his head. "I wanted that. I wanted it so bad I would've done anything for it. I hated myself for that. Your perfect fucking family."

The babies. He must have meant Claire and Julie. Esther's heart ached, searching for the memory of a night on the floor with blocks, but nothing came. It was so long ago. She couldn't even conjure Julie's face.

In the corner of her eye, the shadows throbbed.

Donny continued, "At first, I came back just to get away from my parents and that shitty fucking trailer. Then I couldn't stop. I watched you all eat together and watch TV and laugh and I hated every second of it. I hated *myself*. It was torture. I wanted to touch everything that you all touched. I wanted to breathe that perfect air that didn't smell like cigarettes and piss and spilled beer."

It wasn't perfect, she wanted to argue. They fought. They struggled. But they had each other. Until—

"After a while," Donny continued, "I found other places to be. I found this house. I found her." He closed his eyes for a moment, and when he opened them, they were nearly black. "She understood. It wasn't right. It wasn't fair. So she showed me how to fix it." He turned to Esther. "She showed me how it would all come together, and it did. It was exactly as she showed me. With your mom gone, I bribed a couple of kids with booze I stole from my dad's stash to keep Meg busy, and then I went inside and scooped one of the babies up like she was nothing and brought her back here." Something flickered across his face—regret? But it fell away just as quickly. "It was too cold, I guess. Hypothermia."

Hot tears dripped down Esther's face. She'd seen him that night. Outside her window. And then later, when he showed them the house—

She looked up and he was watching her, watching her thoughts play out across her face. A grin split his lips.

"I didn't plan it, if that's what you're thinking," he said, like he could read her mind. "It was fate. Her grand design." He glanced toward the shadows again, and this time, Esther followed his gaze, unable to stop herself.

There were no eyes, but Esther felt its gaze, cool and piercing. The shadows that made up its thin, sharp body bulged and heaved like storm clouds. She followed the length of one of its spidery limbs to her shoulder where it seemed to go through her, where wriggling appendages burrowed under her skin.

Another of its limbs lingered near Meg's throat, waiting for her to wake up. Waiting to feed.

Donny's expression fell. "Claire loved her too. And she loved Claire. But Claire tried to ruin it. She tried to take her away."

Esther frowned, her mind too sluggish now to make any sense of things. She tried to focus on Meg, to get back that control seeing her sister had brought before, but the darkness had begun to close in again. A creaking sound pulled her attention to the left, where a shadow drifted across the floor, like something gently swaying.

A voice screamed at the back of her head, ordering her not to look.

She didn't listen.

It was Claire, hanging from the ceiling by her neck, her hair almost completely obscuring her face.

The darkness wriggled up Esther's neck beneath her skin. It coated her tongue and her teeth and filled her ears until all she heard was the creak of the rope around Claire's neck, all she felt was the cold, all she saw was Meg's blood.

And she realized.

The shadow creature *was* despair. It was heartache and regret and anger and jealousy. It was fear. It was guilt.

She felt it consuming her, the light of the room growing dimmer.

There was no point in fighting. Donny was wrong. Esther wasn't a fighter.

She closed her eyes and leaned her head back, but instead of hitting the hard wall, her head rested on something soft.

Hands cradled the sides of her face, a finger gently tapping her temple. Tap-tap-tap. One, two, three. She felt lips press to her ear. "Look."

She was looking, wasn't she? No. Her eyes were closed. They were too heavy.

"I can't," Esther said.

"Do it anyway."

It wasn't the words that finally pushed her eyes open. It was her body recognizing the voice before her mind. It was Claire.

As though carried by the sound of her sister's voice, Esther saw through the foggy darkness to where Meg was now leaning up, her injured arm dead at her side, the other furiously working to free herself. No, she decided. They would not die here.

Claire's hands left Esther's face, and before she could wonder, her wrists broke free.

She didn't hesitate.

Ignoring the pain that shot through her chest as she stood, and the grip that threatened to pull her back, Esther launched herself at Donny. He was bigger than her, so her only advantage was that he'd been distracted by Meg. Esther tackled Donny, and they both hit the ground with a sickening crack.

Meg shouted something, but all Esther heard was a ringing in her ears. Donny groaned and groped blindly, clawing her face. Adrenaline pulsed through her as she threw punches, not paying attention to where they connected. In the back of her mind, she still saw Claire hanging from the ceiling, and, as she was punching Donny, in her mind she was hitting the fan that held the rope. She felt nothing. Heard nothing. She saw Julie's tiny body in the middle of the floor, frozen, silent, and she punched harder until someone pushed her back. She blinked away tears, and Meg's face came into focus. Behind her, Claire stood over Donny, who barely moved, his face bloody. She seemed to flicker in and out of existence, like it was him who held her here.

Esther bent down and picked up a lighter that had fallen out of Donny's pocket.

"The gas can," Meg said.

Esther blinked. "What?"

"In the police report. There was a gas can. Claire was going to—"

"—burn it down," Esther finished.

The shadow creature had loosened its grip on Esther, the limbs still close, but it seemed more interested in Donny, whose agony pulsed off him in waves. It was like any other predator—it would always go after the easier prey.

For a moment, Esther had thought that was her.

Not with Meg here. With Claire. Together, they were stronger. Together, they could do anything.

She'd almost forgotten that.

Meg grabbed her face. Forced Esther to look at her. "We have to go."

She started to protest. They couldn't just leave, not with the shadow creature still here. Even if it consumed Donny—Esther shivered at the thought—there would be others. She thought of the mattress downstairs, the food… How long until one of them wandered upstairs and found the hall of doors? How long until the darkness found someone else to lure others to her?

"The gas," Esther said.

They'd smelled it on their way in. But it'd been days since Claire had been here. Would the gas have lingered that long? Would it still catch?

Meg seemed to be reading her mind. She nodded once.

Esther flicked the lighter. The flame danced. And in the periphery was Claire. Here and not. Esther closed her eyes for a moment and imagined Claire was alive and Julie too. They were all here together, the four of them. The Finch girls.

I love you, she thought, and arm looped through Meg's, they ran, stopping in every room to light what they could—insulation bulging from the ceiling like stuffing from a teddy bear, old food wrappers, curtains as dry and papery as callouses.

In the hall where the smell of gas was strongest, Esther held the dying lighter to curls of wallpaper.

A *whoompf* shook the floor, and the hair on Esther's arms shriveled with heat. Without thinking, she grabbed Meg's hand and they ran for the door, barely beating the fire as it chased them down the stairs. Smoke clouded her face, making her cough so hard she saw stars. Blinded by tears and smoke, she tripped on a torn bit of carpet, but Meg was there to catch her, one arm dead at her side. They stumbled through the living room and out the front door, flames licking at their backs.

Outside, Esther gulped the air while Meg pulled her across the yard and to the other side of the street. Doors opened as neighbors peered out, their cries drowned out only when Esther heard sirens in the distance. Across the road, they collapsed into a heap on a damp lawn. They held each other, foreheads resting against one another, as behind them the house of broken doors burned.

CHAPTER THIRTY-THREE

MEG

NOW

Smoke billowed, the air acrid. Meg could still feel the heat of the fire on her skin as the paramedic re-taped her wound.

"Gotta get that re-stitched," he said when she refused to get in the ambulance.

"I will," she said.

He sighed as he ripped a second strip of gauze from the roll. "'Kay."

As he finished, Meg glanced at Esther, who was sitting on the sidewalk, shivering despite the blanket wrapped around her shoulders. On the other side of the street, the house smoldered, the front porch entirely collapsed. Esther stared at it, unblinking.

When the paramedic finished, Meg joined her on the sidewalk. She took her time getting on the ground, still a little woozy from the bleach cocktail Donny had shoved in her face. Esther leaned her head, silently, on Meg's shoulder.

They sat that way for a long time, watching the firefighters continue to hose down what little was left of the house. The whole place had been taped off, and Donny's body already carted off by the coroner. The police hadn't asked many questions—the bruises around both their wrists had been answer enough.

"Do you think she's still in there?" Esther asked.

"No," Meg said, because it was the right thing to say, not because she meant it.

"I need to call Ryan."

Meg nodded.

Neither of them moved.

Part of Meg expected—hoped—for Claire to appear beside them. But which Claire would it be? The rotted thing that plucked memories from Meg's tongue and tormented her with guilt? No, Meg decided, because that hadn't been Claire at all. It had been the shadow creature—the darkness—feeding on her guilt and fear, luring her back to the place where it all began. It had always been with them, from the day Donny took Julie, seeping from his hands through the glass of their windows, into the walls of their home. It was in every kind word they didn't say to each other, in every moment that passed with their pain ignored, shoved deeper inside their bodies to fester.

And there it would stay, burned house or not, until they did something about it.

Wincing, Meg nudged Esther's head up and then stood.

"What?" Esther asked.

"Call Ryan."

"Okay." Then, "Where are you going?"

"To find a ride. I need to tell Mom, and I'm not going to do it over the phone."

"I can come with you."

As much as she was tempted, Meg shook her head. "No. I need to do this on my own." Then, "I'll call you after, okay?"

"You better." She reached up and squeezed Meg's hand. "I love you."

Already Meg could feel it loosening. Already, she was leaving the darkness behind. "I love you too."

Six months later, Meg sat on the grass in front of two polished headstones, face pointed up at the hot sun. Her eyes burned behind her eyelids, but today was the first sunny day in what felt like forever, and she wanted to soak it in.

"Keep doing that, you're gonna go blind," Esther said.

Meg smirked. "A risk I'm willing to take." Sighing, she turned away from the sun and toward her sister, who sat cross-legged on a blanket, a plastic cup of wine in her hand.

They'd been coming to the cemetery, once a week, for over a month. What started as taking a few moments to be with their sisters had turned into a full afternoon affair once Meg suggested they start bringing snacks. The weather eventually improved, and wine inevitably followed. Once in a while they invited their parents. Dad never came—though Meg later learned that was because he made his own visits, in his own way—but Mom joined them sometimes, on her good days. She would argue otherwise, but she still hadn't completely forgiven Meg. She might not ever, and that was okay, because Meg was coming closer every day to forgiving herself.

It helped that Donny was dead, that Krystal was looking at a decade behind bars for her part in helping him. The house didn't quite burn to ash, but after the news outlets got word of what had happened there, folks in the community put enough pressure on the city to have it torn down.

Esther handed her cup to Meg. "Hold this. Don't drink it."

"No promises," Meg said.

Esther dug through her bag while Meg took a sneaky sip from Esther's cup. Sure, she had her own, but wine always tasted better when it was her sister's.

Finally, Esther made the reveal with a loud, "Ta-da!"

It was the Space Mountain snow globe.

Meg laughed. "Where did you find it?"

"I've always had it."

"Seriously?"

Esther nodded, then her expression went deadly serious as she tapped the edge of the base of the snow globe on the top of Claire's headstone. "Hear ye, hear ye, the meeting of the Midnight Society will now come to order. There is something *very* important we need to discuss."

It was Esther's idea to call themselves the Midnight Society when they were young. Meg had thought it was silly then—what sort of midnight society met in the middle of the day? But now, she supposed, that was the point. They'd both loved *Are You Afraid of the Dark?* as kids, but it wasn't until Meg was an adult that she realized what the show was really about. It was about overcoming your fear, your darkness, especially in the moments when it seemed bleakest.

"You're pregnant," Meg deadpanned.

Esther snatched back her wine and took a long swallow. "God, I hope not." Then, "But there are going to be big changes."

Meg fought to keep from panicking. *She's sick,* she thought. *Or Ryan's sick. Or Brandon. Or they're separating.*

"You know that development they're building? Over by…"

By where the house had stood. Meg nodded.

"Well, they extended it by about three blocks before the money dried up. Half the houses are sitting there with dirt yards and unpaved driveways."

"Figures."

"Sucks for them, but it means the houses are selling for cheap."

Meg frowned. "And?"

"And I convinced Ryan to buy one of them. For us to buy one of them." She paused. "We're moving. Soon-ish. Provided the buyers for our place come through." Then, seeing Meg's doubtful expression, Esther raised an eyebrow. "Well?"

"You're sure you want to do that? You want to move closer to…"

"To Mom? To my sister, who would have easier access to my refrigerator and Wi-Fi?"

"Esther. Stop."

"No. You stop." Esther shook the snow globe and set it on Claire's headstone where they both watched the glitter fall. "I'm done giving the darkness any more power over me or my family. That includes you. You don't make it go away by ignoring it or avoiding it. You force it to slink back into the shadows where it came from. You point your finger at it and say *I see you*, and then live your life in the light."

"Unless you're a vampire," Meg said.

Esther laughed, then shook her head. "You're impossible."

"You're right." Meg took the snow globe and shook it again. The glitter was calming. "About it all. I know that. It's just hard."

"It is. But I'll be close by. And I won't even kick you out when you take the last brownie and leave the empty box in the cabinet. Again."

Meg smiled. "Promise?"

Esther reached across and looped her pinky around Meg's. "Promise."

READING GROUP GUIDE

1. The sisters' relationship changes dramatically between the moment before they find the hall of doors and after they venture inside. What might this mirror about our relationship with our siblings as we grow up?

2. One could argue that Esther's personality between childhood and adulthood changes the most of the three sisters. Why might that be?

3. Where do you think Esther's obsessive paranoia originated? Do you think the tapping behavior will continue after the darkness is banished? Why or why not?

4. How might the story have changed if just one of the sisters had been willing to share with the others what she had seen behind her door? Would it have saved Claire? Or was her ending inevitable?

5. In the present day, the keys to their doors often appear to Meg and Esther, seemingly out of nowhere. What might their appearance foreshadow?

6. Much of the conflict in this book comes from the Finch family's refusal to talk to one another, to bury the darkness rather than bring it into the light. Would Donny have had as great an influence over Claire if that had not been the case?

7. Why do you think the darkness clung to Claire in such a literal way, especially as a child? Did her age have something to do with how she perceived the darkness's influence?

8. Though Donny is the villain of the novel, he is as much a victim of the darkness as the sisters. How might his victimhood have contributed to his nature? Was his jealousy of the Finches innate or a result of his association with the darkness?

9. While Esther's and Claire's visions involve only harm to themselves, Meg's vision reveals the deaths of her sisters, birthing the belief that she is a danger to Esther and Claire, rather than their protector. As the eldest, this is particularly detrimental to their sibling dynamic. How important is her own growth to the success of healing their relationships?

10. Though a tragedy, it is Claire's death that ultimately forces Meg and Esther to confront the issues that had fractured their close relationship. If Claire had not died, do you think their relationship would ever have mended?

11. Meg is haunted throughout the story by a twisted version of Claire's ghost. Is it Meg's perspective that makes Claire's ghost seem so much crueler, or is it, as Meg believes, that a person's soul could break as permanently as their body?

12. In the end, the house is burned and the darkness, it is assumed, with it. Is it possible though that the darkness could manifest somewhere new? What is it that you know about the darkness that makes you believe it could or could not? What does your belief mean for the evolution of the darkness and what it represents?

ACKNOWLEDGMENTS

As always, I am eternally grateful to Kim Giarratano for taking my constant panic, complaints, worries, and WHAT IF ideas with kindness. Sometimes I just need to talk at someone, and having you on the other end of the phone is a comfort.

For hundreds of thousands of things, thank you to my wife, Crystal, but especially for allowing me to tie your hands together and watch you try to escape so I could get the beats of that one scene just right. You never ask questions, and honestly, that's for the best.

Thank you to Mark Matthews, Rachel Harrison, Eric LaRocca, Prince Ali, Ally Malinenko, and Trevor Williamson—horror pals for life. See you at StokerCon!

Thank you to my agent, Joanna MacKenzie, for getting me through hard decisions (in and out of my fictional worlds) unscathed. We make a great team.

To Mary Altman, whose keen eye and gentle hand have helped me make this book (and those before) the best versions of themselves. I truly appreciate you.

Finally, to the booksellers, especially those at Magers & Quinn in Minneapolis, who've been an incredible support from the beginning. I am eternally grateful.

Now, on to the next one.

ABOUT THE AUTHOR

Photo © Bert Jones Photography

Katrina Monroe lives in Minnesota with her wife, two children, and Eddie, the ghost that haunts their bedroom closets. Follow her on Twitter @authorkatm.